Ashleigh Bingham lives in Queensland. After a career in family therapy she now writes full time. A love of history and travel has taken her on journeys that provide the exotic settings of her novels.

THE WAYWARD WIND

It's 1867, and when Tom Sinclair learns that his sister has run away, he sails from London, confident of finding her. The trail leads him to Morocco where his fears for her safety are confirmed. Stranded in a country, understanding neither the language nor the culture, his quest seems at a dead end. But help is thrust upon him: Francesca, a sharp-tongued Spanish governess, has spent years in North Africa, and learns of Tom's need for a translator. She snatches the opportunity to join the search for his missing sister — while hiding her own grim agenda in the enterprise . . .

Books by Ashleigh Bingham
Published by The House of Ulverscroft:

WINDS OF HONOUR

ASHLEIGH BINGHAM

THE WAYWARD WIND

Complete and Unabridged

ULVERSCROFT
Leicester

First published in Great Britain in 2007 by
Robert Hale Limited
London

First Large Print Edition
published 2008
by arrangement with
Robert Hale Limited
London

British Library CIP Data

Bingham, Ashleigh
  The wayward wind.—Large print ed.—
  Ulverscroft large print series: general fiction
  1. Runaway teenagers—Fiction 2. English—
  Morocco—Fiction 3. Large type books
  I. Title
  823.9'2 [F]

  ISBN 978–1–84782–398–4

Published by
F. A. Thorpe (Publishing)
Anstey, Leicestershire

Set by Words & Graphics Ltd.
Anstey, Leicestershire
Printed and bound in Great Britain by
T. J. International Ltd., Padstow, Cornwall

This book is printed on acid-free paper

1

London 1867

'Cynthia! Cynthia — look who is sitting over there!' Mrs Houghton-Blake held the opera glasses to her eyes and kicked her heel hard against her daughter's ankle. 'He's back in England at last!'

Miss Cynthia Houghton-Blake turned her head and calmly scanned the tiers of Drury Lane boxes. 'Oh, Tom Sinclair, you mean?' she said, and returned her attention to the stage. 'Yes, I spoke with Tom at Ascot last week. He's been away somewhere in South America.'

'Sir Thomas Sinclair!' her mother hissed, fluttering her fan, 'and he was so attentive to you when you came out. I'll invite him to dinner on Tuesday.'

'Mama, don't meddle! You can't have forgotten that I'm engaged to Clive Sanderson when it was you who worked so hard to bring about that situation.'

'Of course I hadn't forgotten, my girl, but have you forgotten that you have a sister? I must make a good match for Margaret also.'

1

Miss Houghton-Blake turned sharply to her mother. 'Surely you're not suggesting that Tom Sinclair would be a good match for our little Margaret? I think not!' She trained her own glasses on the handsome, good-humoured face of the man sitting on the other side of the theatre. 'He must be at least thirty-four now — and he was always a flirt and a tear-away. Goodness knows what other bad habits he's sure to have picked up while he was away in all those wild places.'

Mrs Houghton-Blake closed her fan with a snap and sank back into her chair. 'A wife can change a husband's bad habits — or learn to ignore them.' She sniffed and gave a sigh. 'Thomas Sinclair, Baronet — he's so good-looking and charming, wealthy, too. Is he still unattached? Oh, Cynthia — bad habits or not — what a challenge for any mother to catch that man for her daughter!'

'Yes, Mama, he's still unattached because he's been very careful to dodge every net cast in his direction. Besides he's not perfect you know — he walks with a limp.'

'Barely noticeable! Anyhow it's a reminder that he survived a dreadful wound in the Indian Mutiny. And such a hero! I've heard tales of how he saved his whole family from massacre.' She sat forward again and flicked open her fan as a thought struck her. 'He

2

must meet your cousin Barbara! She still has her looks — so I'll invite her to dinner on Tuesday, too. Something might very well come of it.'

Tom Sinclair was quite aware that he was the object of close scrutiny by several ladies sitting on the other side of the auditorium and he did what he usually did on such occasions: he left his seat before the last curtain-call, ran down the stairs, slipped a half-crown into the palm of the man at the stage door, and was waiting in the wings by the time the chorus dancers had taken their final bow.

'Tommie darlin', you're back!' He was quickly surrounded by chattering, warm, perspiring, pretty girls. 'We've missed you somethin' awful.'

A painted cheek brushed his. 'Where the devil have you been all this time?'

'Oh, just over the hills and far away, Sally, m'dear.' There seemed little point in naming the rugged territory he'd been surveying for an Argentinean railway line running into Chile. 'But now I'm back, and it's time for us all to hear some champagne corks popping again.'

There were giggles of excitement and several more kisses found his cheeks. 'So, for those of you who have no prior engagement this evening, I'd like you to hurry up and change because there's supper waiting for us in the Palm Court at Langham's.' The squeals grew louder. 'The Prince of Wales might be there, you know, and if you behave yourselves, I'll take you for a ride up to the tenth floor in the new hydraulic lifts.'

He counted about ten girls who'd accepted his invitation, and while they fled, chattering, to the dressing-room, Sir Thomas Sinclair went outside and engaged a convoy of Hansom cabs to carry the party to Mayfair's newest hotel. His entry into the Palm Court with a flock of colourful females wearing their frilliest dresses and feathered hats caused other patrons to turn their heads, but the staff extended the hotel's hospitality with the utmost civility. The gold coins which Tom had already slipped into the appropriate hands ensured that chairs were held for his guests, napkins unfolded, and champagne flutes kept filled while the party enjoyed a splendid supper.

As Tom looked around the polished marble room, so filled with potted palms it looked like an extension of Kew Gardens, he caught the glances of several acquaintances. Some registered their astonishment at seeing Sir Thomas Sinclair in the company of ladies who were clearly not quite ladies, and those who knew Tom better acknowledged him with a wink.

The girls were in high spirits and Tom, always a charming host, moved to sit beside each one in turn, entertaining them with a flow of light-hearted anecdotes — some even based on fact — about his adventures in exotic places around the world.

'I had no idea that building railways could be such fun!' said a lovely redhead, lifting a spoonful of pineapple meringue to her mouth. 'Fancy you going down those Amazon rapids with the natives in a canoe! And chasing buffaloes with the Red Indians in America!'

'But Tommie, darling, do tell us how you were wounded in the Sepoy Mutiny.'

'Well, Peggy,' he said with absolute honesty on this occasion, 'I'm afraid they had to put down the Great Indian Mutiny of '57 without me, because I fell off a polo pony and broke my leg the day before it all started. Never was a fellow less of a hero.' He hung his head, attempting to look guilt-ridden, and they laughed at his performance.

'However my stepbrother, Robert Fitzalan, was heroic enough for both of us. There we all were in a house that was being pounded to pieces by the mutineers' cannon, when Robert rushed out into the night and blew up their ammunition wagon!'

There were sighs of admiration and glasses were raised to Commissioner Robert Fitzalan. The ladies wanted to hear more, but Tom shook his head. He knew he'd already had too much champagne to drink and when he was tipsy it was difficult to keep his feelings under control when he thought back to that period of horror ten years ago.

It was strange how quickly alcohol had the power to unwrap all the bandages he'd wrapped around his memories. The physical pain in his shattered leg was probably the one most easily forgotten, but the deepest hurt had been watching Phoebe marrying his stepbrother, Robert Fitzalan. And after all the delightful ladies he'd romanced in the years since then, it was sheer madness still to be carrying Phoebe's image so close to his heart. Especially after he'd learned that Phoebe was the one woman in the world whom he could never have married.

'Well, my lovelies,' he said, rousing himself, 'let's fill your glasses once more and then I'll introduce you to the wonders of the first hydraulic lifts in London.' The coin he handed to the lift attendant ensured that the ladies had an exciting ride straight up to the tenth floor, and down again so swiftly they were swaying as they stepped out into the foyer — just in time to see the arrival of the Prince of Wales and his party.

'Oh, Tommie, he smiled at us as he went past!' Sally squeaked as he escorted the group to their cabs and paid the drivers to take them to their lodgings.

'You're a darlin' you are, Tom Sinclair, to lay on all this fun for us,' the raven-haired Millie called as the horses pulled away. 'Are you comin' to see us dance again next week?'

'Can't, m'loves, I'm spending a couple of weeks in the country,' he said and waved them off.

When he walked back into the hotel foyer, he was hailed by a friend. 'Safety in numbers, eh?' the fellow said with a laugh as he approached. 'Well, I'm glad to see you back in London at last, Tom. How about lunch at the club tomorrow? I'm keen to hear how you plan to get a railway through the Andes.'

Tom shook his head. 'Sorry, but I'm going down to Tilbury in the morning to meet my mother and stepfather. They're arriving from India with two grandsons who are to be sent to school, and they've taken a house near Sherborne while the lads settle in. I plan to stay down there with them for a week or two, but I'll let you know as soon as I'm back in town.'

Tom's emotions were running high and his throat was tight as he watched the ship carrying his family steaming steadily towards its berth. All sails were furled while the steam engine thumped, smoke billowed from the funnel and the propeller churned the brown waters of the Thames.

His eyes searched the faces lining the rails as the vessel was manoeuvred alongside the wharf and, as soon as the gangplank was in place, he was first aboard, feeling like a schoolboy again as he ran along the deck towards his parents. Julia and James seemed to have changed little in the five years since he last saw them at home on the tea plantation. His mother, perhaps, had a little more grey in her dark hair but she still moved with the grace of a young woman, and though his one-armed stepfather was now over sixty, the years had treated him kindly, also.

'Tom! How wonderful to see you,' Julia said warmly as she held his hands and kissed his cheek. 'Tell me, dear, is there any mail waiting for us at the hotel?' Her question surprised him, and he saw her disappointment when he shook his head.

His stepfather simply took his hand and smiled, but in his eyes Tom could read deep emotion which neither of his parents ever openly displayed. Tom swallowed hard and tightened his grip on James's hand, holding it for a few seconds longer. The affection he felt for Major James Fitzalan was deeper than any he shared with anyone else in the family, for there was no one who understood him as well as James had always done.

Tom cleared the lump in his throat and pretended to be puzzled by the two boys standing between his parents. 'Goodness, Dad, what have you done with my little nephews? Who are these strapping young fellows you've brought along?'

The sons of Robert and Phoebe beamed while James performed the introductions. Young James Fitzalan, aged nine, and Timothy, aged seven, were a fair-haired pair who had inherited all their parents' handsome features. 'How do you do, Uncle,' they said in turn as they shook Tom's hand and the smiles they gave him were so like Phoebe's they made his heart turn over.

'Can you take us to see the Tower of London before we have to leave for school?' Timothy asked eagerly. 'And some Egyptian mummies?'

'Absolutely, chaps. And if we start straight away we'll have time to climb up the dome of St Paul's, too, after we've been to Madame Tussaud's.'

'Tom, have you heard from Diana since you came back to England?' Julia broke in, 'I wrote to let her know when we were to arrive and was so hoping a letter would be waiting for us when we reached Cape Town, or here.'

Tom looked at her in surprise. 'Mother, I've never been able to keep up with my sister's comings and goings. The last I heard from Diana was that she was engaged to some army chap in India — but that seems years ago. What happened to him?'

'Oh, that fell through,' Julia said tightly. 'Last year she wrote to say she'd married a man in Liverpool, but we haven't had a word from her for months.'

'I'm worried about her, Tom,' was all James had time to say before the two Indian servants travelling with them came to announce that the luggage was ready to be unloaded, and they were all then caught up in the flurry of disembarkation.

Tom took his nephews off to explore London, and it wasn't until the servants had put the exhausted boys to bed that he and his parents had an opportunity to talk.

'Tom, I'm becoming more and more concerned about Diana's whereabouts,' Julia said as they sat down to dinner. 'I don't want to intrude in her life, I just need to know that our daughter is safe and well — wherever she

10

is.' She played with the food on her plate. 'I'm afraid that Diana has always been a very headstrong girl.'

'Mother, at the age of twenty-nine she can hardly still be called a *girl*!' Tom spoke more sharply than he'd intended, but he stopped himself from adding that he'd always considered Diana to be wildly reckless, habitually inconsiderate and painfully self-absorbed. 'Perhaps growing up with a younger sister as perfectly behaved as Kate had made her rebellious,' he finished lamely, aware that James had always scrupulously avoided favouring one daughter over the other. 'Who was the army fellow she was engaged to? Did you approve of him, Dad?'

'There was nothing to disapprove of,' James said dryly. 'Captain Roger Copely was charming — perhaps just a little too charming to us all — but when I spoke to others in his regiment, I heard of no flaws in his character. Being bland has never been regarded as a crime, and Diana appeared to be very much in love with the fellow.'

'But when his regiment was sent to Afghanistan, Diana accepted an invitation from his mother in London and sailed off to stay with her,' Julia said with a whiff of disapproval in her tone. 'I mean, if anything dreadful had happened to Roger while she was so far away, if he'd been hurt — '

'Well, nothing did happen to Captain Copely,' said James with a sidelong glance, 'and apparently Diana and Mrs Marietta Copely hit it off so well in Hampstead that they then went on a trip to Italy with a party of her friends. It sounded a very Bohemian group of painters and poets, but we heard regularly from Diana. She seemed perfectly happy, until she broke the news that Roger had jilted her. Apparently, while she was romping through Italy with his mother, he'd eloped with some girl he'd met while he was on leave in Kashmir.'

'Good Lord!' Tom exploded.

'The next we heard from Diana was that she'd come back to London, met a well-to-do merchant from Liverpool and had married him!' James pushed away his half-eaten meal. 'Her husband and I exchanged a few letters after that news reached us, but he came across to me as a very cold fish. Diana herself wrote during her first year in Liverpool, insisting that all was well, but now it's been months since we've heard from her.' Tom sensed the pain this had caused in his stepfather's deep voice.

'I myself, wrote to Mr Herbert at Christmas, asking for news of Diana,' Julia added, 'but his reply simply said that, 'his

12

wife was no longer living under his roof'. I thought — I hoped — he would at least have forwarded my letters on to her.'

James saw the moisture gathering in her eyes and reached for her hand. 'Darling, we mustn't allow ourselves to fear the worst. After all, we've always sent her a decent allowance, so we know she's not destitute.'

Tom silently cursed his vibrant, dark-haired sister for inflicting this painful situation on their parents: selfish, thoughtless Diana.

His stepfather let out a long sigh. 'I have an appointment tomorrow with the attorney who handles the money I send to her each year. Perhaps Mr Maxwell can throw some light on recent developments in her life.'

'I'd like to go with you, Dad.'

James nodded, and a warm look passed between them. 'Thanks, Tom. Yes, I'd like you to come along.'

★ ★ ★

The portly, balding Mr Osbert Maxwell, Attorney of Oxford Street, was indeed able to contribute information regarding Diana, though what he disclosed was of little comfort to James, especially when the ledgers were opened to reveal her current financial situation.

'Major Fitzalan, while your daughter was travelling in Italy, she withdrew every penny you sent to her and, I'm afraid to say, she also asked — twice — for an advance on the next year's remittance — which, of course, I provided.'

'I send her a thousand a year!' James said gruffly. 'What the devil was she doing with it? Was my daughter swindled by that Copely woman and her friends? What do you know about them?'

Mr Maxwell cleared his throat and looked grave. 'I too, was concerned about that particular lady, Major, and I had enquiries made into the background of Mrs Marietta Copely and her jolly little band. Now, while the report stops short of labelling any of these men and women as *malicious*, there was evidence that they were completely irresponsible regarding financial matters. They seem to have left a trail of debts wherever they went in Italy.'

'Stupid, stupid Diana!' James shook his head. 'She must have let them use her as their milch-cow.'

'I'd hazard a guess that my sister's depleted funds had much to do with Mrs Copely's son jilting her and eloping with a girl in India,' Tom said through tightly clenched jaws.

Mr Maxwell gave a sympathetic nod. 'I

understand that particular young lady had inherited an estate which brought in five thousand a year.'

James blew a long breath through his teeth. 'So, there we have it. Diana was short of funds when she came back from Italy — and then rushed into marriage with this man from Liverpool! How in God's name did that come about?'

'I'm afraid I must accept responsibility for their meeting — right here in my office.' Mr Maxwell spread his hands apologetically. 'Your daughter had come to request another advance — just a small one — and Mr Francis Herbert was here to finalize the settlement of his late mother's estate.' He looked at James from under his thick, grey brows. 'Unfortunately, on that particular morning an involved case kept me in court for much longer than I had anticipated, which left Miss Fitzalan and Mr Herbert cooling their heels here for a considerable period. I believe they became better acquainted when he invited her to luncheon.'

Tom curbed his tongue. He could visualise the scene: there was Diana, smarting from the humiliation of a broken engagement and the realization that Mrs Copely's affection had quickly evaporated when the Fitzalan money

15

ceased to flow. Then into the waiting-room came Mr Francis Herbert — and Miss Diana Fitzalan had pounced. Of course, she would have been the one to suggest having lunch together but, to this day, Mr Herbert would no doubt still be imagining that it had all been his own idea.

'So what can you tell us about this man my sister married?' he asked.

Mr Maxwell seemed to choose his words carefully. 'Mr Francis Herbert is a highly respectable gentleman,' he said with a significant look, 'Methodist, aged in his mid-forties, never married previously. He inherited a sound merchant business which has grown considerably in recent years.'

Tom saw James struggling to comprehend why Diana should have rushed into this marriage rather than come to him for help. That was hurtful.

'Mr Maxwell, have you any idea where my daughter could be at this moment?' he asked stiffly. 'Her husband has informed us that she is no longer living under his roof.'

The attorney's jaw dropped in astonishment. 'I'm sorry, Major, I had absolutely no idea of any such thing,' he said. 'I've received no correspondence from either Mr — or Mrs — Herbert for over six months.'

Tom and James left the attorney's office

and walked slowly down the stairs, but James halted in the doorway before they stepped out on to Oxford Street; his face was drawn.

'Oh, God! What the hell has happened to Diana? If she's no longer living with her husband and has run through all her money.' He leaned his shoulder against the doorpost and shook his head. 'Thirty years ago I gave an arm to save your mother from the cut-throats who'd kidnapped her in the mountains of Ranaganj, and I'd do the same today if I could rescue Diana from whatever disaster I fear she's hurtling towards.'

'Yes, Dad, I know you would.' There was a catch in Tom's voice. 'But let me go up to Liverpool in the morning and talk to this fellow, Herbert. You and mother carry on with your plans to take the boys to Sherborne, and I'll follow you there when I have some news of Diana — even if I have to thrash it out of her husband.'

James looked at him deeply and placed his hand on Tom's shoulder. 'It was a fortunate day for me when you became my son, Thomas Sinclair.'

Tom's throat tightened, and he had an impulse to throw his arms around his stepfather and hug him. But any such display would have embarrassed James Fitzalan so, instead, Tom said quietly: 'I love you, Dad.'

He hadn't said those words aloud for thirty years, but the look that came into his stepfather's eyes when he spoke them, made him glad that he'd done so today.

2

When Tom arrived in Liverpool he booked a room in a small hotel and watched the time carefully. He'd planned a meeting with the unsuspecting Mr Francis Herbert to take place after dinner in the man's home, rather than at his place of business. That seemed the decent thing to do, considering the delicate nature of the subject to be discussed, and it was eight-thirty when he knocked at the door of the tall house which had been Diana's last address.

The pinched, nervous face of a young maid in a white cap and apron peered out at him when the door was opened. 'Good evening,' he said firmly, 'would you please inform Mr Herbert that Sir Thomas Sinclair, brother of Mrs Herbert, wishes to speak with him?' Tom used his title rarely, but on an occasion like this, he felt it could be useful.

The girl's eyes widened as she stepped aside and Tom walked into the chilly hall. He pulled a silver case from his pocket and handed her his card.

'One moment, please, sir. I'll see if the master is in.' The maid scuttled away across a

19

dull brown carpet patterned with even darker brown scrolls.

Tom pulled off his hat and gloves and placed them on a table next to a stuffed owl which stared at him balefully from under its glass dome. The stillness of the house hung like a heavy weight in the air; there was no sound apart from the ticking of the clock in a tall brown case standing in the corner. The minutes passed slowly as Tom paced to and fro, his frustration mounting.

He opened a door on his right, and light from the hall streaked into a musty sitting-room, revealing a collection of brown velvet-covered chairs and sofas, and walls hung with pictures in heavily carved dark frames. The carpet with the brown swirls stretched in every direction. He closed that door and opened one on its left. This was the dining-room, where heavy oak furniture stood in battle formation across the hideous carpet; as if defying any whisper of joy to cross the threshold.

He closed this door, too, and was still struggling to comprehend how Diana could have survived for more than a year within these stifling walls, when the nervous little maid returned, almost running. 'Mr Herbert sends his apologies, Sir Thomas,' she recited in a shaking, sing-song voice. 'He is unable to see you as he is spending the evening at his devotions.'

'At his devotions, eh? I'm delighted to hear it,' Tom said, so evenly that few would have guessed that his temper was on the boil. 'Well then, I think this is an excellent time for me to join him!'

The girl clapped her hands to her cheeks and rolled her eyes in alarm as he strode past her and along the brown hallway until he found a light shining from under a closed door. He gave one loud knock before he flung it open and came face to face with the man who had married his sister.

'My apologies for disturbing your devotions, Mr Herbert, but I'll take only a moment of your time,' he said.

Francis Herbert sprang from his brown leather chair and the Bible in his hands slipped to the floor. Shock rendered the man temporarily speechless but the look in his eyes could have turned the Mersey to ice.

'I'm here on behalf of my parents, Major and Mrs Fitzalan, to learn the whereabouts of their daughter, my sister — your wife. We are all most concerned about her.' Tom's first glance took in Mr Herbert's oiled, sandy-coloured hair brushed back from his low forehead, the small, hooked nose and the round eyes that seemed almost replicas of those on the stuffed owl under the glass dome in the hall.

The man was white-faced with outrage, his lips so tightly pinched they had difficulty forming the words that were apparently choking his throat. 'My wife?' His voice came out thin and high. 'I had no wife! That woman scorned the marriage vows she made before God. I gave shelter to a harlot, a whore, a Jezebel, who has chosen the path leading to the eternal fires of hell. God will punish her wickedness.'

'I see. So tell me, where is she now, Mr Herbert?'

'Where is the scarlet woman now, you ask?' His voice reached an even higher pitch, with the words accompanied by a little spray of spittle. 'I'll tell you exactly where she is! She is on the high road to damnation!' The man's face twitched and his tongue shot out to lick the saliva pooling in one corner of his mouth. 'She walks in sin, contaminating the very earth around her, but I refused to permit her to befoul me until she was willing to fall to her knees and repent her wickedness!' He took a step backwards and felt for the arm of his chair before dropping on to the seat, breathing fast. 'Nightly I prayed for her soul to be cleansed, but when she refused to heed His Word, the Lord gave me the strength to escape her carnal snare.'

'Ah, yes, Mr Herbert, I see clearly that the marriage bed brought no happiness to either party. So now that your wife has gone, will you divorce her?'

His owl's eyes appeared to widen further. 'What God hath joined together, let no man dare to put asunder!' His voice rose. 'That daughter of the Devil made her vows before God, so let her burn in Hell for breaking them!' He snatched a brass bell from the table beside him and rang it wildly. 'Get out of my house this instant! Get out, I tell you!' He was still shouting and ringing the bell when the little maid ran in. 'Be warned, you wretched girl, I'll put you straight out on to the street if ever you again open my door to this man! D'you hear me, Nellie?'

The white-faced girl bobbed and threw a distraught look towards Tom.

'Thank you for your time, Mr Herbert,' he said with sarcasm ground into every syllable. 'Meeting you has provided a very clear answer as to why my sister left Liverpool.' He struggled to keep his fists by his side as he left the room and followed the quaking, white-faced maid to the hall. His failure to get a sane answer from Diana's husband was galling; his parents would be even more distressed now when he arrived back with no news of her whereabouts. Damn Diana! Why hadn't she written to them?

He heard a sound behind him and was well aware that Mr Herbert had found the strength to leave his chair and was now standing at the door of his study to watch his visitor's departure.

The maid picked up Tom's hat from the hall table and handed it to him. She was about to pass his gloves when one dropped and she stooped to retrieve it. 'Go to the Silver Dolphin and ask old Billy Burton — he knows,' she whispered while her head was lowered.

★   ★   ★

The next day Tom went for a long walk along the river where a forest of tall masts of the ships lying at anchor in the Mersey stood out against the skyline. He strolled past the docks and the quays lined with warehouses — the largest of which carried the imprint, 'Herbert and Son' painted in high letters. A big clipper was presently tied up at Herbert's wharf, unloading a cargo of wool from Australia, and a hundred yards further along the quay Tom saw the sign of the Silver Dolphin tavern.

He went in and ordered an ale. 'I'm looking for a fellow named Billy Burton. Do you know him?' he asked, and the innkeeper gave a genial grin.

'Everybody knows Old Billy,' he said and nodded to a frail figure sitting alone in a corner, with a seaman's cap on his wild white hair and a peg leg stretched out under the table.

'Give me an ale for him, too,' Tom said and carried both across the room.

'May I join you, sir? I'm Tom Sinclair,' he said and took a place on the bench beside the old man.

The fellow's shaking hand reached for the ale as Tom pushed the mug towards him, but there was nothing feeble behind the pair of bright blue eyes that looked at him questioningly.

'I thank 'e for this, sir,' the man said with a gap-toothed grin, using both hands to lift the ale to his lips. He gave a sigh of satisfaction when he thumped the mug, half-empty, back on to the table. 'And what brings young Gentleman Tom to these 'ere parts, may I be so bold as to ask?'

Tom looked at him steadily. 'Actually, I'm here on a mission to discover the whereabouts of my sister — Mrs Francis Herbert — and I was told last night that you might be able to tell me where she has gone.'

Old Billy gave a cackle. 'Ah! What a picture

to gladden any man's heart that young beauty made when she came paradin' down here in her fine silks, a-twirlin' her parasol and catching the eye of a certain good-lookin' American captain each time his schooner dropped anchor.' He ran the back of his hand across his lips. 'I used to see her slippin' aboard *The Swallow* when her 'usband weren't lookin'. My landlady's daughter, young Nellie, who works up at the 'ouse, swears old Misery Herbert never suspected a thing.' His shoulders shook with laughter and he had to wipe his eyes with the frayed cuff of his jacket.

Tom's heart sank. 'Who is captain of *The Swallow*? Are you saying my sister might have run off with him?'

'Aye, lad, I knows for a fact she did just that. Cap'n McCallum, that's who 'e are, a big, good-lookin' buccaneer who always had an eye for a pretty ankle — and well known around these parts for runnin' the Yankee blockade to bring us our baccy and cotton all durin' the Civil War over there.'

'Is that where they've gone? Back across the Atlantic?'

The white head shook slowly. '*The Swallow* were sailin' south to Africa, with a cargo o'cloth and guns, they say — first port o'call, the Canaries.' He pushed his lips in and out while he pondered. 'It weren't long ago that Cap'n McCallum were runnin' slaves from Africa across to Carolina, but 'e can't do that no more, can 'e, now that the Yankees h'won the war. Maybe he'll take 'em to sell in Brazil?'

Tom groaned, put his elbows on the table and cradled his head in his hands. 'Oh, God! What has Diana got herself caught up in?'

The old man fixed his gaze out of the window and stared at a ship that was hoisting its sails and turning for the open sea. 'The first time I ever laid eyes on your sister, lad, I could tell that she were one who'd always find her course set into the eye of the wind.'

Tom raised an eyebrow.

'Aye, lad — *eye of the wind* — that's what the old ones call sailing to windward. It makes for an easy voyage when the wind comes from behind, fillin' the sails so a helmsman can set a steady course for port. Life itself can be like that for some folk, but there are others who find themselves always headin' into the wind, always havin' to tack to and fro, judgin' the set of the sails just right, hopin' that luck might help catch 'em a current, always battlin' to make headway, and never knowin' when they'll make safe harbour.'

'I see what you mean,' Tom said and slowly

finished his ale. 'I have a younger sister, Kate, who seems to have sailed steadily through life with a following wind to fill her sails. Poor Diana — yes, it's true that she's always been battling into the wind, tacking this way and that.' He stood and reached into his pocket for two sovereigns. 'Thank you for your information, Mr Burton,' he said and put one gold coin into the wizened hand. 'And next time you see young Nellie, give her this for being brave enough last night to tell me where to find you.' He held out the second coin.

'That I'll do, thank 'e kindly.' The old sailor grinned up at Tom and slipped the gold pieces into his pocket. 'Somehow I get a feelin', young Gentleman Tom, that you might be another poor soul who finds his course more often than not set into the eye of the wind!'

'Perhaps you're right, my friend.' Tom shook the man's hand and laughed. 'But you can be sure that I'll keep sailing on until — one day — I find the safe harbour I'm looking for.'

★ ★ ★

When Tom arrived at the house which James had leased, his parents were stunned to hear the news he brought back from Liverpool.

'Mother, I don't know how Diana endured living for even one year with Mr Misery Herbert in that dismal house,' he concluded.

'But now you say that she's run off with an American sea captain?' Julia looked appalled and James put his arm around her.

'If her marriage was so unhappy, why in God's name, didn't she let us know?' he said. 'What do you know about this man she's left her husband for?'

'I know very little, Dad, but along the waterfront Captain McCallum seems to be highly regarded as a seaman, and they say that *The Swallow* is a sound vessel.' He tried to sound encouraging, and didn't mention the captain's slave-trading activities.

An atmosphere of gloom followed them into the drawing-room where afternoon tea had been laid. Julia lifted the teapot and had just begun to pour when Tom drew in a deep breath and, after a moment's hesitation, announced the plan which he'd been reluctantly — *very* reluctantly — toying with all the way back from Liverpool. Pursuing his scheme would mean foregoing an invitation to join an exciting railway venture in South Africa, but all that now paled into insignificance beside his determination to help his parents solve the riddle of Diana's whereabouts.

'Mother, Dad, I'm going to catch the first ship sailing for the Canary Islands and see if I can discover what happened to Diana when *The Swallow* arrived in Tenerife.' He made an unsuccessful attempt to sound enthusiastic.

'Oh, my dear, but what about your work?' Julia said. 'All the plans you told us about?'

He shook his head. 'That's all right, Mother, I've made no firm commitments.'

'My dear Tom, that's most generous of you, and I thank you from the bottom of my heart,' James said as Julia passed him his cup. 'But if Diana sailed from England months ago, what are the chances now of finding *The Swallow* still in the waters around the Canaries?'

'Very little chance, I imagine, Dad, but Tenerife is a good starting point because I have an acquaintance there. Jose Alvarez is secretary to the Spanish governor in Santa Cruz and he should be able to give me information about Captain McCallum. Alvarez knows just about everything that happens in that area, and if he doesn't know, I'm sure he would soon be able to find out where *The Swallow* was heading.'

'Oh, Tom, do you think Diana might have changed her mind and, perhaps, left the ship there?' Julia tried to sound hopeful.

'That might be wishful thinking, Mother,'

Tom said and leaned over the table to put a firm hand on her wrist. 'Look, I'm determined to find out what I can, and if she's sailed down to Cape Town, or to Brazil or Argentina, you have my promise that I won't stop until I catch up with her — somewhere.'

James reached into his pocket and withdrew a photograph. 'Take this with you. It might be useful.'

Tom ran his tongue across his bottom lip as he studied the image of his sister's sensuous face with its high cheekbones, the soft dark hair, smiling lips and eyes that could have captured the hearts of a dozen worthwhile men. What had driven Diana to make many stupid mistakes in her choices of companion? He had very little sympathy left for her at that moment.

'When you become a parent,' James said quietly, as if he could read Tom's thoughts, 'you'll discover that you'll never stop loving your child — no matter what circumstances arise. Tell that to your sister when — if — you meet her.'

★ ★ ★

Three weeks later Tom stood on the deck of a Dutch trader, inhaling the scents of tropical vegetation drifting out across the sheltered

31

waters of Santa Cruz bay as the vessel slid towards its moorings. The mainsails were lowered with a loud flap of canvas and a scream of hemp, the forward cable thundered out, and when the anchor bit, the ship came to rest, straining against the outgoing tide.

'Thank you, Captain, it's been a most pleasant voyage,' Tom said, as he climbed into the ship's boat to be rowed ashore. On the far side of the bay stood the castle, along with a ring of guns and fortifications, and on the other side, the low white houses of the town lay shimmering in the sultry heat.

Once on the jetty, Tom hired a boy to carry his box to an inn where he'd stayed on previous visits. Straight away he wrote a note to his friend, Jose Alvarez, giving him an outline of his reason for coming to the island, and requesting a private meeting at the earliest opportunity. He asked a servant to deliver his letter to the secretary's office in the Governor's residence — grandly known as his palace.

All afternoon a band of tension tightened around Tom's temples as he reviewed the enormity of this cavalier enterprise which he'd taken on so impetuously. What odds would any sane man place on the success of a mission to rescue Diana from her own folly? And even if he did eventually come face to face with his sister, she'd probably laugh at him and tell him to go away. Damn Diana!

As Tom strolled aimlessly through the waterfront markets, buying grapes and figs to eat along the way, he asked himself what the hell he was really doing here, chasing after a self-centred woman who seemed to have thrown all commonsense to the wind.

And the more he thought about it, the more a discomforting answer niggled at the back of his brain. He tried to brush it away, for surely it was quite ridiculous to imagine that lurking behind his rush to mount a white charger and undertake his knightly quest to rescue Diana, might lie some juvenile urge to prove himself to be as resourceful and valiant as his stepbrother, Robert, had been during the Mutiny. A leg fractured in a polo match on the eve of the uprising had rendered Tom useless during that dreadful time, and it was Robert's quick action in blowing up the mutineers' ammunition wagon that had saved them all.

So now was he, Tom, attempting to play the role of family hero to outdo his brilliant stepbrother? He laughed at the absurd thought. There had never been any rivalry between Robert and himself for their father's regard. James had never shown more favour to his own son than he had to his stepson. Had he?

33

He was still wrestling with that uneasy notion when he returned to the inn and found a reply from Jose Alvarez waiting for him. The Spaniard said he was eager to offer whatever help he could to locate Mrs Herbert, and concluded by insisting that Tom should come that evening to dine with him and his wife at their home, where they would be able to talk in private.

The pleasant, sprawling white home of Jose Alvarez was close by the Governor's palace, and only a short walk from the inn. Tom's spirits lifted when he rang the bell at the high wooden gate facing the road, and was welcomed into the cool house.

Señora Beata Alvarez herself came from the drawing-room to greet him. She was a gracious, well-born lady, a decade or so older than Tom, and always dressed demurely with a large gold cross hanging from her neck.

'What a pleasant surprise for us to see you in Santa Cruz once more, Thomas,' she said with genuine warmth, and with a gesture of her hand, invited him to walk with her into the garden.

'I'm afraid that my husband has just sent a message to say that his arrival home has been delayed and — as you and I are old friends — he suggests we dine without him.' She was a quiet woman who usually had little to say in

34

men's company, but her gentle brown eyes missed nothing.

'That is indeed most considerate, *señora*,' Tom said. Was it some news about *The Swallow* which was keeping Alvarez so busy? he wondered, and tried to curb his hopes as they strolled through the lush garden.

He felt comfortable in the company of Señora Alvarez, and their conversation drifted about, pleasant and aimless, as they picked guavas and watched a flock of brightly coloured, noisy parrots returning to their trees. When the last of the daylight faded, she led him into the lantern-lit grape arbour where a table and chairs had been set for dinner.

'Your health, Thomas,' she said lifting her wine glass to him and taking a sip, 'and also to the success of your next venture.' She looked at him shyly. 'Am I correct to think that it is more than planning railways which is taking you back to Argentina? Or Chile?'

Tom smiled at her subtle inquisition.

Beata lowered her eyes. 'Forgive me,' she said with a tiny shrug, 'but all Spanish ladies who live for twenty years on an island so far away from their own dear families, take an extraordinary interest in the lives of everyone who steps ashore.'

He raised his glass to her. 'Actually, *señora*,

I'm not sure yet where I will travel from here, because that depends on whatever information your husband is able to give me about an American ship named *The Swallow*. My sister left Liverpool aboard it.' He frowned and sipped more wine. 'I need to let our parents know of Diana's whereabouts, and that she is well and happy.'

For a moment Beata said nothing while her soft brown eyes looked into his. 'Over the years, I have seen that ship call into Santa Cruz many times. Captain McCallum rarely carries a passenger, however, I remember a tall, dark-haired lady who came ashore with him on his last visit some months ago.' She watched for Tom's reaction. 'Several times I observed them walking together in the town. Perhaps that was your sister? A strikingly lovely, slender woman, as I recall.'

Tom nodded. 'That could well have been Diana,' he said carefully, trying to weigh up whether this charming lady's strict religious convictions on matrimony would be offended if he disclosed the truth about his sister's scandalous escapade. He decided not to take the risk, but slipped the photograph of Diana from his jacket and passed it across the table.

She held it closer to the lamp and nodded. 'Yes. That is indeed the lady who came ashore from *The Swallow*.'

Tom put the photograph back into his pocket. 'Thank you for that information, señora. Now I can write to my parents and, at least, give them the good news that when you saw Diana in Santa Cruz she was well and happy,' he said with little confidence.

Señora Alvarez continued to took at him deeply. 'Your sister gave every appearance of being in splendid health, Thomas, but I know she was not happy.'

Tom's jaw sagged. 'You spoke with her?'

'Oh, no, we did not speak,' she said as her fingers played with the gold crucifix hanging from her neck, 'but I observed her with Captain McCallum. A woman recognizes when another is discontented — the set of the mouth, a certain turn of the head, the stiffening of a shoulder, a hand pulled away from a touch, a stepping aside when the man comes close. All these little signals, and more, I saw clearly in your lovely sister, and I knew she felt no happiness in the captain's company.'

'Forgive me, señora' — Tom's voice was unsteady — 'but what of McCallum? Did you see any sign of affection on his side?'

'I cannot answer that, Thomas, I know little of the ways of men, other than my own dear husband.' She frowned and pursed her lips for a moment as she pondered. 'However, I

37

did notice that Captain McCallum *swaggered* when he walked about our island. I do not think I could ever trust the affections of a man who *swaggers*. She nodded knowingly and sympathy filled her eyes. 'Your sister, I fear, may have found herself in an unfortunate *predicament* with that man.'

To Tom's surprise, their conversation remained focused on Diana's predicament as they dined, with Beata listening intently to Tom's increasingly angry comments about his sister's impulsive, selfish behaviour. He was grateful that Beata voiced no judgement, though she fingered her cross frequently. Time ticked by: they left the arbour and walked back into the drawing-room. And still Jose Alvarez did not return home.

At midnight, Tom could see that Beata was becoming concerned about his long absence, and he was about to suggest that she might wish to retire, when the clatter of hooves in the stable yard brought them both to their feet.

Jose was white-faced with fatigue and his clothes travel-stained as he rushed into the room. 'A thousand apologies,' he said with a courtly bow to Tom, then reaching for his wife's hand, he pressed it to his lips. 'I've been to see Geraldo.'

'Oh, of course!' Beata said and smiled

knowingly. 'Sit down, my love.' She poured wine into a glass and handed it to him. 'What have you learned?'

For a moment the Spaniard sat staring into his wine and Tom sensed that he was not about to be given good news regarding *The Swallow*.

'Captain McCallum sailed south when he left here,' Jose said, taking a deep breath and looking up into Tom's face. 'Of course he was heading down the African coast to buy slaves for Brazil.' He lifted the glass and took a mouthful of wine. 'The Governor's records contained details about all this, but there were many questions which I suspected only one man could answer, so I rode to see him tonight. This man, you understand, attempts to avoid all contact with government officers.'

'Geraldo is an old smuggler who lives on the other side of Tenerife,' Señora Alvarez explained in an eager whisper. 'He hears of everything that happens in these waters. So, my love, what did he have to say about *The Swallow*?'

Jose scrubbed a hand across his chin and gave Tom a worried frown. 'After she left here, *The Swallow* sailed south and ran into a hurricane off the Cape Verde Islands. She was wrecked and McCallum went down with her, though there were a handful of survivors, including a European lady.'

'Dear God!' Tom said. 'Who rescued them? Where were they taken?'

'Ah!' Alvarez took another mouthful of wine. 'This information, you understand, has been gleaned from men who must remain nameless, but it was said that the survivors were picked up by a north-bound Arab trader. The Swallow's American crew were put ashore in southern Morocco and one of the desert tribes there is sure to have captured them for ransom.' He pulled a long face. 'The lady, however, was taken up to Agadir — a trading town — and after that, her whereabouts are unknown.'

Tom heard Beata's gasp. His mind raced and the nightmare grew darker. Was Jose telling him that the Arabs who saved Diana had sold her into the slave trade? For several speechless moments, he and the Alvarez couple looked at each other in dismay. 'Oh, dear God! what am I going to do?' Tom groaned, knowing full well that there was no choice now but to go to Morocco and attempt to uncover Diana's fate.

He reached for Jose's hand and shook it. 'My friend, I thank you most sincerely for your help, and now, can you tell me where to find a boat to sail me across to Agadir as soon as possible? And with your prayers to help

40

me, Señora Alvarez, perhaps there might still be a hope of finding Diana alive somewhere.'

★ ★ ★

When Tom returned to the inn, it took him several attempts to compose a brief letter to James and Julia, and in the end, he avoided all mention of the shipwreck and Diana's rescue by the Arabs. It was impossible to give them reassurance that she was safe, so he simply said that when she'd been seen on Tenerife, she appeared to be in excellent health. Now he'd learned that she had travelled to Morocco and he was on his way to Agadir in an attempt to find out more. He would write to them again at the earliest opportunity.

3

Four days later Tom stepped on to Moroccan soil in the port of Agadir, wondering glumly which way to turn.

He carried with him an official letter of introduction signed by the Governor of Tenerife, a document which also bore an impressive display of big red seals. Jose Alvarez had assured him that even if the Spanish language on the page could not be interpreted by some official in North Africa, nobody looking at such a paper could fail to recognize that the bearer must be a person of some consequence.

The air hung heavy with the smell of drying fish, and the hot sun and chaotic bustle on the streets of Agadir reminded Tom of towns in India where he had grown up. The difference, he quickly discovered, was that while he spoke fluent Hindustani, his knowledge of Arabic was non-existent, and nobody around him appeared to understand Spanish or French, let alone English. Difficulties arose as soon as he tried to find accommodation and his gesticulations were misinterpreted as a request to locate a brothel.

'No, no!' he said quickly and backed out on to the street again with the proprietor following, wringing his hands and whining for him to reconsider. A little crowd of onlookers instantly gathered at the scene and Tom scanned their faces. 'Does anyone here speak Spanish?' he called. 'I need someone to interpret for one day.'

'*Si, señor!*' A good-looking youth pushed himself forward with a show of arrogance. 'I take you to find better place than this! Better girls.'

'No girls. Just a clean bed and a lock on the door,' Tom said, noting that no one else in the crowd was volunteering for the job. 'What is your name?'

'Hassan, my lord,' the youth said. 'I take you to a very good place. Very nice house.' He heaved Tom's box on to his shoulder and set off along a noisy street, past crowded stalls overflowing with brass pots, fruit and spices, long-bladed knives and brightly woven carpets.

'Not so fast, Hassan, I want to talk to you,' Tom called. 'I have business with the Amir and I want an audience with him as soon as possible. How do I go about arranging that?' Jose Alvarez had warned Tom that it was essential to present his Spanish credentials to the Amir without delay, and to obtain some form of official letter to carry with him if he decided to travel further into Morocco.

'You wish to speak with the Amir, my lord? Ah, an audience with the Amir can be granted only by his ministers.' The youth nodded towards the crenellated red walls of the citadel looming over the town from a hill.

'Very well,' Tom said, 'how do I arrange to see one of his ministers?'

A wide smile flashed across Hassan's face. 'All is most simple, my lord. Very early tomorrow we wait in courtyard of palace and meet a minister on his way to Amir's audience chamber. You will see.'

Tom dressed himself with care next morning, determined to make a good impression on the Amir when they met, and slipped the impressive document from the Spanish governor into his pocket. With Hassan curled up all night on the floor outside his door, Tom had slept surprisingly well in the spartan room of the little hostelry, and his spirits were high as they set out just as the first rays of the sun were touching the intimidating walls of the citadel on the hill.

Even now, others were trudging ahead of them up the winding road and gathering at the great, iron-studded wooden gates which were not yet open. Already food and drink stalls were being set up on the roadside and

44

fires lit under cooking pots.

A number of women were amongst the group at the entrance, women whose features were hidden under the traditional all-enveloping Islamic *burka*. Most were dressed in blue or black, but one wore a dusty white garment. And when the gates at last creaked open, the women were amongst the first to swarm into the large courtyard, jostling to position themselves near certain palace doors which stood firmly closed. Eventually guards, wearing red turbans and carrying elaborate shields and long pikes, came out to prod everyone back to some unmarked point on the stone paving.

The women clustered together and their shrill voices rose until, one by one, they settled into cross-legged positions on the stones and prepared to wait. And wait. The figure in the flowing white *burka* was the only one to demonstrate a degree of impatience as she approached first one stony-faced guard and then the other. She pulled a paper from some invisible pocket in her garment and waved it under the nose of each man who, to Tom's surprise, appeared to wilt briefly under the force of her verbal assault.

But it was to no avail and as they shook their heads at her, she turned away and kicked a stone across the courtyard. Tom watched her sit alone with her back to the wall, seemingly ready to spring to her feet should any new arrival try to claim the attention of a minister ahead of her.

Hassan, too, had been watching the woman in white. 'She comes here with a petition for a divorce,' he sneered with the conceit of male youth, 'or she simply wants her husband to get rid of his third wife.'

All through the long wait, the water-sellers and food vendors moved in and out of the courtyard, doing a brisk trade. The sun climbed higher, passed overhead, and began to slide towards the west — with still no sight of a minister coming out to speak to anyone in the crowd of petitioners. Some people were now giving up and starting to drift away down the hill. After standing for hours on hard stone, Tom's leg had begun to ache. The bone that had been crushed in the polo accident — which had indeed been no accident — had eventually mended, but the torn ligaments and muscles around it still had a tendency to complain loudly if too much stress was placed on them.

He pulled out his watch and looked at the time, then swore under his breath. The rules of this idiotic palace game were going to be changed, he decided, and ignoring Hassan's hiss of disapproval, he strode to the first

46

sentry and whipped the Spanish governor's impressive-looking document from his pocket. He opened it and held the parchment six inches from the man's eyes.

'Hassan, please inform this fellow that I am a person of the highest rank, and the Amir will be outraged when he hears that I have been kept waiting out here all day. I demand to see somebody *now* about arranging an audience.'

Tom stepped back and tried to avoid the hostile glances of people who had witnessed his performance. He refolded the paper while Hassan and the guard held a lengthy conversation. Initially, they both spoke sharply, but gradually the big man with the lance began to nod his head, and to look speculatively towards the arrogant Englishman. Men and women sitting nearby strained to listen.

The guard muttered to Hassan, then turned abruptly and went inside, closing the door behind him. Jubilation shone in the youth's dark eyes. 'Ah, my lord, as you will see, your Hassan has served you well. Your wait will soon be at an end.'

Tom shifted uncomfortably from one foot to the other as he heard angry murmurs rise around him. 'Well, it's said that the end justifies the means,' he mumbled to no one in particular, and Hassan grinned at him uncomprehendingly.

Eventually, the guard returned to his position outside the door, inclined his head to Hassan, and after another hour's delay, there was a surge of excitement in the courtyard as the palace door opened again and a turbaned man wearing rich robes stepped outside. The petitioners instantly pressed forward, wailing and fluttering their papers at him, but he merely held up his hand in a futile signal for silence, while the lances of the guards ensured no one came near him. Except Hassan, pulling Tom by the sleeve.

'Come, my lord. The minister will take your petition to the Amir. Quickly, give it to him now and your audience will be granted.'

For a moment Tom hesitated as caution over-rode his desperation to get this matter dealt with. Then he looked at the great ruby ring on the hand that reached out for the Spanish governor's document and, drawing in a deep breath, he handed the parchment to the minister.

'Ask him, Hassan, when I may expect to receive an audience with the Amir. Tell him that I need to get on with my business without delay.'

Hassan stepped towards the man, doubled himself over in a bow while he spoke, and didn't straighten again until the man had given his brief reply. Without so much as a glance at Tom, the official walked back inside the building, accompanied by fresh wails from the other petitioners.

'What did he say, Hassan?' Tom asked, overwhelmed by a feeling of anticlimax. 'When do I meet the Amir?'

Hassan's white teeth flashed as he grinned. 'Tomorrow, my lord. You must come tomorrow. Same as today.'

Before Tom could draw breath, the woman in the white *burka* sprang to her feet and rushed at him. 'Never have I seen a such a foolish thing!' she said, speaking Spanish in the cultured accents of a grandee. 'Have you just escaped from an asylum for the insane?' With both hands on the hem of the veil hanging from her fitted cap, she swept it back to reveal her pale-skinned face, a pair of hazel-green eyes sparkling with fury, and a dark purple bruise on her temple. 'Don't you realize that you'll never see your document again now that you have given it to that man!' A few strands of tightly curled, light-coloured hair clung damply to her forehead.

'*Señora*! I have urgent, important business to attend to, and no time to waste here in Agadir. I simply need the minister to arrange a brief audience with the Amir,' he said defensively. He watched her lips tighten before she dropped the veil over her face again and looked out at him through a grille of cotton cutwork.

'Firstly, sir, let me inform you that my business with the Amir is perhaps even more important than yours and I have already been waiting for more than two days. And secondly, have you considered that the man who was so willing to take your document was probably some servant boldly wearing his master's robe and ring for a few minutes in order to dupe a gullible European?'

A serpent of suspicion crawled through Tom's gut and he looked around quickly for Hassan to confirm that the man wearing the ruby ring had indeed been a minister of the Amir's court.

Hassan was nowhere in sight and Tom felt as foolish as he had when he was six years old and an Indian conjuror had tricked him by taking a precious silver trinket and apparently turning it into a stone.

'Your boy is no doubt already on his way to collect his share of the spoils when your document with the handsome red seals is sold for an exorbitant price to some man in the kasbah — a man who will no doubt use your name and credentials across Africa in one kind of nefarious business or another.' The tirade left her breathless, and she looked as if she was about to lift her veil again, but changed her mind. 'Go home, sir. Get on the first ship leaving Agadir, and go home!'

She made a clicking sound with her tongue and turned away with her white cotton garment flapping around her as she stormed towards the gate. Tom followed at a distance. His thoughts were a whirlpool of disbelief and shock at his own idiocy; he tried to catch sight of Hassan along the road to give the young devil the thrashing he no doubt deserved.

The wretched boy was nowhere to be seen, and the slight, swift-footed young woman easily outpaced Tom on the road into town where he found himself limping more than usual.

Damn! What were his options now? he wondered as frustration threatened to suffocate him. Find another Spanish-speaking scoundrel to lead him a merry dance? Or be sensible and admit defeat? The thought of his parents' disappointment if he failed so soon made him pause when he came to the high, vaulted entrance of the caravanserai — the rest house of travellers — on the outskirts of the town. Was there a chance that someone in here knew of an English woman named Diana being carried against her will along a

51

desert caravan route?

Clinging to that faint hope and trying to ignore the smells assaulting his nostrils, he walked inside the building, pushing his way through the tethered horses and kneeling camels, past bundles, baskets and boxes which were being unloaded. In the dim cloisters surrounding the central arena, merchants and traders lounged on cushions, smoking their hookas and drinking sweet mint tea, conducting their business at an imperceptible pace.

On the far side, he caught sight of the young woman in the white *burka* engaged in an animated discussion with a camel driver who repeatedly shook his head at her. At last, she threw up her arms in a gesture of exasperation and turned away to speak to another man who was unsaddling his beast. Even at a distance, Tom could see this man was rebuffing her also.

He remained standing where he was, and as he watched her walking towards the doorway, it was clear that she was very angry. Her head was down and when she attempted to kick a basket out of her way, she stumbled, lost her balance and almost slipped. It was only then that she looked up and apparently recognized Tom. For several moments she made no move, then she came closer and stood with her head and shoulder turned away from him.

'Don't look at me,' she said. 'It would not do for us to be seen speaking here, but tell me quickly, what is it that you are seeking?' Her voice was so low he had difficulty catching the words.

'I need information regarding the whereabouts of my sister,' he muttered, nonchalantly looking down at his sleeve and brushing away a speck of dust.

'Maybe I can be of assistance. Wait two minutes, then follow,' she said and, without a backwards glance, hurried out into the noisy street.

Tom counted off the seconds like an obedient child, then walked away from the caravanserai. The girl was waiting beside a donkey cart on the other side of the road and, with a faint motion of her head, she signalled him to keep his distance behind her.

He soon found himself shouldering his way through narrow, slatternly lanes and into an area which became increasingly malodorous. At last, skirting the fly-blown carcass of a dog, and springing from the path of a wagon trundling a load of dung to the fields, the girl stopped outside a seedy tavern. 'Go in and wait for me. I risk being stoned if I'm seen talking with you,' she whispered. 'I'll be no more than ten minutes. And watch your pockets.'

Almost at once she was swallowed up by the crowd, and again he did just as she'd instructed, sitting uneasily with his back against the tavern wall, and pretending to ignore the curiosity that his presence in the place was causing. He ordered a mint tea by pointing, and had only just finished it when the young woman, now dressed in drab European clothes, appeared in the doorway and waved to him.

'Ah! There you are! Come along now, I've been looking for you everywhere,' she called in her incongruously rich Castillian accent, while the message in her hazel-green eyes warned him to play along with her game.

She was wearing an unflattering white blouse buttoned to the neck and a serviceable skirt of dark blue-and-white striped cotton. A tooled leather belt circled her thin waist, and her tightly-curling hair was pulled back savagely into a bun. A battered straw hat perching on her crown was tipped forward to shade her face and hide the angry bruise on her forehead. The faded pink silk rose sitting forlornly on one side of it, nodded with each movement of her head.

'I think it would be pleasant to stroll to the beach and catch the evening breeze, don't you?' she said to him, and navigated their way to the sea wall. She perched herself up on it, and he swung up beside her, where for several awkward, silent moments they sat watching the boats of the sardine fishermen drifting home across the glassy waters of the bay.

'*Señorita*, my name is Thomas Sinclair,' he said impatiently, 'and may I enquire what sudden urge has persuaded you to become involved in my business?'

'How do you do, Mr Sinclair. I'm Francesca O'Hara,' she said evenly, 'and, believe me, I had absolutely no interest in your business until I watched that young monkey at your side planning to steal that document you were so carelessly exhibiting this afternoon.' She pushed her hat further back on her head and looked him up and down. 'I couldn't believe my eyes when I saw you walk straight into the trap he set up with the guard and some palace flunkey who'd clearly borrowed a silk robe and a ruby ring to trick you.' She pulled a long face. 'Well, I thought to myself, here's a gentleman far from the shores of home who requires a little tuition in the way things are done in a foreign country.'

He was too angry at his own stupidity to make an attempt to justify his actions. 'This is not my first journey away from England, Miss

O'Hara,' he said stiffly, 'and I couldn't help but notice that you also failed to get any satisfaction from your visit to the palace today.'

'Ah yes, I was most dissatisfied,' she said with heavy emphasis. 'I went to the palace to plead with the Amir to order the arrest of a man who robbed me last month — a man I've known since childhood. He stole everything I owned, and he also took a valuable object from the people who employed me. That all happened in Tangier, but the wretch got away and caught a ship bound for Agadir.' Her jaw tightened. 'I arrived here a few days ago with a camel train, and it didn't take me long to find the house where he was hiding. When I confronted him, he struck me.' She touched the bruise. 'If I'd been able to see the Amir, it might have been possible to have him arrested before he got away again.' She spread her hands in helplessness. 'Now my funds are so low that I can't persuade even the most inferior camel driver to take me after him.'

Her scarcely-believable story, and the matter-of-fact way she'd spoken of the events in her cultured accent left Tom dumbfounded. But she appeared not to notice his reaction as she brushed away an annoying fly.

'So, now please tell me, Mr Sinclair,' she continued, 'what is the nature of the information you said you required regarding your sister? I speak Arabic, so perhaps I can help you — for a small fee? The women who live in a town like this usually hear about everything that happens, and in the *souk* they talk to me quite freely when I'm wearing my *burka*. To the men, I'm invisible.'

Her bruised forehead was high and smooth and her greenish eyes looked at him from a sharp, inquisitive face. While her features were regular, there was no conventional prettiness in them. And Tom could see no laughter lines at all.

He scrubbed a hand across his chin, unsure whether to enlist the help of this intense young woman. On the other hand, how could he afford not to?

'Very well, Miss O'Hara,' he said hesitantly, then drew in a deep breath and pulled out the photograph of Diana. 'I have it on good authority that my sister was on a ship that sank off the Cape Verde Islands about three months ago. She was rescued by an Arab trader and brought to Agadir.'

At the mention of that, Miss O'Hara's jaw sagged and her right hand flew to make the sign of the cross on her flat chest. 'Sweet Mother of Jesus!' she said. 'The poor lady! And your family has not yet received a ransom demand? Was she — may I be so indelicate as to enquire if your sister — '

For a moment Tom left her floundering to find a euphemism for the appropriate anatomical word which a genteel Spanish lady would never utter. Her discomfort gave him a twinge of pleasure.

'My sister is a married lady,' he said at last, and she looked only moderately relieved.

'Well, Mr Sinclair, don't believe what you might have heard about the trade of the Barbary pirates fading into the pages of history,' she said, sounding like a schoolmistress. 'There are still galleys plying these waters with poor wretches chained to their oars, and a European lady is still an object of value in certain markets — even if she has been married.'

She bit down on her bottom lip and, for several silent moments, looked westward across the bay to where the sun was setting, bleeding its colour into a bank of clouds on the horizon and staining the heavens crimson.

She studied the photograph again and her tone was softer when she spoke. 'You said that your sister was brought here three months ago? That's a long time. Has there has been no demand for ransom? Has her husband already tried, but failed to find her?'

'No. My sister's husband is, er — not a young man,' Tom said evasively.

'And so you, yourself, have come to search

for her? Oh, Mr Sinclair, you must love her very much indeed!'

Love Diana? What a question! Had he ever loved her? Yes, of course he had fond memories of playing with her at home on the tea plantation when she was a tiny, dark-haired mischief-maker, constantly trotting at his heels. But then he and his stepbrother had been sent off to school, and after that went to Oxford. There were occasional visits back to India, but by that time Diana was growing into an obstinate young woman with opinions that usually clashed with his own.

No, it wasn't love for Diana that had brought him here; he was unable to share his parents' capacity to offer her unconditional love. 'Everyone in the family is concerned at the time that has elapsed since my sister's disappearance,' he said, evading Miss O'Hara's direct question.

'Yes, it must be a most harrowing time for you all,' she said, holding his gaze. 'Perhaps, Mr Sinclair, I can be of some service to you if I wear my *burka* tomorrow and spend the day speaking with the women in the kasbah. May I take this picture with me? If anyone knows about the arrival of a lady here, they might also be able to tell me where she was taken, and by whom.'

That was exactly what Tom wanted to know, but his reluctance to involve this young woman in his personal concerns made him hesitate. His mind searched for some other option. There was none. 'Thank you, Miss O'Hara, I'd appreciate your assistance,' he said, and pulled two sovereigns from his pocket. 'Take these for whatever expenses you encounter tomorrow.'

Francesca O'Hara looked at him closely and frowned. 'I'd hazard a guess that your sister would most likely have been taken north to the market in Marrakech.' Her eyes dipped away from his. 'But which route would they have travelled?'

She seemed deep in thought, but when she looked up at him again he detected a sudden eagerness in her eyes. 'Mr Sinclair — if I bring news of your sister, will you immediately set out on your search?'

'Yes, Miss O'Hara. Immediately.'

'And am I to assume that you would wish me to accompany you and act as your interpreter along the way?' Her enthusiasm surprised him.

This was not at all what Tom wanted, but after today's fiasco with Hassan, it was clear that he needed to be accompanied by someone who spoke the local language. It was not simply a matter of gender that made him hesitate now, but some instinct warning him that this sharp, outspoken woman would not be an easy travelling companion.

'Before I can make any decision about that, Miss O'Hara, I need to know where my sister is likely to have gone,' he said carefully. 'But what of your own family? Surely they'd feel some concern if you set out to travel with a man they know nothing about?'

'My parents are deceased, Mr Sinclair, and the Spanish family in Tangier who employed me to teach their children, no longer require my services. I'm looking for a new position.' She slid down from the sea wall and brushed the dust from her skirt. 'I'll do my best to find out what I can tomorrow and I suggest we meet here again at about this time so I can tell you what I've learned.'

She was about to turn away when she paused and asked him where he was lodging. She frowned when he told her.

'Please be sure to lock your door tonight, Mr Sinclair. I fear you might already have attracted the wrong kind of attention in this city.'

4

Miss Francesca O'Hara was twenty-five years old and, because of the itinerant nature of her late father's occupation, had moved frequently from one city to another around the rim of North Africa. Intermittently throughout childhood she had been sent across the Mediterranean to receive a Christian education with the good sisters at the Abbey of Saint Casilda near Granada, but she still remained a firm believer that it was Fate which ruled her life.

It had surely been the cruel hand of Fate which, four weeks ago, permitted Otto Heinkler to break into her room in Tangier just at the very moment she was replacing her savings in their hiding place. Seven years of diligent work as a governess with French and Spanish families living in North Africa had gone into creating that cache; only to have her late father's so-called friend run off — with not only her money — but all her personal papers, passport and the irreplaceable little family treasures she had kept in the old leather pouch which she had always taken great care to keep hidden.

62

But now Fate must be smiling again, for surely no gentle Christian saint would have so conveniently crossed the path of an apparently well-to-do Englishman named Sinclair with that of Miss Francesca O'Hara — right at the very moment when her life was looking its blackest.

The call to prayer coming from the minaret in a nearby mosque accompanied her footsteps as she hurried back to the ramshackle lodging house where she already owed money for three nights' accommodation. But her spirits were on the rise, for now Fate was handing her an opportunity to catch up with Herr Heinkler again and, this time, hopefully retrieve what was lawfully hers.

Reliable information had come to her this morning that the German had left Agadir with a camel train which was heading east, towards the desert. No doubt he had a buyer waiting out there for the ancient golden bowl he'd stolen from her employer's house. Heinkler now had more than a day's headstart, but never in his wildest dreams would he imagine that Francesca O'Hara could find the means to follow him from Agadir.

All she had to do was to keep her wits about her and tread carefully so as not to arouse Mr Sinclair's suspicion. Of course, she would do everything possible to help the gentleman find his poor sister but, if she was very clever, he would never come to realize that she also had her own agenda in this enterprise.

Everything now depended on confirmation that the lady named Diana had indeed been carried to Marrakech, for there were several ways to reach that city. The one taken by most travellers led north from Agadir, but Marrakech could also be reached by a longer route which first circled east, towards the desert. And Otto Heinkler had set out in that direction. Could Mr Sinclair be persuaded to travel that way also? How satisfying it would be to surprise *Uncle Otto* and beat him at his own game!

No excitement, or even relief, showed on Francesca's slightly freckled and bruised face as she hurried along the squalid street, but hiding inside her thin frame was a euphoric girl who longed to lift the hem of her skirt and dance for joy. Fate had just presented her with a priceless opportunity, and she was determined that it would not be wasted.

She was hungry next morning when she donned the white *burka*, slipped past the angry landlady without being seen, and hurried into the twisting alleys of the medina. Here she was instantly met by the aroma of hot bread drifting from bakers' ovens.

Veiled women clustered, chattering together in doorways as they waited for a baker to cook the dough they had sent to the ovens earlier. In every community, rivalry was strong amongst households as to which family produced the finest bread, and Francesca soon fell into conversation with a woman who was waiting on her doorstep for a boy to come running from the baker with the family's hot bread on a tray.

When it arrived, the woman — with traditional hospitality — invited the stranger into her house, where Francesca not only sampled the bread and praised its quality, but met the other women of the household — two more wives, the grandmother and several daughters.

As there were no men about, she removed her veil and dismissed their concern about her bruised temple. They were astonished to find that this fair-skinned European not only spoke Arabic, but also showed a remarkable familiarity with their customs.

Several ladies from neighbouring houses were called in to meet the visitor, and while they all sat gossiping in the little courtyard, drinking coffee and eating the bread, along with dates and goat cheese, Francesca answered their questions by spinning a tall tale about her own life which would have earned the applause of Scherazade herself.

Mr Sinclair was her *brother*, she told them, and he'd come to Agadir in search of his cherished *wife*, Diana, who had been plucked from a shipwreck and possibly carried here by pirates three months previously. At this point she showed them the picture of Diana, and it was passed around the group to be admired.

She, Francesca, had come from England to care for her brother, she told them, for the poor man was going mad with despair and needed a great deal of assistance. Why, just yesterday, in his unstable frame of mind, he had been tricked into losing an important document.

Nobody in her audience appeared to notice all the inconsistencies peppering the romantic tale of a heartbroken man searching for his beloved wife. What they were most eager to hear were more details of the English lady named Diana, and the style of married life she would have known with such a devoted husband as Francesca had painted her Mr Sinclair to be. The fact that she personally knew nothing about intimate domestic matters in English households didn't prevent her from weaving an image which had the ladies sighing.

'So now you must see that if my dear

brother's wife cannot be found, he will surely go out of his mind with grief. He needs to discover whether she is alive. Or dead!'

Eventually, the toothless grandmother recalled that some time ago she'd been told by her cousin about the arrival one night of a two-masted dhow carrying a white woman.

Several of the women ran to fetch that elderly cousin from her house nearby and when she arrived she confirmed that she had indeed watched a group of men — she swore they were pirates — carrying lanterns and coming from the beach one night. They'd had a white woman with them wrapped in a shawl which had slipped from her head as she'd passed. The old cousin was shown the photograph and, yes, she assured Francesca, this was indeed the lady she had observed.

'Please tell me, was she bound in any way?' Francesca asked. 'Did she appear to be hurt, or distressed? Where was she taken?'

'She walked quite freely,' the old woman said, 'and I saw her enter the house of Yakub al-Mansur. With my own eyes, I saw him open his door to her.'

'Ah!' chorused the other ladies, and it was clear from their tone that the name carried some significance. The corners of their mouths dipped and they shook their heads. Al-Mansur would have paid a high price for a fair-skinned woman, they all agreed, and would take her to one of the big markets. Marrakech? Fez? Perhaps Algiers?

'Of course, when I saw al-Mansur's wife at the spice market next day,' the cousin hastened to add, 'I asked about the lady who had come to their house under cover of darkness, and she said my eyesight must be failing because there was no lady there.'

The elderly relative was clearly enjoying the attention she was receiving and her gestures became more dramatic. 'But I am no fool, cousins, and when I said that my eldest son, the wrestler, would soon get her husband to talk about this visitor who came to his house in the middle of the night, she told me that al-Mansur had left early that very morning on one of his trading journeys.'

She wagged her head from side to side and glanced around the group with a superior smile. 'Though the wife refused to tell me where her husband had so suddenly gone to do his trading, I saw her in the *souk* a month later and she was wearing three new gold bangles — and boasting to everyone that her husband had been to Marrakech to buy them!'

Francesca's heart raced faster at the mention of that city. This was just the information she had hoped for. 'Do you think he would have travelled directly there by the northern route?' she asked, and her new friends seemed surprised that she would have considered him going any other way.

'You have my profound thanks for giving me that news, Madame, because now it's clear that my brother and I must set out for Marrakech without further delay.' The ladies nodded enthusiastically. 'My heart overflows with gratitude for the help you have all given in this hour of need.' She acknowledged each of the women by name. She always made a point of remembering names. 'But now I must beg for two more favours: Firstly, where can we hire good camels and a reliable guide to take us to Marrakech?'

After a heated discussion amongst the women, one name was agreed upon — Ahmed, the husband of another relative. Two ladies immediately hurried off with Francesca to make arrangements with the cameleer; he was surprised when she insisted that her brother did not wish to travel to Marrakech by the direct route, but via the much longer way leading east through Taroudant.

He tried to discourage her, pointing out that this added at least another five or six days to the journey and, because they'd be travelling beyond the limits of the Sultan's law, they faced the risk of running into bandits along the way.

But she stood firm and when he heard the fee she offered, the man finally bowed to her unusual request and asked no questions. He and his camels would be ready to set out before dawn tomorrow, he said.

When Francesca returned to the courtyard with the ladies, she had one last query. 'My poor brother has been unable to gain an audience with the Amir and as yet we have no permit to travel. Would it be possible — ? Perhaps, you might know someone who — ?'

The ladies needed no time at all to debate this matter. They all considered Abu al-Mumin to be the best forger of documents in Agadir, and within fifteen minutes a party of her new friends were escorting Francesca into his little workshop in the *souk*.

When she and the man had settled on a price for the certificate, she wrote the words for him to transcribe, and along with the name of Thomas Sinclair, went that of his sister, Miss Francesca *Sinclair*.

When it was done, she agreed to pay a little extra for several impressive red seals to be added below the signature of the Amir, which the man produced with a practised flourish.

The forgery was excellent. She was a good judge of this kind of work, because her late father had often tried his hand at it and had usually produced very mediocre results.

She felt very pleased with her day's accomplishments as she hurried back to her lodgings with enough money left from the various dealings to face her landlady at last, and also pay for just one more night's accommodation.

As quickly as she could, she pulled off the *burka* and dressed in her skirt and blouse before running back to her rendezvous with Mr Sinclair at the sea wall. He was sitting with a sketch pad on his knee and her quick glance at his impression of the waterfront scene showed he had a remarkable talent.

'Good afternoon, sir,' she said, trying not to look too smug as she handed the photograph of Diana back to him. 'I'm pleased to report that my day has been a very satisfactory one. Firstly, I have learned that your sister was seen coming ashore here one night about three months ago, and that she was very probably taken to Marrakech by a trader named Yakob al-Mansur. The person who caught sight of her said she appeared to be unharmed.'

His eyes widened. 'Someone actually saw Diana here? And she was taken to Marrakech? Then I must arrange to go there straight away,' he said grimly.

'Of course,' she said, 'that's why I have

71

engaged a reliable guide who'll be ready to meet us outside the city gates before dawn. It will be wiser for us to leave quietly and not allow our movements to be the subject of speculation in the caravanserai.'

It now seemed to have become a *fait accompli* that she would accompany him, and he gave a muted groan.

'And I arranged this for you as well,' she said, taking the forged travel pass from her pocket and handing it to him with a self-satisfied expression.

His jaw muscles slackened as he unfolded it and scanned the script written in Arabic. 'I see,' he said and gave her a sideways glance. 'You have my thanks, Miss O'Hara.'

She gave a faint smile and didn't point out to him that her name had been included there as his sister.

'Well, perhaps now is the time to discuss an appropriate remuneration for your services?' he said. 'So much per day? By the way, how long will it take for us to reach Marrakech?'

'Ah yes, the journey to Marrakech,' she said, cleared her throat and took a deep breath. 'I'm afraid we do have a problem there — but just a small one, I've been assured.' She held his gaze and calmly lied. 'Our guide, Ahmed, has informed me that though the northern route is the most direct, we can't possibly go that way at the moment because fighting has broken out again all along there.' She feigned a shudder and frowned, as if tormented by shocking images. 'The Ghomara and Almohad tribes have been battling over that territory for generations, with both sides carrying out the most dreadful atrocities.' She looked at him quickly to gauge whether he was likely to challenge her fabrication, but he seemed to be convinced.

'So what's the alternative?'

'Our cameleer, Ahmed — whom I'm assured is most reliable — says it should take only a few extra days for us to circle safely through Taroudant and Taliouine, and then approach Marrakech from the south-east. It's a very picturesque route, I hear. You should find interesting scenes to sketch.'

He had no knowledge of the towns she mentioned, and sketching was merely a way he occasionally filled in time. 'If you say that's the only alternative, I suppose I must agree.'

She gave a quick nod and controlled the excitement bubbling inside her. Little did Mr Sinclair suspect that by riding hard for two days towards the east, they might very well catch up with Otto Heinkler in the town of Taroudant. And if they missed him there, there was always the hope of finding him and her precious leather pouch in the next town along the edge of the desert. She hoped desperately that Mr Sinclair owned a pistol, but thought it was probably not a good time to raise that topic with him at the moment.

'Ahmed says that his camels are sound and well rested,' she said conversationally, 'and they should be able to cover up to forty miles a day. Have you ridden a camel, Mr Sinclair? No? It's not difficult once you remember that, unlike a horse, your animal doesn't have a bit in his mouth. You use your legs and your feet on either side of his neck to let him know which way you want to go. I always carry a stick, too, for extra persuasion. Of course, the ring through their noses makes it simple for one to be led, if that is your preference.'

At this point she heard him suck in a breath through his teeth.

'Ahmed says that his camels will have no trouble in walking for ten hours a day. He is most particular about their well-being, and — by the way, Mr Sinclair — for the sake of propriety, I have informed him that I am your sister.' He seemed about to comment, then shrugged.

'Ahmed will bring two sons with him to tend the camels and set up our camp each evening if we don't reach a town. Tomorrow morning, well before daylight, both sons will come to escort us from our lodgings — for our own safety, you understand.'

Before he went to bed, Tom wrote to his parents. It was difficult to maintain a tone of optimism, but perhaps it would be of some comfort for them to hear that Diana was seen to be in good health when she'd left for Marrakech. He told them that he was preparing to ride there now to gather further information, and simply said he had engaged a *competent* person to go with him to be his interpreter.

And now *that* person, along with two sinewy, dark-skinned young men was waiting for him when he silently left his lodging house well before any sign of daylight. The sons took his travelling box by its handles and, without exchanging one word, the quartet hurried off in the direction of the city gate where Ahmed was waiting outside in the dark with seven kneeling camels.

A thin sabre-curve of moon gave just enough light for Tom to watch Miss O'Hara speaking quietly to the cameleer, while his sons tied his box and Miss O'Hara's saddle-bag on to one of the animals transporting the expedition's provisions and canvas tents.

'This is your mount, Mr Sinclair,' she said. 'Climb on to the saddle here, and put your feet on his neck. Don't forget that the back legs will stand up first so hang on tightly until his front legs are straight.'

He complied with her directions and suffered instant discomfort as his animal rose with the moan of protest made by all the camels as they were urged to their feet.

As they moved off in line towards the east, Tom's animal was led by the rope attached to its nose ring while Miss O'Hara rode independently behind him. The starlit hours of darkness passed with no sounds but the steady plodding of the animals' flat, padded feet on the *piste* as they travelled inland.

Tom was still trying to persuade his body to accommodate long hours of the camel's motion when dawn broke and the sun shattered the remnants of night, shooting its spears of golden light into the striated, weather-worn cliffs of the Anti Atlas range around them.

The heat rose as they moved towards the desert, and some hours later Miss O'Hara called to Ahmed for the camels to be halted. They were brought to their knees beside a patch of thorn bushes, which they immediately began to nibble. Tom slid to the ground with a grunt of relief that he could stretch his tortured muscles at last.

'Now, Mr Sinclair, if you will be so kind as

to face the east for a few minutes like the other men, I will face the west to relieve myself,' she said with no hint of coyness. 'I'll call out before I rejoin the party.'

Five minutes later the camels were on their way again, and as they trudged relentlessly towards the deserts, sweat stung Tom's eyes and trickled down his spine. He allowed his thoughts to drift homewards to Julia and James — reminding himself that they were the reason for his making this wretched journey. Damn Diana! His foolish sister didn't deserve the twenty-nine years of love they'd never denied her; but he doubted that he'd ever be able to forgive her.

The camels kept up a steady pace and at last the rugged gorge they had been following ended in a wide, dry valley that opened on to the view of a far-off oasis fed by the melting snows of the High Atlas. A deserted, seemingly inaccessible fort perched on the steep height of a rock-strewn plateau, and far beyond it he saw the outline of the vast Sahara with razor-edged swells of shifting sand stretching to the horizon.

A wind picked up and distant whirlwinds spun, weaving this way and that, like dancers across the sand, while a solitary falcon circled high above them on motionless wings. He turned in his saddle and saw Miss O'Hara smile as she looked up to follow the bird's flight until it was no more than a speck against the blue. If Diana had, in fact, been carried along this route, he wondered if she would have smiled at a falcon flying over the desert?

In the heat of the afternoon, after ten hours' travel, the caravan reached the oasis and the sons erected two little tents in the shade of high palm trees. The cooking fire was started and the camels fed and hobbled for the night.

Tom was delighted to find that Miss O'Hara remained withdrawn and uncommunicative because he was too exhausted to make any attempt at sociability. He stretched himself out in the shade and watched her wander to sit on the other side of the oasis. This girl was one of the oddest he had encountered in all his travels, but he was not sufficiently intrigued by her background to encourage confidences. Although, he admitted, it would be interesting to know where she'd learned to speak Spanish in that clipped, cultured accent. Did she know any English? And what circumstances had left her stranded in Morocco without family or resources?

He closed his eyes and lay with his arms behind his head. They'd arrive in Marrakech in a few days' time, and though he and Miss

O'Hara hadn't yet come to any firm agreement on payment, he intended to treat her generously. He grinned to himself. Perhaps he'd even give her a little extra and encourage her to have some new clothes made. The faded grey blouse she was wearing today must surely be the most unattractive female garment ever produced. And her hat with the flapping pink rose . . .

He didn't realize he'd dozed off until she woke him as darkness was falling and the cooking fire was burning low. 'Dinner is ready,' she called. 'You must eat well because we have another long ride ahead of us tomorrow.'

He grunted and passed a hand across his face, then roused himself to join the circle sitting cross-legged around the food, and already dipping the fingers of their right hands into the communal pots.

Miss O'Hara fell into a long discussion with Ahmed and his sons. The glow of the firelight on her face softened her features somewhat, and when she and the Arabs shared an occasional smile, Tom realized how splendid her teeth were. Yes, her smile was certainly her best feature; it was a pity she didn't smile more often.

Francesca carefully selected a date from the bowl, chewed it slowly and threw the seed over her shoulder. 'As soon as we reach

Taroudant in two days,' she turned to say to Tom, 'Ahmed and his sons will begin to make enquiries in the caravanserai and cafés. Even wearing my *burka*, it wouldn't be seemly for a woman to wander about the town alone after dark.'

Tom shovelled another knob of spicy camel meat into his mouth and nodded.

'By the way, Mr Sinclair, if you have a pistol in your luggage,' she said in a conversational tone, 'it might be advisable to carry it on your belt now. The Sultan's law doesn't reach this part of the land and we need to keep a constant watch out for bandits. And the little towns can be full of surprises, too.'

She gave him a sweetly innocent smile — one that hid the discomfort of knowing that she had deliberately misled him into believing that she had asked their Arab guides to enquire about his sister when they arrived in Taroudant. It wasn't news of Diana that she had requested them to find, but information about the German, Herr Otto Heinkler, who'd come this way recently.

And when she did come face to face with that hateful man out here, how would she persuade him to return her leather pouch and all it held? Would Ahmed and his sons stand behind her?

Could Mr Sinclair's pistol be put to use?

5

Their pace of travel the following day didn't slacken until, late in the afternoon, the next oasis came into sight. Ahmed and his sons suddenly halted their beasts and huddled closer, muttering together as they peered into the distance where a large and apparently ragged caravan was already camped under the trees.

Tom lifted his binoculars. 'Surely there's enough water for everyone?' He passed his glasses to Francesca. 'What's troubling Ahmed?'

She adjusted the lenses, surveyed the scene ahead and called out to the cameleer. He responded briefly, and as they rode on slowly towards the oasis, she kept the glasses to her eyes.

'There must have been a recent attack because some of the men over there seem to be injured,' she said and turned in her saddle to scan the silent landscape in all directions before passing the binoculars back to Tom.

The knot of unease in his stomach tightened as they drew closer to the oasis and Ahmed called out to the men camping there.

Miss O'Hara listened to their responses and pulled a long face when she began to translate.

'Tuaregs,' she said simply. 'This was a rich caravan — a big one — coming up from Timbuctu with black slaves and ivory — maybe gold dust and ostrich feathers and saffron, too. They were on their way to Algiers, but this is all that's left after the Tuaregs attacked yesterday.'

Tom felt decidedly uneasy to think of the legendary Tuaregs raiding into Morocco. *The wolves of the desert*, he'd heard them called. That night sleep was elusive as he lay for hours in his little tent, listening for sounds of approaching danger, while from the other side of the oasis came the groans of the wounded cameleers.

Ahmed roused Francesca and Tom well before dawn and they wasted no time in loading their camels and moving off from the dismal scene on the other side of the oasis.

When at the end of that day the formidable, crenellated walls surrounding the old desert trading town of Taroudant came into view, Tom experienced a rush of relief that they'd reach safety. The caravan was halted by guards at the ornate gateway, and while Ahmed negotiated a fee for use of the caravanserai, another armed man scrutinized

Tom's forged pass. Money changed hands and when Ahmed and one son went off to tend their camels, the other led their passengers to what he said was the best accommodation in town.

'Well, Miss O'Hara, this seems quite acceptable,' Tom said as they were shown to their upstairs rooms in the mud-brick house where the windows of two bedrooms and a sitting-room overlooked a vista of rose gardens, orange trees and pomegranates growing within the town's yellow-brown walls.

Tom and Francesca agreed to bathe in turn and when he was again wearing clean clothes, he sprawled wearily in the sitting-room, lost in thought. 'I wonder if Diana was brought to this place on her way to Marrakech,' he said, rubbing one hand across his chin. 'Perhaps Ahmed and his sons will find someone here tonight who has news of her.'

'Ummm,' Francesca murmured, dipping her eyes away from his. Should she confess now that the only purpose in coming here to Taroudant was an attempt to catch up with Otto Heinkler?

She stood up quickly. 'Mr Sinclair, I'm going to take my travel clothes downstairs to be washed. Would you like me to take yours, too?'

Tom looked up from the couch. 'You don't have to go,' he said with a yawn. 'Call for someone to come up and get them.'

'No,' she said firmly, 'I must speak to the women and make sure everything will be ready before we leave early in the morning.'

He gave a grunt of protest, heaved himself to his feet and collected a bundle of laundry from his bedroom.

Francesca walked downstairs with guilt hanging around her shoulders like a heavy black cloak, inwardly cringing at her growing string of lies. Of course, there was no need to discuss this bundle of soiled garments with the washerwomen, but she did need to ask them if they had done laundry recently for a middle-aged German.

She tried to convince herself that Mr Sinclair would come to understand the reason for all this deceit, once he'd heard her explanation. She'd tell him the moment they reached Marrakech, and then she'd wear her *burka* and search every *souk* in the medina until she'd discovered the fate of his missing sister.

But that would be next week, and now it was imperative to grasp the only opportunity she might ever have to make *Uncle Otto* face his nemesis. Surely Mr Sinclair would see that she had no other option.

She sat on a stool beside the two washerwomen and questioned them as they worked. Yes, they told her, there had been a European staying here two days ago, and he was the first they'd seen for months. But now he'd gone. To Taliouine, they thought. He'd sweated like a pig and the stink of his clothes had drawn the flies from a hundred leagues away.

The women laughed as though this was an enormous joke, but their banter tore open the doors of Francesca's memory and a surge of nausea hit her when she recalled the repulsive stench of Heinkler's body. She shuddered at the memory of it, along with the shocking sensation of his damp, questing fingers trying to slide between her legs when she'd been no more than ten years old. She'd fought him off that day but, because the monster was viewed as her father's friend, she hadn't said a word about it.

Following that frightening episode, she'd tried to avoid being left alone with *Uncle Otto*. But even so, Heinkler had played a secret stalking game with her whenever he had an opportunity, tormenting her naïveté with touches and signals which instinct warned her were vile.

Over time, she learned to hide the revulsion these episodes roused in her, and forced herself to respond to his advances with a cold, dismissive disdain. This had infuriated him even further, and puzzled her father.

But, no, it wasn't Otto Heinkler who'd stolen her virginity when she was nineteen. It was the elder son of the genteel Spanish family in Rabat who'd employed her as governess for the younger children. The young man, whose proud parents boasted he was destined for high office in the priesthood, had caught her on the stairs one evening, dragged her into a room and raped her.

Now, as she pushed aside that sickening memory, she heard the washer-women laughing together about various men they'd known. The stout, elder one picked up the shirt which Tom Sinclair had recently removed, and held it to her nose. She raised her eyebrows approvingly, then threw it teasingly at the girl next to her, who sniffed it, giggled, and handed it on to Francesca with mischief in her smile.

Francesca froze at the earthy, musky, masculine scent of the Englishman's body on the fabric as it touched her nose and perplexed her brain. She laughed nervously, and quickly held the garment at arm's length. 'My brother,' she said and felt a rush of unaccountable warmth flush into her cheeks; she hid her embarrassment by fishing for coins in her pocket to pay the grinning women.

She thought how ridiculous it was for her body to react to his scent in such a wayward manner. While Mr Sinclair would probably be known in his own circles as a *fine looking man*, his physical proximity during their journey had never raised her heartbeat or sent fluttery thoughts through Francesca O'Hara's head. And he was certainly not a gentleman who would be tempted to take advantage of the unique situation in which they found themselves. Anyhow, what feminine allure did her thin body and plain face display to arouse desire in any respectable man?

But her cheeks were still warm and her insides still knotted with confusion when she went to the kitchen, asked for a meal to be sent up to their rooms at sunset, then slowly climbed back up the stairs.

At all costs she must keep on the right side of Mr Sinclair until they reached Marrakech, because without the wages he was going to pay her, her situation would be truly desperate. The pouch stolen by Heinkler had contained not just all her savings and little family mementoes, but also the glowing letters of reference from previous employers. What if the German had already tossed them away? Without those letters, where could she ever find another teaching position? She could never ask her last employers in Tangier to provide a character reference after they'd thrown her out with the accusation that she had colluded with Heinkler by letting him into their house to steal. Clearly someone must have left a door unlocked for him that night, but she was certainly not the one who had done it!

When she neared the top of the stairs, the sound of angry male voices coming from their sitting-room suddenly cut across her ruminations. Spanish was being spoken, though she couldn't catch the gist of the argument. Her heart began to pound as she crept up the last few steps to stand for a moment with her ear to the wood of the door.

Dry-mouthed, she gave a sharp tap before she opened it and saw Mr Sinclair standing with a face like thunder in the presence of four men in flowing white robes and turbans. Three wore bandoleers across their chests and carried rifles; knives bristled in their belts and long, curved swords hung at their sides. But the fourth man bore only a jewelled dagger at his waist.

He was darkly handsome, tall and broad-chested, and his robes distinguished him as the Sherif of the town — the magistrate, the religious leader, the chief of this little kingdom. He stood now in the centre of the room, dangling their forged travel pass from Agadir between his finger and thumb as if it contained something contagious. He turned and studied her with a frown of surprise as she bowed to him and then crossed the floor to stand beside Tom.

The corners of the Sherif's mouth turned down disparagingly. 'So this lady is your charming sister?' His tone was mocking and he flicked the parchment on to the floor, then stood watching them both closely with eyes the colour of gun-metal.

Francesca sensed trouble looming — and any form of trouble now was likely to delay their departure in the morning and lower her chances of catching up with Heinkler. She took a deep breath and bowed her head.

'Your shadow on our floor does us great honour, my lord,' she murmured, keeping her eyes averted. 'Please allow me to apologize for my brother,' she added in a tiny voice, 'and I humbly beg your forgiveness for any lack of respect he may foolishly have displayed — for he is unfamiliar with the ways of the desert.'

She heard Tom's quick, angry intake of breath. 'Not at all, my dear sister,' he said with undisguised sarcasm, articulating each syllable with precision. 'It appears that I have simply neglected to pay a tax which, I have just been informed, is levied on all foreigners who pass through the magnificent gates of Taroudant.'

Extortion was not an unusual practice in situations like this but, when Tom reached into the pocket which held his money, she was dismayed to see a sudden rage flare into his eyes.

'By the way, sir, I would be much obliged if you would inform me' — he spoke in a challenging tone — 'whether you also extracted this tax from an English lady named Diana when she was carried this way by her captors?' His chin tightened and his voice dropped to a growl. 'Or did you demand some other form of payment from her?' His body was already tense, but when his shoulders hunched pugnaciously, Francesca's heart sank.

The Sherif's hands dropped to his sides, his mouth thinned, and he let out a long hiss of fury. While the guards standing behind him were unlikely to have understood the Spanish insult thrown at their chief by the European man, it seemed they all recognized signs of violence about to erupt. Hands flew to the elaborate hilts of their swords, and steel rasped as blades were pulled from the scabbards. With a barely perceptible movement of his head, the Sherif signalled for the

Englishman to be taken, and Tom roared his outrage as the points of three swords instantly rose to touch his chest.

'You can't do this — I'm a British citizen! I'm here to search for my — my wife!' The sword tips pressed harder against his shirt and he took a step backwards. 'Damn you, I must know if a captive English lady was brought this way three months ago! Tell me!'

The Sherif's face was a mask of cold fury.

'Oh, Great Lord, I beg you to have mercy on my poor, afflicted brother,' Francesca cried and fell to the floor, prostrating herself in front of the Sherif. The eyes of all five men in the room instantly turned to look at her in astonishment. 'Mercy, Great Lord, mercy, I beg you,' she wailed loudly and repeatedly until the Sherif stepped closer and touched her head with the upturned toe of his leather slipper. When she looked up at him, tears were racing down her cheeks.

'Oh, I beg you not to punish my brother for his foolish words, noble lord. He knows not what he says, for the poor creature suffers from the madness that inflicts all the males in our family.' Her voice trembled, and she slowly pushed herself up into a sitting position. 'Sadly, a terrible — and peculiarly English illness — overcomes him every year at this time, and his wits are completely lost, lord. In his madness, he imagines all manner of strange matters, and at the moment he believes that he once had a wife named Diana.'

At this point, the corners of her mouth took a mournful downturn while she slowly circled a finger on her temple. 'It is the cold, damp, dark winter in our country that creeps into his skull and stirs this dreadful affliction, my lord, and the only remedy is for my dear brother to be taken away to spend time under a hot, strong desert sun to thaw his brain.'

The Sherif looked sceptically from Francesca to Tom, who at that moment found the wisdom to play along with her. He dropped his jaw, tilted his head to one side, and appeared to be mesmerized by the movement of a beetle crawling along the window ledge.

She shook her head sadly. 'Last year my poor, deranged brother believed himself to be wed to Cleopatra, and we sat for many weeks beside the pyramids in Egypt, waiting for her to arrive.' She climbed slowly to her feet and stood with her hands clasped demurely at her waist. 'But, as it always does in due time, the rays of the warm desert sun melted his madness and we were able to return home, to wait in dread for the next winter's attack.'

The Sherif looked at her more closely, studying the fading bruise on her forehead.

'And this he did to you?'

'He was quite out of his mind at the time, my lord. I beg you to show charity to this poor, suffering creature, and not delay our return to the desert tomorrow.'

The Sherif signalled his men to sheath their swords, and Tom picked up the beetle, holding its body at eye level to watch the frantic movements of the little black legs paddling in the air. 'You want to come home and live with me, don't you?' he murmured, half smiling at the creature.

For a moment the Sherif stared, then stepped closer and placed his hand on Tom's head. 'This is the will of Allah,' he murmured, and recited a prayer for those whose wits have fled. 'Peace be upon you,' he said gravely to Francesca as he and his men turned to leave the room. 'And may you soon find a husband to release you from this heavy burden of care you so nobly carry.'

★ ★ ★

Gossip about the mad Englishman who was travelling in the care of his sister raced through the bazaar and the lanes of Taroudant, and well before daylight a little crowd had gathered at the gates to watch the departure of Ahmed's camel train.

93

'I must thank you, Miss O'Hara, for saving me from having to lose a great deal of money to the Sherif yesterday,' Tom said as they rode away from the town. There was more he wanted to talk to her about — her impromptu performance, for one thing — but Miss O'Hara was still angry with him and appeared to be even more reclusive and uncommunicative today.

By the time they'd settled into their little tents after sunset, he had exchanged no more than a few necessary sentences with her all day. However, he was well aware that she had spoken to Ahmed and his sons at length on several occasions. In this evening's camp she'd seemed even more tense and with-drawn, lost in her own thoughts, and when they sat down to dinner, Tom was surprised to notice her hand was shaking as she lifted a bowl to her lips. Why was she showing these signs of nervousness when the ridiculous episode he'd created at Taroudant was well behind them now?

He yawned and stretched, and had just closed his eyes when, for some reason, his thoughts drifted to the scene he'd witnessed that evening when she'd knelt in the doorway of her tent pulling out her hairpins, releasing the thick mass of tightly curled fair hair from its imprisoning bun and brushing the strands slowly. She'd been silhouetted against the great golden globe of the setting sun, and the light behind her had produced a magnificent halo effect, creating an image of a praying saint in a stained-glass window.

★ ★ ★

Tom smiled to himself as he rolled over and settled down to sleep. Whoever she was, Miss O'Hara seemed a most unlikely candidate for sainthood, though — based on the performance she'd given before the Sherif of Taroudant yesterday — she'd make an outstanding actress.

Sleep eluded Francesca as she lay tensely in her little canvas shelter, looking out at the blazing stars suspended in the vast blue-black vault above them. Her racing thoughts were on the possibility of a meeting with Heinkler tomorrow, and as that moment came closer, she felt her confidence rapidly fading. Her stomach churned. Would Ahmed and his sons help her when she faced the wretch? Hopefully the whole business could be dealt with quietly, without Mr Sinclair becoming aware of how she had lied to him from the day they'd met.

Ahmed had told her that while he was smoking a hookah with fellow camel drivers last night, he'd picked up gossip regarding a German who was carrying an article of great antiquity, and boasting that a rich buyer was coming from the desert to meet him at Taliouine.

Francesca closed her eyes tightly and willed sleep to come. Tomorrow she would be in Taliouine, too, with one last opportunity to face *Uncle Otto* and claim her possessions. The golden bowl was not her concern. He could do what he liked with that now, as long as she could recover her old leather pouch.

All the next day Ahmed followed a *piste* that led them upwards through a remote and hauntingly beautiful landscape of worn limestone slopes where scattered Berber villages looked down from the heights.

Tom's body had gradually adapted itself to the motion of the camel, and he'd even mastered the business of steering the beast by the pressure of his legs. He still had difficulty in persuading it to kneel so he could dismount — and he'd begun to suspect that this was due as much to a stubborn streak in the camel as his own lack of technique.

Tom was an affable man by nature, and after each long day of silent travel he would have enjoyed a companionable chat around the fire in the evening. Communicating by gestures with Ahmed and his sons was limited, to say the least, and while Miss O'Hara translated sometimes, his conversations with the cameleers could produce little more than questions and brief answers. Contrary to his expectations when they'd set out, Miss O'Hara kept her thoughts and opinions to herself, rarely speaking to him at all now.

At the end of another two long days on the camel's back, he was relieved when the walls of Taliouine came into view. As there was no guard at the gate, Ahmed led them straight into the town and along narrow, winding streets to the caravanserai, where one of the sons came to Tom's assistance and eventually persuaded his reluctant camel to kneel.

There were no other travellers in the caravanserai, which smelt of neglect, rotting straw and camel urine. It seemed clear that any importance this town might once have enjoyed as a centre of desert trade had long faded, and many of the close-packed houses within the ochre coloured walls looked dead and deserted, a shabby, crumbling reminder of greater days. The bustle usually found in bazaars was also missing, and the mud-brick lodging house to which Tom and Francesca were taken was barely fit for habitation.

Tom watched Miss O'Hara quickly glance around at the state of their grimy rooms, and accept the situation with a shrug. It appeared to be the view from the open window which most interested her, and for an hour she sat on the sill, peering up and down the street below. Her pale face was expressionless, but he saw the fidget of tension in her fingers as they played with cords hanging from the blind.

He found her lack of communication increasingly irritating. When they'd first set out, he'd been glad of it, but there were certain things about her situation that he would now like to understand more clearly. He was on the point of making an innocuous comment to initiate a conversation — about the type of country they'd ridden through, about the weather, about her quick-witted ploy to divert a potentially nasty situation with the Sherif in the last town. God, what an entertaining dinner-table anecdote that incident would make when he got home!

He came closer and looked over her shoulder at the scene below the window. Two old men sat on their heels against the wall opposite, and the only movement on the street was a yellow dog scratching himself in the shade and a man riding past on a donkey while a woman carrying a baby walked behind him. But before Tom could speak, Ahmed came hurrying into view. Without a word, Miss O'Hara sprang up, brushed past him and he heard her running down the stairs.

He leaned from the window and watched her meet Ahmed, who spoke with apparent urgency and pointing towards the far end of the street. He seemed to be giving her directions. She nodded as she listened, and then by her gestures, it looked to Tom as if she was asking something of the cameleer. For a moment the man hesitated, then shook his head and walked away, leaving Miss O'Hara standing irresolutely on the street, looking towards the far end. After a moment, she ran back into the house.

What the devil had been going on out there? Tom wondered as he listened to her quick footsteps on the stairs. He turned from the window and readied himself to confront her when she stepped back into the room. After all, she was in his employ and he had every right to know what —

She gave him no opportunity to speak. 'Mr Sinclair,' she said, breathing fast as she burst through the doorway, 'will you please be so kind as to accompany me immediately — I mean, there is something that must be done — I must meet someone with a request that will — Oh, Mr Sinclair, will you please quickly load your pistol and come with me?'

'No, I certainly will not! Do you take me for a true idiot, Miss O'Hara? For God's sake, tell me first what this is all about!'

'Oh, there is no time!' she called over her shoulder as she snatched her battered straw hat and jammed it on to her head. 'There is not a moment to lose!' She paused at the door and threw him an anguished look. 'I do apologize, Mr Sinclair. I'm sorry. It was far too much to ask of you.'

Then she was gone, leaving Tom floundering in a quagmire of curiosity and guilt. 'Damn you, Miss Francesca O'Hara,' he muttered to himself as he reached for his gun and a handful of ammunition, which he began loading into the chamber while he ran down the stairs after her.

'What the devil am I getting into?'

6

Miss O'Hara was well ahead of him by the time he reached the street and chased after her, gradually closing the distance between them as she ran through twisting alleys, then turned several corners. At last she came to a high wooden gate where she paused uncertainly for a moment. Then hinges squeaked as she pushed it open.

She seemed unaware that he was only twenty yards behind her as she crossed a courtyard littered with fallen masonry, towards a door that stood half-open. Without a backwards glance, she stepped inside and Tom quietly followed her into an abandoned, crumbling warehouse with a vaulted ceiling supported by columns of ageing stone blocks festooned with spider webs.

Just enough light pierced the holes in the walls and roof to see footprints in the red dust carpeting the stone floor, footprints that told of more than one person having crossed it recently. She was light-footed and moved silently as she followed this trail towards a flight of stairs at the back of the building, and when Tom's riding boots suddenly crunched behind her, she turned in alarm.

One hand clutched her at throat and her chest heaved as she threw him a silencing glance, followed by a quick smile of relief. Then, with a finger held to her lips, she nodded towards steep stairs leading down to a storeroom, from where a faint light was shining. As they moved closer, Tom heard the murmur of men's voices; he tightened his grip on the pistol and held his breath as they crept to the top of the worn steps. From the little he could see from that position, it was clear that someone had been living down there; a saddle bag and a scattering of crumpled clothes lay on a mattress on the floor, and a table with a lamp stood nearby.

They were barely half way down the steps when the volume of the voices rose. Something metallic hit the stone floor, there were sounds of a scuffle, followed by a stomach-churning howl.

Before he could grasp her shoulder to hold her back, Miss O'Hara was leaping down the remaining steps and rushing like a wild thing towards a heavy, bald-headed man wearing European dress. Twitching on the floor as his life-blood drained away, lay a blue-robed Tuareg with a long-bladed knife embedded deep in his chest.

The lamp standing on the table provided a

small circle of light which caught the expression of surprise and fury on the fat European's heavily pock-marked face when he recognized her. 'You!' he roared and tried to snatch at her arm as she slipped past him. 'I'll kill you this time, girl.'

'Oh, no you're not. I know you murdered my father but you're not going to kill me! I've come only to collect what is mine!' Miss O'Hara cried, and rushed to the bed where the saddle bag lay open. 'Mr Sinclair, please shoot this man if he attempts to stop me.' She kicked aside a golden bowl which was lying on the stone floor, and it rattled and scraped its way into the spreading pool of blood beside the tribesman's body. 'Otto Heinkler is a wretched thief who stole something of the utmost importance from me. I know he must still have it in here,' she said as she rifled through the contents of the saddle-bag, releasing the offensive body odour of the German's unwashed clothes into the air.

Tom released the safety catch on his pistol and levelled the weapon at the man, wondering what in heaven's name he would do if the fellow — whoever he was — refused to be bluffed. Surely she didn't expect him to pull the trigger in cold blood?

But that question became purely academic when, only moments later, Tom felt the muzzle of a pistol being pressed into the back of his own head, just at the point when Miss O'Hara up-ended the saddle bag and, with a crow of victory, pounced on a limp, shabby, leather pouch.

The gun being held against Tom's skull was pressed harder. 'Kindly step forward and place your weapon on the table, señor,' a deep voice rumbled in his ear. 'Did you think it was possible to outwit me?'

Tom had been unaware of anyone following them down the stairs, and the voice, so close behind, gave him a start. 'God dammit! Will someone tell me what this is about!' he called, and received no answer. But the expression of terror on the fat man's face as he stared at the new arrival made Tom quickly decide there was no alternative but to re-engage the safety catch and put his gun down on the table as the man had ordered.

He glanced at Miss O'Hara and saw her clutching the limp pouch to her breast, and edging her way slowly towards him. As she passed the golden bowl on the bloodied floor, she kicked it again and sent it rattling and scattering red drops towards the stranger.

'You fat swine, Heinkler, it seems you didn't even possess the wits to guess I'd arrive a day early,' the man growled and Tom felt the heat of his breath on his ear. 'You'll die for this!'

Heinkler whimpered. 'Silis, Silis, this is none of my doing. The Tuareg came to rob me, I swear, and this man brings me business of another kind.' He was sweating now, and it was running down into his eyes, making him blink. 'Silis, Silis — you misunderstand. The only trade I have with the man you are holding concerns the girl here.' He gestured with his head towards Francesca who was now half way across the room. 'As you can see for yourself, she would bring very little at the market but if you wish to have her as well as the bowl, it will be my pleasure to place her in your hands.'

'Like hell you will!' Tom shouted. 'That lady is with me.' He felt the gun move away from his head, and when the man began to walk towards Francesca, he was able to see his features for the first time.

The slender stranger was not young, and although he was splendidly dressed in European clothes and wearing long, exquisitely tooled leather boots, it was impossible to guess his nationality, for his skin was swarthy and he had the face of a hawk. His lip curled disparagingly as he stood before Francesca, pulled off her straw hat and threw it on the floor, then took her chin between his thumb

105

and forefinger to turn her head this way and that. He made a scoffing sound — which instantly became a growl of pain when she jerked away from his grip and bit down hard on his knuckles.

'Don't you realize that Heinkler is a liar?' she cried, backing away as he stood shaking his wounded hand. 'All my life I've known him to be a thief and a cheat — and a murderer! So order him to empty out his pockets and you'll see that he has been up to his old tricks. I'll swear he sold this artefact first to the Tuareg, then killed him so he could sell it again to you!' She nodded towards the body lying in the pool of blood. 'Mr Sinclair and I heard them talking about it as we came down the stairs.'

Although Tom hadn't understood one word of that conversation in Arabic, he hastened to agree. 'Oh, yes, I heard what was going on!'

The man called Heinkler was now the object of the angry stranger's whole attention, and Tom saw the opportunity to snatch his own pistol from the table. But the German, moving with surprising swiftness for such a heavy man, reached it first, then lunged at Francesca from behind and threw one arm around her neck, holding it hard against her windpipe. He pointed the muzzle of the pistol across the room — first in Tom's direction, then at the tall stranger, all the time increasing the pressure on her throat and forcing her to struggle for each breath.

'If you want the bowl,' Heinkler called to the man with the magnificent boots, 'I'll give you ten seconds to lower your gun and put your money on the table.' His words had a brave ring, but the hand holding Tom's pistol began to tremble so violently, he was forced to drop it to his side.

The stranger gave a grim smile, raised his own gun and looked along the sights towards Miss O'Hara, imprisoned against the German. 'You expect me now to pay you good money? Oh, no, you swine, you'll get paid with lead in your stomach.' Miss O'Hara made a strangled sound and the man laughed. 'I'm afraid that woman makes a very thin shield. My shot will go right through her.' His eyes gleamed with a malicious enjoyment as he raised and lowered the muzzle of the gun as if selecting the most effective point to send a bullet.

The fat man sweated. Then his lips curled as terror lent sudden strength to his arm and he swung Tom's pistol up towards the swarthy man. But when he pulled the trigger, the gun merely clicked. He'd failed to release the safety catch, and, in his panic to avoid the shot that instantly spat from the stranger's weapon, he threw himself to one side, tripping against the bedding and tumbling Miss O'Hara on to the floor with him. The bullet that was meant for him hit the wall and ricocheted around the room.

Before the swarthy man could again take aim, Tom sprang forward and kicked the golden bowl as if it was a rugby ball, sending it high towards the stranger. Instinctively the man lunged for it with his free hand. He missed the catch and his concentration wavered.

In those few distracting seconds, Miss O'Hara rolled away from the German and scrambled to her feet, while Tom's boot came down heavily on the man's fat arm, forcing him to loose his grip on the pistol.

Tom snatched it up and released the safety catch as he stepped back with it in one hand, and with the other, signalled Francesca to move towards the stairs. 'Stop this nonsense,' he shouted at the gunman. 'Take the damned bowl, and let that be an end to the whole business. The lady and I are leaving.'

The stranger inclined his head, and had just started to lower his arm when Francesca cried out, 'Watch Heinkler! I saw a pistol amongst the clothes on his bed!' Her warning was too late. The German, crouching beside the mattress on the floor, already had the weapon in his hand, and Tom felt a bullet whip past his ear. He saw the well-dressed stranger's mouth fall open as the shot slammed into his chest, making his muscles shudder with the force of the impact. His knees gave way and he fell forward on to his face while a last breath rattled from his throat.

Tom swung around and, to his horror, saw Heinkler now turning the muzzle of his weapon in Francesca's direction. Tom didn't pause to look along the sights of his own pistol. He raised his arm, pulled the trigger and the next instant, blood sprayed from Heinkler's sweating forehead as the impact of that wild shot threw him backwards on to the floor where he twitched once, then lay still.

'Oh, Mr Sinclair, that was magnificent! You saved my life! Thank you, thank you!' Miss O'Hara gasped, and Tom had only a moment to stare incredulously at the outcome of his lucky shot before they heard heavy footsteps tramping along the floor above them.

They looked at each other in alarm and, without a word, he reached for her hand to drag her away from the light thrown by the lamp, into the shadows on the far wall where a section of bricks had crumbled, leaving a narrow opening. He could hear voices on the stairs as she scrambled through first, still clutching the limp leather pouch, and he followed her into the darkness, stumbling over fallen bricks and timbers littering the old cellar.

Ten yards in, they flung themselves face down in the dust and lay silently huddled together behind a pile of rubble. He held her tightly against him, shielding her with his arm lying around her waist and one leg thrown over the backs of hers. They scarcely dared draw breath as they listened to the angry surprise in the shouts beyond the wall where the three bodies lay.

After a few minutes, a beam of light shone into their hiding place as someone holding a lamp came to stand at the opening in the wall, probing the shrouding darkness where they were lying, not daring to move a muscle. Though the man didn't climb through, he stayed there looking, listening.

Miss O'Hara's body, huddled against Tom's, suddenly went rigid. One of her hands lay positioned on the ground a few inches in front of her face, and in the faint ray of light thrown by the man's lamp, Tom saw what she had just seen: a monstrous, hairy, black tarantula was slowly stepping across the rubble towards her fingers. She made not a sound, not a movement as the long legs slowly crept closer. Closer.

The man with the lamp remained where he

was, peering into the darkness. The spider was an inch from her finger now, and still she made no movement. Tom's palms sweated and his thundering heartbeat drummed in his ears. How much longer could this girl contain her terror? One sound, one sudden movement now would give away their presence. The spider's legs were about to touch her skin. The creature was as large as the back of her hand. At any moment she must surely flinch, cry out. Tom still had the loaded gun in his hand, but how many men would he have to face in that bloody room where the three corpses lay?

Oh, God! The realization hit him that not only were three dead men sprawled on the floor in there, but Miss O'Hara's damned straw hat with the faded pink rose was still lying where the swarthy stranger had tossed it. That's why the fellow with the lamp was looking in here so closely: the men knew that a woman had been in that charnel house. What kind of reception would they provide if she was discovered hiding in this cellar?

The black spider's long, high-stepping legs were moving closer. At any moment her nerve was sure to crack; Tom's mouth felt dry as sandpaper as he watched the tarantula step slowly on to her fingers. Her hand didn't flinch. She seemed not to be breathing at all as it picked its way across her skin, scarcely inches in front of her face — and then ran off to disappear amongst the pile of bricks.

She let out a long, silent breath and slumped against him, shuddering, just as the man with the lamp at last turned away to join in an altercation erupting behind him in the room. The level of noise made by the raised voices in there masked any sound created by Tom and Francesca as they climbed to their feet and picked their way through the darkness towards a chink of daylight coming in through broken brickwork in an outside wall.

It was not difficult to remove more loose bricks to make an opening wide enough for them to crawl through into a roofless space that had once been stables.

'Oh, Mr Sinclair, you were so — so utterly courageous — truly heroic!' Her lips trembled, her voice a whisper and, as she gazed at him, a flush swept up her throat. 'I could never have achieved this alone.' She held up the thin pouch still gripped tightly in her fingers. 'I thank you from the bottom of my heart.'

He gave a dismissive grunt and ignored the wide smile that was lighting her face; he swiftly put the gun into his pocket, dusted himself down and cautiously opened a rear door leading out on to a lane. How far had the sound of their gunshots carried through the town? He looked about. Lengthening afternoon shadows lay on the walls of silent houses opposite. Somewhere a dog barked.

As they stepped outside, all the pent-up tension inside Tom rose to manifest itself in a blaze of anger. 'You have much explaining to do, Miss O'Hara,' he muttered through clenched teeth, and grasped her upper arm roughly to propel her in what he judged to be the direction of their lodging house. 'And I dearly want to know why we've left three men lying dead back there in that store room.'

'Yes, yes, of course — but it will take a little time to explain,' she said breathlessly, 'Could we please slow our pace a little?'

A deep rumble in his throat was his only answer and his stride didn't change. Children playing on the street ran off when they saw the European man and woman rushing towards them. Adults averted their eyes as they passed, a baby crawling on a doorstep was snatched up by its mother and taken inside. It seemed to Tom that a sullen, suspicious atmosphere had settled suddenly over the crumbling, time-worn town, and he was aware of eyes behind shuttered windows watching their progress along the narrow streets.

He was unwilling to accept any of Miss O'Hara's panted suggestions regarding the shortest route back to their lodging house, and dusk was falling before he found himself once again in familiar territory.

It was only when he had pulled her up the stairs and pushed her into an upright chair in their sitting-room that he drew breath to speak. 'Now, Miss O'Hara, I killed a man this afternoon — and I would sincerely like you to tell me why I did so!'

Her chin began to pucker, but she mastered herself, then flushed. 'You did it to save me,' she said and gave him a soft smile. 'You were daring, and dauntless, and — '

Tom snorted and permitted her no chance to continue as he began to pace the room. 'After this afternoon's episode, Miss O'Hara, it is now clear to me that, right from the time of our meeting, you have fed me nothing but a pack of lies! I'll wager there was no tribal fighting to prevent us from taking the direct route to Marrakech. Admit it! You arranged this journey with Ahmed and it has had nothing to do with finding my sister. You have used me and abused my trust, entirely for your own purposes!'

'No, no, Mr Sinclair — please believe that's not entirely correct. Your sister *was* carried off to Marrakech — and we *will* arrive there in a few more days. And once there I will seek out all the information I can about her. You have my word.'

'Your word! Don't make me laugh! I don't know what underhanded dealings you've been involved in, but after today's debacle, do you think I'd ever again believe anything you told me?' He halted in front of her, reached for his wallet, extracted a number of bank notes and held them out to her. He heard her quick intake of breath, but her face remained as blank as a carving. 'Our association concludes here and now, Miss O'Hara. Is that clear? Here, this is your fee.'

When she didn't — or couldn't — lift her hand to take the money, he placed it on the dusty table beside her. 'I won't leave you stranded here in this godforsaken outpost, so I give you permission to ride with us into Marrakech, but that's the end of it!' He shook his head in wordless exasperation.

Her expression now began to waver between contrition, anxiety and satisfaction. 'It was my sincere hope that you would not be inconvenienced by my, er — by my efforts to retrieve this.' She stroked the pouch on her lap. 'And again I must say how truly grateful I will always be for your gallant assistance.' She stood, picked up the money and turned towards the door of her bedroom.

'Oh, no, you don't! I won't permit you to walk away without telling me why I shot that man,' he said, moving quickly to block her path. 'And what was all that business about the golden bowl? What was a Tuareg doing there? And who was the man with the magnificent boots?'

She lowered herself slowly on to the chair again and he stood looming over her. 'The man you shot was Otto Heinkler, a German who called himself a *dealer in antiquities*. The man he killed — the well-dressed man with the superb boots — was obviously a buyer for the bowl. There's a huge trade for that kind of thing in Europe. From his appearance, I would guess that he was either a Syrian or, perhaps, a Cypriot. I have no idea who the dead Tuareg could have been, but I know that Heinkler has used that trick in the past: he'd sell an object, take the money, murder the buyer, and sell it again. It didn't work for him today because it seems that the second buyer arrived a day earlier than they'd arranged.'

'I want to know about the German I killed.' Tom regarded her with unblinking severity. 'What was your connection with him?'

A long hesitation preceded her answer: 'He was someone I'd known for most of my life because my late father — who, I'm sad to say, was never a very astute man — sometimes

116

became involved in Heinkler's activities. And though I've no proof, I know that it was Heinkler who murdered him.' She kept her eyes lowered while she laced and unlaced her fingers. 'That ancient bowl you saw today was unearthed by archaeologists who were excavating a Macedonian tomb a few years ago — and it was legitimately owned by my employer in Tangier. He was the Spanish envoy there, and he had a fine collection of artefacts in the house. The golden bowl was probably the most valuable.'

'And Heinkler stole it?'

She nodded. 'He came into the house one night, took the bowl from its cabinet, then came to my room and took this.' She indicated her pouch. 'Well, he'd always hated me.' Her voice was thick and she had to clear her throat before continuing. 'He was recognized by someone as he got away from the house, but then I was accused of complicity in the theft, and discharged without notice.'

Tom walked across the room and leaned against the wall, studying her with a frown. 'Why do you say the German hated you?'

'He hated me because I detested him, Mr Sinclair; it was a personal matter which began when I was ten years old and we were living in Tripoli.' Her tone indicated that she had no

117

more to add on the subject.

His frown grew more ferocious. 'Very well, I could see that the bowl was valuable, but I demand to know what is so precious in your pouch that you were prepared to have us both shot to get it back.' Even before he'd finished speaking he was striding across the floor with his hand outstretched. 'Open it!'

She gripped it tighter. 'You won't understand.' Her fingers fumbled with the tie. 'Nobody can understand. It holds nothing of value to anyone apart from me — ' He snatched the pouch from her fingers, undid the cord, and tipped the contents on to the red dust on the table. Neither of them was prepared for her eyes to fill as they stared at the four objects lying before them: a little wooden flute, a yellowing lace mantilla, a small blue and gold patterned tile hanging from a velvet ribbon, and a faded, stained parchment. When he unfolded it, Tom discovered it to be an old deed to an estate in France.

'And this is what all the — the nonsense today was about?' His voice rose in disbelief 'You would have had us both killed for *this*?'

'These came from my grandparents. This is who I am, Mr Sinclair, these are my roots. I said you wouldn't understand.' She gathered the items one by one, brushed the dust from them, and put them back into the pouch, while he watched with a hostile curiosity.

Her shoulders rose and fell. 'I did have all my money in here, too, but it's gone, of course,' she said. 'I'd been saving for seven years, and I had almost enough to start my own school somewhere.' Her tongue made a clicking sound. 'And, to make it even more difficult for me to find another position, that wretched man has left none of the letters of recommendation from my previous employers. I was a very good governess, Mr Sinclair, and people always wrote well of me and my work.' She waited a moment, sniffed, then slowly glanced up at him with an unspoken question.

He gave her a narrow-eyed look of disbelief. 'Are you about to ask me to supply you with a character reference? Hah! Do you imagine that anything written by me would improve your chances of gaining further employment? Don't make me laugh, Miss O'Hara! I have come to regard you as sly, manipulative and completely dishonest. Would you wish me to put that down in black and white?'

She clamped her lips together, but there was defiance burning in the gaze that held his. He saw her draw a breath, but before she could speak, the tension between them was broken by a sudden noise of hoofs thundering past the house. They both rushed to the window in time to see a horde of blue-robed and veiled Tuareg horsemen sweeping along the previously drowsy street below.

Her eyes filled with alarm. 'Oh, no! This is going to be the third act in today's drama,' she said and nodded in the direction of the derelict warehouse.

'We'll have to leave this house immediately,' Tom said. 'I have a feeling that our camel train will be pulling out if Ahmed sees trouble looming in town.'

Without a word she went into her room and by the time he'd carried his travelling box to the door, she was already there with her saddlebag, and looking ridiculous with yards of white cotton fabric wrapped around her head and under her chin, in the style of the turban won by Arab men — with one end dangling ready to be pulled across her face in the form of a *haik*.

'Well, I could hardly go back to collect my hat from the warehouse,' she said, lifting her chin, but Tom simply shrugged and took one last look from the window. The street was clear.

'You go ahead of me and I'll make sure you're not followed,' he said and, when she was about to object, he cut her off. 'Not another word, Miss O'Hara! You'll kindly do exactly as I say from now on; you've played your hand and this is no longer your expedition.' With a jerk of his head he ordered her down the stairs and then walked a dozen yards behind her through the gathering darkness.

They had just reached the caravanserai when the sound of gunshots came from the direction of the old warehouse. Ahmed and his sons were already saddling the animals and, for the first time, Tom saw them sling long-barrelled rifles across their shoulders.

Ahmed complained that he was not well pleased to be leaving Taliouine before his camels were sufficiently rested, but he wished to be well clear of the town now that the Tuareg warriors had arrived.

Another burst of gunshots rang out across the houses as the caravan started out into the silence of the desert night and Tom wondered when they would next find an opportunity to sleep.

As the night wore on, Francesca O'Hara, unemployed teacher and out-of-work translator who'd now been consigned to riding at the rear with the pack animals, found her thoughts skittering off into previously unexplored regions, with her emotions falling into a strange chaos that alternated from elation to misery.

Overhead, the sky was hung with a superb tapestry of pulsating stars, but she remained unaware of everything else in the universe but the dim shape of the Englishman riding behind Ahmed. For hours she sat astride her saddle, seeing only the silhouette of Thomas Sinclair as he moved with the rolling gait of the camel, and recalling clearly every detail of his face — the shape of his chin, his mouth when he smiled, the indefinable grey-green colour of his eyes when he was angry.

A shocking new sensation — something she'd never before experienced — tightened in her belly when she remembered how he had followed her to the old warehouse earlier today. How he had saved her life. Yes, she would be dead now if he had not killed Heinkler. That odd feeling — feral and urgent — shot through her again and her breathing quickened as she relived the period in the cellar when Mr Sinclair had shielded her, holding her protectively as they lay hiding in the dark. Her toes curled inside her boots.

How remarkable it was to think that the recollection of Thomas Sinclair's body pressing hard against hers aroused such very different feelings from those stirred by the male predators in the past who had insulted and terrorized her. She still felt nothing but loathing when she thought of the young aristocrat who had plundered her virginity, and her stomach churned with revulsion whenever recollections of Uncle Otto's fumbling fingers came into her mind. In fact, she had spent most of her life avoiding the touch of any man.

But now the memory of lying closely against Thomas Sinclair had become imprinted on her mind, stirring an entirely different sensation. Even though he had thrown a leg across hers, wrapped his arm tightly around her waist, and pressed himself closely against her, she had experienced nothing but comfort in his touch. Safety. How could she ever forget the scent of him, the feel of his breath on her hair, and how his heartbeat had thundered against her ribs while the man with the lamp stood looking for them in the darkness.

She shuddered again to recall those moments of pure, primordial horror when the hairy tarantula had crept across her hand. Spiders were her worst nightmare and it was a miracle that she had been able to contain her panic when every instinct was to cry out and fling the repulsive creature from her skin. If she'd been alone, it would have been impossible to have stopped herself from giving away her position.

But she hadn't been alone, and in order to protect *him*, she'd found the strength to fight down her terror. To save *him* she'd forced herself to endure it silently. For *him*, she had made that miracle happen.

As she thought about that, a slow heat burned in the centre of her being. Oddly, though tears came to her eyes, she also felt a strange urge to cry out with joy. Something had happened to her during that whole terrifying period in the old warehouse, something that had given her the power to do the impossible. She couldn't give a name to that something and it would be pure madness even to acknowledge what she had felt.

And just as impossible to forget it.

7

At dawn the next morning, a howling, hot sirocco roared in from the Sahara, hurling clouds of dust and sand pitilessly against everything in its path. Day and night it screamed, fraying tempers, whipping the hem of Miss O'Hara's old skirt into tatters and discouraging any hope of productive discussion between the riders in the caravan.

No wonder minds were known to snap during the sirocco Tom decided on the third day, as he tried to remove yet another piece of grit from his eye, lying each night in a tiny tent which seemed likely to be blown away at any moment, made sleep next to impossible.

Like Miss O'Hara, he was now wearing an Arab *haik* that he'd borrowed from the cameleers; they'd taught him how to wind it on to his head and under his chin, with one end loose to wrap across his face. Even so, his mouth, nose and ears were constantly caked with sand. There was general relief amongst the travellers when the *piste* eventually turned westward into the mountains, which offered a small degree of shelter from the gale, as well as the knowledge that they were on the final leg of the journey to Marrakech once they'd reached the Tizi N'Tichka pass.

Within a day of setting out from Taliouine, Tom had begun to regret the heat in the anger he'd vented on Miss O'Hara. He'd never been one to hold a grudge and if it hadn't been for the damned gale making life a misery for man and beast day after day, he'd have tried already to clear matters between them. At least he'd have given her a chance to offer a fuller explanation, which he might — or might not — have accepted.

The cash he'd thrown at her had been an appropriate fee for her services, but his refusal to provide a letter of recommendation had been churlish. He was sorry about that because she was undoubtedly a splendid linguist and it was obvious that she needed to find new employment quickly.

Damn! How he wished James Fitzalan were here now so he could talk over the whole business of Francesca O'Hara with him. Faced with this situation, his stepfather would never have been so ungentlemanly and pigheaded towards her. Tom was still grumbling to himself as he hunched his shoulders against the battering wind and set off across the campsite towards the cameleers huddled around the camel-dung cooking fire they'd set in the cleft of a rock.

He was just in time to see Miss O'Hara battling to reach her little tent with a bowl of food. Her clothing was becoming ever more ragged and, with her head and face still tightly wrapped up in yards of cotton cloth, she looked neither to the right or left as she passed him.

Well, until the gale dropped there would be little opportunity for any civilized tête à tête with her, Tom decided as he huddled back in his own tent. But Marrakech was coming closer and as soon as he could find an opportunity to sit down with pen and paper he'd do the decent thing and provide her with a letter of recommendation — praising her linguistic skills, her enterprise, her tenacity and her self-control.

Yes, he had to admit, she had a host of positive attributes, though it would be difficult to think of a situation in which the ability to tolerate a spider crawling over one's hand would be a positive attribute. He couldn't think of any other woman who could have endured that. Except, except — perhaps — Diana. Strangely, a memory shot into his mind's eye and he saw his sister at the age of twelve standing in a corner of their plantation house, white-faced with terror and silently facing a cobra rearing to strike, while little Kate was throwing a fit of hysterics on the other side of the room.

'Be brave, sweetheart,' Tom had heard James say quietly to Diana, and she'd stood there, motionless as a lovely statue, while he'd decapitated the snake with one stroke of his old cavalry sabre. Yes, on that day, his sister had been truly courageous and they'd all told her how proud they were of her.

Dammit! he thought, as the gale buffeted the tent and he closed his eyes for sleep that wouldn't come, he should at least have congratulated Miss O'Hara on the courage she'd shown during the spider incident. He felt badly about that. Who the hell was she, anyhow, this shabby, lost creature who had been prepared to lie and deceive him in order to retrieve a shabby leather pouch holding valueless bits and pieces? Where had she come from? Should it be any concern of his where she was going after this? Wasn't she just another traveller whose course through life seemed to be set into the eye of the wind? Like Diana's? He sighed. Like his own?

★ ★ ★

When Ahmed eventually led his dishevelled and exhausted little cavalcade through the Bab Agnaou into Marrakech, they found the

128

caravanserai overflowing with travellers. Initially, it even seemed as if Ahmed's party might be turned away. There were an extraordinary number of horses installed in the building and, while Tom struggled to clear the grit from his eyes, he caught sight of French soldiers drinking and playing cards on a balcony running around the upper floor.

Suddenly a noisy argument broke out amongst them, there was a scuffle, punches were traded. More men joined in the mêlée.

'Goodbye for now, Mr Sinclair, and thank you.' He turned in surprise to see that Miss O'Hara had already dismounted and was standing beside his camel. She'd pulled the turban from her head and was unsuccessfully trying to smooth her tangled hair. 'Ahmed will escort you to a guest-house — a very good one — and I will find private accommodation while I make inquiries regarding your sister.'

'Now, hold on just a moment, Miss O'Hara, there are certain things I'd like to make clear — ' Tom's camel was still agonizingly slow to respond to his commands, and by the time he'd persuaded the beast to drop to its knees so he could dismount, the girl was already hurrying through the high arch of the entrance with her saddle-bag slung over her shoulder and the ragged hem of her skirt flapping around her ankles. Lord, he thought, as he sucked in a breath between his clenched teeth, was there ever a more irritating woman in the whole of creation? She could even outclass Diana in that respect.

★ ★ ★

The opulent guest-house in which Tom found himself was like stepping into another world — a silent world where the howling wind was refused entrance. A series of apartments with marble floors and silk curtains were set around courtyards, and outside Tom's room, a mosaic-tiled fountain played under scalloped arches in a courtyard filled with greenery overflowing from urns.

Beyond the tall, swaying date palms growing outside the walls, he could see the snow-capped peaks of the High Atlas mountains.

He was watching two richly robed Arabs strolling along a path beside a bubbling water-channel in the courtyard, when a servant knocked on his door to conduct him along a carpeted corridor to the steam bath. Here he was scrubbed and soaked, dried and rubbed down with scented oils, then massaged from scalp to toe by skilled hands that transported him into another world.

The tension in his travel-weary, sleep-deprived body had melted away by the time a striped silk robe was wrapped around him and he was escorted back to his own apartment. Plates of Moroccan delicacies were soon brought to his room, where a great, ornate bed of carved cedarwood waited. When Tom threw himself on to it a little later, he swore that it must have been imported straight from heaven.

He should have fallen asleep instantly, but when he closed his eyes, he began to think again about Miss O'Hara's abrupt departure from the caravanserai. Of course, he should have called after her and insisted on her coming to stay at this guest-house, too. At least for a day or two. He couldn't clear her from his mind. What if she had been accosted by French soldiers on her way to find accommodation in the medina? If she'd cried out for help, would an Arab man have come to her assistance?

He lay for a long time listening to the soft sounds of the fountain splashing outside his window and worrying if she had found a safe and comfortable place to stay. First thing tomorrow morning, he'd write a favourable — even glowing — character reference for her, but where could he send it if he had no

131

idea where she was staying? He raised his head to turn the pillow and try to settle again. And there were certain things about her that he still wanted to understand. Why was she living alone in this country and not in Spain?

She was still in his thoughts when he eventually fell asleep, and when he slowly opened his eyes next day, it was well into the afternoon. He stretched, yawned and rang for coffee. When it arrived, he was surprised to see that also lying on the tray was an envelope addressed to him in a bold, unfamiliar hand. Who knew he was staying here? He drank a cup of the thick, black coffee to clear his head and, when he'd read the note, he had to pour himself another one while he looked hard at the invitation that had been sent by an unknown Frenchman.

Monsieur Jean Cauvet explained in his note that he was also a guest in this establishment, and would be delighted if Tom would join him and two colleagues this evening for dinner at eight o'clock. He added, for clarification, that he was a member of the French government.

Tom was intrigued. It was no secret in Europe that the French government, smarting from the humiliation of losing territory to Prussia in their recent debacle, was eager to establish French colonies in Africa. The

132

tricolour was already flying over Algeria, but what was a member of the French government, along with a company of French soldiers, doing here in neighbouring Morocco? Tom sent a note to accept the dinner invitation.

'My dear sir, what a great pleasure it is to meet you!' Monsieur Jean Cauvet blustered in a phlegm-choked voice as he stepped forward to shake Tom's hand. He was a corpulent, middle-aged man who appeared to be far from well, with pasty skin and dark circles under his eyes. 'Please allow me the honour of introducing my colleagues, Colonel Villatte of the French Foreign Legion, and Monsieur Henri Duveyrier.' He turned aside and tried to smother a wheezy cough in his handkerchief.

Tom shook hands and exchanged greetings with the slender, cold-eyed Colonel, and the tall, exceptionally good-looking, dark-haired man named Duveyrier, who appeared to be about his own age.

Cauvet cleared his throat: 'I saw your arrival here yesterday, Mr Sinclair, and made enquiries of our host. And when I learned your name, I could not delay our meeting.'

'I'm astonished that you would be familiar with my name,' Tom said carefully. He was competent enough in the French language to sustain a conversation, though he knew that his accent was schoolboyish.

'Yes, indeed, we know the name of Sinclair,' the affable, young Monsieur Duveyrier interjected. 'We've all read about your work with Indian Railways and also, er — in California, was it? And just last month we saw your proposed South American enterprise mentioned in a British engineering journal.'

'Indeed?' Tom said cautiously, and took the chair he was offered. 'Of course, it will be some time before anything can begin in the Andes.'

'Have you come to Morocco for an audience with the Sultan?' Cauvet croaked, exchanging a swift look with Duveyrier. 'We have just concluded discussions with him and his Grand Vizier.'

Tom suppressed a smile as he glanced at the expressions on the faces of the three Frenchmen looking at him, and felt a bubble of tension rising in the room. He quickly pricked it. 'Gentlemen, my visit to this country is a strictly personal one, and I can assure you that I'm not here to discuss railways with the Sultan or anyone else.' At that moment the conversation was interrupted while trays of food were carried in, filling the room with heavenly aromas.

Cauvet ushered the group to the table, and

while they passed various dishes to each other and spooned the delicacies on to their plates, all attention remained focused on the banquet.

'Do you gentlemen plan to stay long in Marrakech,' Tom asked conversationally, wiping his mouth with a napkin. 'I noticed a number of French troops in the caravanserai when we arrived yesterday.'

The Colonel answered, 'Unfortunately Monsieur Cauvet has been most unwell, and we have delayed our departure for Algiers until the sirocco blows itself out.' The waxed tips of his grey moustache twitched. 'We've been here for almost two weeks, but we should soon be able to set out again.' His lips took a downward turn. 'My men need to be kept on the move; idleness inevitably leads to a breakdown of discipline in the ranks.'

'And what of your plans, Sinclair? Do you plan to spend long in Marrakech?' Duveyrier asked sociably.

Accepting a cheroot offered by the Colonel and slowly lighting it, provided the distraction Tom needed to decide how much information he was prepared to divulge about his visit to Morocco. Revealing Diana's predicament to this group of strangers was not an option. He couldn't risk the kind of ribald jokes about Diana likely to be tossed around

Parisian dinner tables if the truth of his visit to Morocco became known to these men.

'Actually, I'm simply here to escort my sister, Francesca, on a tour of North Africa,' he said smoothly. 'She has plans to write a book — 'Travels of an English Lady Amongst the Moors', or some such title.' He thought of books he had seen lying in his mother's drawing-room. 'I hear that Miss Ida Pfeiffer's description of her recent visit to the Holy Land has been very popular and I believe an Englishwoman living in Mexico has just published a tale about her experiences there.'

'Your sister's idea is a splendid one, Mr Sinclair,' Duveyrier said with enthusiasm. 'I, myself, wrote a book some years ago when I returned from my encounters with the Tuareg tribes, and it was certainly well received. Actually, I was honoured with the Legion d'Honneur for the work I did in the Sahara.'

Tom looked suitably impressed and murmured his congratulations.

'Indeed, Mr Sinclair, I would very much like to meet your sister while we are all in Marrakech,' Duveyrier said with a polished charm. 'I must say how disappointed I am to find that she is not dining with us here this evening.'

Tom forced a smile. 'I'm quite sure my sister would be delighted to make your acquaintance. However, she is staying privately — with a family in the medina.' He sincerely hoped that she had found such a place. A safe place.

'Excellent!' The Frenchman's handsome face shone with interest. 'That is by far the best way to learn the customs of a native population — as I did when I spent three years wandering through the whole Sahara and living with the Tuaregs.'

'Tuaregs? I understood that their sole interest was in attacking Arab caravans and turning murder and robbery into a lucrative business,' Tom said drily. He was surprised to find how quickly he was developing an irrational dislike of this man.

'No, no, no! The Tuaregs are a wonderful people — most hospitable and generous,' Duveyrier insisted. 'In fact, if I was not so hard-pressed for time, I would be delighted to escort you and Miss Sinclair into the desert to meet some of the tribes.'

The Colonel gave a disparaging grunt. 'A rather risky journey now, I would think, Duveyrier. You must be aware that last month a Dutch lady and her servants were murdered by the Tuaregs when she called to visit them.' He drew savagely on his cheroot. 'And three priests from Algiers have met the same fate, as well as a journalist named Lemay and two

Frenchmen who called themselves explorers. God alone knows how many French soldiers lie buried in the sand after meeting your friendly Tuaregs.'

The Colonel's anger was sheathed in ice. 'I think it's time for the government in Paris to be informed that all the hospitable Tuaregs you encountered on your travels seem to have evaporated, and God help any man now who thinks of building a railway across the Sahara.' He ground the stub of his cheroot into an ashtray and kept his gaze fixed on the ashes.

Tom felt the friction between the Colonel and the two civilians becoming almost palpable.

A spasm of coughing forced Cauvet to leave the table. Duveyrier sat forward in his chair and cast a smouldering glare at the Colonel. 'Sir, I spent three years with the Tuareg tribes, three years — and, as I have assured my friends in Paris, I found them to be the best and noblest of savages! They would *welcome* the coming of our railway. I spoke to them of the advantages — travellers, trade, wealth. Progress.'

He looked across at Tom, who gave a noncommittal shrug, and lowered his gaze to his own plate. So, the government of France, urged on by Jean Cauvet and Henri

Duveyrier, was actually proposing a hare-brained scheme to build a railway line across the shifting dunes of the Sahara? Clearly, it was all part of the race to colonize Africa but, in reality, such an enterprise would be sheer engineering lunacy. Tom kept a straight face, offered no comment and continued his meal in silence until Cauvet returned to the table, spluttering his apologies.

'Dear God, how my lungs plead to be taken back to the sweet air of France, far away from this cursed desert dust.'

'Indeed, the sirocco has blown away any desire my sister might have had to cross the Sahara,' Tom said vacuously, then paused and looked at the three Frenchmen. 'However, there is one matter which holds her particular interest — and that is the present situation in Marrakech regarding European women who are captured and sold into slavery.

Cauvet's wheezing prevented him from making a reply. He gave a little cough and shook his head at Tom, while Duveyrier smiled his apparent relief that the topic of conversation had taken this new tack.

'I can happily reassure Miss Sinclair that there is no longer a market for white slavery in Marrakech,' he said. 'And I'm certain that any European woman brought ashore in one of the coastal cities, would be ransomed quickly and sent home to her family.'

As the Colonel listened, he narrowed his eyes and raised one eyebrow at the elegant young man from Paris who spoke with such bold confidence. The officer said nothing, but Tom read the scorn in his expression. He needed to hear the Colonel's personal views on the matter. How could he arrange to talk with the man privately?

★ ★ ★

Actually, it wasn't difficult at all. Tom walked through the Bab Agnaou next morning, found his way to the open space which Villatte had turned into a parade ground, and stood in the whipping wind to watch fifty grim-faced French Legionnaires, fully armed and carrying backpacks, being put through a lengthy, gruelling drill by their sergeants. After that, the squad marched off into the flying dust to complete a twenty-mile circuit. Colonel Villatte returned their salute, then dismounted and walked back with Tom into the relative shelter of the bustling medina.

'After today's exercise, I don't expect there'll be many in the ranks tonight who'll have the strength to crack skulls,' the Colonel said dryly, 'and I'm afraid the whorehouses will be missing many of their French customers. Coffee, Mr Sinclair?

Tom nodded with a grin, and together they crossed the Place Djemaa-el Fna, weaving their way past storytellers and jugglers, musicians and dancers, watersellers and peddlers, barbers and dentists. The Colonel led Tom into a café, and here they were shown to a private room behind a curtain at the rear where they lounged on cushioned couches and a bubbling hookah was brought for them to share.

'Now Mr Sinclair, can we — as they say — lay our cards on the table?'

Tom shrugged. 'Colonel, I can add nothing to what I talked about last night. My visit here — with my sister — is a personal one, but I'd be most interested to hear why two French diplomats came to see the Sultan of Morocco.'

The Colonel gave a cynical grin and sank back on to his cushions. 'I can assure you, Mr Sinclair, that their mission was a purely diplomatic one. Paris needed agreement with the Sultan in order to map a clear border in the sand between Morocco and Algeria before any railway work begins.' The hookah bubbled as he drew on the pipe before he continued.

Tom nodded. 'I don't suppose that the wandering desert tribes have ever been worried about border lines across the sands.'

The Colonel gave a grunt of agreement. 'This idealistic nonsense about building a trans-Saharian railway to bring trade to Timbuktu is being hailed in France as a brilliant concept. Everyone wants to believe Duveyrier's assurances that the Tuaregs would welcome that kind of intrusion into their tribal life.' He shook his head slowly. 'I'm afraid that promoting this railway scheme has become something of a tonic that the Government dispenses every now and again to relieve the electorate's woes about the dismal state of the economy and the growing problem of unemployment.'

Tom frowned. 'Then, Colonel, may I ask why this diplomatic mission required a whole company of French Legionnaires as an escort? Did they think the Sultan would need some kind of military *persuasion* to discuss the border?'

The Colonel shook his head. 'No, nothing like that.' With his right hand he began to finger one waxed end of his moustache while he frowned thoughtfully. 'It's no longer safe for anyone to travel in this region without a large escort, Mr Sinclair. Tribal tensions are at flash point everywhere following the stampede to send French settlers over to Algiers to set up a colony on the best farmland in North Africa.' The hookah bubbled again. 'They have pushed the Berbers off their traditional land and south into the Tuareg's Sahara — and now the Tuaregs are riding north to plunder far and wide.'

Tom pursed his lips and blew a long breath. 'A band of Tuaregs arrived in Taliouine a few days ago,' he said after a pause, 'but we didn't wait to see whether or not they wanted to be friends with us.'

'I applaud your common sense, Sinclair.' For a moment, the Colonel seemed lost in thought, then he began to groom the other tip of his moustache. 'If you and your sister intend to travel further afield, Mr Sinclair, I most strongly advise you to join a large caravan for the entire journey. Despite our friend Duveyrier's assurance on the topic of white slavery, a European lady is still a tempting target for bandits.'

'Thank you, Colonel. Yes, I'll certainly heed your advice.' Tom drew deeply on the pipe and held the officer's gaze before he spoke. 'Actually, my sister heard a whisper in Agadir that a well-bred English lady had been saved from a shipwreck, then brought to Marrakech several months ago. Now Francesca is determined to discover the fate of the woman. Can you suggest where she might turn to find this information?'

The Colonel was clearly intrigued, and raised an eyebrow. 'I'm certain that any such lady would not be sold at a public auction, but it is quite possible for a young woman to disappear — unrecorded — into some powerful man's household. If she had been carried to Marrakech, her sale would no doubt have been negotiated privately — in which case I doubt she would ever be heard of again.'

When Tom returned to his rooms later that afternoon, he was surprised to find a message from Miss O'Hara waiting for him.

He ripped it open and his forehead creased as he read it. 'Who brought this?' he challenged the servant standing at the door.

'A young girl, sir.'

Tom rubbed his chin in frustration. 'Very well, but when she comes again, I want her to wait for my reply. Do you understand? Hold her here by force if you have to!'

8

When Francesca — tattered, sand-caked and exhausted — had bolted from the caravanserai two days previously, she'd had a clear plan in mind. It was an enormous relief to have money in her pocket again and, after avoiding the clutches of clumsy, drunken French Legionnaires who'd tried to accost her as soon as she stepped out into the street, she found her way to the *souks* and hurried through the twisting alleys, searching for a merchant who sold cloth of good quality.

Making her own clothes had always been a necessary part of life and the nuns in Granada had taught her how to cut fabric and sew it finely. Over the last few miserable days riding through the sirocco, she'd tried to distract herself by calculating exactly what lengths of material would be necessary to replace the worn-out wardrobe that lay crushed into her saddle-bag. And as soon as she entered the *souk* of the textile merchants, she found one displaying the kinds of fabrics she needed.

The first she bought was white cotton for undergarments, then a fawn-coloured twill to be made into a travelling outfit, followed by a practical dark-blue fabric for a skirt suitable for work in a schoolroom. To wear with this, she chose one length of cream fabric and another of blue and white stripe, to be made up into blouses. After that she selected lengths of braid for trimming, as well as suitable buttons and buckles.

When that was settled, she fingered the money in her pocket again and permitted her gaze to drift over the bolts of vibrant silk taffetas stacked on the shelves: temptation niggled. Packed into her saddle-bag was a plain, high-necked, grey silk dress — the kind every governess was expected to wear on the occasions when her employers required her presence in the evening. Francesca's grey dress was now more than five years old; the children in her charge had always told her that it was ugly. She touched the money in her pocket again and temptation won the day.

The range of silk fabrics she examined was bewilderingly wide, in glorious shades of blue, gold, purple, pinks and green. Two sons of the merchant had come from a back room and now hovered beside her, eagerly unwinding yards from each roll and, despite her dusty clothes, draping lengths of the silk over her shoulders so she could judge the colours against her skin.

In the end it was an emerald green taffeta shot with sapphire blue which she found impossible to resist. It shone in the light with the glorious iridescence of a peacock and anyone could see that it was a most inappropriate colour for a governess to choose. But one more quick glance at her reflection in the small looking-glass confirmed her determination to buy it. She took a deep breath and decided to take eight yards.

'What is your best price?' she asked the shopkeeper and they settled down to bargain, drinking mint tea until the business was concluded to the satisfaction of both parties, although it would never do for either of them to have acknowledged that.

When her purchases had been wrapped, Francesca moved on to the next step in her plan. 'Thank you,' she said as she took the parcels, 'and now can you tell me where to find the best seamstress in the city?'

'Madame Zarifa's work is renowned in the highest quarters,' the merchant assured her without hesitation. 'And,' he added with emphasis, 'she is the owner of a new mechanical sewing machine which has come from America! My elder son would be honoured to accompany you to her house, if that is your wish.'

'Thank you, indeed,' she said, and with the

young man carrying the parcels of fabric as well as her saddlebag, Francesca went with him to the end of the *souk* and out into the narrow streets of the medina. Before long, he rapped on a wooden door set into the windowless, mud-brick wall of a house, and it was opened by a woman veiled in black. Her eyes crinkled with pleasure when she recognized the shopkeeper's son.

And they crinkled even more when Francesca spoke to her about the number of garments she needed to have made as soon as possible.

'Yes, yes,' the woman agreed. 'I have daughters and daughters-in-law who are also skilled with the needle, and there is no work here that cannot be put aside for a few days.'

'And I have one more request, Madame,' Francesca asked in a genuinely deferential tone. 'Would you be willing — if your husband agrees — to accommodate me in your house while I cut out the garments and explain how I need them to be sewn? I will pay for my lodging, and I will wear the veil in front of your menfolk. I need only somewhere to sleep until the work is done.'

While the seamstress showed astonishment at Francesca's request, her curiosity was clearly tweaked. 'I am a widow, and at present my son has business which has taken him away from home.' She opened the door wider. 'You are most welcome, madame. There will be no men in this house until my son returns — and that will not be for another week.'

When Francesca stepped through the doorway and into the courtyard, she was met by four shyly giggling young women who also lived in the house. Two were Zarifa's own daughters, and two were the wives of her absent son — and each girl had learned her sewing skills from Zarifa.

The women, who were all dressed in shapeless black, couldn't hide their curiosity when Francesca unbuckled the saddle-bag and sorted through the shabby clothes that desperately needed to be replaced. 'Forgive us, madame,' one daughter tittered. 'We have never before seen what a European woman wears next to her skin.'

When the parcels were opened and the fabrics examined and fingered by the ladies, Francesca explained the items she needed to have made. New undergarments were to be first, followed by the skirt and blouses all of which, she explained, she would cut out as soon as she had bathed and washed the sand from her hair.

Hovering in the background while they were speaking, was a stooped and smiling, dark-skinned woman who stood with a broom in her hands. Nobody introduced her.

With Zarifa's permission, the two young wives took Francesca to their room, and the elderly woman brought warm water, filled a tub and scented it with jasmine oil.

'Temina has been a slave in this house since she was a girl,' one of the young women said matter-of-factly when Francesca asked her name. 'She will bathe you and wash your hair.' The stooped woman smiled broadly and bowed.

Later, when she was dressed in a cotton robe and her thick strands of curls were hanging loosely around her shoulders to dry, Francesca felt sufficiently revived to spread out the fabrics one after the other on a floor rug. Using the old garments as patterns, she got down on to her knees to cut out the various shapes.

But the new clothes were not all to be exact replicas of the old ones. She snipped a fashionable fullness into the sleeves of these blouses, the style lately worn by European ladies in Tangier. And some of her thinness would be taken away, she decided, if more material was allowed in the skirt, then gathered in at the waistline. The scissors in her fingers clicked faster.

And the blouses would also have tucks running down the front — and perhaps she'd even add a little frill to edge their white collars, to be finished with a neat bow at the neckline.

Would Mr Sinclair make any comment when — if — he saw her wearing these new clothes? She sighed, then gave herself a mental shake and pushed away such fantasies. The new outfits were needed to help her find employment. She might never again set eyes on *him*.

While old Temina cooked the evening meal, Zarifa and Francesca discussed the sewing to be done, and as soon they had all eaten, the work began by lamplight. At last, with the five seamstresses sitting together and busily sewing, Francesca decided it was time to tell them her reason for coming to Marrakech. Five pairs of hands stopped their work while the women listened to her with astonishment.

'My brother fears that this lady called Diana might have been sold in the slave market. How can I discover if such a thing happened?'

Zarifa and her two daughters shook their heads, but the young wives exchanged a startled look, which was not missed by their mother-in-law.

'You have overheard my son speaking of this matter?' Zarifa said to them sternly. 'Come, be frank with me!'

'No, it was not our husband, Mother,' said one. 'It was the boy, Ulim — Temina's grandson who works in the slavemaster's house. We met him in the bazaar one day when he was seeking Doctor Tahir.'

While the first wife spoke, the second was talking nervously over the top of her. 'Ulim told us that Minzah, the slavemaster, had bought a white woman from al-Mansur and now he needed Doctor Tahir to come urgently to the Rahba Kedima because this woman had tried to take her own life.'

'Oh, no!' Francesca gasped.

'Ulim said that he had that day seen Minzah accepting a high price for the woman,' the first wife continued, 'but she was half-dead next day when the buyer came for her and the man was demanding the return of his money.'

Francesca's blood chilled. 'Was the doctor found in time? What happened to the woman?'

The young wives again looked at each other uncertainly. 'When we went with Ulim to find the doctor, he was not at his house.' The first wife paused and her discomfort was clear. 'It was most difficult for Ulim to discover the doctor's whereabouts, but eventually a spice merchant who was coming from the house of Zaouia Nassiriya, the magistrate' — she raised her eyebrows and dropped her voice — 'said that he, himself, had witnessed the doctor entering the ladies' quarters there.'

Zarifa gasped and her daughters looked appalled as the second wife continued: 'So Ulim stood under the balcony of the magistrate's house and called out loudly for the doctor. It was a long time before he at last peeked from a window, and when he saw us standing there with Ulim, he vowed to cut out our tongues if ever we spoke of his visit to the magistrate's ladies.' The girl quaked and her mother-in-law had difficulty containing her outrage at the doctor's threat.

'Never will I sew another robe for him or his wife!' she snapped.

Francesca felt her heart sinking. 'But — but — the Englishwoman? Did she live? Madame Zarifa, I beg you to help me learn what happened to her.'

★　★　★

Francesca rose early the next morning, and dressed herself in a black *burka* borrowed from one of Zarifa's daughters. 'Do not wear white, Madame,' the seamstress had insisted. 'Less attention will be drawn to your movements if you appear in the medina

153

looking like every other woman.'

It had been decided that old Temina would be the best one to help Francesca in her search for the white lady. 'She knows the workings of the slave market and some of the people there,' Zafira said, as her daughters applied walnut dye to darken the pale skin on Francesca's hands, as well as on her forehead and around her eyes.

The wind was at last abating, but it was still sufficiently strong to make it necessary for Francesca to keep a firm grip on the black shawl draped over her head and across her face.

'Keep your eyes lowered,' the old slave woman said as they left the house. 'We will go first to the Rahba Kedima — it is the market for cereals as well as slaves — and I will find the boy who runs messages for the slavemaster, Minzah.'

Francesca tried to keep her hazel eyes downcast as they walked quickly along the street, and took only an occasional peek as they passed the shops of artisans busy at their work. The odour assaulting her nostrils told her when they'd reached the dyers' *souk*, and she gave a fleeting glance up at the multicoloured skeins of silk swinging in the wind to dry on canes stretched across the lane. Temina was panting loudly by the time they reached the jewellers' *souk*, then skirted the wool and sheepskin market, before turning into an alley flanked by apothecary shops.

At the end of this was the square where, on one side, bags of wheat and grain were being unloaded from carts, and on the other side, a crowd of buyers was gathering to examine a group of two dozen sullen and ragged men with skin the colour of ebony, and chains around their ankles.

'Please keep your head lowered, Madame,' Temina reminded Francesca as they hurried past the slave auction, and then led her behind the building where for two hundred years and more, shipments of captives had been held in chains while waiting to be sold. A wave of nausea hit Francesca as the stench of human misery drifted from the barred windows, and she looked at Temina. 'Surely she would not have been held in there?'

'Oh, no, Madame, though that was where I was placed when I was brought from the south as a girl,' she muttered. 'But a lady with white skin would be held in there — Minzah, the slavemaster's house.' She indicated a square building standing well behind the slave quarters.

A nervous knot tightened in Francesca's stomach as the old woman eased open the door an inch and put her face to the crack. 'Ulim, Ulim, come quickly; I must speak with you,' she called softly. 'It is I, Temina.'

The sound of running feet brought a broad smile to the woman's wrinkled face and when the door was flung open, she held out her arms to the thin, dark-skinned boy who threw himself against her. 'My grandson,' she said proudly to Francesca as she hugged him, then, from the folds of her black garment, produced a bundle of food tied up in a remnant of white cotton fabric left over from Francesca's new petticoat.

The boy's eyes lit when he began to loosen the knot and saw bread, cheese and apricots, but Temina said he was to eat nothing until he had told them what he knew about an English lady who had been brought to this house some months previously.

Before he spoke, the boy peered across the courtyard to satisfy himself that the slavemaster was nowhere in sight. 'Minzah was very happy when al-Mansur from Agadir brought a white lady — and I heard he paid well for her, though she was most troublesome and would not permit Minzah to touch her.'

'Where — where did he keep her?' Francesca asked apprehensively.

'She was locked upstairs in this house with a serving woman to attend her.' His tone indicated that he considered this to have been truly magnanimous. 'Minzah said that her sale would make him a fine profit.' He quickly pulled at the bread and stuffed a piece in his mouth. 'I was sent with a message about her to the palace of Sherif Abu Fares and the Great One sent his son next day to inspect the lady. I heard Minzah say he was well pleased with the bargain they had struck. The Sherif's son was to return the following morning with suitable garments and a serving woman to prepare her for presentation at his father's palace.'

Ulim shoved a whole apricot into his mouth and Temina cuffed him gently on the ear. 'Eat later!' she said. 'What happened to the lady?'

He chewed quickly, spat the seed and swallowed. 'She cried loudly and threw things about and then she tried to strike Minzah which angered him. He said he would put her in the slave cells — but he did not do so.'

'I heard that she became ill.' Francesca felt her stomach knot.

The boy licked the juice of the apricot from his lips. 'When she learned that she was to be taken to the Sherif's palace the next day, she screamed and cried a lot more, then in the night she found her way downstairs and drank a whole bottle of Minzah's *Path to Heaven*.'

'Opium?' Francesca's heart sank. 'Please tell me, did the doctor come in time to save her?'

'No, not the doctor. Another man.' Ulim pulled at the bread and slipped a piece into his mouth. 'When the Sherif's son came next morning to collect the lady and saw her half dead, he demanded that Minzah return the money his father had paid. But Minzah would not do so and said that the doctor would arrive soon to make her well again.'

'But you said — tell me clearly about everything that happened!' The boy jumped at her sharp tone.

'I was not here to see the man who came, madame, because I had very great difficulty finding the doctor when I was sent to look for him that morning.' He rolled his big dark eyes at his grandmother, who acknowledged his meaning with a guttural sound of disapproval.

'Still behaving like a ram in the rutting season, is he, eh? That fool will play his dangerous game once too often!' she muttered as an aside to Francesca.

The face of a young black female house slave who'd apparently been listening to the conversation, peeped around the door. 'I was here, Temina,' she said, 'and I saw the white lady more dead than alive when the Sherif's

158

son came to collect her. He threatened to cut Minzah to ribbons if he did not repay the high price his father had given for her, but Minzah pleaded that the doctor would soon come and make her well again.' The slave girl's dark eyes widened and she shook her head. 'But the doctor did not come, and it was a stranger who later arrived to make the lady well. Within an hour, she was awake and I saw him carry her away from here.'

'He took her away? What kind of man was this stranger?' Francesca reached out and grasped the girl's wrist tightly.

'I learned only that he was an Egyptian, and a guest at the Sherif's palace. But he left Marrakech long ago, and that lady has gone, too.'

Francesca, too appalled to speak, could only shake her head and look blankly at old Temina — who shrugged.

'We will talk to my daughter — Ulim's mother — who works as a nursemaid in the Sherif's harem. Tomorrow, Madame, we will visit her and try to learn about this Egyptian who performs miracles on half-dead ladies.'

* * *

Later, after several attempts, Francesca wrote a brief note to Mr Sinclair, simply stating she had learned today that an English lady had been seen in Marrakech. She tried to keep her tone optimistic and mentioned that, after a short illness, the lady had recovered sufficiently to travel. Tomorrow, Francesca added, she hoped to gain further details about this.

After the message had been sealed, she sat looking at it in her hand, aware that she'd distorted the true facts in order to shield Thomas Sinclair for as long as possible from the awful truth that his sister had indeed become a commodity in the white slave trade.

She ran her fingertips across the paper that would shortly be touched by his hands, and felt her throat tightening. If only — if only she could deliver some hopeful news to him. Surely he would then come to view her in a more favourable light?

She stood quickly and scolded herself. Her thoughts of Mr Sinclair were unnerving and promised to lead her down avenues where it was dangerous for a woman in her position to venture. Outside, a neighbour's daughter stood waiting to deliver her message.

★　★　★

The following day, Temina and Francesca set out again, this time for the palace of Sherif

160

Abu Fares, located near the Menara Gardens on the other side of the city.

'I wish to see my daughter who serves the children of the harem,' Temina said to the officious young guard at the gate. 'Her name is Adara.'

After much persuasion and a monetary inducement from Francesca, the man agreed to call a colleague who grudgingly took a message to be sent up to the women's quarters.

Temina and Francesca sat on the ground with their backs against the street wall, knowing that it was likely to take hours for Adara to hear that her mother was waiting to speak with her. 'She will need permission to leave her duties,' Temina said, yawning, 'so we must pray that the ladies of the harem are in a benevolent temper today.' Her eyes closed and her head fell forward as she gave herself up to sleep.

Francesca closed her eyes, too, and willed her thoughts away from a certain tall man with dark hair and hazel eyes and on to the yards of brilliant silk taffeta which was waiting for the snip of her scissors. That colour was not at all suitable for a governess and neither was the flowing style she pictured for it. At least she had no freckles on her shoulders. A shawl, she needed a shawl.

Could she allow herself, just for once, to be recklessly extravagant and buy a lovely cream silk one with gold threads in the weave? One with a fringe. A long golden fringe . . .

She didn't realize she had drifted into sleep until she was woken with a start by Temina nudging her arm. 'Come, madame, my daughter has been permitted to leave her duties for only a brief time, and she waits now by a gate at the rear.'

9

Tom just happened to be crossing the main courtyard next morning when the bell rang at the street door and the servant opened it to a small girl standing on the step. The child delivered a note into the man's hand and turned away.

'Wait!' Tom started to run towards her. 'Is that for me? If it is, I want you to take a reply. Wait!' It was clear from the expression of panic crossing the child's face that she was terrified by his loud, incomprehensible words. And it was just as clear that, though the servant knew exactly what the gentleman was demanding, it was forbidden for him to grasp the arm of even a very young female. He shouted after the child as she bolted, but she refused to stop.

Tom gave a hiss of frustration and tore open the message that had come from Francesca. Again it was brief, but he felt a rush of relief to read her request that they should meet at three o'clock that afternoon at the Koutoubia minaret, not far from the Place Djemaa-el Fna. 'I have spoken with a maid-servant who has given me certain information regarding your sister's time in Marrakech,' she wrote, 'but I think it would be best to explain in person what I have learned.'

Tom opened his watch. It was still only ten. He chewed his lip and looked about impatiently, but when he heard the sound of Monsieur Cauvet's wheezing voice in the hall, he slipped into his own suite and closed the door. He'd had his fill of that gentleman's pontifications, and he'd certainly heard more than enough of Duveyner's anecdotes about his extraordinary experiences with the Tuaregs in the Sahara.

When he was sure that the Frenchmen had passed his door, Tom picked up his hat and left the sanctuary of the guest-house to plunge into the bustle of the medina. His meeting with Miss O'Hara seemed a long time off, and when he next looked at his watch, it was only eleven o'clock. He spent time viewing some wood carvers who were at work laying semi-precious stones and ivory into cedarwood screens, and watched the dyers tramping hides into their ancient, dye-filled vats. Then he filled more time by allowing a carpet merchant to almost tempt him into buying a jewel-coloured rug, and another hour passed while he studied a display of illuminated manuscripts in a book shop.

It was still much too early to set out for the minaret, and he wandered aimlessly into a goldsmith's shop. And the moment he did so he saw Henri Duveyrier in conversation with the craftsman and looking very pleased.

'Ah! Sinclair, how good to meet you,' the Frenchman called before Tom had a chance to back out again. 'Now, do give me your opinion on this bracelet.' He held out a circle of delicate gold filigree and winked roguishly. 'Will this win me the favour of a certain raven-haired beauty in Paris?'

Tom simply gave a weak smile. The question was rhetorical. He had no doubt that Henri Duveyrier's good looks, coupled with his reputation as hero of the Sahara, would be enough to bring half the women in Paris clamouring to his door the moment he arrived on French soil.

'Now come and see these delightful little baubles I'm taking home.' Duveyrier indicated a tray holding a collection of gold pins, earrings and small combs. 'I've found it always guarantees a night of romance if I slip some little *favour* under the napkin of a lovely dinner guest whose bed I might be inclined to visit later. It rarely fails to win a lady's heart, you know.' He laughed at Tom's raised eyebrows. 'I recommend you try it, Sinclair, and the prices here are most reasonable.'

'No, I'm not here to buy gold,' Tom said quickly.

The Frenchman accompanied him out on to the street again and, within ten paces, Duveyrier had — with no prompting — launched into a description of a memorable meal that his Tuareg hosts had once given in his honour. 'They have scant knowledge of the Koran,' he announced, 'and their diet obeys no recognizable Islamic code. I found it very strange to discover that while pork is quite acceptable, it is forbidden for them to eat either fish, chicken or eggs.'

Duveyrier, again demonstrating that he was also a man never burdened by modesty, soon began talking about the Tuareg women he'd encountered. He was just revealing that he'd actually had liaisons with three of them, when they rounded a corner and Tom caught sight of Francesca walking away from a display of silk shawls.

At that moment the merchant came behind her with a cream shawl draped over his arm, and whatever he said made her pause and turn to face him. When he held it towards her, she reached out and tentatively stroked its long, gold silk fringe, then stood irresolutely in the doorway for a moment longer before she shook her head.

There was something different about her,

Tom noticed, as she came towards him; then he realized that she was wearing a new skirt and a stylish high-necked blouse. And a new straw hat!

When she became aware of him with the handsome Frenchman at his elbow, surprise brought a rush of colour to her throat and she acknowledged him with a guarded smile as they met.

'Ah! Francesca! What luck finding you here!' Her given name came awkwardly to his lips. Duveyrier whipped off his hat as Tom paused to draw breath, realizing that up until now, all conversation with Miss O'Hara had been conducted in Spanish. Would she understand his far-from-perfect French?

'Francesca, please allow me to present Monsieur Duveyrier.' She inclined her head politely. 'Monsieur Duveyrier, this is my sister.'

The Frenchman looked at Francesca approvingly, took her gloved hand and bowed. 'Enchanted, Miss Sinclair,' he said, 'I've been looking forward to making your acquaintance. Your brother tells us that you are writing a book about your travels, and I'm eager to hear your views on the people you've met along the way.'

Tom was relieved to see how well she contained her surprise and gave the French-man nothing more than a calm smile at his mention of a book.

'I, myself, spent three years amongst the Tuareg tribes,' he rattled on, 'and I've learned to speak their language, which — you might be surprised to hear — has only a little similarity to Arabic. If time would only permit it, I would be happy to arrange for you to meet some of the blue men of the desert. It's the Tuareg men who wear the veil, y'know. Their women go unveiled.'

It was many years since Sir Thomas Sinclair had felt such a strong urge to kick a man in the backsides.

'That is indeed most kind of you, Monsieur Duveyrier,' Miss O'Hara responded quickly, speaking to the Frenchman in his own tongue — and in an accent which was much more polished than Tom's. 'However, I doubt that my brother and I will remain for much longer in Marrakech — because I think I have collected most of the local information I require.' She sent Tom a telling look.

'Oh, Miss Sinclair, you cannot slip away before we've had an opportunity to become better acquainted. I insist that your brother permits us the pleasure of your company at dinner this evening.'

She hesitated momentarily. 'That is most kind of you, m'sieur, but I'm afraid this evening is not possible.' Her eyes flicked away from his for a second. 'Actually, er — it has been arranged for me to witness a private betrothal ceremony. It should make an interesting chapter for my book, don't you agree — Thomas?' She looked up at him and laughed, but it was a nervous laugh.

'Everything you write holds interest for me, Francesca,' he said pointedly. 'You know how delighted I am whenever I receive correspondence from you.'

'Very well, Miss Sinclair,' Duveyrier cut in, 'tell me then, are you free to dine with us at the guest-house tomorrow evening?'

She threw a questioning glance at Tom. He frowned slightly, then nodded. 'Yes, of course, do come — if it's convenient.'

'Thank you. Yes, I'm sure tomorrow evening will suit me very well.' A faint colour rose in her cheeks.

'Splendid!' Duveyrier said cheerfully. 'Now, Miss Sinclair, are you about to make some purchase? Let me accompany you and I guarantee I'll be able to haggle with any merchant and get him to drop his price by half.'

'You are too kind, m'sieur,' she murmured, giving him her most appealing smile, 'but the inclination to shop has suddenly left me. Seeing my brother reminds me of fresh family news which I must share with him, so — if

169

you will forgive my shameful incivility — I need to steal him away from you for an hour or so.'

If the Frenchman was put out by her blunt words, he hid it well.

'Of course, I understand, Mademoiselle Sinclair, and I will not delay you one moment longer.' He lifted her hand to his lips. 'I look forward to becoming better acquainted when we meet tomorrow evening.' He bowed to them both and sauntered to the end of the *souk*.

Suddenly Tom was alone with Francesca, and it was a strange moment for them both. Neither seemed to know where to start as they faced each other in the busy lane.

'I haven't had a chance until now to tell you that I regret the hasty things I said to you in anger,' he began abruptly. 'And I want you to know that I've written a character reference which I hope — I'm sure — will be useful when you apply for a new position.' He patted the pocket in his jacket.

'Thank you,' she said stiffly. 'It was very wrong of me to deceive you about our journey, and I hope you'll accept my apology. I'm doing my best to make up for all the inconvenience I caused, and now I do have a little more information to give you about your sister.'

'It's impossible to talk here,' Tom said, pulling her to one side of the congested alley as a pair of donkeys walked past, pulling a cart loaded with bricks. 'Come, we'll find a café.'

He took her by the elbow and they entered a busy one close by, where he chose a table at the rear. They sat facing each other, while she explained in a low voice how she had found lodging with a seamstress, how she'd learned about Diana's attempted suicide, about the doctor who'd refused to come to her aid, and the stranger who had.

'Yesterday, Madame Zarifa's old slave woman took me to meet her daughter who works as a nursemaid in the harem of Sherif Abu Fares. The ladies living in the palace hear about everything that goes on there, and the maid said she remembers them all talking about an Englishwoman who had made herself ill at the slavemaster's house — after the Sherif had already paid a high price for her.

'She told us that he was an Egyptian gentleman — a guest of the Sherif — who went to your sister's aid. He carried her back to the palace and the maid said it stirred up great excitement amongst the Sherif's ladies because the Egyptian was said to be a holy man who had come to Marrakech to collect a

— oh, some kind of religious artifact.'

Tom looked at her in speechless dismay.

'Temina's daughter heard the ladies saying that the Sherif flew into a rage about the whole matter because he had very much wanted to add this white woman to his harem. When the Egyptian brought her to the palace, however, the Sherif's soothsayer warned that an evil spirit was likely to have possessed her while she lay dying and therefore some kind of purification ritual had to be performed before the Sherif could safely bring her to his bed. If she didn't survive whatever the man planned to do, of course, it would simply prove that she truly was an evil one.'

Tom shook his head and gave a groan.

'Never fear,' she went on, 'it seems the Egyptian claimed that was all nonsense, and then he and the Sherif had a great argument. The upshot of the matter was that the Egyptian bought the lady from the Sherif — they say he paid a high price — but the Sherif insisted that she and her evil must be gone from his palace before the sun had set. I know that this all sounds terribly melodramatic, but I believe it to be the truth.'

'Good God! So where is Diana now?'

'I'm afraid that was something the ladies in the harem didn't know, but Madame Zarifa

— in whose house I'm staying — is sure that the grooms in the palace stables would have heard because they were looking after all the horses belonging to the Egyptian and his servants. Servants always gossip.'

She read the next question in his expression, and answered before he had a chance to speak. 'No, I haven't yet been able to get information from the stables because Zarifa and her daughters are not permitted to speak to men with whom they have no connection. But don't worry, her son is due to return home any day now and as soon as he does, I'll ask him to visit the stables and question the grooms.'

'A few more days?' Tom sat lost in his own thoughts as he played with the empty coffee cup before him on the table. Dammit, he was not prepared to wait a few more days! Francesca had performed a remarkable feat in collecting the backstairs gossip, but enough was enough. Why shouldn't he go to the palace himself — face the Sherif and ask him politely — man to man — where Diana had been taken and by whom?

He drew in a deep, steadying breath, straightened his shoulders and pulled the references he'd prepared from his pocket. 'Thank you, Miss OHara, I greatly appreciate all the help you've provided. In this letter I've acknowledged your tenacity, reliability and honesty.' He gave a wry grin. 'And your new clothes are sure to win the approval of any prospective employer.' His grin widened. 'Indeed, you look extremely, er — *employable*.'

She raised her eyebrows at him. 'Thank you. I appreciate this,' she said as she took the envelope and slipped it, unopened, into her pocket. 'Finding another position with a good family in Morocco is going to be difficult — maybe impossible — after the way Otto Heinkler blackened my name with that dreadful business in Tangier. I think I might go back to Granada and see the Abbess when I've completed my enquiries about your sister.'

'Good Lord! You're not thinking of becoming a nun, are you?'

She gave a rueful smile. 'I could probably accept a life of chastity and poverty — but obedience? I'm afraid not. But I know that the Abbess will help me find new employment, when I explain that Heinkler was behind my problems once again.'

'Are you saying that she knew that German?'

'No, not personally. But, yes, she knows the part the late Herr Heinkler played in my father's life, and in mine.'

He seemed interested, so she drew in a breath and organized her thoughts. 'My father was a portrait painter in Spain, you see — not a very accomplished one, I'm afraid. But he was full of charm and his fees were low — and the ladies were kind to a widower who'd been left to raise a child on his own. I'm afraid, though, his earnings didn't amount to much until he met Otto Heinkler and, unfortunately, became caught up in some of that creature's shady affairs involving stolen artifacts.

'One night in Seville my father happened to be in a room with Heinkler when Heinkler killed a man — an arrest warrant was taken out for Declan O'Hara as well as for Heinkler. I was only three at the time and we all had to escape to North Africa. My father said he'd be arrested if he ever returned to Spain, so most of the time he and I had little to live on — except when he'd go off somewhere with Heinkler and come back with enough money to keep us afloat a little longer.

Firstly, he left me to be raised by a Arab family in Tunis and then another in Tripoli, until I was about eleven. I was very happy with them — but he arrived back one day with enough money to send me off to Spain to be educated in the Abbey of Saint Cresilda near Granada.'

Tom looked puzzled.

'My own mother had been a pupil there, you see, and my father wanted me to have a good education, too.' She broke off and drew in a deep breath, adjusted her hat and prepared to stand. 'Now — about this invitation to dinner tomorrow evening: I assume that your new French acquaintances know nothing about your real purpose in coming to Marrakech? Diana?'

He shook his head. 'No, that's nobody's business but ours. Anyhow, we'll all be parting company shortly and I'd hate to think of the story of Diana's indiscretions being carried back to France and bandied around salons and dining-rooms.'

She agreed. 'But if I'm to continue playing the part of your sister at dinner tomorrow, I do need to know a little about the family I'm supposed to belong to.'

He chewed his lip as he thought. 'Best to keep it simple and just say that we have a mother and stepfather, and a sister called Kate — who is married and has a little boy — and we all live on a tea plantation in the foothills of the Himalayas.'

'Oh, how delightful,' she said, smiling to herself. 'I've only ever lived in Spain and North Africa.'

'Well, in that case my congratulations on

your fluency in the French language.'

She looked surprised. 'The Abbess made sure of that. I've worked for several French families.'

'Are you going to tell me next that you speak English as well?'

There was a teasing note in his tone, but she didn't take his question lightly. 'I taught myself to read and write your language by reading the works of Mr Dickens with a dictionary at my side. But I have never met anyone who could tutor me on pronunciation.'

Her grammar was faultless, but she spoke in an accent so atrocious it was almost incomprehensible. Tom fought to keep a straight face. 'That's a most commendable attempt — and I sincerely hope that one day you'll find a nice English family to practise with.'

'Well, perhaps I shall,' she said, switching back to French. 'Now, at what time should I arrive for dinner tomorrow?'

'Come at about seven,' he said, then hesitated. 'Where are you staying? I'll call to escort you.'

'That's very kind, but please don't bother. I'll order a chair to carry me to and fro. Goodbye until tomorrow.'

She put out her hand, shook his in a

businesslike way, then walked from the café, leaving Tom to worry how much of this latest news regarding Diana could be included in his next letter to his parents. No, he wouldn't write again until he had spoken with the Sherif face to face and learned the true facts about this whole sorry mess. Actually, it was something that should be done without further delay. Enough time had been wasted.

On his return to the guest-house, he found a servant to show him the way to the palace of Sherif Abu Fares. It was only three o'clock when he rang the bell at the big bronze door and gave his card to the guard who opened it.

'Sir Thomas Sinclair requests an audience with his honour, the Sherif,' he said in a firm, pleasant tone. A servant appeared a moment later and Tom was invited to enter the building and shown into an opulent reception room with walls tiled in colourful geometric patterns. He was invited to sit on a silk-covered divan at one end, beside a marble fountain splashing playfully in an ornate alcove.

While he waited, he composed his thoughts for the delicate encounter ahead, reminding himself that the reason for this visit was simply to have a polite man-to-man talk with the Sherif regarding his sister's whereabouts. His strategy would be to plead, with the greatest respect, that as a stranger here in a country where the customs were unfamiliar to him he wished only some help to learn where his sister had been taken.

He was prepared to use every ounce of his charm and diplomacy when he met the Sherif, but the longer he was kept waiting the more doubts about this solo venture slowly began to drift into his head. Had it been a sensible decision to come here alone like this to appeal to the Sherif? Possibly not, he thought as the waiting time lengthened uncomfortably and he began to wish more and more that he had the redoubtable Miss O'Hara here beside him. She'd be furious if she knew where his impatience had propelled him that afternoon.

He smiled as he thought how much softer she'd looked today in her new skirt and blouse. Quite attractive. Her hat was certainly a great improvement on the old one.

A sound in the doorway drew his attention to two men standing there. 'His Excellency will grant you an audience now,' one said with a bow, and Tom was led into a richly decorated chamber with a high, vaulted ceiling, under which an impressive, grey-bearded man with heavily-lidded eyes sat on a gold brocaded divan.

Both he and a slender, younger man, who

was standing beside him, were wearing white turbans encrusted with jewels that flashed with every movement. The atmosphere in the chamber was icy. There was no oriental hospitality on display here and Tom sensed immediately that he had made a mistake in coming.

He bowed low to the older man and almost as low to the younger. The Sherif and his son acknowledged him with cold, silent restraint and the son moved forward to circle their visitor, examining him keenly. Then he addressed the Sherif in Arabic and his father nodded.

'You wish to make a supplication to the Sherif?' The son spoke to Tom in French.

'I have come to plead for His Lordship's help in finding my sister who was brought to Marrakech some months ago.' He carefully addressed the Sherif in what he intended to be a properly deferential tone, and watched the startled expression in the man's black eyes. The old fellow understood exactly what he'd just said, Tom judged, but the son arched one supercilious brow and made a play of translating it into Arabic for him.

The Sherif responded briefly in his own tongue and then he watched Tom stonily while his son translated. 'My father has no knowledge of this,' he said in a tone of

180

dismissal. 'The Sherif does not concern himself with such matters.'

'I see.' Tom was angry at himself for having launched into the business so badly, and tried to imagine what Miss O'Hara would try next. 'Actually, Your Honour,' he said in the mildest tone he could contrive, speaking directly to the younger man, 'I am told that my sister was seen in Marrakech some months ago and perhaps you, sir, have some recollection of visiting her when she became ill in the house of the slavemaster?'

The son's eyes narrowed and he addressed a few words to the Sherif whose first response was a low hiss — before he began to suck his teeth noisily.

'You have been entirely misinformed, Sir Thomas Sinclair,' the younger man said with a cold smile. 'We have no knowledge of such a person. And, indeed, what reason would I have to visit the slavemaster's house?'

That was a blatant lie but Tom masked his anger in bitter politeness. 'Of course, sir, as a stranger in your city I have no answer to that. However, in the name of charity, I beg your help to discover what has become of my sister. If you have information that could direct me to her whereabouts, her father and I would be profoundly grateful.' He made another low bow to the Sherif.

'I repeat, Sir Thomas Sinclair: the woman you speak of is unknown here.' There was acid in the son's voice now.

'I see,' Tom said quietly while the band of tension in his chest grew more uncomfortable. 'But I am sure Your Honour will recall an Egyptian gentleman who stayed as your guest here at the palace. Perhaps he can help me find my sister? Can you tell me in which direction he planned to travel when he left Marrakech?'

For one incredulous moment the Sherif regarded him with a bone-chilling, unblinking stare, before he began to speak to his son in a voice that quickly worked itself into a quivering anger. He threw a look of pure venom towards Tom, hauled himself to his feet, and with his attendants following, swept from the room.

With a gesture that registered his own intense displeasure, the Sherif's son indicated that the audience was now at an end.

'You have asked your questions and you have heard the answers, Sir Thomas Sinclair,' he said and, as he turned to leave, his dark eyes burned like coals. 'I trust you will now heed my words when I say that it would be wise for you to leave Marrakech without delay.'

'Damn, damn, damn!' Tom muttered to himself as he trudged back towards the guest-house with his frustrations gathering like black clouds on the horizon. Damn, damn, damn! He'd achieved absolutely nothing in that meeting and he couldn't have made a greater fool of himself if he'd set out to try! The son's petulant fury and the veiled threat about leaving Marrakech meant that Tom had obviously touched a nerve somewhere.

If he knew where Miss O'Hara was staying he'd go and confess his stupidity immediately — and no doubt get the sharp end of her tongue for behaving like a blundering idiot. He walked through the alleys of the *souk*, knowing that he had no chance of finding her in there, yet at the same time hoping that he might.

He came to the place where they had met that morning and then, a little way ahead, he saw the merchant at whose stand he'd caught a glimpse of her reaching out to touch the long golden fringe on a cream shawl. He'd seen the longing in her touch and her temptation to buy it. And then he'd read the signs of regret and resignation in her expression as she'd turned away.

He walked up to the stall and — after a little half-hearted haggling using his fingers — he bought the shawl for her.

And with that done, he felt in a somewhat more cheerful mood.

10

As soon as she had left Tom in the café, Francesca lifted the hem of her new skirt and ran the whole way back to Zarifa's house.

'Quickly,' she called, laughing, as she joined the seamstresses, 'put aside everything else and let us all work on my silk dress because I'm to dine with my brother and his friends! I said I wasn't able join them this evening — oh! I made some excuse — but I'm sure that if we all work hard, the blue taffeta gown will be ready for me to wear tomorrow night.'

The yards of peacock blue-green fabric slipped quickly under the needle of Zarifa's new sewing machine and, with a series of tucks and darts, the bodice of the dress was moulded to Francesca's slight figure. Each time she slipped into it for a fitting, her spirits lifted a notch. It was going to be a beautiful gown with a décolletage which was modest by fashionable standards, though much more daring than a governess would ever be seen wearing.

The lovely silk shawl with the golden fringe would have been perfect with it, and she wished she'd found the courage today to buy it. But from amongst the treasures in her old leather pouch, she took the yellowing, lace mantilla which her grandmother had made, and set about whitening it. If the neckline of the gown was ever deemed to compromise her modesty, she decided as she looked at herself in the glass, the white lace around her shoulders would provide a perfect solution.

Zarifa and her daughters were determined to embroider all the trimmings with gold thread, and one of them found a length of gold-coloured velvet ribbon on which Francesca hung the precious little blue tile to wear at her throat. 'This came from my grandfather's house in Italy,' she explained, fondling the keepsake. 'My mother's father was Italian.'

★ ★ ★

The household was surprised next afternoon when Zarifa's son arrived home two days earlier than had been expected. He was a big, good-looking young man, and he was in high spirits as he walked into the house with the news that he'd met several Spanish gentlemen in Casablanca and had sold his finely crafted, silver-decorated saddles for a splendid profit.

185

He was at first bewildered to find that a foreign lady was staying with the family. But when he sat down to eat the meal which old Temina placed in front of him straight away, the womenfolk wasted no time in telling him about all the work that Francesca had brought to them, as well as her search for a missing Englishwoman.

'Temina's daughter is quite sure that the Sherif sold this lady to an Egyptian who was his guest at the palace,' Zarifa said to him, 'and now, my son, I wish you to gain entrance to the stables there and learn from the grooms in which direction the man planned to take the English lady when he left Marrakech.'

As the young man listened to the extraordinary story unfolding, his eyes widened. His mouth was too full to speak, so he merely nodded at everything said by his mother, responding with eager little grunts as he chewed.

'Early tomorrow morning, you must make an excuse to visit the Sherif's stables and talk to the grooms,' Zarifa instructed.

He swallowed, then wiped the back of his hand across his lips, belched loudly and pushed his stool away from the table.

'Now is the best time to get into the stables,' he said as he stood up quickly.

'Grooms are too busy to talk in the mornings.' He gave his mother a grin. 'They're sure to invite me inside if I take some of my work to show them.'

He opened a wooden box, lifted out two elaborately tooled leather bandoleers, and held them up for Francesca to admire.

'I shall return as quickly as I can,' he murmured to his wives, investing the words with promise and they both burst into fits of happy giggles.

* * *

The chair that had been ordered to carry Francesca to her dinner engagement was waiting outside the house long before she was ready to leave. Zarifa's son had not returned from the Sherif's stables and as time sped by, Francesca gave up hope of hearing any fresh news that she could take to Tom that evening.

Zarifa and her daughters shared her excitement as they brushed her hair and helped her into the dress. The new gown emphasized her small waist, and the tightly fitting long sleeves covered the dusting of freckles on her arms. When she looked in the glass her heartbeat quickened, for there peering back at her in surprise, stood the image of quite an elegant English lady.

But her roughened, freckled hands were not those of an English lady. When the young women offered to decorate the backs of them with an intricate henna design — a fine tracery with symbols which they said were used only on the most significant occasions — her first impulse was to refuse. A governess would receive a sharp reprimand for crossing such boundaries of culture, but the woman in the peacock blue gown was pretending that she was *not* a governess this evening. And besides, the dye would have faded by the time she presented herself to some prospective employer.

Francesca placed her hands palms down on the table, and Temina carried in the pot of henna. The young women chattered as they set to work with their fine brushes, covering the back of her hands with delicate reddish-brown swirls. When the design was dry, she pulled on her gloves and, with a royal farewell from Zarifa's family and neighbours, she walked out to the waiting chair.

By the time the walls of the guest-house came into view, the knot of excitement in her stomach had turned to nervousness and she felt her heart-beat quicken. How long would it take the Frenchmen to see through her charade this evening?

A shout came from along the road behind

and the chair stopped. Zarifa's son, panting hard, ran up and put his head through the window. Smiling, he spoke to her in low tones.

'Madame, I have the answer to your question. The grooms at the Sherif's palace say the Egyptian guest was known to be the Khafra Bey — a man of high status — he left Marrakech in great haste, carrying a veiled lady on his own saddle. I was told by one who witnessed their departure that she was making no protest as they rode away.'

'Oh! Thank you,' Francesca said, struggling to absorb this rush of information. 'Khafra Bey, you say? I heard someone say that he was a holy man. Did the grooms mention that?'

He looked puzzled. 'No, Madame, his servants said only that their master had come on family business — to find an icon, they thought. The Sherif's grooms heard the Bey's servants grumbling because it had been a long ride to reach Marrakech and they were expecting to rest here. But within two days, the Bey left to return home.'

'Yes, but return home to where?' Her voice was tight.

'One groom heard a servant say that the Bey was riding directly to the port of Oran, from where they would take a ship.'

'To Egypt?'

Zarifa's son scratched a finger under his turban and frowned in thought. 'Perhaps, but the destination was not named, Madame, though one groom said he heard mention that they would sail from Oran to the end of the Mediterranean.'

'Oh, you have done very well! I thank you a hundred times over.' Elation swept through her. 'I will tell all this news to my brother the moment I meet him, and I'm sure he will want to leave for Oran straight away. Someone there is sure to remember where the Bey and his party were going. Thank you again!'

* * *

With the gold-fringed silk shawl draped over one arm, Tom hovered in the lamp-lit courtyard waiting for Francesca's arrival. He wanted to steal a few minutes alone with her before he took her inside to meet the Frenchmen, a few minutes in which to confess his foolhardy performance yesterday afternoon at the Sherif's palace. He was prepared for her castigation. He deserved it, but he hoped she'd understand his impatience; and he hoped she'd accept the shawl.

Just as the bell at the gate rang promptly at

seven, Henri Duveyrier strolled to Tom's side with a casual greeting.

Tom's ingrained social training produced an automatic, civil response, though he wished the Frenchman was anywhere else in the world but here at the moment. One quick glance at the handsome, immaculately dressed figure standing at least an inch taller than him, brought an unaccountable squirm of resentment sliding through his insides.

'Miss Sinclair is to be congratulated on her punctuality,' Duveyrier said in his deep, velvet tone as the chair was carried in. 'Very few young ladies of my acquaintance have developed that remarkable ability.'

'Oh, I think there might be many things about my sister that would surprise you,' Tom said more sharply than he'd intended as they watched the chair placed on the ground.

He stepped forward to greet Francesca and his surprise was instant when she stood before him. Her expression was alive with excitement, making her look quite radiant, and he felt an unstoppable smile spread across his face. Words evaded him as she reached up to remove a white mantilla, and he saw that her hair, instead of being pulled back severely into its usual bun, was styled into a knob on top of her head with her natural ringlets falling softly from it. She looked very much younger, and quite strikingly attractive.

She acknowledged Henri Duveyrier with a smile that was at once shy and triumphant, but before the Frenchman could speak, Tom held out the shawl in readiness to drape across her shoulders. 'You forgot to take this with you yesterday, Francesca,' he said, straight-faced.

He caught the flicker of surprise in her eyes, but she was sufficiently quick-witted to say nothing and turned her shoulder slightly so he could slip it around her. She stroked the long fringe. 'Thank you very much, Thomas. Where would I be without a brother like you to look after me?'

'After all this time, I think we've learned to look after each other very well.' His gaze met hers; she moistened her lips and he saw her eyes sparkle as if she was impatient to speak. But a quick glance at Duveyrier silenced her.

'Permit me to welcome you, also, Miss Sinclair,' the Frenchman said with the easy elegance for which he was always much admired. He lifted her gloved hand to his lips.

'I thank you,' she murmured, then looked uneasily at Tom. When he offered her his arm, she held it tightly and he could sense her nervousness as the trio made their way to a dining-room where Cauvet and the Colonel stood in earnest discussion.

They broke off and both looked approvingly at Francesca when she entered, and Tom felt something akin to pride as he led her towards them. The lamplight caught the sheen of her pale hair and, with each movement she made, the colours of her taffeta gown flashed with the iridescence of a peacock's neck.

The Colonel's cold blue eyes sparkled and he drew himself up stiffly, while Cauvet straightened his tie and tugged his waistcoat over his stomach. When Tom had completed the introductions, the politician bowed to her with an expression of open admiration and began to address her with his usual barrage of words. But the wheezing in his chest quickly curtailed any long speech.

Colonel Villatte fingered the waxed tip of his moustache as his shrewd gaze followed her. He now made a bow. 'From what your brother has told me, Miss Sinclair, you have shown much courage in undertaking this arduous — perhaps even dangerous — journey. The book you are writing should make very interesting reading.'

She gave the Colonel a self-conscious smile. 'Thank you for your kind words, Colonel, but no matter what I undertake, I always take pride in doing a job well — even when I occasionally do find myself in odd situations.' Her fingers played with the fringe of the shawl. 'But I'm sure, sir, that you are a gentleman who has faced real danger, so — perhaps — I could persuade you to spare a little time to tell me some of your experiences out here in the desert?'

Tom saw the Colonel — middle-aged, hard-headed and cynical — warming under her unaffected charm. 'Of course, Miss Sinclair — if you think that the tales of an old warrior might hold interest, I would be delighted to tell you about some of my encounters.'

'And I would be happy to provide the answers to any question you have about the Tuaregs,' Duveyier interjected. 'I lived amongst them for three years.'

'Yes, yes, we all know you did,' Cauvet wheezed, then called for the first bottle of champagne to be opened. With their glasses filled, the politician proposed a toast to welcome their guest.

The four gentlemen raised their glasses. 'To Miss Francesca Sinclair,' they chorused, and her colour deepened further.

When she darted a glance across the room, Tom could read her discomfort at suddenly finding herself thrust into the spotlight like this. And he also noted how she drank her champagne far too quickly.

There was little need for her to initiate any conversation as Cauvet — another gentleman who had never been burdened by modesty — regaled her with anecdotes about his political victories in France.

Not to be outdone, Duveyrier claimed her attention with a story about the Tuaregs' astonishing skill in navigating their way across the desert at night. 'They are truly expert astronomers, steering their way by the constellations,' he said with a dramatic sweep of his arm. 'And they are fond of music, too, though I'm afraid their one-stringed violin may not sound quite as pleasant in an English drawing-room as it does under the brilliancy of the desert stars.'

She laughed politely. Tom was relieved when a servant came into the room to announce that dinner was about to be served, whereupon Cauvet began to organize the seating around the table.

He held a chair for Francesca and, although he directed the Frenchmen other-wise, Duveyrier snatched the one on her right side, while the Colonel positioned himself on her left.

She appeared to ignore their manoeuvres, but when she shot an amused look across the table at Tom he caught a sudden movement of her eyelid. It might have been an involuntary tick, but he took it as the ghost of a wink and suppressed a grin.

Actually, he was becoming increasingly impressed by Francesca O'Hara's performance this evening. There was something unaccountably different about her — apart from the strikingly attractive new silk gown. Not only were her flushed cheeks adding a bloom which softened her features, but she was also displaying a new level of confidence with the gentlemen. But how he wished that she had refused the next glass of champagne.

While the bowls of food were being carried into the room other servants moved around the table. When Francesca's napkin was lifted to spread across her lap, Tom saw a small box which had been lying beneath it on the white cloth. One quick glance at Duveyrier's face told him who had slipped it there.

A little bauble never fails to stir the affections of a lovely lady, the Frenchman had boasted when they'd met in the goldsmith's shop. Tom felt himself begin to seethe. Damn it, if Henri Duveyrier thought he'd begin a little seduction with Miss O'Hara, it would be a chill day in hell before he'd let him have the opportunity.

From across the table he saw her looking towards him with an unspoken question:

196

What should I do with this?

'Francesca, my dear,' he said, keeping his voice toneless, 'open the box and I'm sure you'll find a pretty little bauble from Monsieur Duveyrier. The other day he showed me a splendid collection of charming gifts he's taking home to present to his lady friends in Paris.' From the corner of his eye he saw the Frenchman stiffen.

A pair of long, gold filigree earrings lay on the satin lining of the box in her hands and Tom saw her eyes light up, but she resisted the impulse to handle them. 'How very kind of you, m'sieur,' she said and calmly closed the lid. 'Thank you for this charming souvenir of Marrakech.' She gave him a polite smile and lifted the glass to her lips again.

He should have remembered that Miss O'Hara was no gushing fool, Tom thought as he sat back in his chair, while she sipped her champagne and turned towards Cauvet who was pontificating afresh on the topic of French politics. She listened with every appearance of attention and was refusing to look bored.

For a moment, Duveyrier studied Tom with a lordly nonchalance. 'I see that you enjoy playing the part of your sister's guard dog,' he said, leaning forward and speaking low, 'But be careful, my friend, or you'll one day find yourself chained to your kennel for refusing to let that young lady run free when she has the desire.' He sat back and ran his finger around the rim of his wineglass.

Tom smiled in mock surprise. 'Really? Until now, my sister has always been the one to keep me from falling headlong into mistakes. Now, as a fond brother, I'm delighted to find an opportunity to reciprocate.' He checked himself, surprised to find that this incident had raised his hackles so quickly. After all, Francesca O'Hara was far too level-headed to play a part in any of this Frenchman's game of seduction.

Watching him, Duveyrier laughed without humour.

Good Lord, Tom thought, dragging his attention away from the man's artificial smile, we're behaving like a pair of Highland stags in the rutting season. He looked quickly to see if Miss O'Hara had overheard their exchange, but her attention remained politely focused on Cauvet.

After the food had been served, and her glass again refilled, Francesca slowly removed her soft kid gloves and picked up a fork. That was when the men at the table were surprised by the sight of the intricate reddish-brown patterns decorating the backs of her hands.

'Ah, Francesca, I see you're wearing henna

again,' Tom said flatly, before anyone else could comment. 'That's a particularly beautiful design.'

'Yes, isn't it?' she said, tilting her chin and looking around at the others. 'It was done by the ladies of the house where I am staying.' She took another sip from her glass.

'One more example of your remarkable courage, Miss Sinclair,' Duveyrier said smoothly. 'I know of no other lady who would dare to do something so — so un-European — '

Francesca made no answer, but she threw an arch look across the table at Tom. And she sipped a little more champagne.

'I suspect you have done much travelling, Miss Sinclair,' said the Colonel with a kindly smile. 'I take it that Morocco is not your first journey from home — from England?'

She drew in a deep breath. 'Ah, Colonel, England is not my home. Actually, Thomas and I call India home.' She gave a smile and drained her glass. 'Our parents are tea planters and we grew up in the foothills of the Himalayas. Such a beautiful, beautiful place. Our younger sister is still there — now married — and she has a baby boy. Isn't that so, Thomas?'

He gave a grunt of affirmation and was about to steer the topic on to safer ground

— on to the weather, or —

But Cauvet spoke first, 'How interesting, Miss Sinclair. I suppose it must have been the isolation of the plantation — despite its beautiful situation — which stirred your thirst for travel. I imagine that entertainment is very limited for young people living in the foothills of the Himalayas.'

She lowered her eyelids and gave a benign smile. 'Yes, our entertainment was very limited, wasn't it, Thomas?' A servant came to fill her glass again and she disregarded Tom's subtle signal not to touch it.

'On the plantation we had little to do but ride elephants and hunt tigers — and occasionally leopards. The best way to bag one of those is to leave a bait in a tree and then go out at night with a gun and wait for the animal to come.' Again she lifted the glass to her lips. 'Of course, it's most uncomfortable to be perched up in a tree for hours in the dark, but the snow leopards were quite another matter, weren't they, Thomas? Sometimes we'd climb up to the rocky heights where they live, though one must be very careful not to start an avalanche up there in the mountains.'

'Francesca — I think we should explain that you were very young — perhaps your memories are not as clear as mine.' Tom's stern frown didn't stop her.

'I remember it all, Thomas, especially the cobras which were always trying to slither into the house. I clearly recall Father shooting several each day — and while it was rare for one of the bears to wander down from the forest — '

Tom stretched one leg under the table and pressed his toe down warningly on her slipper. 'Yes, I was very young then, wasn't I?' she said with a sigh of resignation, and took another sip of champagne. 'But I remember how much I missed you when you were sent off to school in England.'

The Frenchmen murmured their understanding. 'You were not also sent to school in England?' Cauvet asked. 'Perhaps that's behind your desire to explore the wider world now.'

'No, m'sieur,' she said, 'it was not my brother who prompted my longing to venture afar. That came from our sister, Diana, who visited Marrakech some months ago. She found it to be a strange and fascinating city.'

Tom's fork hit his plate and he stared at Francesca in disbelief. Good God! How much champagne had she drunk tonight? Her cheeks were very flushed, though her eyes remained clear and sparkling and there was a suppressed excitement in the look she directed at Tom, but he had no idea what message could be lying behind it.

'Yes, Diana made a visit here several months ago,' Francesca went on, looking hard at Tom. 'However our sister is one of those frustrating correspondents who gives very few details about her movements, the last we heard of her was that she was intending to ride north from here into Algeria — to the port of Oran — and find a ship to take her far along the Mediterranean.' She gave a shrug. 'Typically though, Diana omitted to tell us exactly where she was going.'

Tom found his heart racing. 'Yes, Diana travels to the most unexpected places,' he added lamely.

'I'm sure you now want to make a journey to Oran, don't you, Thomas?' She gave a rippling giggle. 'A little sea air is probably just what we both need.'

★ ★ ★

At the end of the evening Cauvet pronounced the dinner a great success. 'I hope we will have the pleasure of meeting you again, Miss Sinclair, before we leave for Algiers in a day or so,' he said. 'My recent illness has been the cause of delaying our departure, but I feel well enough now to set off as soon as the

Colonel's Legionnaires are ready to ride.' He sighed his relief. 'And then — on to my beautiful Paris with the news that our mission to Morocco has been a complete success.'

Francesca was in high spirits and giggled a little again as the four men gathered at the gate to bid her farewell. 'I need to speak with you alone, Francesca,' Tom hissed in her ear as he settled her into the chair, leaning close to wrap the shawl around her shoulders. 'Meet me at the minaret tomorrow morning. Nine o'clock sharp. Are you listening to me, Miss O'Hara? Remember, nine o'clock!'

Her eyelids were heavy. 'Oh, yes, my dear brother,' she whispered on a sigh. 'How could I forget?'

11

Francesca found it hard to lift her head from the pillow next morning. A relentless, thumping headache made her groan each time she moved, and it required an iron will to haul herself upright to face the bars of bright sunlight streaming through the shutters. The thought of food made her stomach churn.

Zarifa and her daughters were already at work stitching the travelling outfit — a divided skirt and a jacket of tough twill which was to be trimmed with brown braid. They were eager to hear all about Francesca's dinner party — but as she tried to recall the evening's events, it seemed that some areas had become very foggy in her mind. What had been real — what had she dreamed? The gentlemen who had all listened closely to everything she'd said? She closed her eyes and rubbed her fingers across her forehead. Had Mr Sinclair really come into her bed while she lay asleep?

Senses older than time cried out to her that she had entered dangerous territory where webs spun by night to catch a fantasy were broken in the morning by cold reality. Last night she had been carried to a place where all the old boundaries surrounding Francesca O'Hara's life had melted away, permitting her to blunder into a world that could ultimately offer her nothing but disenchantment.

She bit down hard on her lip because while other scenes had become blurred in her mind, she could remember so clearly how last night as she lay asleep, Thomas Sinclair had walked — again and again — through her dreams. She had felt him caressing her body and arousing her with whispered promises as they lay together in a scented garden.

She gave a soft groan, hauled herself back from the edge and reclaimed her sanity. 'Yes, Zarifa, the food they served at last night's dinner was splendid, and I saw the gentlemen all admiring my gown.' She showed the gifts she'd been given, and the ladies tried on Duveyrier's long, beautiful earrings, and giggled as they took turns to drape the golden-fringed shawl around their own shoulders.

'I am sure your brother was glad to hear the news that my son brought from the Sherif's stables. Now you will wish to leave Marrakech as soon as possible to follow the Egyptian?' Zarifa indicated the various garments still to be completed. 'Please have no concern, madame, all will be ready by tomorrow evening because I have two more girls coming today to help with the hemming.'

Francesca murmured her thanks and went to complete her dressing. It was a struggle to clear her mind; she splashed cold water on to her face. What had she said to the men at the table? A shaft of recollection shot through the clouds in her mind and she heard herself spinning a string of nonsense about her childhood on a tea plantation — tigers? elephants? She cringed in embarrassment. Oh, dear! Had she really mentioned Diana's name?

Yes, she had — and she had even announced that they must travel to Oran to make further enquiries about his sister. No, no, no! Her arrangement with Mr Sinclair had come to an end. His payment for her work had been generous, he had written a fine character reference, and by tomorrow evening she would have an appropriate set of clothes ready to wear when she went back to Spain to look for new employment.

She brushed back her mane of thick hair and had just pulled it into a bun on her neck when, like a thunderclap inside her head, she recalled Mr Sinclair's request — his order — to meet him at nine o'clock. It was already half past the hour and with a quick apology to Zarifa, she ran from the house and hurried until she reached the minaret where he stood lounging against the wall.

He shook his head slowly at her as she begin a breathless apology. 'No, Miss O'Hara, I'm to blame. I should have had enough sense last night to order a cordial for you,' he said and raised one eyebrow. 'How do you feel this morning?'

'Perhaps even worse than I look,' she said, pulling a long face. 'And I have a vague memory of saying some very strange things in front of your friends — about tigers? cobras? Diana? I'm so sorry. I had no idea what effect a few glasses of champagne could have. Was I a great embarrassment to you? I do apologize. Did the other gentlemen think I was completely mad?'

'No. Actually they were — were not embarrassed — But, tell me clearly now, what have you discovered about Diana's whereabouts?'

She gave him the information that Zarifa's son had gathered from the Sherif's stables. 'Little else seems to be known here about Khafra Bey, or where he came from — but the title of Bey signifies that he is a man of importance. He could be a significant landowner, or the governor of a province, or — '

'But, if they say that he took Diana to Oran, I must go there, too,' Tom interrupted. Although he kept his eyes on hers, she was struck by the fancy that he was looking at something a long way beyond her. Then with a wry smile, he seemed to bring her into focus again.

'Miss Francesca O'Hara, I have a confession to make, and when you've heard what an impatient, incompetent, fool I — yet again — have proved myself to be, I hope you'll take pity on me and agree to work as my interpreter for a little longer. At least until we've made enquiries in Oran.'

She listened in slack-jawed dismay as Tom described his disastrous interview with the Sherif. Then she clicked her tongue at him scolding, 'Yes, I think it would be wise for you to leave Marrakech as soon as possible.'

'Hmmm. Well, I've discussed plans to travel as far as Oran with Colonel Villatte and his Legionnaires when they escort Cauvet and Duveyrier back to Algiers. They're starting out on the day after tomorrow.' He arched his brows and ran his tongue along his bottom lip. 'Would you consider coming to Oran with us? To be my interpreter? I'll pay whatever you ask — and afterwards, you'll be able to catch a ship to Spain. I'll pay for your passage.'

She looked at him silently for a moment, aware suddenly that her heart — in general a very reliable organ — was once more behaving in a most alarming way and making it impossible for air to reach her lungs.

'Please come with me, Francesca. I've just proved — again! — that I can't manage in North Africa without you, and I won't give up the hunt for Diana when we do seem to be getting closer now.'

The flicker of a shy smile came to her lips and she inclined her head as she drew in a deep, steadying breath. 'I see,' she managed to say at last. 'Yes, I can be ready to leave on the day after tomorrow. Oh! And I haven't yet thanked you for the lovely, lovely shawl. I certainly didn't deserve such kind consideration after the shameful way I misled you over the business with Otto Heinkler. And then, when he tried to kill me, you saved my life. Really, Mr Sinclair, you are too kind.'

'Enough! We're talking about a business contract.' He spoke firmly, showing that the subject was beyond discussion. 'I need you to help me find where my sister was taken: you need me to guarantee you a safe journey to Oran.'

'Thank you, that sounds a most convenient arrangement.' She drew in a deep breath, turning her eyes from his to stare at a gaily dressed water-seller who was coming towards them with all his bells jangling.

Should she tell Tom Sinclair that he would probably manage very well without her in Oran? There was a community of French and Spanish families settled there and he would probably find no difficulty in arranging for someone to interpret Arabic for him.

No. She was not going to mention it because he had just handed her an opportunity to spend a little more time in his company. She knew that the deep feelings she had for him would lead nowhere, and commonsense was crying out to her that it was foolish to go with him. Yet, she turned to smile at him enthusiastically.

'And you'll be ready to leave in two days?'

She nodded, then flinched at the pain caused by this sudden movement of her head.

'The Colonel has offered to let me have a couple of decent horses for the journey, so I'll go and have a look at them now.' He raised an eyebrow at her worried expression. 'I gather that you are not a horsewoman? Never mind, you'll find riding presents no difficulty if you remember that — unlike with a camel — the animal is controlled by a very convenient bit in its mouth.' He gave a faintly amused smile and his tone softened. 'I doubt I'll find a lady's saddle in this country, so I hope you have no objection to riding astride?'

That evening, Tom sat down to write to his parents with a full account of his endeavours, so far, to find Diana. As he wrote, his pen flew over the page with thoughts almost too swift for his hand to catch. Miss O'Hara's name appeared repeatedly; at some points he found himself describing her as gracious, gentle and shy, at others, he painted an image of her as a warrior-queen storming across North Africa.

I know very little of her background but, from the moment we met, Miss O'Hara has proved herself to be a most resourceful young woman and, without her assistance I would never have been able to trace Diana's footsteps as far as this. Now we are to leave here under the protection of a company of French Legionnaires who are riding back to Algeria. Miss O'Hara will accompany me as far as Oran — which we should reach in about three weeks — and where I hope to learn from the port authorities wither Egyptian, Khafra Bey, was planning to sail. I will write again with that news as soon as I have it.

With a small scouting party of troops leading the way, Colonel Villatte set out towards

Algeria at the head of the column of fifty Legionnnaires. Francesca rode beside him on one side, with Monsieur Cauvet on his other. The French politician had been understandably anxious about venturing out again into the dust of the desert and, with encouragement from Francesca, he'd at last agreed to adopt the *haik* worn by the Arabs to cover his nose and mouth.

'I'm afraid that headgear will prevent conversation with the gentleman,' the Colonel said to her quietly, and it was only when she caught the twinkle of amusement in his eyes that she realized he'd made a dry joke.

'Then it must fall on your shoulders, Colonel, to enlighten me on all the points of interest we pass along our way,' she responded, straight-faced and using the same tone. 'I'm eager to learn about everything, you know.'

Tom saw the Colonel exchange a particular glance with her, slight and fleeting. 'It will be my pleasure, Mademoiselle.'

Tom and Duveyrier, riding behind the Colonel's party, spoke to each other only when necessary. Tom was pleased with the way Francesca had soon adapted her riding style to the steady horse provided and he noted how often Duveyrier's attention seemed to be fixed on her. Yes, he admitted to himself, she looked very trim in her new travelling outfit with the divided skirt and jacket that emphasized her small waist. Her straw hat, tied on with a scarf the colour of daffodils, framed her face, shading it from the bright sun, and giving her an appealing look of femininity that was not lost on either Duveyrier or the Colonel.

★ ★ ★

On the first two days of their travel, Tom had ensured that he was beside her horse to cup his hands and assist her each time she mounted her well-mannered mare. But by the third day she'd developed the knack of springing in and out of the saddle unaided. The Colonel ordered that when camp was set up each evening, her tent was to be circled by those of Tom and the three Frenchmen, while the Legionnaires were bivouacked around the outer perimeter. The *piste* they were following through the mountains eventually led to the stony plateau at the edge of the silent, shifting desert, then dropped to a chain of oases which provided a well-travelled route towards the north.

They met few other travellers and, as the days passed, Tom wondered if Cauvet and Duveyrier were also aware of the subtle signs

213

of the Colonel's growing affection for Francesca. She rode beside him constantly, but from the little Tom overheard of their conversations there was no whiff of flirtation. She seemed genuinely entertained by what he was telling her about the history, the myths, and stories of the people who lived in this wild, timeless land which he'd helped to conquer in the name of French honour. She sometimes questioned and sometimes challenged him. Sometimes she even made him laugh.

It was only at night, when they all sat eating dinner around the camp fire, that the Colonel's eyes gave him away each time he looked at her. He was twice her age, battle-hardened and cynical, but Tom saw that, though she was making no attempt to play with his emotions, he was clearly captivated by her.

One feature in the landscape, which the Colonel didn't explain to Francesca, was the number of freshly-dug graves they passed as they rode further northwards. Often Tom noted four or five lying close beside each other — sometimes near an oasis, sometimes out in the desert sands. He was aware that Duveyrier had seen them, too, but the Frenchman made no comment, and neither did Tom.

★ ★ ★

After two weeks, Cauvet was clearly becoming exhausted by the long journey and slept — snoring monumentally — at every rest stop, while Duveyrier, finding himself without an audience to impress, withdrew into a cold silence and spoke to his travelling companions only when it became unavoidable.

The growing heat as well as the monotony of the daily march began to cause tension in the group and by now Tom was looking forward to the day when he and Francesca would be able to leave the main party safely and ride into Oran. He was about to take another swig from his water canteen, when they were all startled by the stuttering crackle of musketry in the distance. A few minutes later the scouting party came riding hard towards them across the sand.

The Colonel instantly halted the company and turned to Tom. 'Take your sister to the rear and protect her at all cost, m'sieur,' he said, and before he had a chance to draw breath, the rim of a sandhill two hundred yards to their right was lined with a horde of blue-veiled men silhouetted against the vast, cloudless sky.

Tom narrowed his eyes against the glare of the sun's rays dancing on the long, curved blades of a hundred drawn swords. The sight sent a chill racing through his blood and he felt for the handle of the pistol tucked into his belt.

The Colonel spurred his horse and rode out to meet the scouting party while Cauvet raised his binoculars. 'Damned treacherous Tuaregs!' he spluttered. 'They must have attacked some caravan; see how they're loaded down with booty!'

Tom grasped the bridle of Francesca's mare and was pulling the animal away from the front of the cavalcade when Francesca let out a cry and he looked back to see Duveyrier riding away at break-neck speed towards the Tuaregs on the sandhill. The Frenchman was standing in his stirrups, shouting at them, waving his arms. As he approached, the Tuaregs let out a howl and the horsemen on the flanks of the party began to move down the slope like a pair of enveloping arms, so that by the time Duveyrier reached the base of the sandhill, they were encircling him in a swirling, sword-waving blue ring which obscured him from sight.

The Legionnaires raised their rifles, but the Colonel ordered them to hold their fire and glared towards the throng surrounding Duveyrier. 'Damned foolish exhibitionism!' he muttered to Tom. 'If that man doesn't extricate himself in the next five minutes, we'll attack!'

But even as he spoke, another large band of Tuaregs reached the crest of the hill and moved down to swell the numbers surrounding the position where Duveyrier had last been seen. The French company was now overwhelmingly outnumbered. Tom looked around apprehensively for any rocky outcrop or ditch where it might be possible to find shelter for Francesca if an attack did eventuate. But nothing in the barren landscape offered refuge.

She stood in the stirrups and shielded her eyes against the glare as she watched the warriors. 'Look, we must be outnumbered by at least five to one — but I think it will be all right, as long as everyone simply keeps calm'. Her face was a mask of composure, but when she leaned across to place her hand on the back of Tom's, it was sweating with fear. He turned his hand over so that their fingers intertwined and felt her fingertips bite into his flesh.

'What the devil is happening now?' he muttered when the throng of yelling Tuaregs parted and Duveyrier, straight-backed and grinning, spurred his horse back towards the French party with a large band of blue-robed men riding at his heels.

'Miss Sinclair!' he called and, ignoring the Colonel, he pulled up a dozen yards in front of her. 'Do allow me to introduce some of these gentlemen. What great luck it is to find them so far north, because now you'll have a first-hand anecdote to include in your book about how you came face to face with the legendary Tuaregs of the Sahara.'

She looked appalled at the suggestion as he swung from his saddle and walked towards her. 'Perhaps you would care to dismount? It would be taken as a gesture of friendship.'

'Sweet Mother of Jesus!' she whispered, and Tom felt her grip tighten on his fingers.

'Stay on your horse, Mademoiselle!' the Colonel called and urged his own mount forward. 'Tell your *friends*, Duveyrier, that an English lady does not — '

'No, please Colonel, it's probably better not to provoke them,' she interrupted in a shaking voice, and tugged her hand away from Tom's. 'Please, gentlemen, let me do this. I promise you that I'm not going mad, but I'm prepared to trust my instinct in this situation.'

She swung from the saddle and began to walk towards the blue-robed men, all the while untying the knot of the scarf under her chin, pulling off her hat and taking the pins from her long hair to let the tight, pale curls fall free down her back. The wind caught the cascade and ruffled it, lifting strands to catch the sunlight and making them dance.

The blue-robed men staring at her fell silent. A number of them dismounted and assumed an attitude of cringing affability.

Tom climbed down from his horse and walked a few paces behind her towards the line of Tuaregs flanking Duveyrier. As she closed the distance, Tom drew alongside and found her hand again as they listened to Duveyrier speaking with the warriors in their own clipped, fast speach.

'Splendid manoeuvre, mademoiselle,' the Frenchman called. 'It is your fair hair with its curls which intrigues them. They have never before seen anything like it.'

'In that case, m'sieur, perhaps your friends would like me to offer them some of it? Perhaps you could persuade them that a man who carries a strand of these fair curls will have many sons? a beautiful woman in his bed? his wildest dreams fulfilled?' Tom caught the nervous quaver in her voice. 'I will permit my brother to draw his knife and cut my hair — if your friends would like me to do so.' She pulled away from Tom and stood stiffly alone.

When her suggestion was translated for the murderous Tuaregs, they appeared to accept it with an almost childlike enthusiasm, and several came towards her brandishing their knives.

'No!' she ordered and flung out her arms. 'Stop! Please tell them, M'sieur Duveyrier, that only my brother is permitted to touch me. A black curse will fall instantly on any other man who touches one hair while it is on my head, and he will never father a son.'

She stood before them panting with fear, but her theatrical performance and Duveyrier's translation of her words stalled any further advance of the Tuaregs who crowded around while Tom positioned himself behind her.

He pulled out his hunting knife with deliberate slowness. 'What the devil do you want me to do?' he whispered in her ear.

'How sharp is your knife?'

'Very.'

'Good.' She heaved in a shuddery breath. 'Then tug a handful of my hair and slice it off at my collar. Cut it all off.'

He grabbed a handful and hesitated. 'Are you quite sure?'

'Yes!' she hissed. 'Go ahead — and hurry.'

'If I pull hard, it's going to hurt you.'

'Not nearly as much as we're all going to be hurt if these friends of Duveyrier's grow impatient. Get on with it! Please!'

Her head jerked backwards as he tugged at

the first hank and sawed at it with his knife. It was not an easy task, but by the time he'd worked his way from one side of her head to the other, he'd learned the technique.

Francesca took charge of each bundle of cut hair as Tom passed it to her, and Duveyrier hovered close by, eager to take possession and be the one to distribute her magic.

'Splendid, Mademoiselle,' Duveyrier said as he reached for her gift when Tom's job was done. 'A most noble gesture of friendship.'

The men in blue sheathed their swords and began to swarm closer as the Frenchman started to give out small strands of hair which were quickly snatched away and divided amongst others.

'Just wait a moment, Duveyrier!' Tom ordered. 'Don't give it all away before you ask your friends what they know about the fresh graves we've been passing.'

The Frenchman looked at him dismissively. 'This band is coming from the east. They'd have no information about what has been going on along the Moroccan border.' He bunched the remaining strands in one hand and waved them in victory above his head like a battle-banner. The Tuaregs' ululations registered their excitement and they pressed closer around him.

'Dammit man! Ask them first about the graves,' Tom said forcefully and jerked his head towards the men now watching in fascination as Francesca adjusted her hat and tried to push a riot of short curls away from her face. The blue robed men seemed to view this as humorous and laughingly held aloft the long strands they had been given.

For a young lady who'd said that she was merely following her instincts in this situation, Tom could see that those instincts had proved to be astonishingly accurate. She had transformed the wolves of the desert into her docile hounds — at least for this brief moment.

'Ask them about the graves, Duveyrier,' he repeated. 'Now, damnit! ask them!' The Frenchman shrugged and began what appeared to be a lighthearted conversation while he passed more long strands of fair hair into grasping hands.

But the smile on the Frenchman's face quickly vanished after hearing what the veiled men had to tell him. He pushed the remainder of the hair into the hands closest to him and began to back away towards his horse. He remounted quickly and spurred it towards the Colonel, leaving Francesca and Tom to follow at a dignified pace, while the Tuaregs melted away quietly into the razor-backed dunes.

Cauvet's high-pitched, wheezing voice was the first they heard as they approached the French party.

'Plague? Dear God, Duveyrier! Are you saying that we're riding straight towards the outbreak! Oh, no! We must avoid it — which direction can we take? Turn back, Colonel! Quickly, turn back!'

12

The Colonel pulled away from Cauvet and rode straight to Francesca. 'Oh, my dear, my dear Miss Sinclair! I have never — absolutely magnificent, but the risk — your courage — Oh, thank God!'

Her preference at that moment would have been to throw herself into Tom's arms, sob her relief that the wild gamble had paid off, and be comforted by him. Her insides were a quaking mess but pride soon jammed a steel rod down her spine and helped her to receive the Colonel's praise with an unlikely calm.

'Your sister, sir — I am — ' The Colonel rallied himself. 'Mr Sinclair, we must reconsider our route to Algiers because Duveyrier has learned from the Tuaregs that there has been an outbreak of plague between here and Oran. That region is to be avoided and I intend to swing south for a few days.' Though he was addressing Tom, his gaze didn't leave Francesca's face.

'Colonel,' she said urgently, 'it's impossible to predict how far or how fast an outbreak will spread.' She paused and looked down, pretending to study the tops of her dusty boots. 'At least that's what I've heard, or read — somewhere — in a book. Of course what would I — a new arrival in this land — know of such matters? But I'm sure it will — '

'What did Duveyrier's friends say about the outbreak?' Tom interrupted her. 'I assume that explains the clusters of graves we've been passing, yet we've met no signs of sickness along the way.'

'God alone knows where it will spread,' the Colonel said, still speaking directly to Francesca and making no attempt to hide the warmth in his gaze as it drifted over her face. 'Our best plan would be to bypass Oran, avoid all settled areas and keep to the desert until we understand how far the sickness has travelled.'

Tom looked uncertainly at Francesca, then back to the Colonel. 'Yes, I agree, sir, and I would be much obliged if you would be kind enough to escort my sister to safety. However, I'm afraid that my business in Oran can't be postponed, I must still make my way there as quickly as possible.'

Francesca narrowed her eyes at him. 'Thomas, I think you and I should discuss this matter privately.' Speaking quietly, she excused herself from the Colonel, walked her horse a little distance from the Frenchman, then dismounted and stood stiffly while she waited for Tom to join her.

The day's heat was growing and the wind was fitful. It gusted, blowing dust into her eyes, making her blink; her heart pounded and sweat trickled down her face. She felt a terrible hysteria rising inside her and thought for one moment that she might scream. The notion of leaving Tom Sinclair so abruptly was more than her heart could bear. What would he say if she admitted her deep, tender feelings for him? Feelings which she knew could never be returned, but were none the less precious. For the first time in her life, she was in love with a man — hopelessly in love — and it had changed her views on everything.

'Mr Sinclair, do please consider what you've just suggested to the Colonel!' Her voice quavered. 'His plan is quite wrong and, besides that, I refuse to travel further into Algeria alone with him. I intend to go with you to Oran.'

'My dear,' he began, and instantly regretted his patronizing tone. He cleared his throat. 'Look Francesca, the Colonel must know what he's talking about because he's lived in this country for twenty years and — '

'Oh, for heaven's sake,' she said through tightened jaws, 'I've also lived in this country for twenty years — on and off. And I've lived in cities which have been visited by the plague — Tunis and Tripoli — and while I have no more idea than anyone else does about the cause of the sickness, I've seen how it can pass from one person to another — unless the right precautions are taken.'

'Francesca, with the plague moving towards Oran, travelling there with me is quite out of the question. I can't — '

'Oh, why won't you listen? The desert itself can guarantee no safety. Just ask those poor creatures lying back there in their graves. Strict quarantine is the only answer to staying alive — a long quarantine, if that's what is necessary.'

'There have to be more factors involved than just that,' he said, trying to strike a calming note. 'No, it will be best if you stay with the Colonel's party. He'll take care of you and eventually get you safely to Spain.'

'No thank you, Mr Sinclair, I don't want anyone to *take care of me*, and if you go off to Oran, I certainly don't want to travel any further with the poor Colonel.' He saw a glint of something in her eyes — perhaps anger, perhaps fear. 'Can't you see that he — he is working up the courage to ask for my hand? I may have had little experience in matters of that kind, but a woman can read a man's signals and I don't want to play games with the affections of a good man.'

He looked at her speechlessly.

'Are you blind, Mr Sinclair? Can't you see what will happen if you make me his responsibility? He will — oh! he won't take advantage of the situation, but it will make matters between us very *complicated*.' She played with the knot of the scarf tied under her chin. 'I've grown fond of the Colonel and I have no intention of hurting his feelings.'

'Are you saying that you'd rather face the plague than face the romantic overtures of Colonel Villatte?'

'It's most unkind of you to joke about such a thing, Mr Sinclair,' she snapped. 'The Colonel is a very worthy man — and I find him not unattractive. I'm probably just the sort of wife he needs, y'know, but I'm not going to be because I have every intention of going to Oran and completing the work I set out to do for you.' The intense look in her eyes warned him that the subject was closed.

She took a deep breath and lifted her chin. 'Besides, when it comes to surviving a plague, I do know what I'm talking about, and you'll be glad to have me there will you.' *Please, please, let me come with you*, she silently begged.

He frowned and again shook his head at her.

She gave a hiss of frustration. 'Listen, all we need to do when we reach Oran, is to find lodging in a *Christian* household, because Christians will take precautions to avoid catching the illness. The Mohammedans won't practise any kind of quarantine because they believe that it is Allah who decides whether they live or die, and they must do nothing to thwart His divine will. They take no preventive measures against catching any kind of sickness and go wandering about the country spreading it in all directions.'

His look of indecision fuelled her anxiety further.

'After coming so far in a quest to find your sister, do you really want to run the risk of losing the last link now because — perhaps — the man who knows which ship was boarded by the Egyptian's party is about to panic and flee from Oran? And when you have no knowledge of the language, how will you make enquiries about the lady travelling with him?' She was manufacturing problems as she went along. 'It must now be months since the Bey passed through Oran, so you could find difficulty locating someone on the waterfront who still remembers which ship he took. And if you do find that person, how will you make arrangements to follow your sister?'

She wiped away the perspiration on her

cheek and waited for him to challenge her. But he simply chewed on his bottom lip, and continued to frown. She was still determined not to tell him that he'd find Spanish and French people residing in Oran, and someone amongst that group would surely be able to assist him with translations. She looked away. How soon would he realize that she'd been lying to him again — this time by omission? Eventually the time would come when every pretext to remain in Tom Sinclair's company would have been exhausted and it would be impossible to conjure up a further reason to delay their parting. Inevitably, when there were no more pieces of the Diana puzzle to solve, it would be time for them to go their separate ways. But that moment didn't have to have occurred yet. *Please God, not just yet.*

For several more heartbeats he stood frowning down at her, then he shrugged. 'I've always heard that the Irish were a stubborn breed, Miss O'Hara,' he said. 'Very well, climb back on your horse and prepare to ride to Oran, while I dash the romantic dreams of a French military hero.'

'Oh!' she said, and looked worried as she swung back on to the saddle. 'Shouldn't I say something to him, too? Apologize?'

'Not if you're my sister!' he said, and

remounted. 'An English lady leaves delicate matters of this nature in the hands of her elder brother.' His face softened as he studied her sitting straight-backed on the horse. 'Y'know, Francesca O'Hara, I agree that you are *just* the kind of woman who would have made a very fine soldier's wife.'

'And am I to take that as a compliment?'

Her attempt at nonchalance neatly masked the elation churning inside her. She had got her own way in this debate! But he said nothing more as he swung his horse around and rode straight to the Colonel. They spoke closely for some time, then a sergeant was called and ordered to select a six-man escort with a pack animal to accompany Mr Sinclair and his sister on the three-day ride to Oran.

The suddenness of the whole operation left Francesca time to exchange only the briefest of farewells with the other Frenchmen, who were both eager to turn south immediately to travel through the desert.

'My dear, dear young lady,' Cauvet wheezed and took the cotton scarf from his face in order to bring her hand to his lips. 'It has been a delight to have known you, and please allow me to applaud your fortitude, your — ' Another spasm of coughing prevented him from finishing.

'Thank you M'sieur Cauvet,' she responded

and turned her smile towards Duveyrier. 'And farewell to you, too, sir. I must thank you again for your gift of the lovely earrings — and I promise that I will never forget the day you introduced me to the fearsome Tuaregs — and I lived to tell the tale!'

As soon as he, too, had kissed her hand, she faced the Colonel. He was stiff-backed, but the expression in his clear blue eyes made her throat tighten. It was the way that Tom Sinclair sometimes looked at her when he appeared in her dreams. She blushed and felt her heart thumping so wildly she feared the Colonel might hear it.

'I wish you a safe journey back to England, Mademoiselle,' he said, 'and also my felicitations. May you and your betrothed enjoy a long and happy life together.'

So, Thomas Sinclair had cooled the Colonel's ardour by inventing her engagement to another man! Francesca felt a stinging sensation under her eyelids. 'Thank you, Colonel. And thank you from the bottom of my heart for all the kindness you have shown towards me during our journey. I will never, never forget you — '

She had to clamp her lips together to stop them from trembling, but she dropped the reins and held out both hands to him. Watched by one Englishman, two gentlemen from Paris and fifty Legionnaires, Colonel Villatte reached for her fingers and held them tightly. She thought he might lift one of her hands to his lips, but when he didn't, some impulse made her urge her horse forward a step, then lean from the saddle to kiss him firmly on his lips. She heard his sharp intake of breath and his grip on her fingers tightened even more.

'You will always have a very special place in my memories, Colonel,' she whispered. 'Adieu.'

★   ★   ★

The hard ride to Oran provided Tom with occasional reminders of the risk — the madness? — it was to be making this journey. Within hours of parting from the Colonel, they encountered the first signs of illness when they passed an Arab caravan where it had stopped to bury a victim. The six Legionnaires making up their escort kept their eyes straight ahead and hurried their mounts past the scene.

Tom exchanged a glance with Francesca, but neither made any comment.

Later that day they came upon the swollen, fly-blown corpse of a young man lying face-upwards. An army of black ants was crawling in and out of his open mouth which was crusted with sores. His head was pushed to one side by a red swelling the size of a large pomegranate on his neck, which had split to ooze puss and blood into the sand.

At Tom's insistence, the Legionnaires dug a grave facing Mecca, then rolled the body into it. They all knew that once the sun had set, the animals of the night would come scavenging.

Travelling north towards the coast, they pushed their weary horses through the long, hot days and into the night. When an isolated place to make camp was found, a makeshift shelter was erected for Francesca, while the men slept under the stars, rolled up in their blankets. Tom positioned himself protectively between Francesca and the Legionnaires, and the man placed on guard ensured that no intruder came close to their camp.

During the day, other travellers they met along the way hurried past without the exchange of customary greetings, and the sight of freshly-dug graves became more frequent. When the party at last approached a cluster of little farms on the high ground above Oran, they caught the sounds of lamentation drifting through the plantations of fig and date trees.

In the distance, beyond the trees lay a

picturesque view of the small town. An ancient citadel and kasbah crowned the hill overlooking the port and white, flat-roofed, close-packed houses spilled down little streets to embrace a wide, blue harbour. Cupolas topped the town's mosques and baths and, amongst the dazzling whiteness of other buildings, a small Spanish-style church with a tall cross stood out like a beacon.

Tom pointed to it. 'Perhaps the priest down there can give us the name of someone in his flock who'd be prepared to provide safe lodgings,' he said, and Francesca agreed.

As they rode into the town, it was impossible to ignore the sombre pall that hung over the place and the arrival of a European man and woman with an escort of French Legionnaires brought some people to watch nervously from doorways. But many of the houses they rode past looked bleak and deserted; dogs growled from the shade and a cart carrying a corpse to the graveyard scattered a flock of hens pecking in the dust.

The door of a house flew open as they passed it, and a well-dressed European man and woman, each carrying a small, tearful child ran down the steps. There was surprise and fury in the looks that both parents threw at the new arrivals. 'Go away!' the man shouted while the woman ran, stumbling down the hill after a handcart loaded with travelling boxes. 'You will not be permitted aboard! I don't care how much you can offer.'

Several servants of the household — all wailing — came to stand in the doorway to watch the departure of their master and mistress. They regarded the Legionnaires with alarm, and quickly retreated into the house, slamming the door behind them.

'Why are you leaving Oran?' Tom called to the man, and urged his horse to trot alongside him as he hurried after his wife towards the quay. 'Sir, my sister and I have come to do business in Oran and — '

'Then you are mad, señor, both of you. The sickness is spreading like a forest fire, so find yourself a boat and get away before it's too late!'

'Surely not every European is leaving Oran?' Tom felt his anger rising. 'And besides, what port will permit you to land when you've come straight from a plague area?'

The man answered with an angry grunt, but when they reached the quay, Tom was appalled to see at least twenty men, women and children pushing their way noisily aboard a two-masted, lateen-rigged Arab dhow which was already making ready to sail.

'Where is this ship taking you?' Tom said, leaning from the saddle to speak to a grey-haired man who was struggling to haul a barrel towards the boat. 'Anywhere away from here,' he cried. 'We have engaged this vessel, so find yourself some other!'

Francesca drew her horse alongside Tom's and they watched the Arab crew swiftly untie the hawsers, set the lateen sails, and turn the little boat away from the quay and into the eye of the wind.

'Oooh! How wrong I was to imagine that the non-Muhammadans here would demonstrate some sense of responsibility,' she said despairingly. 'They'll be taken to land in some isolated bay on the other side of the Mediterranean, and then — who knows what will follow?'

The sergeant leading the escort of Legionnaires made it clear to Tom that he had fulfilled his orders to deliver the English couple safely to Oran, and he was eager to take his troops away from this plague town as quickly as possible and back to the desert.

Tom agreed, and the party rode back to the steps of the church. When Tom and Francesca dismounted from the borrowed army horses and their baggage was unloaded from the pack animal, the Legionnaires rode off.

'Well — ' Tom said wearily, glancing up at the façade of the building, 'this seems the place to start. Let's hope the priest here will know someone in his flock who'd be willing to provide us with safe lodging — that is, if they haven't already run off.'

Francesca picked up her belongings and held open the heavy, wooden door for Tom as he carried his box into the dim interior of the church and deposited it on a back pew. Every sound echoed around the empty walls. The one candle alight on the altar was burning low, and when a draft from the open door caused the flame to give a final splutter and go out, it seemed like an omen. A shudder ran through her and, as they walked the length of the aisle, she sensed a hushed and terrifying foreboding hovering over them.

The door leading to the priest's robing room stood closed and, after a moment's hesitation, Tom crossed to it and tapped softly on the wood. When there was no response, he turned the knob and eased it open a few inches. A pungent smell like rotting fruit rushed out at them. Instantly, Tom mumbled an oath and stepped forward in an effort to block Francesca's view into the room.

But he was not quick enough and she caught a clear glimpse of the priest's twisted body on the floor just a few yards from the door. He lay on his back, staring wide-eyed at the ceiling; and his grotesquely contorted face was blotched with red shapes like rings of rose petals blooming under his skin.

'They left him! All those people who called themselves Christians ran away and left him here to die alone!' Francesca whispered with a sob in her voice.

'Panic is a powerful force, and so is self-preservation,' Tom said and put an arm around her sagging shoulders to urge her aside while he closed the door.

He continued to hold her as they walked back down the aisle. Who was left here now to bury the priest? Suddenly the door on to the street swung open and two small, elderly ladies, accompanied by several male and female servants, bustled inside and then stopped in surprise at the sight of two strangers in the church.

Both the ladies were dressed in heavy mourning, with black lace mantillas half-covering their faces.

Francesca and Tom murmured a greeting, which the grey-haired ladies barely acknowledged while they looked in bewilderment around the empty church. 'Surely we're not too late for Mass?' said one and began to sob.

'Of course we're not!' the other red-eyed lady scolded, grasping the back of a pew to steady herself. 'Besides, you know very well that Father Sebastian would never begin a special Mass for our dear brother if he saw that we were not here.'

'No, of course — not when it was he who laid dear Alfonso to rest just two days ago.' They cast watery, agitated glances around the empty pews, while each fingered a large gold crucifix hanging from her neck. Tears trickled down their lined cheeks and they looked helplessly from Tom to Francesca.

'It was all so sudden, you see. Our dear brother was struck down just three days ago — right before our eyes.' They spoke together, one lady talking rapidly over the top of the other. 'He felt a little unwell one morning, and the next he was fever-stricken, crying out with pain and his body covered with great swellings. He died in agony and ranting like a madman. We did everything we could for him and we were most careful that the bread was always cold. Hot bread can bring on the fever, you know. And we would never touch the skin of a peach or the shell of an almond. Some say that the sickness can be conveyed on the scent of flowers, but I assure you that we had no blossoms in our house.'

'Yes, it is a frightening mystery how this terrible sickness is caught,' Francesca said gently. 'May I offer my deepest condolences to you both on the loss of your brother.' She turned her head and threw Tom a look of concern.

He guessed what must be rushing through her mind. If the sisters had nursed their brother as he lay dying with the plague two days ago, were they now both carriers of the infection?

Tom drew in a deep breath. 'Ladies, I'm sorry to be the bearer of more sad news, but poor Father Sebastian has also become a victim. The illness has taken his life, too; he's lying in the robing room.' He tried to deliver his news as gently as possible, but even so the ladies broke into a paroxysm of sobbing and needed his and Francesca's assistance to sit.

The three female servants hovering in the background also began to weep, falling to their knees in the aisle and crossing themselves repeatedly. A rotund male, who appeared to fill the role of general factotum in the ladies' household, rushed down the aisle to investigate the priest's corpse behind the closed door.

Again a wordless message passed between Tom and Francesca. Their most urgent need now was to find lodgings where they could put themselves into isolation and play a waiting game for two weeks while they watched each other for symptoms of the dreaded illness to develop: a sweating fever, painful swellings, blotches under the skin, delirium. The prospect was terrifying.

Francesca crouched beside the oldest of the wailing female servants kneeling in the aisle. She put a calming hand on the woman's arm and drew her to the back of the church where they could speak quietly. At first, it seemed to Tom that the maid was too distressed to comprehend what she was being asked.

But at last Francesca was able to report that the woman had given her the address of a house owned by a Spanish couple who'd fled from Oran without paying the servants the wages they were owed.

'She's sure that the servants would let us stay in that house — if they were offered sufficient money. Of course, we'd need the guarantee of everybody working there that our instructions for setting up a strict quarantine would be followed to the letter.'

★　★　★

An hour later, heaving their luggage with them, Tom and Francesca climbed the steep, winding street to a modest, flat-roofed, white house which stood in the shadow of the citadel on the hill.

The surprised male servant who opened

the door to Tom's knock was fluent in Spanish, but he was uncertain about his authority to meet a request for lodging — until Tom reached into his pocket and withdrew a fistful of gold coins.

'Who has been left in charge here while your master is away?' he asked and shook his hand so that the coins clinked enticingly in his palm. The young servant's agitated expression brightened and he invited Tom and Francesca into the hall, which was still in a state of disarray after the sudden departure of the master and mistress.

'Have any of the servants here shown signs of illness?' Francesca asked.

'All who live under this room are indeed well, señora,' the man said, twisting his hands together nervously, 'although two nearby houses of Muhammadans have been stricken.' He made a sign of the cross on his chest. 'And four more bodies were carried yesterday from the citadel.'

'But what precautions did your master and mistress take to keep the illness away from this house? Quarantine? Fumigation?' Francesca asked, but the servant simply shrugged his shoulders.

'Tell me,' Tom said, 'why were all those people in such a panic to leave today? And how did they persuade the master of that dhow to take them on board?'

The servant gave another half-hearted shrug. 'News came last night that Father Sebastian had been stricken and the white people of his congregation ran from house to house declaring that it was the hand of the Devil at work in Oran. A dhow came to the quay to unload grain and the people pleaded with the captain to take them away.'

'And, naturally, the Arab was not concerned about where he might carry the infection, so he agreed to take them on board, if they could meet his price,' Tom added grimly. 'I'm sure he was happy to accept their gold, or their *señoras*' jewellery.'

Francesca looked squarely at the young man. 'Well, it seems to me that until the day your master returns, you have been left with an empty house and no wages.' The servant watched her tensely as she scrutinized the lack of order around them. 'Please call the others who are employed here so they can also hear what I have to say.'

Three other male servants immediately shuffled in from the next room and looked apprehensively at the new arrivals.

'My name is Señorita Sinclair,' she announced, looking at each man closely. 'My brother and I have travelled from Morocco and we now require rooms upstairs. We intend to remain alone there for two weeks to ensure that no illness has travelled with us. All unnecessary furniture and carpets must be removed and I want the walls and floors to be washed down thoroughly with vinegar before we enter.'

Tom noted the impressive authority in her tone and jingled the coins in his hand again to encourage the servants to heed her message. But, he thought to himself grimly, what guarantee could they honestly give these men? What if either he or Francesca had already been infected by close contact with the two elderly women in the church barely an hour ago?

Before parting from the grieving Pinella sisters, the ladies had described in vivid detail how they'd both been at the side of their bachelor brother, nursing him throughout his last tormented day on earth as he thrashed and raved, cursed and cried out in agony. They had breathed in his foul breath; bathed his sweating, cracked and crusted skin; held his tortured body on the bed when he seemed likely to throw himself from it.

All logic screamed to Tom that loving women must surely be the next ones to succumb to the plague. And just an hour ago he'd seen Fancesca supporting one of the sisters in her arms when the poor lady seemed about to collapse. And he'd felt the breath of the other on his face as he'd assisted her to a pew.

Oh Lord! how could he and Francesca *not* have been contaminated by them?

Only time would tell, he thought, and felt his heart sinking.

13

Francesca went through the house like a small whirlwind, inspecting each room. 'If you wish to remain employed,' she said to the four assembled servants, 'it is absolutely essential that you follow all my instructions to the letter.'

Tom jingled the money in his pocket again and the men instantly vowed to do exactly as requested. It was at this point that he realized how much lighter his purse was rapidly becoming.

'To make sure that no illness enters this house,' Francesca said as she looked each man in the eye, 'everybody must remain indoors. However, if anyone wishes to leave now, he may. But he will leave without wages and will not be permitted to return while my brother and I remain here.' No one appeared to doubt her words.

'But for those who choose to stay — and receive the wages which my brother will pay — you must not permit any visitor to put a foot *inside* this door, nor be tempted to step *outside* yourselves, until we give our permission for you to do so.'

She must have been a very impressive teacher, Tom thought as he watched the servants cling to everything she said. 'Food is to be ordered from this window overlooking the street, and be delivered to the doorstep where a bowl of vinegar and water must be waiting for one of you to wash every purchase before it is taken to the kitchen. You will then bring the merchant's account to the landing outside my bedroom, and washed coins will be sent down to him.'

Tom leaned a shoulder against the wall as he listened.

'I also require an immediate supply of camphor, myrrh and aloes, as well as a small quantity of gunpowder,' she went on. 'This is to be placed in a large glass jar and every part of the house is to be fumigated daily with its odour. If any letters arrive, they must be instantly fumigated also, and all domestic animals and birds are to be banished from the building.' She paused to draw breath. 'If any one of you feels feverish, or develops a cough, I must be told about it immediately. Is that clear? *I am the one to be told.*'

She instructed the cook on how their food was to be prepared, then asked for writing paper and reading books to be fumigated and taken up to the spartan rooms in which she and Tom had chosen to be quarantined on the second floor of the house. Each bedroom door opened on to a landing, and from here a steep staircase, which was little more than a ladder, led up to the flat roof above them. From that height they had a wide view over the town and the bay in one direction, while the other aspect was dominated by the looming walls of the citadel sprawling on the crest of the hill.

Neither Tom nor Francesca had raised the question of what was to be done if one, or both of them, developed symptoms. If he should die out here on the northern rim of Africa, who would inform his parents? Tom pondered bleakly as he climbed into bed that evening. And what of Francesca O'Hara? What was to be done if she caught the sickness?

He tossed on the pillows and told himself that these maudlin ruminations were just the product of exhaustion brought on by the weeks of hard travel from Marrakech. His spirits would be restored after a good, long sleep.

But sleep refused to come and as he lay with his fingers locked behind his head, staring at the moon shadows on the walls, doubts about his entire crusade to rescue Diana took a stronger grip on his mind. Defeat was staring him in the face, and perhaps Oran was going to be as far as the trail would ever lead. If only he and Miss O'Hara had reached this port before the plague had struck, before the whole social structure of the town had disintegrated.

Well, that was hardly her fault, he told himself. Without her, he'd have been forced to turn back after the first day in Agadir.

He closed his eyes, recalling how bedraggled she'd looked when he'd first met her and how, once in her new clothes, she'd charmed the Frenchmen in Marrakech and warmed the heart of Colonel Villatte on the long ride into Algeria. That public farewell kiss she'd given him had revealed a surprising tenderness in her character. And reminded him again of how little he really knew her. Would she kiss him like that, too, when it came time for them to say farewell? What had caused her impulse to cut off her hair to placate the Tuaregs?

For so slight a girl, she'd shown enormous stamina in all their travels. And not once had she grumbled about the discomforts and inconveniences they'd faced along the way. In fact, only once before had he encountered such a self-possessed and uncomplaining young woman: that had been Phoebe.

He sat up instantly and swung his feet to the floor. Damn! Why should the memory of his half-sister come back to punish him here and now? How strange that thoughts of Francesca O'Hara had suddenly brought Phoebe to his mind. Never in his life had he encountered two women with such little similarity. Certainly not physically. He'd fallen headlong in love with Phoebe's sensuous, ethereal beauty the moment he'd set eyes on her sitting on the veranda in Delhi, and —

It was madness to recall the sensations that Phoebe had stirred in him ten years ago. He'd never been able to find that magic again with any of the other lovely, witty, eager girls he'd known since then — and he'd certainly looked far and wide.

He pushed all the old memories back into the deep recesses of his mind as he stood and stretched, frustratingly wide awake now. He opened his bedroom door, crossed the landing and climbed the stairs to the roof.

Francesca was already there, perched on the parapet and gazing out at the silent sea. When she heard his footsteps, she adjusted the shawl she was wearing around the shoulders of her high-necked night-gown, then turned to acknowledge him. With no pins or combs taming her shortened hair, it was drifting around her face in a soft disorder that was quite enchanting.

'I couldn't sleep, either,' she said, and looked back at the sea. 'I kept thinking of that disgraceful scene on the quay this afternoon. Oh, Mr Sinclair, I truly believed that the people of Oran would be sensible and remain in their houses until this sickness had passed.' He recognized the undertone of acknowledged fear in her voice.

He gave a murmur of agreement and sat up on the parapet beside her. 'Nothing could have stemmed the panic we witnessed. It would have been like ordering that moon to stop rising.'

The full moon, huge and flat, was just coming up over the eastern horizon and sending a path of light over the bay, towards them.

'Isn't that a remarkable sight?' she said. 'My father would say: 'God is putting a silver path across the water to lead us from our troubles'.'

'What a very convenient piece of Irish blarney.' He felt tired and defeated and anxious. 'Sorry, I didn't mean to — '

'Don't apologize. My father could manufacture a saying to suit any situation,' she said drily.

They sat for a little longer without speaking, then she gave a little huff of frustration. 'I do hope there is someone left down there who remembers where the Egyptian gentleman took your sister.'

'Well, we're not going to give up hope yet,' Tom said with more conviction than he felt, while he continued to watch the path of moonlight growing wider. 'Y'know, where I come from in India, they say that good luck will follow moonbeams across deep water. Look down there now and you'll see that they're pointing straight to the quay. Yes, our answer is down there somewhere and we have to find a way of getting it.'

She looked at him, half-believingly at first, then she gave a little laugh. 'You've just made that up!'

'Have I? Well, don't you agree that while we're incarcerated up here, there might be someone down in the town — perhaps a merchant who calls at this house — who could ask about the Egyptian for us? It seems somewhat late now for me to be coy about trying to keep my sister's troubles a family secret.'

She hesitated. 'Hmmm, yes of course, but — ' She gave a self-deprecating murmur. 'If I sound unenthusiastic about involving someone else, it's only because I particularly wanted to be the one to discover the final piece of the puzzle — especially as I started out so badly with misinformation about the route to Marrakech.'

'Miss O'Hara, you didn't *misinform* me, you *lied* to me!' The severity of his words was undermined by a chuckle.

'Yes, I admit I did,' she said, looking down at the toe of her embroidered slipper. 'But I hoped that the information gathered in Marrakech would start to win back your trust.' *It wasn't only your trust that I was hoping to win, Mr Sinclair, foolish female that I am.* She pulled the shawl with the long fringes more tightly around her shoulders.

'Of course, you have my trust,' he said, 'and I do think that now we're about to spend the next two weeks together in quarantine — '

He didn't finish, for though it was well past midnight, their attention was caught by a movement of people coming towards the town — a silent procession leaving the gates of the citadel and winding its way down the road.

'Shhh,' she said, slipping quickly down from her perch on the parapet and pulling him by the arm. 'We mustn't let them see us up here. Stand in the shadows while they go by.'

They remained motionless as the cavalcade of shrouded women and their attendants approached. She leaned closer to him and whispered: 'Look at those huge stone walls of the citadel up there — built to keep out invading armies and yet quite useless against whatever force delivers the plague. Our cook told me that the sickness is raging up there and the ladies of the Amir's harem have been given special permission to leave their seclusion tonight and walk down to pray at a shrine in the Great Mosque. This has never, never happened before and it's a measure of the Amir's desperation. If you peep down there — carefully now! — you'll see they're surrounded by their eunuchs and black slaves, who've been ordered to kill any man in the town who might try to look at these wives and concubines as they pass.'

Edging forward an inch, Tom and Francesca were able to see the ladies and their escorts walking below. He felt a shiver run through her.

'It's hard to keep pretending that I'm not terrified of the situation we've walked into here,' she whispered, and he instinctively put an arm around her shoulders.

She didn't resist when he pulled her to him and for some time after the street was empty again they remained as they were, with her head against his shoulder. He sensed the warmth of her body under the thin cotton nightdress and felt her heart beating. It intrigued him pleasantly. Her freshly washed skin and hair carried the scent of flowers, and there was a tightening in his chest when he lowered his head closer to her curls.

It took only five seconds to rally his commonsense and let out the breath he didn't realize he'd been holding. He dropped his arm, and she stepped away from him quickly.

Tom cleared his dry throat and ran his tongue across his lips. 'I was about to suggest earlier that if you and I are to spend the next two weeks up here, we should agree to use Christian names. My family and friends call me Tom.'

'Oh, yes! Very well, *Tom*. I am Francesca Estelle Maria Consuela Isobella Paloma.' She caught him trying to hide his smile. 'I'm afraid my parents had nothing to give me but a string of family names and a few family keepsakes that I carry in my leather pouch.'

'As well as enough courage to fill the Bank of England. Never before in my life have I met anyone to match you, Francesca Estelle Maria — er, Consuela Isobella — um?'

'Paloma.' Her smile seemed to eclipse the light of the moon, and suddenly he found the prospect of spending two weeks in isolation with this young woman was looking much less daunting.

★　★　★

By the time Tom emerged from his bedroom next morning, Francesca was already discussing household arrangements with the head servant who was standing at the bottom of the staircase. She had drawn a bench across the top of the stairs to act as a barricade to their quarters and she remained behind it as the cook came up with a breakfast tray and put it down beside the bowl of vinegar and water already standing there.

'Thank you,' she said. 'Is everybody downstairs well this morning?' She was reassured that this was the case. 'Good, now as soon as the rest of the house has been fumigated thoroughly, I want the jar to be brought up here, so I can see to these rooms, also.'

She picked up the tray and turned to see Tom coming towards her with his field glasses hanging from their strap around his neck. 'Why don't we eat breakfast up on the roof?' he said, and when she nodded, he took the tray from her.

They perched uncomfortably on the parapet to drink coffee and eat their boiled eggs, dates and bread, then took turns to use the binoculars to scan the town and the surrounding hills. The sun was sparkling off

257

the blue bay, but no ship of any kind was in sight. The yellow plague flag hung limply from its pole on the quay.

It was Tom's suggestion that they would be more comfortable on the roof if they brought up the table and chairs from his room. It was a struggle to get even this small setting up the ladder-like stairs, but they managed it between them and when they sat facing each other across the table, he gave a grin.

'This reminds me of school.' He raised his brows at her. 'Look, Francesca, as we're to be imprisoned up here for two weeks, I have a suggestion — or rather, a favour to ask.'

Her eyes danced with interest and she leaned forward to rest her elbows on the table.

'I'd like you to teach me to speak Arabic,' he said.

'That's a splendid idea,' she said, and a flush crept up her neck. 'And I also have a request — a favour to ask you.'

'Name it. Anything.'

'I would like you to teach me how to pronounce English words correctly. You know that I've taught myself to read and write your language, but you're the first English person I've ever met.' She looked at him eagerly. 'It would broaden my range of opportunity in finding employment and I might be able to find work with an English family, if I could make myself understood in your language.'

He grinned at her. 'You're not one to miss an opportunity, are you?' His tone was teasing, but she was too caught up in her own thoughts to recognize this.

'The world is full of people like me who can only survive by grasping opportunities,' she said, then looked at him and gave a shrug of apology. 'I'm sorry, Tom. You've provided more chances for me than anyone else has done in my whole life — please don't think I'm not very grateful.'

He held her gaze. 'I'd still be in Agadir if you hadn't taken the opportunity to come to my aid that day. So, shall we settle for Arabic lessons in the morning and English conversation after lunch?'

They began in high spirits as soon as Francesca had written down the 28 letters of the Arabic alphabet and given him his first lesson in pronunciation. This was followed by several colourful phrases to be used in the bazaar.

'Yes, you're making satisfactory progress, Thomas Sinclair,' she was saying, straight-faced when, to his relief, they heard their lunch tray being placed on the bench on the landing. 'I think that in another two or three years you'll be quite proficient in the language.'

'Please, *señorita*, I beg you not to joke,' he said, playfully slapping his palm against his forehead. It made her laugh.

They moved the table to follow the afternoon shade and, after they'd eaten, he held back a smile as he watched his demanding teacher become an anxious pupil.

'I'm sorry, *señorita*, but your grand Castillian accent will have to be sacrificed, because the first task in our English lesson will be to master the letter *h*,' he announced, and they sat huffing that sound until her efforts satisfied him.

'Good,' he said, 'now try this: *How heavy is this rock?*'

She watched his mouth intently as he carefully enunciated each word. Then she took a steadying breath and attempted to repeat them.

He, in turn, watched her lips and tongue as she struggled with the task. Her mouth was delightfully shaped, he noted, with full, soft lips, mobile and well-coloured. 'Fine effort!' he said, straightening himself on the chair. 'Your *how* and *heavy* are not bad at all, but we'll have to work hard to get rid of that trilling *r* and the lisping *s*.'

He was grateful that there were no

neighbours to overhear the odd sounds flung to and fro across the little table on the roof as Francesca struggled to train her tongue to follow his instructions. At times she became frustrated, but he refused to end the lesson until he was satisfied with her effort to say: *I trust the health of your great yellow hound is sound.*

He grinned his approval and tipped his chair to balance at a gravity-defying angle on its back legs. 'You've done very well, Francesca. Tomorrow we'll deal with the letters *v* and *z*.'

She gave a theatrical moan and slumped with her elbows on the table and her head in her hands. 'And tomorrow morning we'll ignore the health of your *great yellow hound*, and I'll teach you a few very effective phrases to use when a swindler in the market is trying to part you from your money.'

When he began to laugh, she joined in, too. Again he was struck by how her face was softened by her wide, white smile and the tendrils of unruly hair falling on to her forehead.

'Y'know, Francesca, from the day we first met, I've been intrigued by your Spanish accent. Was your family from Castile?'

'The O'Haras of Castile? Good heavens, no!' She laughed afresh.

'Well, then, how do you come to speak Spanish like a grandee?'

'Oh, that's a long story.'

'So?'

She gave a grin and brushed her hair away from her face. 'Well, if you must know, it all began when Grandfather Patrick O'Hara — a hungry Irish farm-boy — joined the British army and went to Spain with Wellington's infantry to fight Napoleon.'

Tom leaned closer.

'However,' she said, whispering, 'after four years of facing shot and shell, Grandfather Patrick had had enough. When Wellington turned *north* to chase the French over the Pyrenees, Patrick turned *south* and kept walking until he reached the little town of Almagro, where he met a lovely lace maker. The mantilla I wore to dinner in Marrakech was made by her. Did you notice it?' He nodded. 'Well, they were married and Patrick set up as a carpenter in the town. That little wooden flute in the pouch was his.'

'And he never did go back to Ireland?'

'No, they stayed in Almagro and had one son. That was my father and he grew up to become a painter. He was very handsome and charming, though his work was far from first-rate. But that was how he met my mother Estelle when she'd just left school.

She sat to have her portrait painted by him.'

For a moment she gazed with unseeing eyes across the rooftops. 'My mother's family had escaped from France at the time of the Terror, and all they could bring with them were the deeds to their little chateau in Normandy.' She rallied her thoughts and looked quickly at Tom. 'I'm the keeper of that document now, even though the chateau was burned to the ground on the orders of Robespierre and the mayor of the town soon confiscated the family's land for himself. Those deeds are totally worthless, of course, but to me they're a reminder of where I've come from and who I am. Like the Irish flute, the Spanish lace and the Italian tile — those French deeds are all part of me. When Heinkler stole everything, I was left feeling — oh! abandoned, nameless, lost. And lonely.' She bit down hard on her bottom lip.

'Well, tell me, then,' he said quickly, to distract her thoughts, 'where does an Italian tile fit into the O'Hara family saga?'

She blew a long breath through her lips, then shrugged. 'My French grandmother fell in love with an Italian merchant and eloped with him. But they say that it was a true love affair. That little blue tile I wore on the ribbon around my neck in Marrakech came from their house in Ravenna. My own mother

263

brought it with her as a keepsake when they sent her to be educated at the Abbey of Saint Casilda near Granada.'

'Not Castile?'

'Patience, please! My mother met and married my father not long after she left the Abbey, but she died before I was three. She'd always wanted me to be educated there, too, but my father fled with me to North Africa when he and Heinkler were accused of killing that man in Seville. Most of the time in Africa, my father's earnings didn't amount to much, but when I was about eleven he and Heinkler went off somewhere and — what do you know? — suddenly we had money to spend and I was sent off to Granada and put into the care of the Abbess of Saint Casilda — who was from *Castile*!'

Her story left Tom stunned. 'Was the Abbess aware of all that business?'

'Of course, she was no fool. The Abbess was a very grand old lady from a noble family. She might have spent fifty years within the walls of the Abbey, but she kept in touch with the world outside.'

'Intriguing,' he said. 'Did she ever meet your father?'

'Oh, no. He thought he'd be arrested if he ever set foot in Spain again,' she said, 'so he wrote to the Abbess and put me on a boat

264

when I was eleven. I had no trouble finding my way to Granada.'

She spoke as though this was a perfectly logical solution to her father's dilemma and there was no self-pity in her tone. Tom clamped his jaws and thought it best to keep his opinions to himself, though he could feel the veins in his neck standing out. She didn't appear to notice.

'The Abbess took a particular interest in my education, and she was shocked to discover that my father had left me to be raised by Arab families.' She smiled to herself and looked across to the blue water of the bay. 'Believe me, I was very happy growing up in those big, good-hearted families, but they weren't Christians and so I arrived at the Abbey speaking Arabic more fluently than Spanish and knowing nothing about the Mother of Jesus.'

Her story left him speechless, and his thoughts flew back to the sons of Robert and Phoebe, who'd been brought to England and delivered to their new school by fond grandparents. He was appalled by the image of an eleven year-old girl sailing off alone to find her own way to an Abbey in Spain.

'The Abbess herself took charge of my education, and what a challenge that was for her,' she said with a laugh. 'She warned me that it was essential to become proficient in every subject and be prepared to earn my living as a governess when I left the Abbey. She said I'd never be able to depend on my father to take care of me and, right from the start, she insisted that I practised speaking Spanish with her own grand Castillian accent. *It will give you an advantage when you are out in the world, and it will set you in a class apart,* she often used to tell me.'

'Ah! Now I see!'

'Well, the Abbess was right, you know, because — while my academic credentials were sound enough — I know that some employers engaged me because they thought my aristocratic tone of speech would add a degree of refinement to their children's education.'

She spoke jokingly, but Tom didn't laugh.

14

By the time he woke next morning, Tom's enthusiasm for mastering the Arabic language had begun to wane. Anyhow, there seemed little point now in pushing on with the lessons, he decided with a degree of relief, especially when he lifted his head from the pillow and heard Francesca speaking rapidly from the roof to somebody down on the street.

He dressed quickly and, unshaven, was about to climb the ladder, when she clambered down and met him with a bright smile. She held a small basket tied to a length of twine.

'Good morning, Thomas.' They had agreed last night that all conversation was now to be conducted in English. 'I am happy to see that you have risen, for I have speak — er, spoke — with a seller of melons who will go immediately to the waterfront and ask for knowledge of the Egyptian Bey and where was his destination.'

Tom nodded his understanding, then looked questioningly at the basket in her hand. 'Ah — ' she paused briefly, constructing a reply. 'I will lower this and he will place in it his message when he returns. Then everything will be fumigated.'

'Yes, of course,' Tom muttered, quickly calculating how much he should pay the fellow if he came back with an answer. But, would it be a truthful one, or some fabrication calculated to extract a little profit from a disingenuous stranger?

'Thank you, Francesca. It will be interesting to see what he can learn.'

But no message came back from the melon-seller that day, or the next, or any other day.

Despite trying to keep themselves occupied with language lessons, time hung heavily, and they'd soon read the books brought up from the rooms below. She filled several hours each morning quietly writing what she called a journal, while he often sat on the parapet with the sketch pad on his knee, drawing views of the domes and minarets of the town and the towers and crenellations of the citadel on the hill.

'I think your work is much better than my father's,' she said when he showed her some of his sketches.

But there were other pages which he didn't display: they were the ones covered with quick drawings of a young woman sitting at a table, writing a journal. Sometimes her head was tilted forward, with her concentration clearly on the pen in her hand. And sometimes, when she was gazing out towards the town, her profile was turned to him. It was a pleasure to sketch her rounded forehead and straight nose. The chin? Well, if she wasn't quite so thin, perhaps the stubborn line of that chin would be less obvious. Perhaps.

But on a few occasions, her thoughts appeared to be drifting far away and she sat looking towards him, and past him. In those brief minutes his pencil flew across the paper in an attempt to capture a sensuality he'd not previously recognized and which he found impossible to reproduce accurately.

★ ★ ★

'Oh, how sad. The melon-seller died yesterday,' Francesca translated for Tom five days later when she leaned over the parapet to speak with a man below. 'This fellow is a carpenter and he says that he is — was — a neighbour of the melon-seller, and before the poor man departed from this life, he asked this friend of his to keep his promise to us.'

She saw Tom's surprise. 'That's the way

269

things are done in this part of the world. The melon-seller made a promise to us and the carpenter is honour-bound to fulfil it for him. If he feels himself becoming ill, he will pass the request to some other neighbour or friend.'

It was clear from the frequent cries of grief drifting across the roof-tops that the plague had taken hold of the whole town. The sounds of lamentation were frequently accompanied by the snarls of dog packs roaming the streets and by the rumble of carts arriving with loads of timber for the coffin maker, and other carts trundling away from the town several times a day with bodies for the graveyard.

Francesca kept track of their time in isolation by putting a mark on the wall each day before the sun went down. By the time nine days had passed, Tom's language lessons had long since lapsed, but she continued to practise her English during their lengthy discussions on everything ranging from family life on his parents' tea plantation; to steamships and ornithology and theatre productions in London.

And sometimes she made him laugh by mimicking some of the overbearing people whose children she'd taught. '*Señorita, you will be dismissed instantly if you ever again*

270

allow any of my daughters to eat a persimmon,' she squeaked in the tone of an outraged madre, while wildly fluttering a sheet of paper like a fan. 'Surely you must be aware of how this fruit — when eaten under the hot African sun — will encourage the most unseemly secretions to be produced within the bodies of young females gently raised in Spanish households?'

Tom snorted. 'Well, thank you for that information, Francesca. I had no idea that persimmons could be blamed for some of the lively behaviour I've seen displayed by young Spanish ladies in South America!'

Sometimes he drew maps and told her about the far-flung places where he'd lived and the railways he'd helped to build. But, it was his descriptions of family life on the tea plantation that most fascinated her. 'Tell me more about how your mother and sisters spend their days. Do they sew? Or paint? And when you and your stepbrother were permitted to go into the jungle beyond the plantation, was there no danger of being eaten by tigers?'

'Yes, there were tigers to watch out for,' he laughed, 'but we were safe enough on the back of an elephant. Besides, my stepfather always sent along a few men with rifles when we rode out there.'

'And your stepfather — you are very fond of him, I think?'

'Yes, indeed.'

'Your mother must be very happy.'

A wave of nostalgia hit Tom as he pictured James and Julia strolling hand in hand through the garden, sitting together on the veranda in the evenings, and closing their bedroom door firmly at night.

'Tell me all about them again,' she asked and he repeated the story of a man and a woman who'd broken the rules of society thirty years before when they'd fallen in love while each was already married.

'My mother says that it was Fate who had arranged their meeting and, when the inevitable happened, it was as if two planets had collided, illuminating their whole universe forever.'

For a moment he found it hard to continue and chewed down on his lip while he looked away from her. 'Actually,' he said at last, 'I witnessed the very same thing happening to my stepbrother, Robert, when he and Phoebe first met at a party in a Raja's palace.' He took a steadying breath. 'At the time, my stepbrother was District Commissioner of the princely state of Ranaganj, and when I took Phoebe up there for a visit — '

He stopped abruptly. Dear God, he was

272

speaking of the unspeakable! That excruciating episode in his life was closed, and nobody — apart from his stepfather, of course — had ever known how deeply it had hurt him.

'You were in love with this Phoebe yourself? But she refused your hand and, instead, chose Robert's?' Francesca's words were deadly accurate. 'I can well imagine how hurtful that must have been.' She looked unflinchingly into his eyes.

He had to clear his throat. 'Yes, I felt hurt at the time, and it's an understatement to say that I was angry about it. I was wildly jealous — and I behaved in a totally ungentlemanlike way. Anyhow, that was ten years ago and it's all forgotten now.'

She looked doubtful. 'Have you never again fallen in love?' Her tone carried no sentimentality.

'Yes, of course I have,' he said, attempting to be flippant. 'I've been in and out of love a dozen times — all most enjoyable.' Actually, he felt uncomfortable now to think about the reputation he'd gained amongst the ladies he'd kissed, so he threw Francesca a question of his own: 'What about your own plans? Doesn't every young lady have marriage in her sights?'

'Governesses don't marry,' she said and he saw her small breasts rise and fall. 'My plan is

273

to open my own school and teach generations of Spanish girls to speak perfect English.'

'Well, you'll be speaking like a duchess, by the time I've finished with you, *señorita*,' Tom said, relieved that the conversation had taken a lighter tone. 'You'll be able to convince everyone who hears you that you've been brought up in the grandest house in the land.'

'No, thank you, I have no wish to be anything other than I am,' she said briskly. Then he caught the laughter in her eyes. 'Although, I must admit that I really enjoyed being your sister in Morocco. But I wonder if those Frenchmen would have shown such courtesy towards me if they'd known that I was actually the daughter of a man wanted for murder in Spain, and the granddaughter of a British army deserter?'

Tom grinned back at her. He was finding himself increasingly charmed by her candid outlook on life and her sense of humour. At times he was aware of a strong tug of affection towards her, but he was careful to keep that to himself. Any admission of warm feelings would only complicate matters when the current crisis in Oran was over and it was time for each of them to go their separate way.

Although he said nothing about it to Francesca, his last hope of finding Diana had evaporated when the carpenter failed to return and no other townsman had come forward to keep the melon-seller's promise to help them.

Well, he told himself as he climbed into bed that night, he'd done everything he could to find Diana, and he'd failed. As soon as the plague had passed, he'd buy a passage on the first ship sailing away from Oran and make his way back to England. James and Julia would understand and they certainly wouldn't mark it as failure on his part.

Francesca? He owed her much more than the wages he'd thrown at her all those weeks ago, and as soon as could contact a British Consulate and cash a cheque, he'd make sure the money found her, wherever she went. The thought of her setting out alone again made him uncomfortable. Was there some way he could assist her to find new employment?

★ ★ ★

Each morning Tom and Francesca assured each other that they were still showing no symptoms of illness and she checked that the servants were also remaining well. Merchants brought deliveries of food and oil — and the latest news. Nothing that had been touched by an outsider's hands was brought into the house until it had been washed.

Tom's cash was running low and that evening when he counted the remaining money in his pocket, it occurred to him that no household bills had been presented for days.

'I haven't seen an account all week,' he said to her. 'How much do we owe?'

'Nothing,' she said offhandedly, and set out the draughts board they'd improvised. They played with this by lamplight most evenings, using buttons for pieces. They'd been less successful in trying to create a pack of playing cards from pieces of writing paper.

'Hold on a moment, Francesca,' he said, pausing before he moved his first button on the board, 'I saw a fresh delivery of your fumigation concoction arriving two days ago and I can recall what I paid for the first batch. I know the price of everything is soaring — and I've seen other merchants delivering supplies, too.'

'I assure you that there's nobody outside waiting for payment,' she interrupted, keeping her eyes on the game.

He anticipated her next move and took her piece. When she again fell into a trap, Tom realized that her concentration this evening was wavering badly. He looked closely at her face as she chewed her lip and studied the board. Out of nowhere, he was hit by the obvious answer to his question.

'Francesca, you've been using your own money to keep us afloat, haven't you?' She didn't answer and, with great deliberation, moved her next piece.

'It's most generous of you, but I don't want you to do that. Especially when I recall the less than gracious manner in which I gave it to you after that debacle with Heinkler.'

She merely gave a little smile and didn't look up.

'Now I don't know what to say, Francesca — apart from giving you a promise to repay every penny as soon as I can.'

She made a quiet murmur and kept her eyes averted.

He sat back in his chair and shook his head. 'Francesca O'Hara, I think you must be the most *extraordinary* girl I've ever known.' Even as he spoke, he felt something tightening in his chest, something that came with the realization that until that moment he'd been measuring his feelings for her by some *ordinary* man-woman yardstick. Why had he refused to recognize the effect that her uniqueness was having on him?

She smiled and slowly raised her eyes to meet his. He was stunned by what he saw, for in their depths he read a message that sent a pulse of dark excitement racing through his blood. Miss O'Hara was no player of flirtatious female games — that he knew for a certainty — yet there was a clear invitation contained in that innocent look.

The breath caught in his throat and, as he held her gaze, he found himself floundering in a new tension that had suddenly started to hum in the air around them.

Something intangible which had been hovering between them for weeks, was suddenly taking on a shape of its own. It's name was desire. And it took him utterly by surprise.

'You owe me nothing, Thomas. There is no debt between us,' she said with a poignancy that swept away his last ounce of resolve to keep his feelings tightly furled. Without a conscious thought, he reached across and placed his hand on the back of hers, knocking aside the buttons on the board as he did so. When she made no move to pull away, his thumb slid down to stroke the soft skin inside her wrist and he saw her lips part as she drew in a sharp breath.

Careful! Think of what you're about to do, a feeble voice inside his head warned. But the moment stretched and they both remained as they were, hands joined across the table, gazing at each other with a kind of bewilderment. The last call to prayer for the day floated from the minaret beside the Great Mosque, but Tom couldn't hear it above the ocean-roar of his own pounding blood.

Some barrier between them was magically evaporating like a morning mist and he almost laughed aloud with the joy of it. He stood, dry-mouthed and, not slackening his grip on her fingers, he slowly drew Francesca to her feet as well. The look she gave him was luminous and she came towards him willingly.

He caught her around the waist, pulling her to him until they were hip to hip, chest to chest and, when he lowered his head, their breath mingled as they stood almost mouth to mouth.

In that moment the world stopped spinning and nothing existed but a tall Englishman and a small Spanish woman who found themselves poised on the brink of something that was ready to carry them swiftly to a place beyond her comprehension. But it was a place that was not beyond Tom's comprehension. God, how he ached to take that leap with her and permit his feelings to sweep them deep into some dark ocean of rapture.

But, tempting though it was, he couldn't take that step with a girl who was surely still an innocent. That would be utterly unfair. So he stood as he was, trying to steady his racing pulse as he held her, allowing the moment to stretch endlessly, knowing that he must bring it to an end yet incapable of doing so.

He told himself that all he needed to do was to offer a few clichéd, polite words of apology and back away. But his mind was blank. He didn't want to apologize, and he was still floundering in indecision when she raised her head a fraction so that her lips touched his.

And, like a flame put to kindling, desire flared in him. He took a long, shaky breath and slowly brushed his mouth to and fro across hers. He felt her body tremble, then press closer against him. The tip of his tongue began to trace the outline of her lips, the taste of her entered his blood like wine and went straight to his head. His awareness began to spiral out of control; he could barely think, he could only react. He made a sound in his throat, his arms tightened around her more and he planted his mouth hard over hers, possessing, searching.

She closed her eyes and clung tighter, while a feverish flush of pleasure as old as time rose up from the centre of her being. His intimate contact raised no alarm within her body. Indeed, she wanted more of him, and it seemed the most natural thing in the world to slip her hands across his shoulders and up the warm column of his neck. Her fingers slid into his hair, urging his kiss to deepen. And deepen.

This was the glorious moment that had so often woven itself into her wild fantasies, but tonight she wasn't dreaming. Tom Sinclair's touch, his taste, his scent were all gloriously real, as was the heat spreading through her in slow, languid waves, lapping at every secret corner of her body. This was everything she'd dreamed of and more.

She gave a groan of delight when she felt the warm velvet of his tongue invading her mouth, slowly stroking, seeking. The taste of him was intoxicating and she became possessed, fuelled by heat and magic; she abandoned herself to him, lost in the heat of his kisses.

When his breathing grew ragged and his mouth became even more demanding, a shiver of pleasure shot up her spine. If this had been any other man, panic would have taken hold and she'd be fighting now to put a distance between her body and his. But this wasn't any other man. This was Tom — the man she'd loved from afar — who was now holding her close. It was his hand which was exploring her, stroking up and down the line of her spine.

When it came to rest on her bottom she instinctively pressed herself harder against him and felt his arousal. A great rush of excitement washed over her. This man desired her! He hungered for her! She leaned into his embrace and kissed him back with abandon.

And when at last he slowly raised his head and broke the kiss, she stood panting in his arms, her head against his chest, awash with weakness in the wake of their sensual rush into passion.

She pressed her lips together as if to capture his kisses and her heart sang because Tom Sinclair had wanted to make love to her tonight! She knew that intuitively, and she, herself, had been ready — almost ready — to give herself to him, if he'd asked her. Now it was a strange sensation to stand in his arms, trying to define whether the maelstrom inside her was made up of *disappointment* or *relief* that he hadn't asked her? Mainly disappointment?

No, no, no! It was *relief* that she felt! Her head was clearing sufficiently now for her to realize how different these glorious moments shared with Tom had been, compared with the assault that she'd been forced to endure when her virginity was plundered six years ago. She'd fought hard that night to repulse the loathsome creature thrusting himself into her, but it had been hopeless. Horrible and humiliating.

Yes, it was truly a *relief* now to know that Tom Sinclair still remained ignorant of her shame. For a few precious moments in his arms she had forgotten that she would always carry the brand of *damaged goods*, and no respectable man would ever consider taking her as his wife.

Never, never, never again must she allow her emotions to run riot as they had done tonight with Tom. There was no need for him ever to be told what had happened to her, and when he eventually went back to England, it would be some small comfort for her to know that the awful secret remained hers alone.

She opened her eyes and found herself drowning in the depth of his gaze. What was there to say at a moment like this? she thought, struggling to regain her wits. She took a step backwards, but not too far, for now he was running the back of his hand softly down her cheek.

'Francesca?' he murmured, tilting her chin. 'I hope — ' He had absolutely no idea what he should say. They had blundered into a realm that had been clearly signposted No Trespassing! and the discoveries made along the way had astonished him. How could a man of his age and experience permit himself to be swept into a situation like this with a girl who was so clearly an innocent? Yes, he'd grown deeply fond of her, but he could never take advantage of that friendship.

Her physical response to him, however, had not only been surprising, it had also been both delightful and dangerous. A game of that kind could very easily become addictive. And that would be most unfair to Francesca. Wouldn't it?

'Well, Tom,' she said breathlessly, and much too brightly, putting her hands on his chest to push herself away. 'I really didn't expect to receive such warm thanks for my little contribution to our financial situation.'

'Francesca, if I have — I mean, if you think — '

'Please, Tom, stop now, before you insult my intelligence.' She gave a brittle laugh. 'What happened tonight was simply the result of being forced to play too many silly games of draughts, and there's no need for either of us to apologize, or ever mention it again. We'll simply have to create a new diversion to occupy our time tomorrow evening. Any suggestions?'

In fact, they avoided spending any time at all together after dinner the following evening. Tom said that he had some writing to do in his room, and Francesca, feigning weariness, went to bed and prayed for God to send some ghastly retribution on to the Spanish swine who had stolen her hope of ever finding love and happiness with a man like the one who had kissed her last night.

* * *

The numbers of people struck down by the plague was still growing, sometimes it appeared that whole families had been wiped out leaving no one to bury them. Francesca heard from their servants that the two elderly Spanish ladies who had nursed their plague-stricken brother, had themselves died a few days after their sibling.

Tom was feeling the frustration of their quarantine more keenly than she was. 'Look, in only another four days our prison gates will be opened,' he said, raising his brows at her. 'Don't you think we might be allowed a little time off for good behaviour?'

She frowned for a moment. 'It's very tempting, but I don't think we can take the risk. So far, everybody in this house has stayed well, but if we break our own quarantine up here, even by a few days, it will give a message to the servants that they can break rules in the rest of the house, too.'

They looked at each other and both heaved a loud, theatrical sigh. 'I can't argue with your logic, but tell me, ma'am,' Tom said good-humouredly, 'is there one subject on God's earth that's left for us to talk about in the next four days?'

'Hundreds!' she said. 'I haven't yet told you anything about how to cook a camel's intestines in barley water, or the very delectable way of serving the eyes.'

He grimaced and made a play of clutching his stomach as he turned away.

Neither he nor Francesca had made any mention again of their rooftop embrace. She had more books brought up from the shelves in the sitting-room and Tom spent longer periods sitting by himself, sketching.

Fewer people were out on the streets these days. The yellow plague flag fluttered over the port and, as no ships called in to unload provisions, food supplies were becoming short and prices were continuing to rise. The bazaar was almost deserted, while packs of hungry dogs scavenged though the town, and crows gathered on the minaret beside the mosque, watching, waiting.

This morning Tom and Francesca had observed several wailing women wandering aimlessly along the street in front of their house; women who appeared to be so demented with grief that they'd torn their veils to expose their faces in public and allowed their hair to hang loose and dishevelled.

Two evenings ago, a slave, screaming from the ravages of the plague, had thrown himself from the high walls of the citadel. And a man with great swellings on his neck collapsed to lie groaning for hours outside their house until he was picked up and carried away.

'Come away, it's best not to watch what's happening down there,' Tom said, urging her away from the parapet yet again. 'There's not a thing we can do to help.'

But it was impossible not to take an occasional look, and late next morning they watched a young woman stagger into the town with a small child clinging to her skirts. For a time she sat on the ground with her back to the wall of a house opposite theirs, coughing violently while the little boy clambered across her legs, whimpering.

There were a few people on the street when the mother with the child first settled, and two black-robed women who were passing, paused to speak to her. They moved on when she shook her head. Francesca watched anxiously as the hours passed and the child's crying grew more insistent. The woman dragged herself to her feet, took a dozen steps, then fell to the dust where she lay, occasionally groaning and writhing as the hours passed.

'That child can't yet be two years old!' Francesca whispered as they watched the boy crawl around and over his dying mother, trying to rouse her, pulling himself on to her breasts, poking his fingers into her mouth, and eyes and ears.

'There's not a thing we can do to help,' Tom said.

'Oh, where are the relatives? Why doesn't somebody come looking for them?' She thumped the parapet with her clenched fists. 'That baby has not eaten all day. Tom, I can't bear it!'

He caught the tone of her voice and pulled her away from the parapet. 'Francesca, don't even think about going down there yourself. You know damn well that the woman — and probably the child, too — is highly contagious. We can do nothing, *nothing* to help them.'

A few minutes later, he walked back to the parapet, then gave a groan. 'Oh, God! She's not moving at all now. I think she's gone.'

The child's wail started again on a low note and rose swiftly to a high pitch, wavering like an infant version of the mullah's call to prayer from the minaret.

Tom heard Francesca's gasp, and felt her fingernails bite into his arm while her other hand pointed towards the bazaar. 'No, no, no, no, no!' she hissed, and when he turned, he saw a pack of pariah dogs scavenging along the street, coming in the direction of the screaming child.

She spun away from him and started for the stairs, calling over her shoulder 'I'm sorry, I'm sorry Tom, but I can't bear it. I'll have to go down and get that baby off the street. If those dogs reach him, they'll tear him apart!'

'No, not you Francesca!' he shouted as he ran after her and grasped her by the arm. 'You wait here, and I'll go. You're not to go near him!'

'You're being thick-headed,' she cried, pulling away and pushing past him to reach the stairs before he did. 'Don't you see that I'll have to bring him up here and stay in quarantine with him for another two weeks.'

She was half-way down the stairs now and Tom was only two steps behind. 'Then I'll stay up here with him, not you! You will not put a foot outside this house. Are you listening? That's an order!' He caught up with her as she raced to pull aside the bench at the top of the stairs.

'Please try to be sensible!' she called back to him as she started down the stairs leading to the reception rooms. 'What do you know about caring for a small boy? I'm the one he'll need up there in quarantine with him.'

He managed to lay a firm hand on her shoulder before she reached the front door and spun her around to face him. 'And what if he's already ill? Please think about the consequences of bringing a plague sufferer into this house. Let's both be clear-sighted about the risk we're about to take — not just for ourselves but also for the other poor souls living under this roof.'

'I know, I know,' she said in a voice shaking with agitation. 'But I think everyone else in the house should be safe if I take the boy straight upstairs into quarantine. You can move into a room down here, and — '

The sound of their raised voices brought the wide-eyed head servant into the hall, where he stood listening and wringing his hands.

'And what happens if we go out there now and find that the child — the child whom we've seen climbing all over his dead mother — is already showing signs of plague?' Tom yelled.

'If — if — Oh, I don't know. I'll look after him up there, and — '

'Dear God, Francesca, if you were to become ill I'd never be able to — '

But the time for indecision was brought to a sudden end when the sounds of the approaching dog pack sent a chilling reminder that the child would be dead shortly if they didn't act now.

Tom looked around quickly, but he could see no walking stick or weapon of any kind in the hall, so he snatched the cloth from the hall table, sending a collection of religious statues crashing to the tiled floor. He flung open the door to the street and, with Francesca hard on his heels, he ran across the road, roaring and flapping the white cloth at the snarling dogs.

Initially, they were startled and distracted, backing away from him with their hackles up and teeth bared. But almost immediately they began to circle in closer, snarling.

Francesca ran to the filthy, hysterical child clinging to the skirt of his mother. Thank God he'd be too young to remember the hideous sight of this poor, dead creature, was her first thought as she snatched him up.

Holding him at arm's length, she ran towards safety while Tom backed towards the house, struggling to keep the dog pack at bay, and the servant's sandaled feet danced a nervous tattoo on the doorstep as he watched the drama.

'Out of the way!' Francesca ordered as she set the thrashing child down at the entrance and began to strip his clothing. 'See that all these things are burned immediately and bring warm water and towels to my room. Food for the child, too!'

She ignored the servant's indignant grunt and heard Tom arrive behind her. The street door was closed and, carrying the naked, screaming child away from her body, she ran past the other horrified servants and up the stairs.

'Stand back!' Tom shouted at them as he made to follow her. 'My sister and I — and the child — will remain upstairs in quarantine for a further two weeks, and the household routine is to be continued down here. Is that understood? And try to discover who this child belongs to, and whether he has any family left living.'

He reached the top of the stairs and pulled the bench into position again to form a barricade.

The servants down there had good cause to be angry, he thought, as he stood at the door of Francesca's bedroom and watched her trying to calm the baby's storm of weeping while she examined him for signs of fever and the dreaded, rosy rings of the plague under his skin.

It would be a miracle if his little honey-coloured body wasn't carrying the seeds of infection, Tom thought grimly. And he and Francesca must bear the responsibility for bringing any sickness into this house.

Damn! What were the chances now that any of them would ever get out of here alive?

15

Nothing would pacify the child, even after Francesca had bathed him thoroughly in the bucket of warm water, which the lowest ranking servant in the house had delivered with a telling thump on to the bench at the top of the stairs.

'I'm afraid our popularity in this house has slipped badly,' Tom said as he picked up a towel and crouched beside the howling baby, trying to catch a flailing limb to dry it. 'Well, I must say that it's a relief to see that he seems to be showing no symptoms — so far. I suggest we — Oh! quickly, Fran — is there is chamber-pot handy?'

She produced one from under her bed and watched in astonishment as Tom adroitly held the child over it while he relieved himself.

'There, that's better, little man, isn't it?' he murmured, throwing a glance at Francesca. 'You didn't think I'd know how to do that, did you?' He grinned when she shook her head. 'Well, I can't claim to have had a lot of practical experience, but I've acquired a clutch of young nephews in India who've taught me the basic principles.'

He settled himself into a chair, holding the frightened child on his knee, while Francesca cut a hole in a towel and improvised a miniature Roman tunic to slip over the boy's head. He immediately buried his face against Tom's shirt and continued to sob silently, while Tom gently stroked his thick, dark hair.

'Hungry, little man? Look at what Aunt Fran has in that bowl. Maybe now you'd like to eat some of this lovely mush — whatever it is?'

Francesca drew up a stool beside Tom's knee and spoke soothingly in Arabic, but the child's weeping continued. Then she began to sing a tune with strange, off-key notes that sounded alien to Tom's western ears, but he felt the child's breathing steady gradually. The shaking little body began to relax and he turned his head to look about. His eyes, round and dark like ripe grapes, fixed on the bowl in Francesca's hand and his expression became a combination of suspicion and craving. She scraped the spoon noisily around the bowl, and the child's lips trembled as he leaned forward to peer into it. Then he opened his mouth a fraction and she slipped a spoonful of gruel on to his tongue.

His eyes didn't leave her face while he

swallowed it quickly, then opened his mouth wider for more.

'What shall we call you?' she crooned softly, smiling as she watched him swallow another spoonful. 'What is your name? Is it George? No! Is it Antonio? No! Is it Siegfried? No! Is it Abu?'

Her sing-song name-game kept him distracted until the bowl was empty and then he lay back, limp and passive, in Tom's arms. Gradually, his eyelids grew heavy and began to droop, yet he fought sleep and looked repeatedly towards the door, as if expecting it to open at any moment. As if expecting his mother to appear.

When silent tears started to fill his big, dark eyes again, Tom reached into his pocket and produced a handkerchief to wipe them away. Then, humming softly, he rocked the boy in his arms until, at long last, his eyelids closed.

Francesca watched the pair in silence; the ball of emotion in her throat would have made it impossible to speak, even if she'd found the words to express what she was feeling. Tom Sinclair was the most *extraordinary* man she'd ever known, and every moment — God help her! — she was falling ever more deeply in love with him. He was tender and patient and strong — it took a truly strong man to reveal the tender side of his nature, as Tom was doing now with this nameless baby.

She stood up quickly, pretending that there was something of interest to be seen from her window, which looked on to nothing but the roof of the next house. It was going to be difficult to keep her feelings for Tom hidden during the extra time they had committed themselves to spend up here in quarantine. But somehow — for her own sanity as well as his — she must keep him from seeing how intense her feelings for him were becoming.

It was a relief when she heard heavy footsteps coming up the stairs, followed by the sound of their dinner tray being clattered down on the bench.

'Put the boy to sleep in my bed while we eat our meal,' she said, briskly stowing her riot of feelings behind a wall of efficiency. 'I'll have some bread and milk sent up later in case he wakes in the night.'

Tom settled the sleeping child on her bed, then carried their meal up to the table on the roof. He lit the lamp while Francesca busied herself laying their cloth and setting out the cutlery.

They both glanced towards the parapet, then back at each other. 'You stay here while I take a look,' he said, and she held her breath while he crossed the roof, then rejoined her quickly.

'His mother is no longer lying down there,' he said, pulling his chair up to the table. 'Someone has taken her body away, so surely they'll come looking for the boy tomorrow.'

'Of course they will,' she said, with little conviction.

That evening she went to her room early and stood at the bedside for a few moments, watching the little boy lying deeply asleep on her sheets and smelling of her flower-scented soap. He was on his back with his arms and legs flung wide, but though he didn't wake, his whole body gave a sudden jerk and he began to whimper.

'We'll keep you safe, little one, and the dreams that trouble you now, are sure to fade with time,' she whispered as she knelt beside the bed and stroked his head until the rhythm of his breathing steadied.

Tom was watching her from the doorway. 'There's a spare bed in my room. He can sleep in there with me, if you'd prefer,' he whispered.

'Leave him where he is,' she answered over her shoulder. 'There's plenty of room for us both in my bed, and if he becomes frightened in the night — ' She looked at Tom, and shrugged at his frown of concern. 'I know you want to tell me that having him sleep beside me will increase my chance of becoming ill — if, indeed, he is carrying the sickness, but — '

She spread her hands in a gesture of helplessness and her chin began to pucker. 'I don't know — He doesn't understand what any of this is about, and he's missing his mother. It just seems so heartless to — What will become of him if his — ? Perhaps I could take him with me when it's time to leave, and maybe — ' She couldn't go on.

This was the first time Tom had seen her completely at a loss, vulnerable and frightened. 'Francesca,' he said, taking a few paces into her room, 'we're in this together, remember? Whatever happens, I'm here to share it with you.'

As she stood to face him, her lips trembled and she passed a hand across them, embarrassed by her moment of weakness.

He took a few more paces into the room, held her shoulders and kissed her on the forehead. Then his hands began to slip to her waist, heating her with their touch. 'I want you to know, Francesca, that whatever happens, I won't leave Oran until you — '

She sniffed as she swung away from him, then straightened her shoulders and presented him with a manufactured smile. If she felt his hands on her body like that again, she knew she'd fall to pieces. So she turned to the sleeping child, and briskly finished Tom's sentence for him. 'You were saying that you won't leave until — until I have a new teaching appointment in view? Is that it? Thank you.'

That wasn't at all what Tom had had in mind to say, but he'd found it impossible to put plain words to the feelings stirred in him when she'd lowered her guard momentarily and given him a glimpse of her confusion and uncertainty. He thought he'd come to understand the character of Francesca O'Hara thoroughly, but she'd just shown him that there were still aspects that had an uncanny power to disturb him.

★ ★ ★

That night, Tom began a letter to James. It might be his last, he thought grimly, for there was no denying that the act of bringing this baby into the house with them was akin to playing a game of Russian roulette. If his little body were carrying the plague bullet, which of them would it strike first? Under the circumstances forced on them this afternoon, what else could they have done but rescue the child?

He dipped his pen in the ink and started to write. If he was still alive in two weeks' time he'd tear it up, but if he was already dead when ships once again began calling in to the port of Oran, he hoped that someone in this house would post it to England.

With his emotions running high, his pen flew over the pages with thoughts flowing too rapidly to be captured and presented in an elegant form. Sheet after sheet of paper was quickly filled with the account of his attempt to find Diana, coloured by descriptions of Francesca O'Hara's remarkable skills in collecting information for him along way. He gave copious examples of her stamina, generosity and ingenuity. And he also explained how she came to be alone in the world.

At this point he put down the pen, stretched, and linked his fingers behind his head while he pondered on how to express in words the deepening tenderness he felt towards Francesca. Was it love? The feelings she aroused in him were quite unlike any others he'd experienced in a line of romances over the last ten years. What was different about his feelings for Francesca? Even though she'd so fervently returned his kisses two nights ago, she'd made it clear that she was not to be considered a candidate for any further romantic dalliance. Did that mean never?

He scratched his head and picked up the pen again. He was too weary to wrestle with the question, so dipped the nib back into the inkwell.

'*Dad*,' Tom concluded, '*as you can see from what I've told you, Francesca is completely alone and if I should not survive, I beg you to do whatever you can to see that she is not left destitute. The Abbess at Saint Casilda near Granada is the only person likely to know how to contact Francesca, if she has been lucky enough to walk away from the hell we have become trapped in here.*'

He felt drained when he at last put down the pen, folded the thick letter and addressed the envelope. His watch said that it was more than two hours past midnight, but when he turned out his lamp, he saw a light still shining under Francesca's door. Although there was no sound coming from the room, he couldn't resist the impulse to see if the baby was keeping her awake.

Quietly, he turned the handle and eased the door open just far enough to look in at both Francesca and the child sleeping soundly. The boy's little honey-brown body was cuddled into the curve of hers; her cheek lay against his head and one arm was wrapped around him.

His eyes swept over the sinuous lines of their bodies and Francesca's hair on the pillow, his gaze lingered on her expression of contentment. His throat tightened, and the tender image became indelibly printed in his mind. *Woman and child.* How lovely her face looked in repose. Who would ever have guessed that the abrasive, scheming young woman he'd encountered at the start of his quest in Agadir, could become the gentle girl lying there with a baby in her arms. This was the woman whose kisses had made his blood sing two nights ago, the woman whose flight into passion had matched his own — and made him lust for more.

Had she really changed so much physically in the time since they'd first met? Was it merely something to do with the new clothes and colours she was wearing and the fact that her hair was no longer scraped back into a tight bun at her neck? Were his eyes deceiving him, or had his perception of her altered so radically because she'd allowed him to see her softness and vulnerabilities, too.

Before he turned out the lamp, he reached down and pushed back a sweep of hair falling on her cheek, recalling the day she had ordered him to slice off her tresses to placate a tribe of desert warriors. What other woman in the world would have had the imagination or the courage to do that?

She stirred at his touch, and her eyelids fluttered. Then she sighed, snuggling the baby closer — and Tom felt a tug on his heartstrings. The life of a governess was spent raising other women's children, loving them, watching them grow and then saying goodbye.

That thought was still in his mind as he went back to his room and climbed into his own bed, waiting for sleep to come. What was going to happen if the child lived and no relative arrived at their door to claim him? The image of Francesca asleep with the baby in her arms haunted him. It would be almost impossible for a governess to raise a child on her own. But if she had a husband? What if he were to offer her his hand?

He gave a groan, settled into his pillow and tried to still his thoughts. It was pointless to concern himself with problems concerning the future until Fate had made its decision on whether any of them would still be alive next week.

★ ★ ★

They called him Akil. That was the name he responded to instantly when Francesca

304

played her name-game with him the next day. 'Akil?' Tom said to him and the big brown eyes that were puffy from crying, turned to him straight away. 'Yes, he seems to recognize that name.'

Though he ate whatever food was given to him, the child remained withdrawn and miserable. They took him up to play on the roof and, though they tried to devise games, he showed little interest in them. Initially, he spent most of his waking hours clinging to one or other of them, often with his face buried in Tom's shirt, or snuggled into Francesca's arms, and reaching up to play with her tendrils of fair hair.

★ ★ ★

After a time, his tears dried and he began to climb down from their laps, and toddle to and fro around the roof, collecting any leaf or piece of debris that had been blown in, building towers with them or carefully storing them in a box that Tom provided.

Akil continued to remain free of symptoms and, as the days passed, he grew more accustomed to his new surroundings. Sometimes they heard him give a happy gurgle when Tom did something to amuse him, or when Francesca played a haunting, off-key

North African melody on her little flute. A big, black beetle which landed beside them one morning provided splendid entertainment, with Tom and the boy crawling to and fro across the floor after it, and putting obstacles in the insect's path to tease it.

When the creature had eventually had enough, it spread its wings and flew away, leaving Akil to howl his disappointment.

'Cheer up, old chap,' Tom said, scooping the boy into his arms. 'Do you want to fly, too? Come on!' He held Akil above his head and the child squealed with excitement as he was spun around until they were both dizzy.

Initially, Francesca was kept busy cutting up a well-worn bedsheet and stitching several little tunic-like garments for Akil. Then Tom tore a long strip of the fabric and fashioned it around the child's head in the style of a *haik* which he'd been taught how to wear in the desert.

And when Tom presented himself on the roof wearing his own *haik* with the end drawn mask-like across his face, it set a new game in motion. Together he and the boy trotted around the floor on make-believe horses, uttering blood-curdling, warrior-like whoops.

Sometimes Francesca played an Irish jig on her flute while Tom and the child skipped and hopped to the rhythm. She was ridiculously happy in this make-believe world, so different from anything she'd ever known and it was becoming increasingly difficult to keep her eyes from following Tom as he laughed and romped with the boy. In all her years of working with families, she'd never encountered a man who could tolerate the company of a small child for more than a few minutes, even if it was his own.

It remained a mystery to her why a man like Thomas Sinclair was still unmarried. Surely he must have met many well-bred ladies who would have been delighted to wear his ring and bear his children. It was hard to understand why the girl called Phoebe had rejected his offer. How could any woman in her right mind not see that Tom Sinclair was the most amiable man who ever walked the earth? Handsome, too. Her palms grew moist and her toes curled in her shoes as she remembered the feelings that had overwhelmed her on the night they'd embraced under the stars. Even thinking about it now brought a flush to her cheeks. Tom Sinclair had found her a desirable woman that night —

He caught her gaze, and she lowered her eyes quickly in case he was able to read in them just how much she still stupidly hungered for the impossible.

★ ★ ★

The servants' hostility towards them gradually settled as the days passed with no signs of sickness appearing in any of those living at the top of the stairs. 'We have advised every merchant who calls that a motherless boy waits here,' the head house servant announced. 'Perhaps soon his family will come.'

'Just look at our score on the wall now,' Francesca called as she added another mark to the tally of their days in quarantine. 'It will only be another four days before we can all safely present ourselves downstairs.'

He nodded at her and tossed Akil a ball that he'd improvised from a rolled-up sock and string. The boy squealed as he tottered across the floor after it, but Tom's attention was distracted by the sound of a cart rumbling past the house.

Francesca heard it, too, and ran to where he was standing at the parapet. 'Look, there's only one coffin on the wagon today, and there was only one taken out to the graveyard yesterday, too.'

'Perhaps this means that the end of the plague is in sight?'

'It's certainly a good sign,' she said, 'but we'll still have to be careful, because it could flare up again if — Oh!' She stopped suddenly when two black-clad, veiled women crossed the street, stood in front of the house, and looked up towards them. 'Quickly, Tom, quickly,' she called excitedly, 'bring Akil over here and lift him up! Perhaps these ladies are from his family!'

She leaned over the parapet, waving. '*Salem aleikum* — Peace be with you. You have come for the baby?' she called and Tom held Akil high for the ladies to see. 'Observe how well he is, and thriving, God be praised, though his poor mother . . . ' Her words dried when the women's only response was to shake their heads.

'What is it?' Tom asked, straining to catch the gist of whatever Francesca and the women were discussing in Arabic. He should have paid more attention during his language lessons, he told himself as he saw, first, the colour drain from Francesca's face and then watched her breathing quicken as the women continued to explain something, which then caused her to laugh and clap her hands.

'What the devil is it?'

'It's about Diana! They have brought news of the Egyptian and your sister!'

'But — but — ' he spluttered. 'Tell me — '

'Oh, this is wonderful! I must get some money for them,' she said, making for the stairs. 'Wait here until I come back. Lean over the parapet and say *Salem aleikum* to them a few times.'

Tom did as he was instructed and, after Francesca had lowered several gold coins to them in the basket, she and the women exchanged polite farewells.

'Well,' she said, spinning on her heel and facing Tom with a lift of her chin, 'the melon-seller's honour has been upheld, and the information we asked for has been delivered. Our visitors have just told me that the Egyptian gentleman and Diana were seen aboard a boat that was bound for Rhodes. And from there they were sailing to an island not far away.'

Tom shook his head. 'But — slow down — how did those ladies learn all that?'

'Well, as the melon-seller promised to do, he started to make enquiries, but then he became ill, so asked his neighbour, the carpenter, to continue. And the carpenter tried, until he became another victim. But before he died, he asked his uncle — a fisherman — to keep the promise.' She rubbed her palms together gleefully. 'After all this time, it was only last night that the uncle learned of the Bey's destination. He asked his wives to bring us the news.'

'Whoa!' Tom said, scratching his head.

310

'There seem to be several pieces missing here. It's months since the Bey and Diana sailed away from Oran, so where did this local fisherman get his information? Can you be sure that the story is genuine?

'I'm prepared to believe it.' As Akil was showing signs of weariness, she picked him up and settled in a chair with him on her lap.

'Tell me, Fran, did the fisherman himself see the Egyptian?'

'No, he heard the story from a friend who had heard about it from another fisherman — and — Oh, Tom, the information has taken all this time to reach us because it's an involved story, but I'll try to make it as brief as possible.'

Tom pulled up a chair next to hers.

'Months ago, well before the plague arrived, fishermen all along the northern coastline here were out in their boats when a great storm struck. Some boats limped back to their various ports, but others were sunk or wrecked, and now, of course, whenever fishermen in this region happen to meet now, they exchange stories about the terrible things that happened during that calamity. And that's why our fisherman chanced to hear only last night about an Egyptian with healing powers who had brought one young man back to life after his body had been

311

pulled from the water during that storm. Surely that must have been our Egyptian?'

Tom gave her a sceptical look. 'How can you be sure that the man who performed the miracle was Khafra Bey? Did our fisherman speak to the man who was plucked from the jaws of death?'

She shook her head. 'Our man heard the story from another fisherman, who said that he had been told all about it by a fisherman from Tangier whose son's life had been saved by the Bey.' She was speaking fast and starting to sound impatient.

He gave a grunt and raised one eyebrow at her. 'Isn't this how myths and legends begin? A mysterious figure suddenly appears — '

'Don't be too quick to jump to conclusions,' she interrupted, 'When I was in Marrakech I heard the Bey referred to once as a Coptic holy man. Don't forget they said that he was the one who had revived Diana when she almost killed herself with an overdose in the slavemaster's house.'

'He's a Coptic Christian?' Tom's forehead creased and he chewed down on his lip as he tried to recall what he'd heard about certain healing gifts belonging to members of that ancient church. 'So what was the miracle he performed on the fisherman's son from Tangier?'

'Now listen: the man's boat was blown far out to sea by the storm. The mast was smashed, the craft was overturned, and the fisherman's son was almost drowned. He was unconscious when his father dragged him to a scrap of floating wreckage and held him on it for — well, for a long time. Even though the boy's breathing had stopped, his father refused to give him back to the sea.' Akil's little body twitched; he gave a whimper in his sleep, and Francesca pressed her lips to his forehead before she went on.

'Well, it seems that miracles do still happen, Tom, because just when the fisherman thought all was lost, a ship sailed into view and he and his dead son were taken on board. His tale of how an Egyptian appeared on deck and brought the boy back to life, may have become somewhat embroidered with all the re-telling since then, but' — she drew breath and paused for dramatic effect — 'the fisherman also said that when he went below deck, he saw an unveiled lady — a European lady — sitting there.'

Tom frowned thoughtfully.

She clicked her tongue at him and raised her brows. 'Well? Surely you must agree that it was Diana?'

He gave her a narrow look. 'It's possible, I suppose, but how long ago did all that

313

happen? Four months? Five? Aren't we just clutching at straws?'

'We've been clutching at straws from the start!' she said. 'But this latest news points directly to Rhodes, because that's where the fisherman and his son were put ashore, and they heard that the boat was sailing on to a small island close by. Tom, all you have to do is get to Rhodes and after that you should have no difficulty locating the Egyptian's island.'

'Yes, I suppose so.'

He knew that his lack of enthusiasm was related to the fact that Francesca had just made it clear she would not be going any further with him.

16

Francesca's news left Tom pondering. The gossip was third hand, but if the facts were accurate, it put fresh life into the hunt for Diana. Perhaps it hadn't just been a quixotic adventure, after all. What a relief it would be now to tear up his farewell letter to James and write a more optimistic one. Well, guardedly optimistic, anyhow.

He stood slowly and took a step towards her chair. 'All right, let's suppose that the unveiled woman travelling with this Egyptian was Diana.' He felt his enthusiasm rising and something tightening in his chest. 'After all, how many Egyptian gentlemen have been escorting European women around the Mediterranean recently?'

Her eyebrows raised a fraction and her lips twitched at the corners.

'Francesca, you're remarkable, and — ' He leaned over the sleeping baby in her arms, inclined his head and kissed her cheek. His impulse had been to kiss her firmly on the lips, but he'd thought better of it. Now he stood looking down at her with his heart pounding and he had to clear his throat before he could say any more.

'Without you, my sister's fate would have remained a mystery and — and I only wish that I could find the right words to tell you — tell you . . . ' *how very much I've grown to love you.*

He sucked in his breath and applied a brake to any such blundering, schoolboyish outburst. She'd shy away and laugh at him if he told her what he was feeling. Ever since they'd left Marrakech he'd been trying to deny to himself that he was falling in love with her. That realization might have crept up on him as slowly as fading sunlight on a winter's day, but he was in no doubt now that his sentiment was very real.

He felt himself staring at her like an idiot, and took a steadying breath. 'Well, Francesca, as I was saying, I — I can't find the right words to express my gratitude for everything you've done,' he finished lamely.

She gave him a sweet, though somewhat distant, smile.

'Er — would you like me to take Akil?' He held out his arms, but she shook her head and held him closer to her breast.

'Thank you, Tom — but, no. Goodness knows how much longer I'll be able to have him with me like this.' When she smiled at the child, her face was suffused with tenderness.

'In all honesty, I was actually relieved today when the ladies said that he was not the reason for their visit, because it meant that Akil could remain ours for a little longer.'

Ours! He watched her closely. 'And what will we do if he remains unclaimed when the time comes for us to leave here?'

Her eyes remained fixed dreamily on the child. 'Do you think it would be possible for us to keep him?' she asked with a catch in her voice.

Tom's heart leapt. She was still using the inclusive *us*. Was she suggesting that perhaps he and she would not go their separate ways after this? His mind whirred with possibilities.

'Perhaps we could keep him with us, Francesca — if we were to become husband and wife.'

His voice was so low it made her wonder for a moment if she'd heard his words correctly. She gave him a startled look and shook her head. 'Oh no, Tom! That wouldn't be fair — I couldn't ask you to do that. Besides, you have your work to complete, your career, and — and your family — and you must find Diana and hear whether she wants to return to your parents, or — '

He started to interrupt her, but her frown stopped him. 'If Akil's family doesn't come, I've been thinking seriously about taking him back to Morocco and finding a nice Arab family to raise him for a year or two until I've earned sufficient money to start my own school. Then, when I'm independent — '

'My dearest Francesca, please listen to me! I admire and love you, and there's nothing I want to do more than look after you and the child. I'd be honoured if you would agree to be my wife.'

Her eyes widened in alarm and the colour drained from her face; she held the sleeping child higher, like a shield. 'Ooh! Thank you for your offer, Tom,' she said in a tight voice. 'I am much obliged, but marrying you is quite out of the question.' She lowered her head and rested her cheek against the baby's forehead.

He dropped on a knee beside her, took her chin between his thumb and finger and tilted her head back, willing her gaze to meet his. 'Francesca, I'm fit and healthy in mind and body, I'm financially comfortable, and I have come to truly love you. I want to spend my life with you, so why do you say that marriage to me is out of the question? Just give me one reason why I should take that as your final answer.'

As she stared at him, a shadow crossed her face and she simply shook her head.

'Oh, come along, now, Francesca — you

know that you can trust me. After all, we've come to understand each other very well during our travels.' Her lips trembled, but she still made no comment.

'All right,' he said, trying to inject a lighter note into his voice, 'I'm ready to admit that there have been times along the way here when you and I were, perhaps, not the best of friends.' Her eyes dipped away from his. 'However, I thought matters between us warmed up delightfully during our brief interlude up here under the stars not long ago.'

He thought she was about to speak, but she tightened her mouth and kept her eyes focused on the baby. But he caught sight of the moisture on her lashes.

'Dearest Francesca, just look at the situation we're in,' he said. He was pleading now. 'Remarkably, we've somehow been able to spend weeks together in relative harmony up here in quarantine. We've rarely quarrelled, so surely that proves we've learned, at least, to tolerate each other's imperfections? Come along now, isn't that a reasonable foundation for any marriage?'

She shook her head.

He stood up, and ran a hand roughly through his hair and gave a groan. 'I'm sorry, Francesca, please forgive me. What I said was utterly crass. I wanted to woo you gently, I wanted you to hear that I've come to feel — '

She quickly looked up and levelled her gaze at him. 'Please, please say no more about it, Tom.' Her voice was controlled, the words cool and precise. 'You asked me to give you the reason why I will not accept your very kind offer of marriage, and I'm afraid there is only one way to say it: I don't want to marry you, Tom. I don't want to marry anyone. I'm sorry, but I just don't want to, and that's all there is to it, so please don't raise the matter again.'

Her answer left him dumbfounded, and there was a long moment of stricken silence as they stared at each other.

'Well,' he said at last, pulling himself together and heaving a long, theatrical sigh. 'I suppose I must thank you for keeping your answer brief and unambiguous. The whole subject will now be completely erased from my mind.'

He pulled out a handkerchief and made a pantomime of dusting an imaginary blackboard. Better to play the part of a clown and disguise his frustration, he thought, than to press her further on the matter. She gave him a weak smile and he made a bow to her. Why had his mention of marriage instantly raised her hackles in such a way? She was not a cold woman — far from it. How could he ever forget the fire lit by their embrace — the fire in her that had almost stretched his restraint beyond endurance.

Ah, no! Protest now as much as you like, Miss Francesca O'Hara, he thought. You're a truly passionate woman, and it wasn't *you* who stalled our flight into intimacy that night.

I don't want to marry you, she'd told him. He narrowed his eyes and studied the enchanting image of her sitting with the sleeping child in her arms. *I don't want to marry anyone.* He turned away from her, pulled the sketch book and pencil from his pocket, perched on the parapet and began to draw the child in her arms. *You might try to lie to yourself, Miss O'Hara, but you can't lie to me.* His pencil moved swiftly over the page. *You were made for love and loving, for marriage and children. One day you'll admit it and I'll be waiting. You're about to discover that I'm a very patient man.*

★ ★ ★

The topic of matrimony was not mentioned again, and when the time came for their quarantine to end, Tom and Francesca conducted an audit of their combined financial resources.

Money to pay the servants' wages was put into one envelope, household expenses for another week went into the next, but it was difficult to estimate how much would be needed to buy their passage on ships to carry them away from Oran once the port was open again. He would sail east to Rhodes; she and Akil would sail westwards. Perhaps to Tangier? Tom carefully made no comment about that.

When their period of quarantine came to an end and the bench at the top of the stairs was drawn aside, the head house servant greeted them with the good news that for the last two days, no further deaths had been reported anywhere in the town.

'What a relief!' Francesca said, giving him the wages owing to the servants. 'And thank you all for your splendid care in keeping the sickness from crossing this doorstep.'

The man cast a quick, eloquent glance towards the child. His master and mistress were the only ones in this house who had defied the rules. But God had been good to them and had not allowed any sickness to enter with the baby.

Akil was wide-eyed and eager for Tom to set him down to explore new territory, and he toddled around the drawing-room peeping behind chairs and reaching for knick-knacks on shelves.

'What news have you had from neighbouring towns? How far has the sickness spread?' Francesca asked. 'My brother and I must make plans to leave Oran as soon as boats start calling in to the port again.'

The servant seemed unsure. 'Some say that there is sickness all the way west into Morocco, and ships no longer call into Tangier because of the plague flag flying there.'

Francesca and Tom exchanged a frown. 'Obviously I can't go back there just yet,' she said.

'And what's the situation east of here?' Tom asked. 'Has Algiers been affected? Or Tunis?'

'No, señor, travellers say that the plague has not struck in that direction.'

'Well, in that case,' Francesca announced, in a my-mind-is-made-up tone which Tom now knew better than to oppose outright, 'I'll revise my plans and wait for a boat sailing for Tunis. I'm not unfamiliar with that city and I'm sure I'd be able to find employment there, as well as somewhere for Akil to live happily, until — '

Tom wisely passed no judgement on her choice of destination. 'Tunis, eh? Yes, I need to visit the British Consul in Tunis and arrange for him to cash a cheque so I can repay my debts.'

'Tom, I really will be all right, you know,' she said firmly. 'I have that excellent character reference you wrote, and I'm sure there'll be money enough left to keep Akil and me afloat for a month or so.'

'Very well,' he said, so submissively that she shot him a questioning glance. He smiled back at her blandly. 'Why don't we all take a stroll down to the quayside and see if we can glean some news about shipping?'

She ran upstairs to get her hat and when she came down, Tom was already standing in the open doorway with the boy in his arms. They were both looking across the street to the place where she had snatched the child from his dead mother.

'How much of that day would a little fellow of his age remember?' Tom asked in a subdued tone. 'It's been two weeks since we brought him over here with us.'

One glance at the distress in the boy's wide eyes and at the bottom lip that drooped and began to tremble gave them the answer. 'I think the poor little darling must remember quite a lot,' she said.

At the sound of her voice, Akil leaned away from Tom and reached out his arms to her.

She held him and he clung to her tightly with his face buried in the curve of her neck.

'Come along, Tom, let's get away from here; perhaps we'll find something along the quay to distract him.'

They walked down the hill in silence, passing a mere trickle of people on the street that was once bustling and noisy with the cries of vendors and the sounds of craftsmen hammering in their workshops.

The sparkling blue bay that lay ahead of them was empty, apart from two fishing boats far in the distance. A few nets were stretched out along the beach and several small craft lay idly on the sand. At the far end stood the quay where four weeks earlier they had watched the herd of panicking Europeans stampede aboard the dhow that carried them over the horizon. Where were those people now?

She sat down on the beach with Akil and poured a handful of sand through her fingers. The child wriggled from her lap and ran his hand through the sand, too. He began to laugh and clutching her arm for support, climbed to his feet; then he let go and toddled towards the water lapping the shore.

Tom studied her face as she waited a moment, then they both stood to follow the child who was now running — running away from her. Tom's heart ached as he imagined what thoughts must be in her mind as she rushed to snatch the boy before he tumbled into the water. This episode must surely be a foretaste of things to come, for no matter how deeply she loved him, or how much of herself she gave to him, Akil would never truly belong to her. His roots came from a world where she could never be more than a visitor, a world that, sooner or later, would draw him away, leaving her with empty arms once more.

She picked up the happily squealing boy at the water's edge, and her eyes met Tom's. 'I know he'll run off one day to a place where I won't be able to follow,' she said with a flare of defiance. 'But for as long as he needs me, I want to make him mine.'

'Indeed,' he said matter-of-factly, 'and I want to assure you that I have every intention of playing a part in young Akil O'Hara's life, too. The financial part, perhaps?'

The wind blew a strand of hair across her cheek and as she brushed it back, he caught a look in her eyes that held more than gratitude. 'Thank you so much,' she said, in a tone that warmed his heart. He was aware of a deep well of love inside Miss O'Hara that was just waiting to be tapped.

Tread softly, foolish man, he told himself.

Give her time. Be patient.

Another visit to the quay the next day still produced no news of shipping, and later they walked to the bazaar with Akil riding on Tom's shoulders. The atmosphere in the town was sombre, with grief and exhaustion written on the faces of people who passed each other without a greeting.

But though many stalls in the market stood empty, others were beginning to open for business again. Farmers' carts had started to trundle in with supplies of fruit and produce, and Francesca was able to buy fresh peaches and eggs and a haunch of goat meat to take home for the household.

Each time they came back to the house after an outing, Akil began to whimper, and cling tightly to Francesca while his gaze remained fixed on the place where his mother had died. Today was no different.

'It still surprises me that a child his age can remember what happened over there more than two weeks ago,' Tom said, running his hand fondly over the boy's head. 'You're a bright little button, aren't you?'

Francesca murmured agreement as they entered the house. 'I'll take him up for a bath now and join you later,' she said to Tom and rang for warm water to be sent to her room. She was almost at the top of the stairs, following a servant carrying the pitcher, when there was a loud knock on the street door. She hesitated, trying to catch the gist of what several unfamiliar male voices below were saying, when Tom came to the foot of the stairs and called to her.

'Can you come down and bring Akil with you?' His voice sounded unsteady. 'There is a gentleman here who is — I think — looking for his grandson.'

She grasped the banister and stared at Tom speechlessly for a few heart-beats. He took the steps two at a time to reach her, and kept a steadying hand under her elbow as she walked down, holding the child on her hip.

Waiting in the small sitting-room and almost filling it, were three large men dressed in flowing white robes with tooled leather bandoleers and heavy belts inlaid with silver. They were all handsome, hawk-nosed, dark-eyed sons of the desert, who held themselves with stiff dignity. The eldest of the group wore a well-trimmed white beard, and when he saw the boy in her arms, his face lit with joy.

While a maelstrom of emotion battered her insides, Francesca presented a picture of serenity as she carried Akil towards him. She smiled graciously at each of the men, while every instinct screamed a warning that she was about to face the dreaded moment when her foolish dream of making this child part of her life was about to be popped like a bubble. How many times in the past had she been forced to say goodbye to children she'd grown to love? Now her smile didn't slip; she was well rehearsed in playing this scene.

'Allah be praised!' murmured the three visitors, and Francesca felt the little boy in her arms tense with excitement, then squirm and wriggle to be set down on the floor. He toddled to the white-bearded man, who had dropped to one knee with his arms outspread.

'Suliman, my beloved!' the man called. 'Suliman!' He embraced the child and tears spilled from his eyes to run unashamedly down his brown cheeks.

'Suliman?' Francesca's smile slipped. 'Sirs, I believe this child bears the name of Akil. He has answered to it constantly during the time he has spent with us.'

Once again, Tom was at a disadvantage with the language, and Francesca quickly translated for him. 'Oh, yes, indeed,' he agreed. 'He is named Akil.'

The two younger men seemed puzzled. 'Your Honours, this is the child of our sister, and his name is indeed Suliman,' one insisted.

The other nodded towards the white-bearded man, who was now on his feet with the child clinging to his neck. 'It is our father — Suliman's grandfather — who himself bears the name of Akil. He has a special love for this child, and the child for him.' The boy had turned his back to Tom and Francesca, and was gurgling happily while he tugged at the white beard.

'Yes, that special love is clear to see,' she said, fighting to hold her composure. 'My brother and I were distressed that we could offer no help to his poor mother.' As gently as possible, she explained how they had rescued the boy. The grandfather wept.

'May the blessings of Allah be upon you for your charity, Madame,' said one of the younger men. 'His mother was our sister, and married to a man whose family lived in Oran.'

The second uncle took up the story. 'The husband brought her and Suliman — their firstborn — to visit his parents here, but when they did not return to our village and we heard that sickness had broken out in this region, we set out to find them and bring them home.' He shook his head slowly. 'We found the parents' house deserted. A neighbour said that all had been taken to the graveyard — except a young woman who had fled with a small child.'

The other uncle took up the story. 'We

have spent days searching for news of Suliman and his mother, and it was only now in the bazaar that we learned of a motherless child being cared for in this house.'

Francesca took a deep breath and widened her smile. 'While the sickness raged, my brother and I remained in quarantine here, so it was a simple matter for us to bring — Suliman — to stay with us. We are delighted that he has remained well also.'

'Allah is merciful indeed,' the grandfather said repeatedly at he listened to her story. 'Our beloved child has been restored to us and our family will forever be in your debt. Honoured Friends, our wells are your wells, your friends are our friends, your enemies are our enemies.'

Francesca felt herself crumbling. Breathe deeply, breathe deeply she told herself. Smile, smile brightly and say goodbye quickly. She was aware of Tom moving closer to her and she instantly stepped aside and froze. Any touch of sympathy now would be her undoing.

'May blessings rain on your house for a thousand years,' the grandfather named Akil murmured as he turned to leave with the boy still clutched against his chest.

'Goodbye, Suliman,' Francesca whispered as he passed, and the boy's big, dark eyes were wide with happiness as he peered at her over his grandfather's shoulders.

'Akil,' he lisped and snuggled his head against the old man's neck. 'Akil.'

The two uncles salaamed deeply to the Europeans and followed their father through the door. Their white robes swirled around their ankles as the trio strode along the street to where three horses were tethered.

Francesca and Tom stood watching from the doorstep as the men mounted and, with the boy seated on the front of his grandfather's saddle, they clattered up the hill, past the walls of the citadel and disappeared from view. Back to the desert.

'Akil,' Francesca said almost to herself as she stood gazing after them, along the empty road. 'Akil was his grandfather's name. How extraordinary.'

Tom put an arm around her shoulders to urge her back into the house, but she pulled away from him and turned her head aside as soon as the door had closed behind them.

'Maybe, when the name Akil came up in your game with the boy, it stirred fond memories of his grandfather,' he said, desperate to find some way to breach the icy wall she had erected between them. 'I know it's hard to make sense of such a thing, but perhaps he felt some kind of comfort to hear us call him by that name.'

'You might very well be correct,' she said, avoiding his eyes. 'Anyhow, it's most satisfactory to know that the child has been reunited with his kin. That's where he belongs. I was stupid to think that he could have been happy growing up with someone like me.' She picked up the bell and rang for a servant. 'Excuse me, Tom, I'm going up to take my bath now and I think I'll dine in my room this evening. I really feel quite weary.'

Not for one moment did her composure slip as she walked stiffly away.

Tom waited, listening for the sobs that he was sure would come, but all he heard was her continuing, defensive silence which tore at his heart even more than crying would have. He wanted to hold her and tell her how much she was loved.

For some time after going to his own bed, he lay wide awake, promising himself that in the morning they would have a serious talk about plans for the future. And he would insist that she allow him to continue playing a part in her life.

Damn! he swore under his breath as he swung his feet on to the floor. This was too important to wait until morning.

17

Tom opened Francesa's door quietly and went to the edge of her bed. The shaft of moonlight slicing through the window gave her face the appearance of marble as she lay on her back with her arms outstretched, with a stream of silent tears running, unchecked, over her cheeks. He touched her shoulder, a gentle, reassuring touch, but she flung herself away and turned her back to him.

'I'm here with you, Fran. I loved him, too, and I understand how you feel, I truly do,' he murmured, stroking her hair. She covered her face with her arms and curled herself into a tight ball. Her distress deepened and the great, gut-wrenching sobs could no longer be contained. She tried to speak, but Tom could barely catch her muffled words.

'Go away, and don't say you understand — because you can never, never understand!'

For a moment he hesitated, then impetuously sat on the edge of the bed, reached across and scooped her into his arms, holding her in a half-sitting position against his chest. At first she was stiffly resistant, but the surprise of his action silenced her storm of tears.

'Very well, perhaps I don't completely understand how you feel, so, right now my dearest Francesca, I want you to tell me what it is that I should know.' He spoke with a gentle firmness, but she simply shook her head and gave a fresh wail. He rested his cheek against her hair and then, as if she was a frightened child, he began to rock her gently to and fro in his arms.

'Please don't close me out of whatever it is that distresses you. I feel sad, too, that we have had to say goodbye to our little Suliman. But this is more than just about having the child taken away by his own people, isn't it?'

When she made no response, he gave a deep sigh and pushed aside a thought that he was about to let his heart outrun his commonsense. But he couldn't stop himself now.

'If you remember, Francesca, it was not long ago that I asked you to be my wife; you turned me down, and said not to ask you again.' His pulse started to race. 'Well, I am going to ask you again — and again and again — because I've grown to love you with every fibre of my being, and I want us to spend our lives sharing — '

'Stop it! Stop it! I've already told you that I

don't want to marry you!' She lifted her head, and scowled at him, then sniffed and tried to pull away.

But he refused to release his grip. 'No, my dear, I'm not going to stop asking you until you help me to understand why I shouldn't.' She pushed her hands against his chest, but he held her tighter. 'And don't give me the lie that you don't love me!'

Frustration cracked in his voice. He brought his mouth down hard on hers and held it there until he felt her resistance fading and her body growing limp.

'There, that's just a taste of what I feel for you,' he said when he drew back and broke the kiss, leaving them both struggling for breath. 'So now, my love, tell me again that you have no desire to become my wife!'

Slowly her breathing steadied and she heaved a sigh that was more like a groan. 'All right, but please take your hands away from me — please! — I must have a moment to — Oh! go and sit over there in that chair near the wall — ' Though her voice was frail, an uncanny calmness settled about her, and he moved reluctantly to do as she asked.

She sat upright on her bed and pushed the tangled hair away from her face. 'Oh, Tom, I can never marry you, never.' Her voice was a mere whisper, and there was enough

336

moonlight coming into the room for Tom to see the distress in her face. He struggled for the self restraint to remain sitting where he was.

'You see, Tom, when I was nineteen I had a position teaching the younger children of the Spanish Consul in Rabat. It was a pleasant family, and the parents were very proud of their older son who was in Rome training for the priesthood. The parents were sure he was destined for a brilliant future in the Church, and when they said he was arriving to spend a holiday with them — ' The words suddenly stuck in her throat. 'He was about my age, but so very self-assured and full of charm — '

When she began to falter again, Tom's heart sank and a great, gut-searing rage seized him. His fingernails bit into his palms. Dear God, he knew exactly what was going to come next!

'You don't need to say any more, sweetheart,' he said quietly as he rose from the chair and crossed back to the bed. 'He — he attacked you, didn't he? That bastard hurt you and then threatened that if you breathed a word to his doting parents, he'd tell them that it was you who had led *him* into sin.'

Her breath came in huge, stomach-heaving gasps, then with her hands folded tightly across her breasts and her head bent low, she began to rock to and fro.

He made a soft sound in his throat and sat down on the edge of the bed again. 'Oh, Fran, I'm so terribly sorry that you were forced to endure that — but in no way can you ever be blamed for what happened. Absolutely not! And my guess is that, until this moment, you have never told another soul about it. Am I right? You've carried that burden all alone?' She gave a little nod and he pulled a handkerchief from his pocket. She buried her face in it.

He waited a moment. 'Well, thank you most sincerely for confiding in me,' he said in an artificially level tone. He paused again and, for a few heartbeats, sat wondering how to delicately phrase the next question.

'I'm honoured that you have sufficient trust in me to unburden yourself at last, Francesca,' he said calmly, 'and may I now, as your closest friend, be permitted to ask if — if you later suffered any consequence of that wretched event?'

She took the handkerchief away from her face and blinked at him with astonishment. 'You mean — ? Did I find myself — ? No, thank God! I would have killed myself if that had happened.' She shuddered and tears began to roll again. 'But — but anyhow, don't you see — how he has ruined me? He has ruined my whole life. How can any respectable man ever want to marry me now? It would be impossible!'

Tom felt a great bank of dark fog lifting and sunlight suddenly bursting into his life. Now he knew that the obstacle which she saw keeping them apart, had a name, a face, and a solution.

He took her hand and lifted her fingers to his lips. 'My love, I am angry beyond words that you fell prey to that loathsome creature, nothing would give me greater pleasure than to give him a public horsewhipping and to see him defrocked.' She sniffed hard, and he felt her fingers grip his hand. 'However, I want to assure you that my feelings for you have not been changed in any way whatsoever, and that my offer of marriage still stands.' He deliberately dimmed the growing excitement inside him by keeping a neutral tone in his voice. 'I truly love you, Fran, and I always will.'

She edged herself a few inches across the bed so there was more room for him to sit beside her. 'But how could you ever feel — ? I mean, knowing that another man has — ?'

'Oh, Fran, Fran,' he said on a long sigh, then paused to gather his thoughts. 'Look, settle back against the pillows and let me tell you a true tale of what happened to a girl named Julia. By the way, can you give me just a little more room?'

She did and it seemed a perfectly natural move for him to swing his feet up on to the bed and lie beside her with his fingers laced behind his head on the pillow while he began his story.

'Now, you see, years ago Julia was a schoolteacher in England. The only living family she had was a wealthy uncle and aunt who had a big house in the country, and when Julia was nineteen, she was invited to stay there to attend her cousin, Harriet's, wedding. However, on the night before the ceremony, the bridegroom came into Julia's bedroom and attacked her — the way you were attacked.'

'Oh, how appalling!' Francesca raised herself on one elbow and looked down into Tom's face. 'What a wicked, horrible man!'

'Yes, he certainly was. He had an aristocratic title, but not a shred of decency or honour,' he said, slowly stretching one arm in an invitation for her to lie against his shoulder. She accepted shyly and snuggled against him as he continued. 'But Julia wasn't afraid to make a hullabaloo about what he'd done, and she woke the whole house that night. Even threatened her uncle that she'd tell the workers at his mill about the vile creature her cousin was about to marry.'

'How brave! I could never have done that.'

'Well, that courage led to even deeper troubles for Julia because, before she was able to get word to anybody outside the house, her uncle and his doctor colluded to keep her quiet by drugging her. And then they bundled her off on a ship bound for India.'

She gave a gasp of alarm.

'Luckily, on the long voyage out there she was befriended by a kindly, middle-aged merchant and his sister who were travelling back to their home in Delhi. Of course, she told them nothing about what had happened in her uncle's house, but after they'd been at sea for a few weeks, Julia realized that she was carrying a child.'

'*Holy Mother!*' She sat bolt upright. 'If I'd found myself in that situation, I think I'd have thrown myself overboard.' Tom pulled her back on to his shoulder.

'Yes, Julia did have something like that in mind, but the merchant's sister was a very wise and sympathetic lady. So, when she made her brother aware of Julia's predicament, he offered her another option to suicide. Marriage. He was more than thirty years her senior, a man whose legs had been crippled in infancy by a paralysis, but he'd grown to be a man who was greatly respected by all who knew him. Quite wealthy, too. Besides, he'd become truly fond of Julia during the voyage.'

'So, she accepted his offer?'

'Yes, they were married when the ship reached Cape Town, and when they arrived in India, she was welcomed ashore as his wife. Nobody ever knew that he was not the father of the child she bore.'

'Oh, how wonderful! And was the marriage a happy one?' She craned her neck to peer at him closely.

'Yes, m'love. Julia did find deep happiness in that marriage. I know, you see, because Julia was my mother, and I was that child she didn't want to have.'

'Oooh!' She sank her head on to his shoulder again, and edged closer, sliding one hand on to his chest. Comfortingly. 'Oh, thank you, Tom, that was a wonderful story. Do you remember the man who called you his son?'

'No, I'm afraid not; I was probably about the age of our little Suliman when he died of injuries after an attack on a palace in Northern India where our family was staying. Yet, somehow, I do feel I know him very well — not just from what my mother has told me — but also from the fond recollections I hear from people whenever his name is mentioned in India.'

They lay quietly for a few minutes with his chin resting against her forehead. 'So, now tell me, Miss Francesca O'Hara,' he whispered, 'how deeply does my lack of pedigree concern you? Could you ever consider marriage to a man whose presence in the world is the result of one utterly despicable act?'

'Oh, Tom — I — you must never think — '

'Just answer my question, Miss O'Hara,' he said. 'Will you please now consider my offer of marriage. Yes. Or no?'

A tremor ran through her. 'Oh, yes, yes, yes, yes, but I still can't believe that you really do want me.' She snuggled closer. 'Ask me again — please — say those words again, just so I know that I'm not dreaming.'

'Francesca O'Hara, you are a remarkable young lady whom I've grown to love deeply and it is my earnest wish that you will do me the honour of becoming my wife. Nothing that has happened in your life could ever change the way I feel about you, and I can promise that my family will welcome you with open arms.'

'A family!' She felt his words take root in her heart. 'So, I'm not dreaming after all! Oh, yes, thank you, I'd be — be perfectly delighted to marry you, Thomas Sinclair.' She hugged him. 'I started to fall in love with you weeks and weeks ago and, of course, how you came into the world doesn't matter to me one jot. The only important thing is that you're here and that by some miracle you say you love me.' She sniffed and rubbed her damp face against his shirt. 'I'm so happy, I don't know whether to laugh or cry. I didn't think it was possible to do both at once, but — ' She stopped. 'Tom, I promise never to raise this subject again, but please tell me how you came to know about your mother's dreadful experience with that — that man who married her cousin. Surely she didn't tell you herself?'

'Heavens no! And she still has absolutely no inkling that I'm aware of all that.' He touched his lips to her forehead. 'My stepfather told me, and now I've told you, but there's not another soul in the world knows about it. Nobody has ever suggested that I'm not the natural son of Sir Thomas Sinclair of Delhi.'

'Oh — and thank you for trusting me. You know that I will never, never mention it.' She hugged him again and lay quietly for a time, digesting everything he'd told her.

'Tom,' she said at last, 'may I ask just one more question before this subject — I promise — is closed forever?'

'You can ask me anything at any time, sweetheart,' he murmured, relishing their closeness.

'It seems rather strange to me that your stepfather would talk to you about that awful time in your mother's life. Why did you have to be told the details of such a very, very private matter?'

He blew a long breath between his teeth. 'Why? Well, Fran, ten years ago it became imperative for me to understand exactly whose blood was running through my veins.' His arm tightened around her. 'I assure you that my stepfather was extremely reluctant to discuss my mother's ordeal, but he had to make me understand why it was impossible for me to consider marriage to a lovely young lady named Phoebe Grantham.'

He felt Francesca tense.

'You see, m'love, despite everything, Cousin Harriet's marriage did take place as planned on the day following the attack on Julia. And though the bridegroom took himself off to live in Venice not long after the honeymoon, their brief union did manage to produce one child.'

'Oh!'

'Yes, Harriet had a daughter who was named Phoebe and, against all the laws of

345

nature, she was as lovely as her mother was plain and as sweet-natured as her father was despicable. She grew up to be a spirited young lady who clashed with her mother on just about everything — especially on marriage plans that Harriet was making for her.

'So, as soon as Phoebe turned eighteen, she threw those plans into disarray by finding a way to marry a childhood friend, who unfortunately met his death in a riding accident a couple of years later. Then, not long after that, a matter of business brought the widowed Phoebe out to India, and, frankly, from the moment I set eyes on her, I was a lost man. She was the most beautiful creature I'd ever encountered, sweet-natured and capable, too, and I left her in no doubt about my feelings when we set off to visit my stepbrother, Robert. He'd been appointed District Commissioner of a state called Ranaganj up in the mountains.

'I knew Phoebe only by her married name, so when I wrote to my mother and stepfather and told them that a young widow called Mrs Grantham had captured my heart and that I had hopes of marrying her, the name held no great significance for them. But when they discovered that Phoebe was the child of Harriet and her husband — and therefore my half-sister — of course, they rushed to put a stop to any marriage plans.

'As it turned out, they had no need to worry on that score, because Phoebe had already made it perfectly clear that she had no romantic feelings for me and we could never be more than friends. It was my stepbrother, Robert, she fell in love with, and he with her. Instantly. Yes, they were made for each other.'

Francesca stroked his chest consolingly. 'You must have felt very hurt at the time.'

'Hmmm. Hurt? Perhaps. Jealous? Definitely. However, I was sufficiently arrogant at the age of twenty-four, to imagine that I'd have no trouble at all in finding another girl to share the kind of love that seemed to radiate from Robert and Phoebe. And, y'know,' he gave a soft chuckle, 'it's the kind of love which still lights the looks that pass between my mother and stepfather.

'Well, Fran, I looked hard and long, but I couldn't find the right girl to share that kind of love. I've spent the last ten years of my life travelling across the world looking for her, but all the time I've found myself sailing constantly into the eye of the wind — steering one wrong course after another, making little headway, sometimes finding myself a little lost, always trying to locate that one mystical, uncharted harbour where it would be safe to furl my sails and drop anchor in calm water.' He pressed his lips to her forehead.

'It's taken me all that time to discover you, Francesca O'Hara, and now the journey is over. With you, I've found my safe harbour, and I'm here to stay.'

She curled herself closer against him. 'I'll go with you to the far corners of the world — ' She hesitated. 'Your parents! How will you ever explain who I am and the way we met? I'm not proud of the lies I told to persuade you to chase after Otto Heinkler.' Her forehead creased. 'When I think of it, I can't imagine how you could possibly have fallen in love with someone like me.'

He grinned. 'I admit that the beginnings of our relationship were somewhat unconventional, but I think I've now gained some measure of how your delightfully cunning brain works.' He held her hand and rubbed his thumb to and fro across her knuckles. 'Believe me, my lovely Francesca, I don't want anything about you to change because I love you — utterly — just the way you are.' He gave a murmur of pure contentment. 'And one day, when you're ready for me, I'll show you just how very much I do love you.'

'I'm not afraid of you, Tom,' she whispered as she slowly slid one leg over his.

'I'm very glad, sweetheart.' He could hear his heart pounding. Take it slowly, slowly the sane side of his brain pleaded as he threaded his fingers through her hair. She caught his hand and brought it to her mouth to nip his knuckles, and it was almost his undoing.

'I was miserable just a few hours ago,' she whispered. 'I could see nothing ahead for me but long, lonely years but then, by some miracle, you came into my room and offered me — *everything*.'

'The Wheel of Life has turned, love. For us both. And tomorrow we'll start to make plans — exciting plans — '

'The first thing we have to do is to find a ship bound for Rhodes. We haven't finished our search for Diana yet.' He smiled at a touch of the governess which still lingered in her tone.

'You're absolutely right, ma'am,' he said, 'but there'll be no more talking tonight; we both need to catch a few hours' sleep before morning breaks.' He kissed her lips softly, then eased himself away from her and swung his feet on to the floor. 'Tomorrow, sweetheart, tomorrow we'll make plans for this year, next year and all the years to come — '

'Ah, yes,' she murmured and yawned. 'And tomorrow I will come to your bed, and you will teach me how to make very beautiful love.'

Tom was grinning as he went back to his own room, but sleep proved to be elusive. Images of Francesca whirled continuously through his mind as he lay recalling random incidents that had occurred in the long weeks since they'd set out together from Agadir. At what point had he begun to fall in love with this extraordinary young woman? There was no doubt in his mind that she was now the one woman with whom he wanted to share his life, though he could recall many times when the feelings she'd evoked in him had included frustration to fury. Though he'd often been impressed by her quick thinking and tenacity, there had never been a time when love for her had struck him like a lightning bolt. Certainly not the way it had done the moment he'd met Phoebe.

Perhaps, with Francesca, it had begun when she'd had the wit to give the audacious performance which convinced the Sherif of Taliouine that she had a mad brother who needed to feel the heat of the sun on his skull. He felt himself grinning as he recalled that scene, then he remembered the time in the cellar when she'd not flinched a muscle as the hairy, black legs of a tarantula had stepped slowly across her hand; that image still sent a

350

shudder through him.

And he'd never forget the sight of her standing before the horde of Tuaregs on the sandhill and ordering him to slice off hanks of fair hair to present to them. She'd said that she was acting purely on instinct at that moment, but she'd provided a remarkable diversion, if indeed those tribesmen had been inclined to attack the French column.

Of course, she'd looked extremely attractive in her new clothes when she'd dined with the Frenchmen in Marrakech, and it wasn't just the champagne that had made her sparkle. Duveyrier was obviously a man who flirted with every woman he met but Colonel Villatte — the tough desert fighter — had been truly touched by something he'd discovered in her during their ride from Marrakech. He had very much wanted her to continue to Algiers with him — and perhaps remain with him forever.

He recalled the moment when she'd parted ways with the Colonel and, in front of the whole French column, had said farewell with a kiss.

Now it dawned on Tom that, even though he hadn't realized it at the time, *that* was probably the moment he'd fallen in love with her. Why that moment? he wondered as he tried to settle his head comfortably on the pillow. The very public kiss had certainly roused no jealousy in him, but some warm feeling — some vague sense of satisfaction had stirred in his blood — a feeling of victory because she'd chosen to travel with him to Oran. What a fool he'd been not to recognize that she must have already been feeling an affection towards him, even though he'd given her little enough reason for it.

The shawl with the golden fringe? Yes, buying that for her and witnessing her happy surprise when he'd wrapped it around her shoulders had given him a jolt of pleasure. So, perhaps that was when his love for her had begun?

Love! Tom tossed on his pillow. How thick-headed could a man be when the answer to that question had been staring him in the face for so long? Falling in love was one of life's miracles! No thunderclap had suddenly shaken the heavens when he'd fallen in love with Francesca O'Hara. For weeks she had tested him, just as he had tested her, and drop by drop he had discovered the kind of pure love that he'd never known before.

Love! From the day they'd met, it had been quietly and steadily soaking into his heart and soul like a spring of fresh water seeping through the earth's deep, rocky layers, filtering out every impurity until, at long last, it came rushing to the surface to reveal itself as a crystal clear, life-sustaining oasis — one that was named Francesca.

Who could tell where the first drop of his desire for her — or her for him — had sprung from? Anyhow, that was of no consequence now, because the pool of mutual love which had so inconspicuously risen to the surface now lay sparkling ahead of them — and it was wide and deep and, oh! so very inviting. Tom smiled as he drifted into sleep with images of Francesca floating in their life-giving pool, beckoning him to join her.

★　★　★

The first glimmerings of dawn were streaking the sky and poking faint fingers of light through the window when he was roused by the bedcovers being pulled aside. Dreams disappeared and his eyes flew open as a slight body slid into bed beside him.

'This is tomorrow, Tom, and I want you to teach me what I should know,' Francesca whispered. For a moment, everything seemed extraordinarily still, as if the whole world was holding its breath, waiting.

'Oh, Fran!' he spluttered, opening his arms to her. 'Come, lie close to me. Just let me hold you, sweetheart, and nature will be our teacher, I promise.'

'But I don't even know where to begin.' He saw the naked longing in her eyes. 'I don't know what I should — I mean what if — ?'

'No talking, that's the first rule,' he breathed and when his arms closed around her, she snuggled into him, sighed, and with an unconscious sensuality, nuzzled her cheek against his bristly jaw. He tried to hold on to his sanity.

'But, am I allowed to say how very much I love you?' she asked in a tiny voice while her fingers slipped slowly across his shoulder, up the nape of his neck and into his hair, stroking his scalp with an erotic feather-light touch that sent an instant flash of fire through his body. 'I fell in love with you such a long time ago.'

'No words, sweetheart. Words are superfluous when we hold each other like this.' His body, hard and masculine, touched lightly against the full length of hers. His breath was short when he bent his head and kissed her lips, then summoning all his resolve to carry her very slowly and tenderly and protectively into the unexplored realms of sensation, he slipped her night-gown over her head.

'Don't be frightened, Fran,' he breathed as he stroked her breasts and kissed them reverently.

She seemed in no need of such reassurance; her response to his intimacy was instant, and it was joyous. And as his expert hands and lips continued to explore and worship her body, she gave herself to him, surrendering completely to the moment as a power — elemental, primitive, passionate — swept them up into another world. A long sigh of delight came from deep in her throat and he felt her body under him come alive, heated, nerves afire. Soon it began singing to him — singing her own, instinctive woman-song, the one as old as time itself — and the ripples of ecstasy spread through his body.

Time lost all meaning as the heat of their passion flared and swirled, sucking them into its glorious flame, until they reached the threshold beyond which the world fell away and nothing existed but a plunge into the white heat of the void.

'Oh, yes,' she sighed. 'Oh, my love, yes.'

18

Next morning Señor Sinclair and his sister were late coming down to breakfast. The servants had heard the *señor* whistling while he was dressing, and they noted that both the *señor* and *señorita* were very hungry when they at last arrived at the table.

'Could you bring more toast and honey, please?' Señorita Sinclair asked with a sweet, happy smile. 'And another pot of hot coffee? Is there still a peach or two left from yesterday?'

Her brother was in excellent humour, too, the servant reported to the other staff. 'And the *señorita* asks for all their laundry to be done without delay.'

'Yes, they'll be leaving now that the yellow plague flag has gone from the harbour.' The cook pulled a long face at the prospect of losing their undemanding guests, and facing the return of the owners of the house.

The head house servant consulted the notebook in which Señorita Sinclair had insisted that he must record every payment she and her brother made — money spent on household necessities, as well as the staff wages. Nobody here was looking forward to the return of the Fernandez family with their endless demands and reluctance to pay accounts — or wages.

While their clothes were being laundered and packed, Francesca wrote a letter of appreciation to leave for the mistress of the house, explaining their reason for taking refuge in the family's home, and applauding the service given to them by the servants. 'My brother and I are most grateful for the use of your establishment,' she concluded. 'And we leave no outstanding debts.'

Later, when Tom and Francesca strolled arm in arm to the waterfront, they saw a small ship already sailing into the bay, and this long-awaited event had brought a group of eager merchants to the quay.

Francesca spoke to one of the men, then translated for Tom. 'He says that this is a Portuguese boat which calls occasionally to buy salt for Lisbon. It won't be any use to us, but I'm sure an eastern-bound vessel is bound to arrive soon.' She squeezed his arm.

He smiled at her excitement. 'Yes, m'love, but with our funds about to hit bedrock, I'm afraid we might have to do some hard talking to persuade the master of any boat to take us on board.' He pulled out his gold watch and held it in his palm. 'I could put this up as a guarantee until we reach a British Consulate somewhere and get my funds replenished.'

'No, you must never part with your father's watch!' she scolded fondly. 'We might not be able to travel first-class, but I'm sure we'll have enough to pay for our passage.'

The heat of noon persuaded them to sit in the shade while they watched the Portuguese boat tie up at the quay. As soon as the portly, flush-faced master of the little vessel stepped ashore, he was rushed by the salt merchants, all anxious to do business.

But the negotiations dragged on and grew heated. The captain was clearly not pleased with the amount of salt available, nor with the price being asked. Finally, he shouted at the merchants, turned on his heel, and stormed back along the quay towards his boat.

When he caught Tom's eye, he seemed unable to resist the opportunity to stop and vent his spleen.

'These people are all the same,' he said, gesticulating angrily towards the merchants. 'Look at them — they make excuses that sickness has cut the trade routes and supplies have gone elsewhere! I know this game! If I agree to their extortion and pay the figure they want, just watch those camel-loads of salt suddenly appear as if from the clouds! Do they take me for a fool?'

'I imagine this has been a difficult time for business,' Tom said mildly, and felt Francesca squeeze his hand. 'My sister and I have been isolated here for over a month, captain, and we're anxious now to get to Rhodes. Do you know of any ships sailing in that direction soon?'

'Rhodes?' The seafarer gave a dismissive shrug. 'Take whatever vessel you can find sailing east, señor. Plague has broken out in Algiers, but I hear that Tunis is still open. If you reach there, it might be possible to find a ship to take you on further.'

For some time, the captain stood talking with Tom and Francesca, all the while keeping the merchants in view from the corner of his eye. He gave Tom a sly wink and excused himself when he saw two of the men approaching and before long negotiations were resumed.

By the end of the day, a cargo of salt had been loaded for Lisbon, and when the vessel sailed next morning, it was also carrying the letter that Tom had written to his parents in England. It would be posted in Lisbon, the ship's master assured him, and he calculated that it could well reach Sherborne in fewer than two weeks.

'I've told mother and dad all about our engagement,' Tom said as they watched the ship's sails slipping over the horizon. 'They'll soon know that you were the one who found Diana's trail and how clever you are, and brave, and pretty, and loving, and how you've rescued me from more mistakes than I care to remember.'

She flushed shyly.

'Oh, Francesca, I can't wait for you to meet my parents; I know they'll love you as much as I do.'

★ ★ ★

Their luggage stood packed and waiting for another four days before the next ship came into the bay. It was an Arab dhow and from the roof of their house Tom kept his binoculars trained on the activity along the quay where water barrels were being taken from the hold and filled at the pump, while a small party of men set out for the market.

'It looks to me as if this boat has called in simply to pick up fresh supplies,' Tom said. 'I doubt they'll stay long in port.'

'In that case, we must get down to the quay straight away and find out where they're heading.'

Tom and Francesca looked at each other and grinned. 'We certainly won't be asked to pay a first-class fare on that vessel,' he said, 'but it might get us on our way!'

They ran down the stairs, calling for the servants to pack up the last of their belongings and follow them down to the quay with their luggage. She snatched her hat and, with the cord of the old leather pouch wrapped around her wrist, they set off at a trot towards the boat tied up at the quay.

It was a typical one-masted working dhow, small, badly in need of paint and heavily loaded with deck cargo as well as passengers. Most of the people on board had clambered down a rope ladder to buy food from the vendors who had quickly set up their stands on the quay when they saw the boat sailing into the bay.

'Tom, dear, I have a confession to make,' Francesca said, puffing a little as they approached the vessel. 'Call it force of habit, but life has taught me always to keep a little cash aside in case of an emergency. Here, take this.' She passed him her pouch.

When he shook it and heard the reassuring sound of coins jingling, he laughed. 'Fran, if I wasn't already so much in love with you, I'd — '

She put a hand on his arm and nodded towards a tall, lean old man peering gravely at them from the rail of the boat. His beard was dyed red, but his eyebrows and lashes were long and white. 'He must be the *nakhoda*, the captain, and he doesn't seem very pleased to see us.' She slipped her arm through Tom's. 'If you have no objection, my dearest, I think there will be fewer complications if I introduce us now as husband and wife.'

She smiled up at the man's brown, weathered face and explained to him in Arabic that she and her husband were looking for a ship to take them to Rhodes. Was this fine vessel sailing in that direction?

Tom saw no change in the man's stern expression as he continued to study them standing together, but when he gave an answer, Francesca smiled with glee.

'Splendid news! The *nakhoda* said that, Allah willing, he is sailing east to Tripoli, and he is prepared to take us. That's at least half way to Rhodes and it shouldn't be difficult to find another boat from there to take us on further.' She squeezed his arm. 'Oh, this is marvellous, Tom, because you'll be able to go to the British Consulate there — and I can show you where it is because I once lived in Tripoli when I was young.'

Tom bowed to the elderly man, recited a flowery phrase of profound gratitude in the little Arabic he remembered from Francesca's lessons and, when she and the *nakhoda* had settled on the price of their passage, they counted out the money from her pouch. 'See, we still have a little left!' she whispered with a hint of smugness.

By the time the servants from the house arrived at the quay with their luggage, Señor Sinclair and his lady had already climbed the rope ladder up the side of the vessel and were standing on the deck amongst the cargo of piled-up boxes and bales.

One visit to the cabin allocated to them below deck — a dark, tiny space, thick with the horrendous stench of the bilge — had been enough for them to decide to find sleeping space on deck.

There was time for only a brief farewell with the tearful servants before a ram's horn was blown and the other passengers, along with the remaining crew, came scrambling back on board.

The evening was hot and airless as the sun slipped over the horizon and the dhow was cast off from the quay. The crew, working to a rhythmic chant, hoisted the great triangular sail up the raked mast just in time for a chance breath of wind to catch the canvas. The vessel began to drift slowly forward, so slowly that only a gentle straining of timbers assured Tom that they were under way.

He stood at the rail with Francesca,

holding her close. 'Happy, sweetheart?' he breathed.

'Happier than I thought I could ever be.'

'This is just the beginning, I promise. We have a whole new life ahead of us now — a life together.' The boat began to slide across the polished water, changing tack in the wayward breeze. 'I'm going to take you to places you've only dreamed about, or — if you like — we can settle down and grow tea, or cabbages, or violets. Fran, my dearest love, I promise that you'll never again have a worry in the world.'

She saw that he was about to kiss her and pulled back a fraction. 'Not just now. Look.'

He turned his head and saw the other passengers, who included four veiled women, all standing about the deck in little groups and staring at them expectantly.

'Right at this moment our travelling companions are very curious to know who we are and where we're going,' she said. 'It's hard for Europeans to get used to the custom, but in this part of the world it's considered to be very good manners to ask all kinds of personal questions of people you've just met.'

Tom acknowledged their audience, then watched their expressions warm as Francesca began addressing those closest to her, while others listened. She said something which made them chuckle and several groups then set about rearranging bales and crates on the deck to make a private space for the newcomers to lay their blankets.

'I told them that we've only just been married and that you're taking me to meet your family,' she said. 'They've offered their felicitations and now they want to make sure we'll be comfortable on the deck. And secluded. At least a little bit.'

'My heartfelt thanks to you,' he said in halting Arabic to the line of faces staring at him. 'I must say, Señora Sinclair,' he muttered from the corner of his mouth, 'this was not quite the kind of honeymoon I'd envisaged for us.'

She giggled. 'It's not? Well, I can't think of anything more delightful than floating for a thousand miles on a calm sea and lying together every night under the stars. You'll see.'

A feeling of unity and fellowship quickly sprang up on the ship, not just between the passengers, but with most of the crew, too. They talked openly to each other about their families, their illnesses, their struggles and hopes.

The *nakhoda* remained an aloof and dignified figure, living aft on a little platform from which the helmsman steered the dhow by means of a long oar: it was he who gave the call to prayer five times daily and led the chanting at night in his old, croaking voice. The passengers treated him with great deference, and sometimes when everyone was resting, he sat amongst them reciting a tale about the wit of some merry thief of old, or the wisdom of a great king.

The ship's cook was a huge, pock-marked African of slave origin who took pride in pounding and blending the ingredients for each meal which he cooked over an open fire up in the bows. Inevitably sparks blew down on to the cargo, but there seemed to be nothing highly flammable in the boxes and there was always someone close by to put out fires before any took hold. After a few days, Tom learned not to panic.

On the rare occasions when there was work to be done, everyone came together to heave on ropes and join in the chanting. Each day several men trailed fishing lines behind the dhow, adding their catch to the menu, and at mealtimes all hands were dipped into the common dish.

Often in the evenings someone would produce a stringed instrument and strum plaintive African melodies to the accompaniment of a drum. At other times groups formed spontaneously to sing folk songs, and Francesca occasionally played Irish tunes on her flute.

Tom provided popular entertainment by doing quick sketches of the interesting faces of their male travelling companions. And one evening a veiled young woman was taken below to a stifling cabin by her sister, where she quietly gave birth to a daughter.

'That brings back memories of our little Akil, doesn't it?' Tom said as the baby's aunt carried her on to the deck the next day to be admired.

'Only happy memories, I promise. We did enjoy having him with us for that time, didn't we?' She leaned her head against his shoulder.

'Hmmm, and once we're married, my lovely lady, we might well decide to begin our own family straight away.' He lay his hand, warm, strong and possessive on her wrist, and the smile she gave him was all the answer he needed.

As the boat sailed on, one Mediterranean day melted into another, but this time Francesca simply forgot to count them. On some days the great triangular sail filled with wind and billowed at the mast then, just as suddenly, the breeze drained out of it and the canvas hung down loosely and they didn't move at all. Sometimes the rim of Africa was visible off to starboard, other times they seemed to be floating in the middle of a vast watery nowhere.

Francesca was quietly amused to note that while Tom had been a unimpressive student of Arabic when she'd tried to teach him at the start of their quarantine in Oran, now that he was surrounded by that language and no other, his ear was also quickly picking up conversational phrases used by the men on the boat. And, with friendly patience, these men were constantly encouraging him to join in their conversations and share their jokes.

A canvas awning over the deck provided the passengers with shade during the day, and seven weak lamps lit the deck after nightfall. These usually ran out of oil after a few hours and with only the stars looking down on to their personal nest, Tom and Francesca found a comfortable degree of privacy as they lay together each night.

'I don't care if this journey never ends,' Tom whispered as he slid his hands under her nightgown to stroke her skin. 'This is pure joy. You're pure joy.'

Her body relaxed against his and she rolled into his embrace, lifting her lips to his. He kissed her softly then, as ever, the kiss deepened and the warmth and generosity of her response shook him — as it always did. How many women had he kissed since his youth? He didn't know and he didn't care. None of them had been Francesca.

★   ★   ★

On the last few days of the voyage, a steady following wind sprang up to fill the dhow's sails and allowed the helmsman to set a straight course for Tripoli.

'We could take this as a good omen for our life together,' Tom said while they lay listening to the sea slapping against the wooden hull as the dhow picked up speed. 'We're no longer fighting into the eye of the wind, m'love. You and I are sailing right on course now. And that's the way we'll keep on going.'

19

Tripoli, the town that for centuries had watched the Barbary corsairs sweep out of the harbour to plunder coastal towns and shipping, now lay quietly shimmering in the glare of sunlight bouncing off the white-walled buildings which ran down to embrace the bay. Francesca pulled her hat down further on her forehead to shade her eyes as the dhow drifted towards its mooring.

Several other vessels lay at anchor; an American flag flew on one sleek clipper and a Dutch one on another ship. 'If I recall correctly,' Francesca began, as she screwed up her eyes to peer at the buildings on the shore, 'the house where my father and I lived for nearly a year was over there on the northern edge of the town. There's a Roman arch built by Marcus Aurelius still standing up there. The British Consulate is located just over in that direction.' She pointed to the left.

'Where?' Tom asked, trying unsuccessfully to identify a likely building. 'I should go up there and make myself known to the Consul without delay.'

When he turned to Francesca she couldn't

contain her giggles. 'I'm afraid it's been a long time since either of us has had a good look in a mirror.' Her shoulders shook. 'Before you visit the Consulate, my love, I strongly advise you to take a deep bath and make an urgent visit to a barber.'

He laughed with her. 'Good Lord, Fran, however are we going to find a decent inn, or some hotel that will be prepared to take us in, looking like this?'

'A pair of vagabonds with almost no money?' She doubled over with laughter. 'When I was here with my father, he would sometimes sit on the quay over there and try to entice European ladies to pose for a portrait. I think you would have more success with your sketches.'

'And, perhaps, you could sit on the other end of the quay and offer lessons in English pronunciation. Have I told you lately how impressed I am with the way that your Spanish lisp has almost disappeared?'

'Thank you, sir, but — '

The anchor splashed into the water, announcing that the long journey had now come to its end. The lethargy that had kept the passengers shackled to the deck for weeks, now vanished and in its place a general urgency erupted to clamber down the rope ladder and be rowed ashore.

Farewells were brief and once their luggage had joined them on the quay, Tom — using his newly-honed skill in speaking a little Arabic — arranged for them to be escorted to a comfortable hotel.

It turned out to be a small, pleasant establishment and though the manager refrained from voicing his doubts about offering accommodation to this dishevelled couple standing at his desk, his worried frown spoke clearly.

'My wife and I require rooms until we are able to arrange a passage to Rhodes,' Tom said. With a dash of bravado, he pulled out his father's gold watch and laid it on his palm at an angle which displayed the baronet's crest etched on the case. The manager's demeanour underwent a rapid change.

'Sir Thomas and Lady Sinclair,' Tom announced, overloading his tone with pomposity, 'and we would be obliged if a bath could be brought up as quickly as possible. Yes, and I require a barber also.' He caught the laughter in Francesca's eyes; she was enjoying his performance.

'Ah! and one more thing, landlord: please send up a menu. Lady Sinclair and I will dine in our rooms this evening.'

★ ★ ★

The changes brought about by thorough bathing, clean clothes, the skill of a good barber and a sound night's sleep in a comfortable bed, allowed the hotel's manager to regard his new guests in an entirely different light when they appeared downstairs at noon the next day. The gentleman looked most distinguished in a freshly pressed, lightweight suit and his small wife — while not exactly a pretty woman — seemed to radiate an aura of happiness that quite eclipsed any imperfection in her features.

'Are you quite sure you won't change your mind and come to the Consulate with me this afternoon?' Tom asked as they stood at the door of the hotel. 'Couldn't you visit your friends tomorrow? Are you sure they will still be living in that house?'

'Tom, dearest, I have no idea whether I'll find the Alamiin family today or not, but it's only about a twenty-minute walk through the medina. I could do with the exercise and, besides, I think you should deal with your financial business in private.'

'Francesca, that's a ridiculous statement to make. There's no reason for you to feel uncomfortable hearing about my money matters. Don't you know that everything I have is yours?' He stopped when she put a finger on his lips. He took it away, then stooped to kiss her. 'Very well, then, go and visit your friends, but don't get lost and don't stay away too long. Promise?'

She nodded and he dug into his pocket for their last remaining coins. 'Here, you might want to buy — a glass of tea, or — '

'Thank you,' she said and smiled at him adoringly, then slipped the money into her pouch, and walked off briskly towards the old part of the town. She stopped before turning the first corner and lifted her hand to blow a kiss.

He waved back to her and, after she had gone from view, he stood where he was for a few moments, holding on to a ridiculous hope that she would change her mind and he would see her come running back to him.

When she didn't he fought the urge to chase after her. Instead, he gave his waistcoat a tug and turned in the opposite direction to find his way to the British Consulate.

★　★　★

Mr Albert Graham, the British Consul, was genuinely delighted when his secretary informed him that Sir Thomas Sinclair had called.

'Sinclair, the railway builder?' he asked, extending his hand, and when Tom nodded, he pumped it harder. 'Good God, man, what are you doing here? You're not involved in that nonsensical trans-Saharian line through Algeria that the French have been braying about, are you?'

Tom quickly shook his head. Mr Graham was a small, balding man, in his middle years who bristled with efficiency. Tom took an instant liking to him.

'It's an honour to make your acquaintance, Sir Thomas, and of course there will be no difficulty at all in arranging whatever cash you require,' Mr Graham said, ushering Tom into his study and ringing for refreshments to be brought. 'How long have you been out in this region? Are you aware that there's been another outbreak of the plague along the coast? But luckily we haven't seen it here.'

'Yes, I know all about the plague. We were in quarantine for more than a month in Oran,' Tom said, and the Consul's brows lifted when he heard his guest use the plural *we*.

'I take it that you are not travelling alone?'

Mr Graham had an open, friendly face and, for a split second, Tom felt the inclination to tell him the entire story of Diana's folly and the reason he was anxious to reach Rhodes. But he couldn't bring himself to mention it. Family business was best kept within the family.

'No, I'm not here alone,' he answered with a smile. 'I'm escorting my fiancée, Miss Francesca O'Hara. She's writing a book about her travels amongst the Moors, and at this moment she's off somewhere visiting a family in the medina.'

'How splendid! I would very much like to make her acquaintance,' said Mr Graham affably. 'You and your fiancée must come to dine with us here tomorrow evening. My wife is always eager to welcome fresh company.'

Tom grinned inwardly. Since they first met, Miss O'Hara had been known as his sister, then as his wife, and now here in the Consulate she'd become his fiancée. Well, soon they'd be officially married and all this nonsense would end.

'Thank you, Mr Graham. Francesca and I will be delighted to dine with you and Mrs Graham tomorrow,' he said with genuine pleasure, and took the chair offered by the Consul.

'Now, Sir Thomas, I'm keen to hear what impressions you've formed during your travels across North Africa. Did you strike any difficulties with the desert tribes? And Whitehall has heard about a French delegation conducting talks with the young Sultan of Morocco. Are you aware of what that was all about?'

Tom told him what he knew and they settled down to a lengthy discussion on the French policy in Algeria. Suddenly a startlingly loud rumble from somewhere outside drew both men to their feet. 'Cannons?' Tom said in disbelief, peering through the window. 'Thunder?'

'Most unusual to have a storm at this time of the year,' said the Consul, and quickly went to the drawer in his desk where his binoculars were kept.

* * *

As Francesca wound her way through the medina, it wasn't long before she began to wish that she had Tom beside her. She should have waited for him to pay his visit to the Consul, and then he would have been here with her while she navigated her way through dark and narrow lanes, past workshops and cafés where men sat smoking their pipes and playing cards, past schools and mosques and weavers hunched over their looms.

After centuries of invasions, earthquakes, raids and wars the beautiful order of the old Roman city had become blurred. Each historical convulsion had erased part of the city plan as buildings were destroyed, then rebuilt again and again. The neighbourhood where Francesca had lived happily for a year seemed familiar, yet unfamiliar. Some old houses had gone, and many others had been altered by the addition of another storey, which cast even darker shadows along the lanes.

Old memories were rekindled as she walked quickly through the *souk*. A shiver skittered down her spine and she involuntarily cast a glance over her shoulder. Then she took a deep breath and scolded herself. Otto Heinkler was dead. *Her* Thomas Sinclair had seen to that, and never again would he prey on her as he had delighted in doing whenever he'd found her out alone on these streets.

She'd always left the house of the Alamiin family dressed as demurely as their own daughters, yet on countless occasions she'd felt herself being stalked through the medina by *Uncle Otto*. If she didn't remain on her guard, Heinkler would try to create some opportunity to slip his fingers under her garments to touch her soft, youthful skin.

She looked at the tinsmith's workshop now as she walked past, recalling the day the sweating German had caught her arm and dragged her behind that building. He'd pinned her against the wall with one shoulder while his hands fumbled with his buttons to expose himself before her. How strange that she could still remember the odour of that part of his body.

She shuddered and hurried on. That day, he hadn't wanted to end the episode there, she knew, but terror had lent her enough strength to wrench herself away from his grasp, and she'd bolted up to the bakery here on the corner where her friend and protector, Leila Alamiin, was shopping. Leila was only two years older in age, but decades ahead of her in wisdom. She was being prepared to marry at thirteen.

Francesca now experienced the old feeling of relief when she found herself at last standing on the doorstep of the Alamiin house, swinging the shabby leather pouch from her wrist. She'd been truly happy living here amongst the family of the leather merchant, and she'd always treasured the pouch he had crafted for her in his workshop.

She knocked on the street door and looked up at the face of the old house. Sometime in the last fifteen years it had grown by one more storey, as buildings often did here when the size of families increased.

She knocked again and at last heard the clatter of sandals approaching on the tiled floor inside. The woman who opened the door held the veil across her face, but she dropped it instantly and gave a cry of astonishment the moment her eyes met Francesca's.

'Hello, Leila. Yes, it's me — Francesca O'Hara.'

The woman gave a squeal of delight as she threw her arm around Francesca's shoulders while her eyes overflowed with happy tears. 'Am I dreaming? Can this be true?' she laughed.

It was a much heavier Leila than the girl Francesca had known fifteen years earlier. She was now a handsome woman carrying one small child on her hip, while another clung to her robe and two others hovered behind.

'Oh, this is so good, so good! What are you doing here? Is your father with you, or are you married? Have you got children? You must come and stay with us — come, come upstairs quickly and speak with mother.'

Two other young women and several more children came to stare at the visitor, but Leila shook her head at them. 'Not yet, not yet!' she ordered and the ladies took a step back, smiling shyly at the visitor. 'These are the wives of my brother — you remember Karim who shared the same day of birth as you?'

Francesca nodded. 'He and my father will return home shortly and you can talk with these wives later because you must come upstairs straight away. Oh, how delighted mother will be to see you! She is not so well as she was when you were here and she cannot leave the house.' Leila dropped her voice. 'I fear she is failing, but seeing you again will lift her spirits. Oh, my dear sister, come with me. This is so good, so good!'

Several of the children trailed behind Leila and the pale-skinned visitor up the three flights of stairs to the top storey of the house. The young ones clustered in the doorway watching in wonder as the strange woman approached their grandmother with great familiarity.

'Mother, look who the great Allah in his mercy has sent to visit you,' Leila said to the thin figure lying on the bed. 'See, it is little Francesca O'Hara who has come back.'

Francesca's throat tightened as she sat beside the motherly woman who had so willingly included her in the Alamiin family circle. 'Mother Alamiin, I am very happy to see you again,' she said, and the woman smiled, straining to lift herself on to one elbow and peering closely into the lightly freckled face.

'Yes! It is truly my dear Francesca, but you

are still too thin! Where is your father? Have you a husband?' Speaking was clearly a struggle for her. 'How many children? Leila has six — and four are boys!'

'My father died a long time ago, Mother Alamiin, and I have no husband and no children.' Francesca's voice was unsteady. 'You know that I was never as clever or as beautiful as your Leila.'

The woman dropped back on to her pillow and clicked her tongue, though there was a sparkle in her eyes. 'Not yet married? I always said that your father made a foolish mistake in sending you away to the Spanish nuns.'

'Well, now I'm here to tell you that I have found a truly worthy man — handsome and brave, too — who has asked me to marry him. And that is exactly what I will do, just as soon as it can be arranged, though I don't know that I will ever be able to equal the number of children that Leila has blessed you with.'

After a time, the other wives and several more children drifted into the bedroom to meet Francesca and gossip about the neighbours — many of whom she could still recollect.

The laughter they shared was suddenly interrupted by a loud grinding roar, a terrifying sound that seemed to come from all around them. Leila and her mother screamed as the floor, the bed, and everything around them began to shake. Jars and dishes rattled, tumbled from shelves and crashed to the floor. The roar grew louder and they felt the whole house tremble, then begin to sway violently.

'Downstairs! Run quickly Leila,' Mother Alamiin cried. 'Take the children downstairs!'

Screaming in terror, Leila and the wives scooped children into their arms, while others locked themselves around the legs of their mothers, immobilizing them.

'Mother! I can't leave you!' Leila cried.

'Do as your mother says and get the children downstairs, Leila,' Francesca shouted over the roar of the quake and the cracking, breaking sounds coming from every part of the house. 'Go, go! I'll bring your mother. Hurry!'

Without a conscious thought that she was doing so, Francesca slipped the cord of the leather pouch over her wrist before she pulled aside the embroidered cover and put an arm under the grandmother's shoulders, heaving her awkwardly to the edge of the bed. 'Can you stand?' Even as she was asking the question, Francisca knew the answer.

The old woman wailed as she was half carried, half dragged across the room. Even though Leila's mother was emaciated, Francesca found it impossible to pick her up and carry her down the first steep, swaying staircase. Her own legs threatened to give way and she had to cling to the wall with one hand when the treads began a precarious sideways tilt. She held Mother Alamiin tightly around the waist, heaving her as gently as she could from one step to the next.

'Try to keep both arms around my neck, Mother.' Francesca was panting as much from terror as exertion when they reached the head of the second staircase. 'This one isn't quite so steep, so it will be easier. Please, please try to hold on to me.'

The woman croaked and coughed, and Francesca felt the frail arms slipping away from her. The air around them was thick with dust and shards of failing plaster and bricks and through all the roaring, cracking, grinding bedlam, came the sound of screams. Inside the house? Outside?

In desperation, and with her own heart thundering, Francesca heaved the woman up and carried her ineptly over one shoulder. Now she could move a little faster down the staircase, keeping one hand on the banister to steady herself while the house groaned and shuddered. *Oh, Tom, I need you, my darling Tom. I need you to help me!*

There was only one more flight after this, she told herself. Keep going. One foot after the other. Keep going. Don't stop. *Tom is waiting. Tom loves me and once we are married, I will never let us be apart again.*

The house shook convulsively, choking and blinding her with its dust and flying debris. The horrendous noise made her ear drums ache. She put her foot forward to feel for the next tread on the stairs. There was nothing there. The staircase had gone, and she and the old woman were tumbling into the void, plunging into chaos, falling, falling, landing with a bone-jarring, mind-numbing force amongst rubble.

She had no idea how long it took her to regain her senses. A moment? One hour or ten? She couldn't breathe. The air was thick with dust, and the cries of children and louder screams filled her ears. They were coming from nearby. She tried to swallow and fought for breath. Something trickled down her forehead and into her eye. It stung. Blood.

She screwed up her eyes, then tried to open them a crack. Through the heavy veil of dust in the air, she could see a chink of daylight above her. The top two floors of the house had collapsed. Where were the other members of the family now? Who was still alive here amongst this devastation? Who would come to help them?

Sounds of loud moaning were coming from nearby. 'Leila?' she croaked, but there was no answer. A child was sobbing. Then it ceased. From all around her came screams and groans and cries for help and, by turning her head a fraction, she could see the body of Mother Alamiin crushed and half-hidden under fallen masonry.

A severed leg was lying only yards away, and through the stifling dust Francesca saw the dismembered corpse of a man. Was that Leila's husband? And another man was lying further off. His head was crushed under a great beam and brain matter was leaking on to the rubble.

'Leila?' she called again, but the only answer was the rumble of an aftershock deep within the earth, announcing that further devastation was on its way. The taste of terror was bitter in her mouth. *Oh, Tom! Where are you? Are you lying hurt, too? Oh, Tom, I love you and I want to be with you.* She whimpered and braced herself as the crumbling walls around her began to shake again. Further bricks, shattered timbers and household detritus crashed down, and something heavy struck her chest. The crushing pain of it made her cry out but there was nobody to hear. There was no crack of light now. It was dark and she was entombed. Alone.

This was a nightmare, she told herself, just a nightmare, and soon she'd be awake again with Tom beside her, saying that he'd found a boat to take them away — to Rhodes, to anywhere — She moved her hand and felt the reassuring touch of soft leather under her fingers. Her grandparents, her family were still here with her. They would lend her strength, but her head felt as if it would burst with pain.

She could do nothing but wait. Someone would come soon. Tom would come to dig her out and carry her away. She had to stay awake and fight the urge to escape into sleep. The pain was real and it told her that she was still alive. That was good. She must hold on to that pain. Time seemed to stretch endlessly, and a deep weariness began seeping into her. She was cold and tired, so tired, and it was becoming difficult to cling to consciousness when she felt so cold. How long had she been lying here? Hours? Days?

Gradually, one by one, the screams and groans and sounds of weeping stopped, and she felt the silence of death filling her ears. She tried to cry out: 'I'm not dead, and I'm not going to die. Go away. Tom will find me.

I'm not going with you, I'm going to live!'

But Death was an old player at this game, a seducer. *When the pain becomes too much to bear, my dear, simply let go — just for a moment — and allow yourself to drift over the edge towards a place where peace awaits you. No more pain. Just close your eyes and put out your hand to me and I will come . . .*

'No! You will not have me!' She thought she had screamed the words aloud, but no sound came from her throat. Her dry lips moved and, when she gave an involuntary sob, an unspeakable pain shot through her rib cage.

She would *not* give up her life! She would *not* permit herself to drift to the edge. Never. Never. But, dear Lord, how tempting it was becoming. *Tom! Tom! Help me!*

20

The earthquake shook the Consulate and while several pictures fell from their hooks and a number of porcelain teacups and crystal glasses were shattered, the solid, single-storey building itself suffered little more than some cracked masonry and a few loosened tiles. The quake, followed by the aftershock, was over in less than five minutes. Mr Graham timed it.

'Well,' he said, 'that's the first one I've experienced since we arrived here three years ago. I wonder how the rest of the town has fared?'

Tom had the Consul's binoculars already trained on to the great cloud of dust rising in the direction of the medina. 'Francesca, my fiancée — Oh, God! Look at the devastation over there in that area.' Shock drained all colour from his face. 'Mr Graham, she was going up there somewhere to visit a family named' — his brain seemed frozen — 'um, named Alamiin. I have no exact address — but I think she said it was located not far from a Roman arch.'

He thrust the field glasses into the Consul's

hands. 'I must go up there and find her immediately.' As he turned abruptly to leave, his face was working with emotion.

'Yes, of course, m'dear fellow, but steady on just a moment,' Mr Graham said, putting a fatherly hand on his shoulder. 'Let me send a couple of men with tools up to the medina with you.' He poured a brandy and handed it to Tom while he called for Stephen Wilkes, his secretary, and rapidly explained the situation to him.

'I'll go with you,' Wilkes said to Tom. 'Just give me a moment to organize some men to bring tools.' He rushed off and was back again within minutes. 'Right, sir, we're ready.

'I'll follow on your heels as soon as I can, Tom,' the Consul said as he walked with them to the door, 'just as soon as I confirm that we've no injuries here amongst our people. Then I must telegraph a report on this quake to my counterpart in Alexandria, and he'll relay it on to London. By the way, is Miss O'Hara a British citizen?'

Tom shook his head. 'Not yet.'

★ ★ ★

Stephen Wilkes had not been stationed long in Tripoli, but he had learned his way about the town, and steered Tom through the earthquake's havoc, towards the still-standing Roman arch. Two gardeners from the Consulate followed with long-handled shovels.

Remarkably, some buildings in the old town remained standing while others around them had collapsed into piles of rubble. Along each lane they met dazed and often injured men and women, who had crawled from some ruin where others still remained trapped. The sounds of distress came from all directions, and in desperation people had begun scrambling over collapsed houses, clawing at piles of rubble with their hands, frantically attempting to reach those still lying inside.

Bodies were being dragged from under the remains of some buildings, and carried away to be placed near the Roman arch, which had withstood this earthquake, as it had all the others since Marcus Aurelius had it erected well over a millennium and a half ago.

'Please, can you direct me to the house of the Alamiin family?' Tom asked repeatedly of shocked and dazed people they met picking their way through the devastation. Daylight was beginning to fade. 'Do you know where the Alamiin family lives?' he pleaded to a woman who was sitting quietly in a gutter, rocking a dead baby in her arms.

With unfocused eyes, she stared towards the mountain-like pile of rubble at the end of the lane, and smiled calmly. 'That is the house of the Alamiin family,' she murmured. 'The family is all there.' She bent her head again and began to croon softly to the baby.

Two men were already on the wreckage that had been the Alamiin house, struggling to heave away heavy masonry and beams. As the party from the Consulate ran up to them, a woman's body was carried out, and then a child's, before a cry of alarm went up as part of a wall started to crumble, sending the rescuers scrambling from the debris.

'Slowly, slowly!' a voice roared, 'or we'll all be killed.'

'It's too unstable to work on from this side,' Tom shouted, assessing the structure with his engineer's eye, though he wondered if these distraught men were able to understand what he was saying with his meagre command of their language.

'Wait! Listen to me! Don't do any more there until we find props of some kind to take the stress and prevent anything more falling.' He looked around quickly. 'Mr Wilkes, will you take your men and try to find a few solid beams — or anything that can be used to support this wall.'

He called to other men who were standing

about, dazed. 'You, start over here and clear these bricks away — carefully now.' The Alamiin home appeared to be amongst the ones most severely damaged by the quake.

By the time it was dark, the Consul and several of his servants had arrived with lamps and torches just as Tom was about to make an attempt to squeeze through a tight gap he had clawed in the rubble. His nails were torn, his fingers bleeding.

'Quick, give me one of those small lamps,' he said to Mr Graham, and pushing the light ahead of him, he lay on his stomach and using his elbows, edged his way into the darkness.

'Francesca, where are you?' he called repeatedly as he pushed his way through a tight tunnel, desperately clawing aside debris in his way. The air was hot and stifling and frequently his hands slid in congealed pools of blood, its metallic odour mixing with the ever-present dust.

'Francesca, I'm here! Can you hear me?'

The only answer came from the unstable building — the creaks and groans of shifting weights, the occasional rattle of more falling plaster and bricks. Inch by inch, he struggled forward until he came to a point where his path was blocked by an obstruction too heavy for him to shift. He swore in frustration.

'Francesca, can you hear me? I'm here, I'm here, my dearest.' He wept.

'My dear fellow, you can do no more tonight,' Mr Graham said with genuine distress when Tom scrambled from the wreckage. 'Come back to the Consulate tonight and start your search again tomorrow.'

Tom sat on a ledge and, with his elbows propped on his knees, he put his head in his hands. 'I can't! I can't leave her out here alone!' His shoulders shook. 'Oh, God, I'm not going to let her die! Do you hear me, God? She is not going to die!'

Mr Graham spoke quietly with Mr Wilkes and sent him back to the Consulate to inform his wife about the situation. 'And when you return, bring enough food and blankets to get us through the night,' he called after him.

Then he sat down companionably beside Tom on the ledge. And because he was a wise man, he remained silent, knowing that Tom would eventually open up and start to talk. And talk —

'Dammit, Mr Graham, I've lied to you!' he began savagely. 'Francesca O'Hara is the most extraordinary woman in creation, but she didn't come here with me to research some inane travel book. It's entirely my fault that she might be lying dead somewhere in there.'

The Consul said nothing, but gave a soft murmur of interest.

'She's been travelling all the way from Agadir with me because I have a very foolish sister named Diana who left her husband and ran off with an American sea captain. He went down with his ship off the west coast months ago.'

Mr Graham's murmur conveyed increasing interest.

'My sister's life was saved, but Francesca learned that she'd been sold into the slave trade and taken to Marrakech.'

The Consul looked at him quickly. 'Did your family not receive a ransom demand?' he asked. 'That's the usual practice — though, thank God, it doesn't happen as frequently as it did in years past.'

'No, our parents have heard nothing at all about her for months, and of course they're most distressed. I came out here to locate Diana, but it became an impossible task for me because the men involved kept her whereabouts a close secret. It was only Francesca's amazing ability to find people with scraps of information which has led the trail as far as this.'

'Are you saying that your sister was

brought here to Tripoli?' Mr Graham sounded worried.

'No, not here. Francesca heard that Diana had been taken to an island somewhere near Rhodes, but Tripoli was as far as we could get once the port of Oran was opened after the plague. That's the reason we were anxious to get on with the next leg of our journey as quickly as possible.'

Tom didn't notice that all the time he was speaking, Mr Graham had been scribbling names into a notebook on his knee.

'Remarkably,' he went on, 'Francesca learned that an Egyptian named Khafra Bey paid money for her in Marrakech, and then took her to some little island near Rhodes.'

The Consul made a note of that and slipped the book back into his pocket while Tom hung his head and dug his fingers into his hair. 'Dear God! I feel so wretched. I've failed to find Diana, and now Francesca is lying somewhere under there — maybe only yards away — yet I can't get to her.' He gave way to a sob. 'I can't tell you how much I love her, how much I've grown to love her. There is no other woman in the world who has the courage and the wisdom that she has. And the tenderness and devotion — '

Tom's voice broke several times, and his narrative grew more and more disjoined as he talked through the night. The Consul listened to Francesca's entire life story, Tom's own story, every detail of their journey from Agadir, about the hair she'd given to the Tuaregs to divert their attack in the desert, the French Colonel who had lost his heart to her, the rescue of a baby during the plague in Oran . . .

Mr Graham dozed off occasionally, but Tom seemed not to notice, and as soon as the first grey light came over the hill, he roused all available workers and the task of digging into the ruins of the house began again.

By midday, two dazed and injured children had been brought from the ruins and taken away by relatives. The grim remains of a woman and two men were removed later in the afternoon, and prepared for burial.

'Francesca!' Tom croaked, 'Francesca, where are you?' He felt the borders of his sanity wavering dangerously and forced his exhausted body to work faster. 'I know you're here. I'm coming, sweetheart. Wait for me, wait.'

The sun was dipping towards the western horizon when a cry went up from a young man. 'A woman! I have found a woman!'

Tom scrambled across the rubble and his heart seemed to stop when he looked down to see Francesca lying motionless. Was she

397

still breathing? Her face and blouse were covered with dried blood and, with help from the youth who'd found her, Tom eased away a heavy wooden chest which was pinning her legs. Were the bones broken?

'Fran! I've found you! I'm here to take you away! You're safe now.' She made no response. 'Look at me! Please, Fran, open your eyes! Look at me!' He brushed the dust and plaster from her face and other men came to remove some of the debris around her.

'We'll put you on a stretcher and find a doctor, and then you and I are going home. Straight home to England. Oh, Fran, can you hear me?'

'Come, let us lift her — carefully, now,' urged Mr Wilkes, coming to Tom's side. 'We'll carry her to the Consulate. Mr Graham has already gone back to arrange for Miss O'Hara to be looked after there and he'll call Doctor Peake to come and see her.'

Tom nodded numbly then carefully worked his arms under her and began to lift. Dear God! she still had that damned pouch caught on her wrist. His own exhaustion left him barely sufficient strength for the task of heaving her up, but he grimly refused any offer of help and clutched her possessively to his chest. Her breathing was shallow, and she lay against him like a rag doll as he stumbled through the rubble with Stephen Wilkes's steadying hand under his elbow.

He lay her on a makeshift stretcher and she was carried back to the Consulate where Mrs Graham, a capable, sweet-faced lady had a sick-room waiting. As soon as Tom arrived with Francesca, the Consul's wife firmly took charge of the patient and, with the assistance of her own maid, she bathed Francesca and prepared her to be examined by the doctor.

Afterwards, she sat with Tom as Doctor Peake gave his opinion on Francesca's injuries. It was clear to her that Tom was refusing to hear the lack of hope in the tone behind the doctor's words.

'Yes, doctor, you say that her ribs and the abrasions will heal, but has there been damage to her spine? Why isn't she moving? When will she open her eyes?'

'Time and patience, Sir Thomas. Time and patience. That's what is needed in cases like this.' Doctor Peake had had little sleep in the last twenty-four hours. 'Leave Miss O'Hara propped slightly on the pillows and see if she will take a little warm broth. I will call to see her again tomorrow.'

Tom sat on the edge of the bed, picked up Francesca's hand and began to rub it gently between his own. 'I'm here, Fran. Can you hear me? I won't leave you, I promise.'

Mrs Graham left the room and talked to Mr Wilkes about arranging for their luggage to be brought from the damaged hotel. When he returned with it, he was also able to mention to her quietly that Tom and Francesca had been staying at the hotel as husband and wife.

She nodded sagely and had a bed for Tom brought in and placed close beside Francesca's.

'Goodness knows what lies ahead for the poor girl,' she said to her husband that evening, 'but I thought he would want to be by her side through it all.'

'Helen, my love, you are the very best of women,' he said and put his arms around her tightly. 'Doctor Peake's remedy is time and patience, eh? Well, let's hope he's correct.'

They looked up when Mr Wilkes knocked on the door with news that the earthquake-damaged telegraph line to Cairo had been repaired, and the clerk was at this moment receiving a message from the Consulate there.

'Well, that's good news indeed,' Mr Graham said. 'I'll come into the office shortly.'

Then, when the secretary had left the room, he picked up his notebook from the desk, and beckoned his wife to sit beside him on the sofa while he began to turn the pages. Her eyebrows raised higher and higher as her husband divulged Sir Thomas Sinclair's confidential business.

'Helen, my dear, I am about to overlook the fact that I am employed as a servant of Her Majesty, and do a little private meddling in matters that are no business of mine at all.'

He lowered his voice and told her what he planned to do.

When he'd finished, she cupped his face in her hands and kissed him soundly. 'Oh, Albert, you are the very best of men!' she said, and together they walked into the telegraph clerk's office.

* * *

The daily routine surrounding Francesca didn't vary. At ten each morning, Mrs Graham and her maid came to bathe her and change the bedclothes, and as soon as that was done, Tom replaced the soft leather pouch under her pillow. 'She'll know it's there,' he said. 'It's most important to her.' Sometimes he placed it under her hand on the bed covers.

Doctor Peake listened to her heartbeat and checked her reflexes, asked what she'd been swallowing, lifted her lids to examine her pupils and pronounced no change in her condition. And each day Tom pleaded with him to do more. 'Look at her! She hasn't even opened her eyes!'

'But, as I have said, sir, the heartbeat is steady, and there has been no change in her condition. Now that in itself is a good sign that there has been no further deterioration. Time and patience, sir. Time and patience is the answer.'

'She's losing weight every day!'

'Perhaps you could try a little egg custard in the evening, made with a dash of brandy. Yes, try that.'

Occasionally she stirred and gave a soft sigh. Tom slept beside her at night and stayed at her side throughout the day, talking to her, reading to her. He became convinced that she could hear his voice, and he chose a variety of books that he knew she'd like from Mrs Graham's shelves. 'I'm here, Fran. I'll always be here, I promise, and one of these days when you open your eyes, you might very well find yourself looking at an old man with a long white beard.'

'Tom, dear, I'll sit with Francesca for an hour or so while you take a breath of air outside with my husband,' Mrs Graham urged gently. 'A little exercise on the terrace will do you good and I promise to call if she stirs.'

Tom lifted himself wearily from the chair and patted her hand. 'I won't be far away, sweetheart,' he said and smiled his thanks to Mrs Graham as he walked outside to join the Consul on the terrace overlooking the harbour. He had to shield his eyes at first from the glare of the bright afternoon sunshine sparkling on the water.

'Ah, good to see you, Tom,' the Consul said. 'Care for a brandy?' He didn't wait for an answer and went to a table where the glasses were waiting. Tom stood, empty-eyed, looking at the profusion of flowering geraniums spilling from large earthenware urns standing around the perimeter of the terrace.

'Do you know that I was with Francesca once when a tarantula the size of a plate — '

'Amazing! Now, Tom, let's sit over here in the shade and — and — ' Albert Graham was under strict instructions from his wife to keep Tom's mind away from any topic involving Francesca for at least one hour each day.

He looked around quickly for some new diversion. 'Ah, now, what a picture the bay is this afternoon with all those craft moored out there. There was a Royal Navy frigate in yesterday and — Oh! just look at the beautiful lines of that vessel coming in towards us now. A private yacht, I'll be bound, and what a beauty, eh? Now that's the way to travel! A steam engine to turn a propeller, as well as two masts carrying sail!'

The Consul was pleased to see that the in-coming boat had caught Tom's interest.

'Yes,' he answered, 'a vessel like that could probably make six knots — or even more — through all weathers. Once that steam engine was fired-up, there'd be no worry about where the eye of the wind might be set.' He drained his brandy quickly. 'That's just given me an idea, Mr Graham — why didn't I think of it before?'

The Consul held his breath.

'Don't you see?' Tom hauled himself to his feet. 'If I could find a steam ship to take Francesca back to England, she'd be able to get the best medical attention in the world there. I know that Doctor Peake is doing all he can, but she needs to be seen by — by someone who's a specialist in this area.' He began pacing to and fro. 'Who can I ask about finding a fast ship from Tripoli, Mr Graham?'

Albert Graham looked at Tom and sighed. 'Leave it with me, Tom. I'll make enquiries in the morning.'

★ ★ ★

'Well, sweetheart, we're not going to be here much longer,' Tom said as Francesca swallowed the last spoonful of egg custard and he wiped her lips. 'You and I will soon be sailing for home, and mother and dad will be there to meet us, and we'll — ' He bit down hard on his lip and tried to ignore the fearful doubts that had sometimes begun to drift into the back of his mind, like smoke seeping under a locked door.

No, no! He must never give up hope that Francesca would live to be fit and well again. He kissed her lightly on the forehead and slipped the pouch under her fingers. 'Hold on tightly, love. I'll never let you go.'

In the world outside, the sun had set and darkness enveloped the town. He turned up the lamp standing on the table beside her bed and opened the book he'd been reading to her. He must cling to the belief that she could still hear his voice.

'Now, where did we get to last night?' He rubbed one hand over his sunken, red-rimmed eyes and cleared his throat. 'Ah, yes, here we are: Pip and Estella are together again and they're talking about Miss Haversham.' He held the book in one hand and with Francesca's limp fingers in his other, he began to read aloud.

At times, the words on the page became

blurred and his head dropped forward with a jerk. His eyes were heavy and it was an increasing struggle to keep them open.

After a time, he lifted his head to stretch his stiffening neck and in the shadows beyond the circle of lamplight, a movement caught his eye. Someone was standing at the door of the room.

'May I approach?' The unfamiliar male voice was soft and very deep.

'Who — ?' The book slid from Tom's hand as he stood, and tried to make out the silken-robed figure coming towards him across the room. The stranger was a tall, olive-skinned man, with a light dusting of grey in his short, dark hair. He carried himself with a quiet dignity and approached Tom with his hand extended.

'I am Khafra Bey, Thomas. Your sister and I were married a short time ago, and so you and I have become brothers. I regret that we meet here under such troubled circumstances.' He was a lithe, handsome man of middle-years, with warm, dark eyes that looked directly into Tom's. 'We came here as quickly as we could.'

Light-headed with fatigue, Tom numbly took the large, firm hand offered, and told himself that he must surely have slipped into madness. 'I don't — '

'May I see Francesca?' the velvet voice murmured, and when Tom gave a grunt of agreement, the Egyptian moved to her bedside, lifted her hand from the leather pouch, and held it between both of his. He simply stood, looking down at her, saying nothing.

Tom felt all the exhaustion and anxiety and confusion which had been churning inside him for the last two weeks, now building up into the rage of helplessness. He looked around wildly, filled with a desperate need to do something physical. Punch his fists into flesh. Thrash something. Hurl curses at the heavens. Shake the universe with his bare hands.

From the corner of his eye he saw another figure now standing in the doorway; the shock of it convulsed him.

It was Diana!

And his first impulse was to kill her!

21

She came to him hesitantly, his tall, luminescent sister, swathed in glorious salmon-pink silk, and now drifting slowly across the carpet as if she had stepped straight out of some dream.

Tom's fury held him rooted to the floor and his chest heaved. 'Oh, God damn it, Diana! Why didn't you write to them?' The words exploded from his throat like cannon shot; his body shook. 'All you needed to do was to send them just one bloody letter!'

She was an arm's length from him now, with the lamplight touching her face and turning the tears on her cheeks to drops of diamonds. 'Yes, and I am truly, truly sorry, Tom. But mother and dad have forgiven me and I hope you'll be able to do so, too. One day.'

Tom stared at her, slack-jawed, then shook his head, trying to clear it. 'Are you telling me that they already know where you are?'

She nodded. 'Yes, I wrote and told them about everything. And also that I was to be married to Khafra Bey.'

Tom threw back his head and gave a bark

of derisive laughter. 'Are you insane, Diana? I had a conversation with your husband not long ago, and he was alive and well in Liverpool!' He swung to challenge the Bey, who was still standing beside Francesca. 'Have you been informed that my sister is already married to a Mr Francis Herbert?'

The Egyptian kept his gaze on Francesca's face. 'That marriage in England was never consummated, Thomas,' he said with quiet certainty, 'so it was annulled here. My family has belonged to the Coptic faith since its beginnings, and that is the church in which your sister and I exchanged our marriage vows.'

The Bey gently replaced Francesca's hand on the covers, smiled at Diana and walked to stand beside her. 'Thomas, your sister and I have received several letters from Major and Mrs Fitzalan since our marriage. Of course, they're now most concerned about you and Miss O'Hara.'

Tom grimaced and shook his head. 'Oh, Lord, what a débâcle this whole thing has become!'

Diana moved closer to Tom and tried to touch his arm, but he jerked it away from her.

'In the last letter that arrived from father, he said that you'd written to him from Oran, telling him how Francesca had been so clever in following my path, and about her fortitude — '

'Ah, yes,' Tom cut in bitterly, 'do let's talk about Francesca O'Hara's courage and tenacity, about her sacrifices and generosity. She has been my guiding star from the start of this chase to find you, Diana' — his voice rose, and shook — 'and look at the price she's had to pay! Look where she is now!'

'Oh, Tom — I can't tell you how very sorry I am. Of course I regret all the stupid mistakes I've made in my life and I'm ashamed to think of the worry I've caused mother and dad. And I'm especially sorry that Francesca has been hurt now.'

Tom swung away from Diana and her husband and went to sit at Francesca's bedside again. He had to swallow hard before he could speak. 'Don't dare ask me to forgive you, Diana, because I'm far from ready to do that while she is lying here, barely alive!'

★ ★ ★

Tom anticipated a restless, sleepless night when he later climbed into bed. He was still shaking with anger as he started to compile a mental list of all the questions he wanted to throw at Diana and her husband at their next meeting. Who was this man Diana had married? What had been his intentions when he bought Diana from the Sherif? How the devil had they learned that he and Francesca had arrived in Tripoli?

There were other matters also troubling him about Diana's journey. But within five minutes he'd fallen straight into a deep, long, dreamless sleep and even before he opened his eyes the next morning, he knew he'd slept late.

He could feel the warmth of sunlight on his face, and heard voices coming from the other part of the household. He reached across to Francesca's bed and took her hand, which was the first thing he did every morning as soon as he awoke.

It was an effort today to lift his lids, an effort to think of what was lying ahead for him. His anger at Diana was still there; he could feel it sitting like a lead ball in his chest.

Gradually he became aware of a slight pressure on his fingers. Was he dreaming? He propped himself up quickly and looked across at Francesca. Again he felt a movement in her hand and scrambled out of his bed to sit on the side of hers, laughing like the madman he felt he'd become.

'Oh, Fran, Fran, you've come back to me! You're back!'

Her eyelids fluttered and as he peered closely, he was sure he saw her lips move.

A knock came on the door, but he couldn't lift his gaze from her face as Mrs Graham tip-toed into the room, and placed a cup of tea on the table beside him.

'Look, Mrs Graham! Look at her! Khafra Bey has worked another miracle!' Francesca's eyelids gave a definite flutter and he felt her fingers deliver a featherweight squeeze to his hand.

'Tom, dear, Doctor Peake is just arriving.' Mrs Graham passed him his robe. 'Here, slip into this, then drink your tea, and I'll bring the doctor in to see Francesca.'

'Yes, yes! Get him in here quickly. I just saw her trying to smile — and look at the grip she's got on my finger. Oh God! Oh God! She's going to live. Where's the Bey? I must give him my thanks.'

It took Mrs Graham's firm persuasion to move Tom away from Francesca's bed while Doctor Peake performed his examination; and when that was completed, he stepped back with a satisfied smile. 'Splendid! As I said at the beginning, time and patience — patience and time — would be the remedy, and here we are! I'm delighted with the results, though I'm sure you realize, Sir Thomas, that your fiancée will need a great deal of continued nursing for her strength to recover.'

Tom blew his nose hard on a handkerchief. 'I think you should know, doctor, that Francesca was visited last night by a gentleman — an Egyptian of the Coptic faith — and I have no doubt that it was he — with some ancient power — some healing gift — '

The doctor raised his eyebrows and gave him a patronizing pat on the shoulder. 'Yes, yes — the power of prayer. Very proper, even useful at times.'

Tom shook his head at the man, and glanced at Mrs Graham. She was giving him a sweet, condescending smile, too. 'And I do believe I detect a little colour in Francesca's cheeks this morning,' she added encouragingly. 'Oh — quickly doctor, look! She's opening her eyes.'

Tom pushed the others aside and leaned closer as Francesca struggled to keep her lids open. After several attempts, her gaze at last remained fixed on his face. She smiled and her lips moved to silently speak his name.

★ ★ ★

'Mrs Graham,' Tom said wearily when Francesca was sleeping soundly again, 'I need to speak to my sister and her husband to have a few questions answered before I lose my mind completely. I can't make head nor tail of what the Bey did last night when he was with her. Where are they staying? And I can't imagine how they came to know that we had arrived here in Tripoli.'

'Tom dear, I can give you very simple answers to two of your questions, so come with me,' the Consul's wife said, taking him firmly by the arm and leading him to a table set for lunch on the terrace.

'Now, first you wanted to know how your sister and her husband knew where to find you?' Tom held the chair for her and she signalled for their wine to be poured. 'Well, we have a telegraph line now and, after you'd confided all your worries to my dear Albert, he took it upon himself to telegraph the Consul in Cairo and ask him to make discreet enquiries in Egypt about a gentleman known as Khafra Bey.'

Tom looked at her in astonishment. 'He did? Wonderful!'

'Please understand that this is not at all the kind of thing my husband would normally do — but under the circumstances — ' She paused while a servant brought the luncheon dishes to the table and then withdrew. 'You see, Tom,' she went on, 'let's just say that we were both most concerned about you and

Francesca, so when an encouraging report came back from the Consulate in Cairo, we took it upon ourselves to advise Khafra Bey and your sister that you were here.'

'Oh — what did the report have to say about the Bey?'

'Simply that the family is a very old and highly respected one. Wealthy, too. They've been members of the Coptic Christian faith for centuries and have several estates outside Alexandria.'

Tom's forehead creased. 'Not on an island near Rhodes?'

'Oh yes, the family spends the summer months on their island,' she said, 'but their estate is just outside Alexandria. That's where my husband's counterpart in Cairo sent our message to the Bey about your arrival here.' She gave Tom's hand a reassuring pat. 'This was all done very unofficially, I assure you.'

'Yes, I'm sure and, er — But everything has happened so quickly since then — I mean — ?'

'We are living in a world that is growing faster every year, m'dear: telegraph lines, steam engines — 'There was a sparkle in her eye as she pointed to the sleek vessel which Tom and the Consul had admired sailing into the bay yesterday.

He blew a long breath through his lips.

'That yacht belongs to Khafra Bey? And, of course, they're living on board now?'

'Yes. And I've asked them to join us for dinner this evening.' She watched closely for his reaction.

His chest heaved as he put down his knife and fork, then walked to the other side of the table to kiss her cheek. 'You're a wonderful diplomat and a true friend, Mrs Graham, and when our first daughter comes along, Francesca and I are going to name her *Helen*.'

★   ★   ★

A new calmness settled around Tom as he waited for Diana and her husband to arrive at the Consulate. Francesca had spoken his name aloud this afternoon, and she'd eaten a little solid food at last. She was propped up on pillows now, but Doctor Peake had given permission for her to sit in a chair for a short time tomorrow, if she felt inclined.

Hope. What incredibly restorative powers lay behind that one little word, Tom decided, and he smiled inwardly when he thought back to his frame of mind just twenty-four hours ago when his hope was on the point of cracking and Diana's sudden arrival had stripped his emotions bare.

Yes, there still remained bridges to be rebuilt between him and his sister, but it was an effort that he must make for the sake of their parents. Perhaps the old, flighty Diana he remembered was now a changed woman after surviving so many frightening events. Perhaps.

He stood under the portico, awaiting the arrival of the Consul's small carriage which had been sent to the quay to carry his sister and her husband to dinner. Again Diana's beauty took his breath away as he watched her alight. She threw him a nervous glance as he stepped forward and offered his hand.

'I want to apologize for the way I spoke to you last night,' were his first words, even before he'd offered her a greeting.

'Nobody knows better than I do how sometimes things are said and done that we'd sooner forget.' She took his outstretched hand. 'My husband and I were overjoyed today to hear that Francesca has turned the corner. May we see her later?' A spark of the old, mischievous Diana flashed in her eyes. 'I especially want to thank her for removing the name of my older brother from the perennial list of Debutants' Delights in London. It's high time you mended your ways and settled down, Thomas Sinclair.'

'I was only waiting for you to set the

example, younger sister,' he said in the same bantering tone and squeezed her hand tighter. 'Francesca is expecting you to visit her after dinner, but please don't mention my scandalous past to her — at least until we're safely married.'

'I promise,' she laughed and lifted her cheek for him to kiss.

Tom's chest tightened as he turned to Khafra Bey. He wanted to throw his arms around this big, gentle man. Or kiss his feet. Or do anything that would convey just some of the overwhelming gratitude he felt was owing to this stranger who had saved Francesca. But when he tried to speak what was in his heart, the words tangled on his tongue. 'Thank you,' was the only intelligible sound he could produce.

It wasn't till after dinner, when Mrs Graham and Diana had gone to sit with Francesca, and the Consul had found an excuse to absent himself for an hour, that Tom and the Egyptian had the opportunity to sit quietly together on the terrace.

'Sir, before one more moment passes,' Tom began, 'I beg you to tell me about yourself, and — and the ability you have to — well, we've heard such tales of your healing powers, and when I saw for myself last night how you were able to bring Francesca back from a place where I couldn't reach her . . . '

The Bey's brown eyes looked into Tom's. 'Tell me, my brother, what did you see happening at Francesca's bedside? I'm sure it was nothing that you, yourself, have not done every day since she was injured. I gave her love and prayed to the God I worship.'

'Even if I had your faith, sir, I'd still believe that it was more than mere coincidence that only hours after you'd touched her, she began to regain consciousness.'

'Whether my God had a hand in it or not, I believe your fine Doctor Peake insisted all along that the outcome would depend on time and patience.'

Tom laughed with him. 'Patience, sir? When you know me a little better, I think you'll discover that there's very little patience in my character, and I — '

'Ah, Thomas,' the Bey interrupted in his deep, soft voice, 'I feel that I already know you very well. Your stepfather has written to me at length about the man you are, and the love he feels for you.'

'He has? Well, I assure you that it's no greater than what I feel towards him,' he said with a rush of emotion. 'I've spent my life trying to be just half the man he is.'

They studied each other for a moment. 'I think you and I are alike in many ways,' the

Bey said quietly. 'I had those same deep feelings for my grandfather; he died not long ago.'

Tom murmured his condolences.

'Yes, my grandfather was recognized in our country as a truly great man.' He smiled to himself as some recollection flashed into his mind. 'He was always deeply religious and, like his own grandfather before him, he had a leaning towards mysticism. On the day I was born he announced he'd had a vision that I would be a wanderer through life, until I came upon an icon which would lead me to a place of contentment.'

Tom attempted no comment.

'Well, I *have* been a wanderer, Thomas,' he said with a chuckle. 'I have had business dealings that have taken me on many long and profitable journeys — to the east and to the west. Not long ago I had business with the Sherif in Marrakech, and I was there in his palace when a great furore erupted concerning a white woman whom the old Sherif wished to establish in his ladies' quarters.'

For a moment he glanced away, seemingly lost in thought as he sat stroking his chin. 'Suddenly, it was as if I could hear my grandfather's voice urging me to go to this woman in the slavemaster's house.' He looked back earnestly into Tom's eyes. 'I assure you that hearing my grandfather's voice was an entirely new phenomenon, and I felt impelled to follow his command — even though it went against everything in my character to intrude into matters that were not mine. But when I found Diana there and looked into her face, I knew straight away that *she* was the icon — the flesh and blood icon — that I'd been sent to find.' He spread his hands. 'I can't explain what happened, but I know it was meant to be, just as my grandfather had foretold.'

'I don't doubt you, sir,' Tom said. 'But we heard that she was dying, and you'd revived her.'

'Did I?'

'People in that house believed her to be near death.'

'People believe what they *think* they see, Thomas. Actually, on that day, the effects of the draft she had swallowed were already wearing off when I found her. Now, that in itself is a miracle, but it was news which I chose to keep to myself because, the moment I set eyes on Diana, I fell in love with her. I told her so that day, and vowed that I would take care of her — always.'

Tom frowned at him in wonder. 'I have never seen my sister looking lovelier, or more contented. But how can you say that you have no healing powers, when I saw with my own eyes how you touched some flicker of life in Francesca last night and brought her back to this world?'

The Bey gave an amused smile and shook his head, but Tom refused to be convinced and pressed the argument further:

'Well, let me assure you that there are men all along the coast who are still talking about the day a fisherman's son drowned in the great storm and his body was brought aboard your boat. They're convinced that he was dead and that you revived him.'

The Bey smiled and again shrugged his shoulders. 'Believe me, it was the boy's father who had already saved his life. All I offered was a place to recover and regain his strength. A little time and patience again, you see, Thomas? Time and patience.'

★ ★ ★

Three weeks later the Bey's yacht slipped swiftly across the Mediterranean with its engine thumping steadily and the sails filled by a following wind. The sea was calm and the ship's roll barely noticeable as the coast of France came into view.

On the deck, Tom and Diana stood at the

stern rail, deep in a lengthy discussion, while Francesca lay dozing in a chair with a rug across her legs.

When she woke, she was startled to realize how close they were coming to the port of Marseilles, and how close she was to meeting Tom's parents at last.

In just a short while this vessel would tie up at the quay, and Major and Mrs Fitzalan would come aboard. Her heart raced. Very soon she was to meet the Julia and James whom she felt she knew so well from listening to Tom's long, affectionate tales about their lives. She wanted so much for them to love her, too.

It had been Khafra Bey's suggestion that Tom and Diana's parents should cross from England to France, then travel by train to meet the yacht at Marseilles. He had arranged it. And then, with the Major and Mrs Fitzalan on board, they would all sail to Alexandria and visit Khafra Bey's family estate where she and Tom were to be married.

The wealthy were able to make life seem so simple, she thought wryly, and wished she had a little more control over the tears of happiness that washed into her eyes each time she thought about her new family. The pouch of her own little family treasures lay packed safely away in her cabin; she was putting down new family roots now.

She tried to still her racing heart and lay with her eyes closed, until Tom and Diana's discussion became heated and their voices grew louder. Francesca gave a hiss of irritation when she heard Diana again describing the elaborate wedding in Alexandria which she was determined to arrange for her brother and his bride.

'No! That's a ridiculous notion, Diana! Only you would think of that!'

'Oh, heavens! Why must you always be so stubborn!' Diana's voice quavered. 'Why won't you listen to my perfectly reasonable suggestion? It would be beautiful.'

Francesca cringed when she pictured herself becoming the centre of the extravaganza which Diana was planning, but at this moment she was still too weak to add her own voice to the argument. But the matter was really of no great consequence, because she knew exactly the kind of simple ceremony that she and Tom would have. Tom's sister had yet to meet the fit-and-well Francesca O'Hara who always refused to buckle under any kind of pressure to do something that was an anathema to her. Diana could argue as much as she liked: Francesca and Tom would have a small, family wedding.

Yet, in recent weeks she had grown truly

fond of Tom's mercurial sister. Diana was generous and effusive, impulsive, determined to win every argument, and very much in love with her husband. It hadn't been difficult for Francesca to take Diana's measure, and now she was quite confident that, once her strength had returned, she'd have no trouble in meeting Tom's sister on equal terms.

She would certainly never argue head-to-head with her, as Tom was trying to do now. There were more effective ways to persuade a woman like Diana to consider another view. Would Tom never learn?

When Francesca had had enough of their futile argument, she pulled aside the rug, and stood to find another chair further along the deck. After a few steps, she found it difficult to keep her balance and was relieved to see the Bey coming towards her.

'Ah, Francesca! Here, let me offer you a little assistance,' he said, holding out his hand.

'You're very kind. Thank you,' she said as she took it, then stood for a moment looking at his hand holding hers. She increased the pressure very slightly and caught the expression that came into in his eyes.

'I want you to know that I *did* feel your touch on my hand when you came to my sick-room at the Consulate that night,' she said softly. 'At that time, I seemed to be travelling somewhere far away, and it was so very cold — or perhaps it was more like a strange feeling of emptiness — but when you touched me, it all changed. I remember a sudden sensation of warmth. Of wholeness. I won't ask you for an explanation because I don't need one.' She pressed his fingers. 'I will always be convinced that you have a gift, and you have my deepest thanks for using it that night in my room.'

He gave her a knowing smile, then shook his head as the voices behind them grew louder. 'Come along now, Francesca. Let us simply ignore them,' he advised cheerfully as they began to walk. 'I grew up with three sisters and there are still times when we also forget that we are no longer children.'

'I've never known Tom to be so — so petty,' she said, instantly coming to his defence by saying, 'That's not like him at all!'

'Ah! I have personally encountered one or two of Diana's difficult moments,' the Bey said and raised one eyebrow meaningfully, 'but we have come to understand each other perfectly now.'

'Very well, Tom, go ahead then, if you must,' Diana's raised voice couldn't be ignored. 'But I'm telling you that it will be quite unnecessary!' Even the sound of her feet running towards the saloon, followed by

426

the slamming of a door, didn't break the flow of the Bey's conversation.

'I think, Francesca, that both brother and sister are greatly excited this morning, and more than a little nervous at the prospect of meeting their parents face to face again,' he said, bending to speak softly into her ear.

'I'm nervous, too.' She looked down at the pretty blue silk dress that had been made for her in Tripoli, then reached up to touch her hair which had now grown sufficiently for Diana's maid to style it. 'I do want Tom's parents to approve of me.'

'They couldn't fail to be charmed by you.' He took her to a chair from where she could watch the crew furling the sails while the engine drove the boat slowly towards its mooring.

Tom came to stand beside them, craning his neck as he scanned the busy quayside, and within minutes Diana had reappeared on deck to join them at the rail.

'Tom! I think I can see them waiting there by that building.' Her voice rang with emotion. 'Look, look, I'm sure it's mother and dad.' She was almost skipping with excitement as the vessel drew closer.

Tom placed one arm around her waist in a brotherly fashion, and waved wildly with the other at Julia and James who were now clearly in view on the quay.

At last, with a clatter and a rattle, the gangplank was lowered and Diana was the first to bolt down it and throw her arms around her mother. They stood, tearfully locked together as Tom brushed past and ran towards his stepfather.

'Dad!' His voice cracked and he reached out a hand. But James ignored it and stepped closer to embrace him. Tightly, warmly, and very publicly, his stepfather held him against his heart while Tom clung to him.

'Tom! My dear boy, thank God you're safe! Your mother and I are so very, very proud of everything you've done.' His grip tightened further, before he then relaxed it and stepped back so he and Tom could look into each other's damp eyes.

James smiled deeply. 'I can't tell you how good it is to be with you again. We haven't seen enough of you in recent years.'

'I've missed you too, Dad. I can't tell you how much I've missed you.'

'Perhaps you and Francesca would like to come back with us to the plantation? A long visit?'

Tom's smile broadened. 'Perhaps a very long visit.'

'Dad! Hurry up!' Diana called from the top of the gangway.

He acknowledged her with a wave. 'Well now, Tom, I believe your mother and I have some new family members to meet. From everything I read in your letter about the delightful Francesca, I feel I already know her very well,' he said, glancing up at the deck where Julia was about to shake hands with Diana's husband. 'But, tell me, how the devil do I address a son-in-law with the name of Khafra Bey?'

They shared a laugh, then with an arm thrown around his stepfather's shoulders, Tom led him gleefully up the gangway.

We do hope that you have enjoyed reading this large print book.

Did you know that all of our titles are available for purchase?

We publish a wide range of high quality large print books including:
Romances, Mysteries, Classics
General Fiction
Non Fiction and Westerns

Special interest titles available in large print are:
The Little Oxford Dictionary
Music Book
Song Book
Hymn Book
Service Book

Also available from us courtesy of Oxford University Press:
Young Readers' Dictionary
(large print edition)
Young Readers' Thesaurus
(large print edition)

For further information or a free brochure, please contact us at:
Ulverscroft Large Print Books Ltd.,
The Green, Bradgate Road, Anstey,
Leicester, LE7 7FU, England.
Tel: (00 44) 0116 236 4325
Fax: (00 44) 0116 234 0205

Other titles published by
The House of Ulverscroft:

WINDS OF HONOUR

Ashleigh Bingham

The Honourable Phoebe Pemberton is beautiful and wealthy, but is the daughter of the late, disgraceful Lord Pemberton and Harriet Buckley . . . Phoebe escapes her mother's plans to teach her the family business of wringing profits from the mills. She dreams of running away, and, when she learns of her mother's schemes for Phoebe's marriage as part of a business transaction, she calls on her friend Toby Grantham for help . . . But Harriet's vengeful fury is aroused, leaving Phoebe tangled in a dark and desperate venture.

THE WELL-TEMPERED CLAVIER

William Coles

A schoolboy at Eton College, with not a girl in sight, seventeen-year-old Kim's head is full of the Falklands War and a possible army career . . . until the day he hears his new piano teacher, the beautiful but pained India, playing Bach's *Well-Tempered Clavier*. Kim's life is destined never to be the same again. A passionate affair develops and he wallows in the unaccustomed thrill of first love. Twenty-five years on, Kim recalls that heady summer and how their relationship was so brutally snuffed out — finished off by his enemies, by the constraints of Eton, and by his own withering jealousy.

THE HEROINES

Eileen Favorite

At the Prairie Bluff boarding house in
Illinois, Emma Bovary has arrived unan-
nounced and distraught . . . Anne-Marie
and her daughter Penny attend to their
guest. The house rule being: *Never meddle
in the lives of the heroines* means that,
besides tea and sympathy, nothing can be
done for Emma. Penny's adolescent angst
is no match for her mother's attention to
these ethereal creatures. Hurt and frustrated Penny strikes out and when she
arrives at the forbidden woods, she
disobeys her mother's second rule, *Never
to enter.* Now she exists in a world of real
heroes and villains, an unwilling heroine in
her own terrifying story . . .

HOUSE OF SERENITY

Susan Shaw

Family life, for Emily and her mother, had meant being in the thrall of her domineering father. She'd been compelled to go to university and then forced to marry a student friend, Howard. But her husband is too much like her father, and the marriage is a disaster. But then, she discovers a grandmother, and that she has inherited a legacy. Things are about to change for Emily . . .